A Mankind Witch

A Mankind Witch

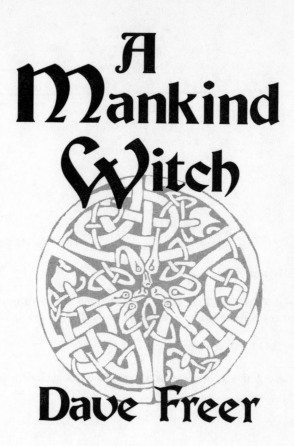

Dave Freer

A MANKIND WITCH

A Baen Books Original

Baen Publishing Enterprises
P.O. Box 1403
Riverdale, NY 10471
www.baen.com

ISBN: 0-7434-9913-1

Cover art by Gary Ruddell

First printing, July 2005

Distributed by Simon & Schuster
1230 Avenue of the Americas
New York, NY 10020

Production & design by Windhaven Press (www.windhaven.com)
Printed in the United States of America

10   9   8   7   6   5   4   3   2   1

DEDICATION

To the memory of loyal companions. If there are no dogs in heaven, let me rather go to wherever they are.

ACKNOWLEDGMENTS

As the first solo novel I have done for some time I felt very alone doing this. Working with Eric Flint and Mercedes Lackey has been very supportive. Nonetheless, my friends and coauthors continued, kindly, to support me this time, too, with advice and encouragement if not with writing the awkward scenes.

My greatest thanks go to my wife, Barbara, who not only fixed my appalling grammar, but also tolerates a husband who has half his head inside Norse myth. I also want to thank the following people: Sioban Finlow-Bates and Dag-Harald Skutlaberg for information about the vegetation and conditions in Norway in winter; my friend Gunnar Dahlin, for help with Skåne; Annette Grahn, for names and maps of the same area; and Jody Dorsett, for some advice on explosives. Mike Kabongo, Tania Shipman, Traci Scroggins, Judith Lasker, all did a terrific job as first readers and helped me polish this tale. My thanks for their help and encouragement.

Grendel is dead.

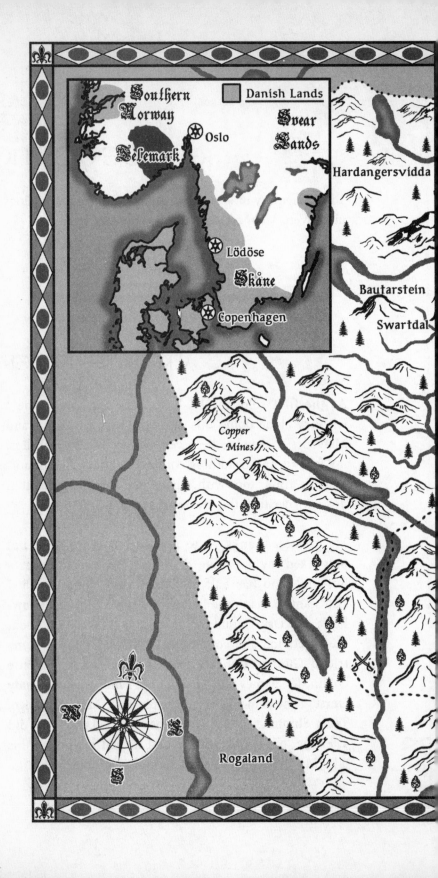

PROLOGUE:
PLAYERS VARIOUS

Biscay, July 1538

*C*air clung to a spar floating in the open ocean, out of sight or scent of land. The rain had stopped now, and, as the spar rose with the swells, he looked around for other wreckage. Other heads in the water.

He saw nothing but white-capped gray sea.

The loss of his crew cut more deeply than the loss of his ship.

He drifted. And clung. The cloud-tattered morning turned to a slate-skied afternoon. There was no longer hope left in him. Just relentless determination, beyond any logic or faith.

And on the wings of evening, a dragon came out of the sea mist.

Lying, bound with coarse rope, on the ribs in the bow of the longship, Cair knew that it had been no dragon. A dragon would have mercifully devoured him then and there.

"They say," said the prisoner next to him, in broken Frankish, "That you are a man-witch. That any other would have drowned. They found no others, nor any sign of your ship."

Cair let none of his instinctive scorn show. Primitive superstition!

Instead he said nothing, keeping as still as he possibly could in his patch of relative warmth.

He remembered little of the rest of the voyage. It was blurred with fever and exhaustion. But he was aware that the other prisoners avoided even touching him.

Kingshall, Telemark, July 1538

"The poor girl. I feel so sorry for her. She's stunted, you know. They say . . ." and the honeyed voice of Signy's stepmother dropped, but not so low that it couldn't be heard clearly through the thin wooden wall. "It's the *dokkalfar* blood on her mother's side . . . The woman died in bearing the girl. That's a sure sign of the ill-fortune that goes with meddling in *seid*-magic. And only the one scrawny girl-child, Jarl. Anyway, it is not important. She is of the royal line even if she probably will never bear children. She's far too small. She spoils her complexion with sunlight. And she has no womanly skills. I mean, look at her embroidery! It's appalling. No, your master would be wise to look elsewhere."

Signy's nails dug into her palms. She dropped the frame of crooked stitchery that confirmed the truth about her skills with a needle. She knew perfectly well that she had been supposed to hear every word. That it was meant to wound. That didn't stop it hurting. Dowager Queen Albruna seldom missed the opportunity to try and belittle her . . . And seldom failed to do so. It wasn't hard. Signy knew that she was no one's idea of a shield-maiden. She was too small, too wiry, and as gifted with the womanly skills of fine weaving and delicate stitchery as a boar-pig. She couldn't even see her threads in linenwork, let alone do it. But, by Freya's paps, she'd sooner die than let the queen mother see any sign of how her barbs stung.

She scrambled to her feet in a tangle of limbs, kicking over a footstool. That was normal, too. Her stepmother hadn't said that Signy was as graceful as a pregnant cow on an ice patch—yet. But she would, as usual. Then the shaming, half-true stories would follow.

Albruna could enjoy needling her stepdaughter. King Hjorda

wouldn't care: he'd take her if she had two heads and tail. He wasn't interested in Signy as a woman: she was merely wanted as a claim to the throne of Telemark. As long as her brother was unwed and without heirs ... she had value. And if that vile old goat Hjorda could get a son on her, he'd have a better claim to the throne than Vortenbras did. She was a very valuable trading piece at the moment, and Albruna was holding out for a high price. Signy knew that was why she was still here, an old maid of twenty-four. She was waiting for Hjorda to increase his offer. Albruna would go on belittling her, pretending to try and put Hjorda off, until the price went up enough.

Signy spat, trying to rid her mouth of the sour half-vomit taste that the thought of her father's old foe engendered. She touched the wire-bound hilt of the dagger in her sleeve. She'd sworn on both Odin's ring and Thor's hammer, that she'd see King Hjorda dead in his marriage bed. Her father's honor demanded that. Then she would die herself as her own honor required. But not for the first time she wished that she really was the *dokkalfar seid*-witch's daughter that Dowager Queen Mother Albruna accused her of being, every time she wanted to make sure the princess had not a friend in the royal household. If Signy had had any powers, dark or no, she'd have turned her stepmother into a rat in a nest of vipers long ago. The gods knew, she'd tried. But her participation in any charm, any piece of *galdr*, guaranteed that it wouldn't work. She could make any charm backfire, let alone fail.

"Come now, Your Highness," said Jarl Svein, his voice as smooth as oiled silk, "a princess of the blood of two ancient houses, no matter how suspect the bloodlines are, is a jewel of value."

Abruna gave her characteristic sniff of disdain. "I've always had my doubts about her blood. Seriously, King Hjorda would be wiser to look elsewhere. How can someone of our lineage be so graceless? She's as clumsy ..."

Signy had been told to wait until she was called to meet Hjorda's emissary. But she knew what was coming next. She'd rather face the inevitable whipping than stay a moment longer. After all, what was one more whipping? They hurt less than words anyway. She could be in the friendly comfort of the stables in a hundred heartbeats. She darted out of the door of the antechamber ...

To have her passage blocked by a large woman with thick buttermilk-blond braids. "Where do you think you're going?"

Such an insolent question from a thrall-wench! Signy raised herself up to her full height, and did her best to look a princess in every one of those meager inches. Even as she did it, she knew she was failing. "It is none of your business, Borgny." She hoped she'd kept the quaver out her voice.

Mainz, late October, 1538

"It's already snowing in the north, Uncle," protested Manfred. "Surely it'll wait until summer. Or at least spring." There was not much hope in his voice. When the Holy Roman Emperor made up his mind, even Prince Manfred of Brittany obeyed. He was even learning to do it with not more than a token protest.

"You're big enough to keep out the cold," said Charles Fredrik, dismissively waving his own large hand at his oxlike nephew. "And I want this sorted out before spring comes and more trouble starts. You, Erik, and Francesca will travel together to Copenhagen. Francesca, it will be your unenviable task to soothe the Danes down. The Knights of the Holy Trinity are still the bulwark of our defence against the Grand Duchy of Lithuania, and, with Jagellion on the throne, we need them more than ever. The last thing I need is them involved in a messy little land squabble with the Danes up in Sweden. At the moment the Knights are subdued because of the way they were used in the Venetian affair. They know they came very close to feeling the full weight of my wrath. The Abbot-General has agreed that there is a problem in Skåne. He has agreed to allow you to act in his name there, provided that we also deal with the Danes." He grimaced. "Which may be more tricky than knocking a few Knights' heads together, Francesca. They are stiff-necked about that independence of theirs, even if they are a vassal state. It's not something that you would be advised to mention."

Francesca, or, as she now styled herself, Francesca de Chevreuse, although this was not the name she'd been born to, shivered artistically. "Your wish is my command, my Emperor." She dimpled, looking at him with her eyes provocatively half-lidded. "Forgive the shiver. It's the thought of all that ice and snow, and me without any good furs to keep it from my skin." The former Venetian courtesan was a voluptuous, warm, creamy-skinned beauty. She liked to show that skin, and was well aware that even the Emperor liked to look at it.

Charles Fredrik chuckled. "We'll have to see that you are appropriately equipped. We can hardly have our Imperial special emissary turning blue in public. See to it, Manfred. Let Trolliger have the reckoning. Why do I get the feeling that suppressing them militarily might have been cheaper?"

Francesca acknowledged this with a smile and a small bow. "I shall try to restrain Manfred from spending more than the cost of a troop of cavalry, Your Highness."

The Emperor shook his head. "I hope you absorbed the lesson, Nephew."

"What?" asked Manfred, rubbing his solid jaw. "Never to go shopping with Francesca? My purse learned that a while ago, Uncle."

"Besides that. Explain to him, Francesca."

She turned to Manfred. "He means I have not wasted my effort on fighting the inevitable, the Emperor's orders, but instead got the best out of it that I can."

"Huh," said Manfred, gloomily. "What *can* I get out of it? To think I asked for you to send me away from this pile of stones before winter set in properly. I had somewhere warm in mind, before the bishop-general insisted on me coming back to some freezing chapter house in Prussia. Even Erik got chilblains in that first winter."

The Emperor turned his attention to the third person present at the interview. Erik Hakkonsen had not said anything yet. But then the tall, spare Icelander seldom said more than he had to. The Clann Hakkonsen of Iceland had provided personal bodyguards for the heirs of the Imperial House Hohenstauffen's *wanderjahre* for centuries now. They were far more than mere bodyguards. They were the final arms instructors and mentors for the princelings. Their loyalty was not to the Empire—Iceland was part of the League of Armagh, owing no fealty to the Holy Roman Empire, but to the House Hohenstauffen, personally. It meant that they, and only they, treated the scions of the most powerful Imperial house in the world like troublesome children, from time to time. Charles Fredrik knew that he owed his personal survival—and the survival of the Empire—to Erik's father. Erik had done as much for Manfred. When the Hakkonsen spoke, the Hohenstauffen listened. But Erik just shook his head and smiled wryly. "He still complains too much, Godar Hohenstauffen. Even if that affair in Venice did help him to grow up a bit. A bit of hard riding in the cold will be good for him."

Telemark, Norway. All Hallow's Eve. A convocation high on the barren vidda.

The hag spat into the balefire. Green flames leapt as the stream of spittle hit the burning fungus. She wiped her chin with the back of her broad hand, and then turned again to face the *draug* she had raised. Needs be it must be one of the dead of this place. Midgard's dead for information about Midgard, after all. She'd brought the body up here, after her slaves had hauled it out of the bog where she'd laid him, facedown, with his throat cut.

And they thought that his body lay in his ship mound in honor! A seeming was quite adequate to fool these Midgard lice. And she was the mistress of seemings.

"Speak," she ordered.

The *draug* gurgled horribly at her. Her hard green eyes narrowed as her son stepped forward, ready to cuff the dead thing. Bah. Blows, even blows from one such as he could not hurt the dead. But she could. Her *galdr* would burn it like a whip of fire. She waved her hulking child back, back to his *björnhednar* guards.

She raised her arms to begin the chanting . . . and realized that the *draug's* defiance was merely a problem of the cut throat. Or maybe it was defiance of a sort. The *draug* hated her, hated her with a helpless fury that could drive it to act even against the pain she could inflict with her *galdr* chants. She took a handful of clay and mended it. "Now. Speak. Defy me if you dare. What is it that holds us back? Why did the raid fail?"

"The *draupnir*," he croaked. "The oath."

Of course. It was obvious now. The oaths sworn on that thing would be binding, even if the swearer had no intent of honoring them. She should have guessed. But the thing had that about it which repelled her. Odin's temple yard was not a place she went to if she could possibly avoid it. The one-eyed one's priests were less affected by seemings than others, even if she'd seen to it that the present high incumbent was near to blind with cataracts. With certain protections her son should be safe from it. And if not—well they would find a way to break the oath. Or cause it to be broken.

Lightning split the sky, and the thunder echoed among the high places. Big drops began to hiss on the balefire. Now that she had what she needed, Bakrauf began dismissing the spells that had given the *draug* the seemings of life. It fell like a child's broken doll, tumbling onto its side by the fire. The face of the dead kinglet was twisted into the rictus of a smile. She considered it, thoughtfully. *Draugar* thus compelled could not lie. She kicked the body, and gestured to the *björnhednar*. "Take him back. I may need him again."

She turned away, the firelight glinting briefly on the cunningly wrought silver ornaments in her ears. They were perfect, down to the last hair, and no small part of her power over the *björn-hednar* rested in them.

Then she strode back downhill, away from the stone that marked the gateway between her place and this, back toward the halls of men in the valley below. Behind her, her son followed. The pelting rain and even the hail did not worry her. Troll-wives have no objection to rain. It is bright sunlight they avoid.

CHAPTER 1

"ou speak Frankish?" the karl translator asked, when the guards deposited him in front of the throne in the high thatched hall.

More fluently than you, thought Cair. But he put on a show of concentration. Nodded earnestly. "I have small." Cair was still not even sure where he was. Some remote little kingdom in Norselands seemed a fairly sure bet. But now came the difficult bit. He had to lie, and lie fluently.

"Vortenbras King he says have you kin who would pay *blot* . . . blood price for you? Ransom." Faced with Cair's blank look, the karl tried again. "Give him money for you."

Cair wrinkled his forehead in a show of effort. "You tell him-King, me poor man." If word went out that some Norseman was demanding a ransom for Cair Aidin . . . Well, even in the fleets of the corsairs there were a good few who would pay for him . . . dead. If word got to one of the Holy Roman Empire's spies that the Redbeard was a prisoner here—they would pay generously. Very generously. They would keep him alive, too. Their torturers were good at that. Dead people felt no pain. When he'd last heard, the Republic of Venice also was offering five hundred thousand ducats for his head. "Me poor man," he repeated. It would mean slavery, but that was better than the alternatives. He would have some chance of escape from slavery. And for some obscure reason the slaves here appeared to be left entire. The threat of castration might have persuaded him to try his luck at escaping from the gilded but carefully guarded cage they would put a high-value prisoner into, instead. However, he'd made sure of that already—all that happened to slaves was a branding. And, once branded, slaves didn't appear well guarded at all. Perhaps the Norse trusted to the remote wildness of this place.

The bearlike man on the throne spat disgustedly at the translation. Bellowed something obviously derogatory in Norse. It was like enough to Frankish to have a haunting familiarity. "What him-King say?"

"Vortenbras King say you too old for good thrall. Not enough work in you before you go die. And too small to plow with."

Too old! He was thirty-five. Not a young man, true. But in his prime! Then Cair understood the implication of the second part of the statement. He'd heard of that, yes. Poor places where they plowed with teams of men or women instead of horses. They did that in the high Atlas, apparently. But for one such as he to be put to such a use by these primitive barbarians!

The hulking bear of a man snapped an order. Cair found himself being dragged backward, by the hair, by his translator. He had to turn and follow, stumbling. He was going to have to learn this language. Fast. And he was going to have to restrain himself from killing idiots like this hair dragger.

"Where are you taking me?" he asked.

"To be branded. Then," and the disdain showed in the man's voice, "you go to be woman's slave. Signy."

Cair thought—by the tone—that the last word was probably some kind of Norse insult.

"What your name, slave?" demanded the stable master in mangled Frankish, looking down at him as he sprawled on the soiled straw he had been shoved down onto.

His new-burned flesh throbbed. Cair added that to the reckoning. But right now he had to survive until that reckoning came due. And that meant that he had to stop being a corsair admiral—and become an anonymous slave. He was not Cair Aidin until he stood on the deck of his own ship again. The barbarians couldn't pronounce his name anyway. He bowed his head. "Cair, master." He would be that, and think of himself as just that, until he was free.

"A good name for a thrall," the stable master grunted. "Get up. Move dung," he pointed to a wooden shovel. "And learn our tongue."

Cair, the new slave, shoveled horse dung. That was another thing they'd pay for, when he escaped. But for now he was content to bide his time. To study his captors and the place he was captive in. When he made his break, he intended to be successful. And, if he had to bring half of the Barbary fleet here, he'd burn this place around their ears. The "palace" and its halls were wooden. The roofs were thatch. They'd burn well. They thought that being this far from the coast would save them. Nothing would.

But after a few days of captivity, Cair—the new thrall—was somewhat less sanguine about it all. The first thing that struck him was that they'd scarcely give a slave this much liberty if escape was a real possibility. He soon realized that, beside the brand, there were other trammels set on a thrall. And one of them was that, here in the north, he was a small, unarmed fellow. Among the corsairs he'd been of average height. It was not something that had worried him, previously. With a sword in hand, or a ship to command, he was the equal or the better of any other man. Here he was utterly forbidden to even touch either a ship or an edged weapon. A few older, very privileged thralls had belt knives. Small belt knives.

Besides being a mere small unarmed slave-thrall, at the bottom of the Norse social order, he also found he was at the bottom of the pecking order for slave-thralls. He was a woman's slave. And not just any woman. Signy.

You didn't, it would appear, go any lower, around these parts. Being the lowest of the low meant that you got the worst of everything, from sleeping quarters to food, if you could call it that. They were teaching him the job with a good supply of buffets, blows, and occasional buckets of filth. And even other thralls were free to hand out a good beating if they felt like it.

On the second day, still struggling with the language, and still wracked by the last chill of fever, Cair found this out the hard way. He wasn't even too sure what he'd done wrong. All he knew was that he was getting a fiercesome beating with a broken stave for doing it. And the fact that he'd dared to strike back was making it worse. The thrall doing the beating was heavier, taller, and better fed than most of them. He was one of Queen Albruna's slaves—not supposed to be in the stables at all. The other thralls stood and cheered and jeered. There wasn't much entertainment in the stables. Certainly no one lifted a hand to stop it.

The fight was going badly. And then it was going worse. The big fellow kneed him in the crotch, and as Cair's head came forward, he cracked it down against one of the stalls.

Cair swore, amid the blur of pain . . . and then the hitting stopped.

Cair managed to stand upright. Blood was streaming from his nose, and the world was definitely out of focus. But the big tow-haired thrall was no longer laying into him. And the stable was oddly silent. Cair closed both eyes and then tried opening them again. His vision was still far from normal, but he could see the thrall, stretched out full length on the stable floor. His head appeared to have turned into a heavy wooden bucket.

That was quite enough for Cair. He was plainly either dead or concussed, and in either case he was going to sit down. Now.

He slumped against the wooden stall partition. He was vaguely aware that some of the other thralls had hauled the buckethead away. But he felt too sore and sick to care. And no one had come to drive him to his feet to work again. He drifted away to somewhere between concussion and sleep.

He awoke to find someone kneeling next to him. Lifting his head. Holding something to his lips. "Drink this."

He sipped. It was a clay dipper of water. He tried to work out who was giving this nectar to him. The light was bad in the stable by now, not that it was wonderful at any time, but evening was plainly close.

It was a woman. Not a thrall he'd seen before. A scrawny lass who had plainly been crying. He sipped some more and then tried to sit up. Quite involuntarily, he groaned.

"You've taken quite a beating, by the looks of you," said the woman, critically. Not particularly sympathetically, but kindly enough. "Can you stand up?" she asked.

Cair tested his limbs. "I think so. I'll try."

"Good," she said. "This is Korvar's stall. He doesn't like being put elsewhere. Come. Up."

She hauled at his arm and he staggered to his feet. She made no attempt to support him, but he did manage to grab the stall edge and steer his way out. The woman appeared more concerned at fussing around the stall, and leading an elderly warhorse across to it, than watching what he was doing, so he sat down again. But his head was clearing, slowly. She patted and soothed the horse. "Next time don't bleed in this stall," she said to Cair, sharply. "The smell of blood gets Korvar overexcited." She leaned over and kissed the horse's muzzle. The horse twitched and sneezed. She laughed. "There, you big old silly. Settle now." Eventually, she came out of the stall, and looked critically at Cair. "There is some horse liniment I made up for strains up on the shelf in the corner. I've found that it helps a bit for the bruises. Then you'd better get across to your quarters, before you get another beating."

It was only after she'd left that it occurred to his muzzy mind that she'd addressed him in Frankish. Not just Frankish but good Frankish. Spoken as a highborn noblewoman would, not some stable girl. But he'd thought no more of it. His head throbbed and so did his ribs. He'd roughly slathered some of the horse liniment on himself. It burned in the raw places, and woke him more thoroughly, but perhaps the herbs in it would do him some good. He'd staggered over to the stinking hovel where he'd been told to sleep. It was small, dirty, crowded, smoky, full of vermin . . . and oddly silent when he'd crept in. He'd found a space easily enough, and slept.

Getting up the next morning was even more torture. The bruises had set, and for all that it was midsummer, it was still cold at first light. He chewed on his coarse rye crust and supped the weak, sour small-beer handed to them in the garth outside the kitchen. In the kitchen, the morning's work had plainly begun well before, and the noise was enough to make him retreat from it. He chewed cautiously. His mouth was sore. Looking around he realized that he stood in a little island of silence, while the other ragged thralls jostled and talked—in muted voices, true, among themselves. And across the yard he caught sight of the tormentor of yesterday. He had a dirty bandage around his head. And the minute his eyes locked with Cair's, he shied away.

Cair's own head had bled, and his hair was matted with dried blood. But it was only when he'd helped to lead the horses out to the paddocks down beside the water, and took the opportunity— along with one of the other two thralls—to wash his face in the cold water that he could wash it clear gingerly. And peer at his reflection in the water. He didn't think, all things considered, that he looked that terrifying. So, on the way back up to the stables, he ventured to ask what was going on. The other man who'd bothered to wash had spoken peasant Frankish to him yesterday. He was presumably a Frankish prisoner taken on one of the locals' raids. "Why is everyone behaving as if I have the plague this morning?"

"I haven't done anything to you," said the other thrall, warily.

"Except kick me and trip me facedown into the dung heap yesterday," said Cair.

The thrall held up his hands pacifically. "But I didn't know, then."

"Didn't know what?" asked Cair.

"That you were a man-witch." Even after the rudimentary wash by the lakeside, the man's face was none too clean. The dirt was the only bit of color on it, right now.

Cair was about to deny this latest piece of ridiculousness when it struck him that it might be useful. These were pagans, after all. They weren't likely to accuse him of trafficking with the devil. "Who told you?" he asked, doing his best to look threatening. He raised one eyebrow, a trick he'd practiced and used to some effect on prisoners himself. If this was the only coin he had to play, well, then he would play it with skill.

The thrall's eyes widened, and he looked ready to bolt. "I saw, yesterday, what you did to Eddi. And I've heard from Piers that one of the other new captives says you were floating on the sea, miles from the land."

Now, thought Cair, *all I have to do is find out what I "did" to Eddi,* who was presumably the person who had given him the bruises that hurt so devilishly this morning. Whatever it was, Cair hoped the bastard was at least half as sore as he was. He ached. Even his aches had aches. He could use any reputation that would stop this from happening again. There were a few tricks he could use to foster the story. There were a fair number of things a civilized man knew to be science that these ignorant pagans would take for magic. But for now he kept his mouth still and let the tongue of rumor speak instead. From experience, he knew that it always spoke louder than any mere man could. He and his brother had cultivated rumors of the Redbeards' uncanny successes, and of the folly of resisting them, for just that reason.

Even the Venetians were inclined to run, and, when cornered, surrender rather than fight. It always made for easier victories if the victims were half paralyzed with fear before they even went into the fight. Logical thought did not come into these things, thought Cair wryly. "See you behave yourself today, and you won't get what you deserve. I'll stay my vengeance. For now."

The thrall nodded so eagerly that his head was in danger of parting from his shoulders. "Nobody will give you trouble. I promise."

"Good. Now show me what I am supposed to do around here. I don't want more beatings." He saw instantly that this had been the wrong thing to say, and rectified it immediately. "My powers are low now, too low after my magics at sea, calling the king's ship to me, to undertake great workings again. But I can still manage to deal with the likes of Eddi. Or you. However, I am here for a greater purpose than to waste magic on thralls, if I don't have to."

The thrall nodded. "We'd better go and muck out then. Signy never says anything, except if the horses are badly looked after."

There was that name again. He'd taken it for a Norse insult the first time he'd heard it. This thrall and the others in the stable yard put a fair degree of disdain into it. "Who is this Signy?"

"The old king's daughter. King Vortenbras's sister. Half-sister."

It was curious that these slaves would even dare to treat someone that high-born with anything but the very greatest respect, or even omit a title. They certainly spoke the name of Vortenbras's mother with hushed deference. It appeared that how much respect a thrall got from his fellows was largely determined by who owned you. Thus the sooner he, Cair, got himself transferred to the service of some more important personage, the better. It would make life more comfortable, until he could escape.

"They say that she is a *seid*-witch," said the thrall with disdain. "Or at least the queen does. But I never saw any sign of it."

During the rest of the day, Cair gradually pieced together a great deal from his new informants, Henri, once a fisherman from the coast of nearby Helgoland, and Thjalfi, their half-witted companion in labor. Thjalfi had no problem repeating the story, over and over again, of Eddi and the bucket. It would appear that Thjalfi had, prior to Cair, been Eddi's favorite kicking target.

By the way the moonling smelled, Cair wished that Eddi had kicked him into the water. Thjalfi had no Frankish, but he was slow of speech as well as wits, and he repeated things endlessly. As a learning tool he was an asset, if a noisome one. If Cair understood Thjalfi right, Cair had called Eddi "Buckethead" and a string of strange and obviously magical words. And the bucket had come from nowhere and landed on Eddi's head.

The Berber-coast obscenity Cair had yelled at Eddi hadn't been "Buckethead." But it did sound similar. Luck and a falling bucket had been on his side. Now he just had to capitalize on it.

From Henri he learned a great deal more. King Vortenbras of Telemark's hall was some fifteen leagues from the coast—for just the reason that Cair had surmised. Once the small Norse "kingdom" had had its seat on the coast. And inevitably had raided far and wide . . . and brought down the wrath of the Danes and Holy Roman Empire on its king's hall. Now, with the royal hall tucked into the mountains, beside what had been an ancient holy site, silver coming from the mountain mines, and a treaty with the Holy Roman Empire, Telemark under King Vortenbras was a growing power. Rumor had it that the limits of this power irked the king. He was looking to stretch them, folk said.

Then, as the afternoon drew in, Cair got another surprise. As he was carrying in a load of straw, a woman spoke in Norse, plainly giving some instruction. Cair felt that he ought to know the speaker. He peered up from under his load, and saw Henri and Thjalfi bowing. "Ja, Princess Signy."

It was the woman he'd taken for a thrall-wench the night before.

Her dress was indeed shabby for a noblewoman, but in the clearer light he could see that it had been, at least once upon a time, a good riding habit. She wore some jewelry, too. Poor stuff, but if he had noticed those bracelets he'd never have mistaken her for a thrall. Her hand rested on the head of one of the hunting dogs that seemed to slope around everywhere in this place. She was inspecting the stable, and pointing to a tag end of a halter rope buried in the bedding straw. Cair was standing a great deal closer to it than she was, and he could barely see it. The woman must have eyes like a hawk.

She was a slight little thing compared to most of the women he'd seen here, fine boned, they called it back on Lesbos, where he'd grown up. Her hair was so strained back and tightly braided that it was virtually invisible from the front. He put down the net of hay. Bowed, considering the ramifications of his encounter last night. What had a noblewoman—who had plainly been crying—been doing in the stables after the household was abed? Cair was a thinker. Life, especially to a master of ships and men, was a chess game and you had to think at least five moves ahead if you wished to win. "Pick that up!" she snapped at him—in Frankish. "Don't you watch where you put things down, thrall? They told me I had a new stable-thrall that spoke no Norse and was too old for good work, but I didn't expect you to be an idiot, too. I suppose I should have. They always give me the insolent, sick, lame, and lazy. I don't care elsewhere, but you'll learn to do a proper job with the horses or I'll have you whipped. Even if I have to do it myself. And learn to speak Norse."

Picking up the hay, hastily he did his best to bow again. But she was no longer paying any attention to him. Instead she'd gone with Henri to inspect some saddle galls on the rough-coated bay. Her voice as she talked to the horse was now as gentle as it had been waspish a minute ago. And if she'd recognized him, she'd not given any sign of it.

Afterward, when she'd left, Cair found himself doing some further cleaning of the two stalls that the princess had been dissatisfied with. He'd already come to realize that her section of the huge stable was cleaner by several degrees than the other parts. He was also aware that the horses in this part of the stable were old. Several of them were definitely beyond work.

Henri grumbled. "It's only those of us in the stables that she makes work. Those house-thralls of hers are the laziest bunch of sluts you've ever met. The queen's women work their fingers raw. But not Signy's. No. Half the time they tell *her* what to do. And the queen lets them! But I'd swear the mistress spies on us down here. Look at Vortenbras's men. Half the day they can sleep in hay loft. The only time I thought I'd try that she turned up and nearly pulled my ear off. And we get the worst food and everything."

"That is going to change."

Henri blinked at him. "No, it's not. The king doesn't love his half-sister."

Cair stared pointedly at him. "I have my powers. Do you want your head in a bucket?"

Henri gaped at him. "You mean . . ."

"I mean the Princess Signy wants her horses cared for. A fine and beautiful noble lady must have what she desires." Cair was much more observant than his fellow peasant horse boys. He'd looked up, just briefly, a few moments before. Above the stalls, the roof beams had been layered with rough timber to make a sort of ceiling and junk store. The timber didn't fit too well. And through one of the cracks Cair had glimpsed a piece of embroidery that he'd seen earlier.

CHAPTER 2

Kingshall, Telemark

It would have been difficult for Cair to have said just when he had moved into the role of man-witch. His facial color—in a region where the slave-thralls had scant contact with the wider world, and had mostly never seen anyone with Mediterranean coloring and curly black hair—helped. To the ignorant, anything different was to be feared. It had probably started with his knowledge of elementary physical chemistry. Perhaps the king and his hearthmen were better informed, but the slave-thralls regarded very nearly everything as magic. Cair was a hardened empiricist who had studied with not one, but two, of the leading philosophers of the age. He was familiar with the works of Averroës, and had had long conversations with Biringuccio—one of his brother's captives, and now a trusted master metallurgist in Carthage. He had dabbled in alchemistic experiments himself, making distillations, aqua regia, aqua fortris, and iron vitriol. He'd experimented with different mixtures of black powder—these barbarians still bought theirs, and used precious little of it. He had a firm grasp of mathematical thought, particularly geometry. It had been useful to him both as a commander of ships and in siege work. He'd spent many hours in debate of these and other matters with others of his social order in the Barbary states. It was what a gentleman did in winter, after all. It was that or drink and fornicate.

And yet his most spectacular results had come from a small piece of badly flawed amber, and the minds of his audience. The amber he'd found down by the riverside. Perhaps this country was where it came from. Or perhaps it had once been a piece of bead. All Cair knew was that he'd had the marvelous attractive properties of rubbed amber displayed to him before. He'd jammed the amber into a knothole in a piece of twisted wood. It looked like some ancient piece of a bear's eye. He rubbed it with a piece of scrap wool plucked from a dog-rose thorn. He had been absently rubbing it when two of the other thralls came up to him. "Hear tell you are a *balewerker*," said the one, in atrocious Frankish. Cair was getting used to the Norse brand of the Germanic languages, and could understand a bit more than he let on. He understood the aside, or at least the gist of it, which was "this should be good for a few laughs."

Balewerker—"evil-worker" was one of the titles given to Odin. The pagans were quite content to have their gods capable of both good and ill, and you'd better respect them or you were likely to experience the ill side. It reminded Cair of the mildly scandalous story of the young woman whom the priest had caught bowing when he mentioned the devil. The young woman of negotiable morals was hauled before the senior priest, who had demanded to know whether she worshiped the devil. She was shocked, but pointed out that a bit of respect didn't cost anything and might help her one day. The priest wasn't amused, but Cair had been. And now he faced the same. If he was a good enough "*balewerker*" he'd get respect. If not . . . the beating of a few days ago might be a minor one.

"I have some small powers, yes." He went on rubbing the amber thoughtfully.

"Hah. Show us then," said the one with the scarred face, and fine, wispy hair. The man's breath reeked of ale. It was early in the day for that sort of tippling, especially from a mere thrall. Odds were he'd been raiding the brew house, and thence came his courage.

"It is never wise to waste power. You never know when you may need it," said Cair, in fair to battered Norse.

Scarface snorted. "By Odin's ring, you're full of wind. I'll—"

"But," said Cair calmly, "I will show you something." He chanted a few appropriate words in Latin—after all, it was easier to use real words than mere garbage. He held up his piece of driftwood. The amber eye winked in the August sunlight. "This is a thief-finder. The guilty one's evil will seek to come to the finder. See. If you are innocent nothing will happen."

He began at the man's neck, chanting his Latin. And was rewarded by the sharp hiss of indrawn breath from the other thrall. "Stand," he snapped as the man sought to turn and bolt. "See," he said to the other thrall, as the beer thief's hair began to rise. With a piglike squeal the beer thief turned and bolted, closely followed by his companion.

Cair went back to the stable. He knew that at least one pair of eyes had been watching, and that the story would grow. It probably wouldn't resemble the truth in the remotest, but as long as they left him alone, he could see to getting himself out of here, and back to his ports along the African seaboard of the Mediterranean.

But in the stable something changed his plans, at least in the short term. King Vortenbras and some seven of his men came in. "Saddle up for us," Vortenbras bellowed. The huge man had a voice that made even the stones shiver. "Move, or I'll whip you myself."

"And not many will survive that," snapped one of the others. "We've a runaway thrall to hunt."

Cair worked as fast as he could. It still didn't keep him from a casual blow from one of the hearthmen for some imagined tardiness. Soon the bunch surged away laughing, following the dogs.

Cair heard the story later. Thirdhand, but still with the elements of truth. Promised the beating of a lifetime, a young thrall had fled in the night. When they found him gone, they'd hunted him with dogs. Somewhere out there they'd caught him. "Lars was clever. He ran in the water and they lost him. But King Vortenbras, he smelled him out. He led the dogs down the shoreline until they found the scent again. And they found him, and they tore him apart. Vortenbras himself ripped the man in half," said the wide-eyed teller.

Well, that was exaggeration, of course. But doubtless the dogs had ripped him apart. Cair decided that fleeing on foot—or even on a horse, would be foolishness. Let him loose at the coast with a small boat, and he'd chance it. But from here . . . well, right now that was not a possibility. Trusted thralls did accompany their masters. So Cair slipped into the role that primitive superstition had cast him into. He became an expert at the vague statement. If you predicted general ill fortune, sooner or later something would oblige. It was a bizarre thing for a rational man to have to do.

It did move him up the pecking order. And it made getting the very best for the princess's elderly horses easier. He'd finally got to the bottom of that: most of them had been her father's old horses. Vortenbras had taken the younger ones, but only Signy's intervention had saved the old ones from slaughter. He learned, too, the secret sign that Signy was in her stable hideout. There would always be two or three of the house dogs around. Apparently, they had to be shut out of the royal hall before the queen could have Signy beaten. But it appeared that other than dogs and horses, the shabby little princess had no friends in this house.

By gradual degrees Cair became a backstairs magician and the master of cheap tricks. In a similar fashion, the Barbary corsair found that somehow he'd moved from his original plan to use the princess as a stepping stone, to being her loyalist.

It was the old dog that finally did it.

Signy came down late in the afternoon, after the other stable-thralls had gone, her hand on the old dog's neck. Cair was standing in a dark corner of the stable, next to the feed store, carefully loosening a rock, which would give him a hiding place for the things he needed to steal for his escape. Now he stood dead still. It was dark back here.

Cair had noticed, over the last week, that this, her most faithful companion, had abruptly stopped coming down here with her. Now he could see it was only loyalty that had made it make the effort to walk. Something was plainly very wrong with the old dog. The beast shivered slightly as it leaned against her, pausing. Then she led it to an empty stall, and it lay down with a little whine.

Cair could swear that he'd made no sound, but somehow the princess knew that he was there. Princesses did not belong in stables. They did not wear old—if once good—garments. They did not walk around unaccompanied by anyone but their dogs. She used to sneak out in the predawn and ride alone, too, Cair knew—something she was almost certainly not supposed to do, by the care she took to have the tack back in place when the thralls came to work. A princess wasn't even supposed to touch tack! She was, by any definition, odd—a breaker of the rules of her society. And Princess Signy added to her oddness by an almost inhuman ability to know where people were. She called him.

She was kneeling next to the dog, her face oddly white—she was always a little too sun-browned for a noblewoman, and her eyes glittered strangely.

"Will you hold her still? I can't miss and I don't want her to know what I intend to do," she said in a dead-flat voice.

So Cair sat with the old bitch, gently stroking her. He had had an old grazehound back on Lesbos when was growing up that had been a bit like this old girl. She'd also followed him everywhere. He'd spoiled her, or so his brother had said.

"It has to be done," she said in that same voice, lifting the ear to expose the ear hole.

Horrified and fascinated he watched as she drew the knife from her sleeve and stabbed hard, pushing the blade in through the ear hole.

The old bitch never even whimpered.

But Signy did. And then, as she pulled the knife out, tears were streaming down her face. "She couldn't swallow anymore . . . a canker in her throat," she said hoarsely.

The hand that didn't hold the knife stroked the white-flecked muzzle. "I grew up with her. I . . ." She choked and let the shaking hand on the dead dog's flank say it all. She bent over and kissed the dog's nose, ignoring the blood.

"But couldn't someone else do this for you?" he asked. No noblewoman would do such a thing!

She stared blindly at him, not seeing past the tears. "She gave me all of her love and loyalty. How could I give her anything less? How could I let someone else kill her? It had to be done as quickly and cleanly as possible. How could I not be with her?"

He nodded. It was an attitude he simply had to respect. He sought for words of comfort, without any thought but to ease her distress, speaking not as a thrall to his noble mistress, but as one dog lover comforting another. "She is young now, free from pain, chasing down the deer in the eternal fields," he said quietly.

"Are there dogs in Odin's host?" she asked, obviously desperately seeking reassurance—even from a thrall.

That was a hard one. One he had debated and decided on long before, at the death of his own childhood hound. He gave her as honest an answer as possible. "Princess, I am not of your faith, but if a god cannot recognize and reward such love and loyalty, how can he be a god? If there are no dogs in heaven, let me rather go to wherever they are."

He took the knife from her hand and cleaned it on one of his rags, and gave it back to her. Signy sniffed. "I don't know what to do with her now," she said in a small voice. "She just hurt so. I had to do it."

Cair touched her, awkwardly, on the shoulder. He hadn't lived here for this long without coming to realize that to do so held possibly fatal consequences. "I will deal with it, Princess. I will bury her down at the edge of the paddocks. The dogs all love that spot. Let her always be there."

She nodded, blindly. Sniffed. Bent over and kissed the dog's gray head once more and stood up. "Thank you," she said guiding herself along the stalls with an outstretched hand, eyes obviously too blurred to see.

Cair knew then that he was, against all the trammels of logic and common sense, her man. It fought with his rational desire to get out of here, and back to his ships and his palace in Algiers. Admittedly, the chances for escape hadn't been good so far. But he knew, in his heart of hearts, that he could have contrived something soon. He stayed on, as the weeks became months, knowing that he was stupid to stay. He was unused to dealing with such feelings about anyone, and not sure how one did cope with them.

To have acquired such a devoted slave seemed to have made no difference to Signy. He was not really sure she even noticed.

By harvest, he had unofficially promoted himself to head of her household servants. He was undisputed lord of all the yard servants. But the house-thralls, mostly women, were a different matter. Still, they would learn. The thought amused him. Cair Aidin, slave-thrall, faker of magics, lord of the backstairs. How the mighty had fallen!

He had quite a neat repertory of tricks by then. If he could gain access to some more chemical substances he'd have a few more surprises ready. But it was amazing what you could get away with in a bad light, with a few threads of gray horsehair, if you had a gullible enough audience.

One thing Cair found passing strange, and not a little unpleasant. He'd been a popular man among the damsels of Carthage and Algiers. Women had swooned at his feet. Naturally, he hadn't expected them all to swoon at his feet here. But they'd left him entire. He'd even wondered at first if he was supposed to service the princess. You heard stories. Well, perhaps beautiful Amazons enslaving men for certain explicit purposes was always a daydream of scruffy sailors that no woman would look at twice, without their price in hand. But he'd never thought of himself in that category. Here—although as a *balewerker* he had increasing cachet, although it also lent fear—women regarded him as odd looking and a little undersized. Even Thjalfi got more attention than he did. Humph. If he'd thought about it, he'd have been less keen on making the moonling-midden wash. And as for Princess Signy, well, he was pretty sure he was regarded as yet another one of her horses. She treated him like one of them, these days. And unless you were very odd indeed, you did not consider a horse as a mate. He was a thrall. And she was a princess of the royal house. He was pretty sure that she was unaware that Cair was actually a man. He was just a thrall. A slave.

CHAPTER 3

Skåne, Sweden, 1538

*P*rince Manfred of Brittany stared out at the steel-gray sky. His oxlike frame blocked nearly all of the weak sunlight from the narrow window. Still, the sunlight wasn't making it any warmer inside the chapter house. The place was at least relatively warm and dry, even without sunlight. There wasn't much else you could say for it. Still—the bleak view outside was scarcely more inspiring than the Spartan interior of this place.

He turned back to face his companion, who was busy having his armor straps adjusted. Both men wore the cross-embossed steel of the Knights of the Holy Trinity, the militant monastic arm of the Holy Roman Empire. Manfred wore armor with the appearance of negligence. A man his size was designed to carry ninety pounds of steel plate on his body. "I suppose it would be as futile to suggest that we should just stay here, warm and full of wine, as it would be to suggest we go back to Francesca in Copenhagen?"

Erik shrugged. "I look forward to your explanation to the Emperor Charles Fredrik. He did expect you to sort out this mess, personally. But I'm sure he'll quite understand that you didn't want to get cold." He felt that he was getting better at handling Manfred. A couple of years of being the prince's bodyguard and mentor had given him enough practice. And being back in full armor made the Icelander irascible. So did the plains of Skåne. Flatness brought out the worst in him, he decided.

Manfred grinned. "I'd let you tell Uncle. You two would have such a good time complaining about the youth of today, you'd soon forget to be mad at me. It's cold out there."

Erik checked the Algonquin war-hatchet he insisted on carrying as well as the standard broadsword. It was the best copy he'd been able to get the imperial swordsmith at Mainz to make of the weapon he'd destroyed on the Woden, outside Venice. It wasn't as good, but short of venturing to Vinland again, it would just have to do. He shrugged again. "The palace at Mainz is just about as cold. And he'd keep you there. Last I heard he had planned to fill the place with dowagers and to move every drop of liquor out of the place, next time you were there. You were begging to get away a month ago, even without that."

Manfred acknowledged the hit. "I was hoping to get sent to Aquitaine. Or back to Venice. Not to the frozen north," he said wryly. "And I thought I could keep Francesca with me."

"We go to where the Empire has problems," said Erik, dryly. "Not to where we've already fixed them. The Emperor said that Francesca should stay in Copenhagen, and you should come and sort out the problems here from the other side. Besides, the cold is good for you. Gets the blood moving around the body."

Manfred grunted. "I've got more body to move it around. And I didn't like the old lecher saying Francesca would operate better without me around."

A tall gray-haired knight limped stiffly into the room. "We are ready to proceed, Prince. We don't keep our horses standing in the cold." Von Tiblaut did not bow. Officially, the militant holy order gave scant deference to worldly rank. And the proctor-general of Skåne was making it very clear that as far as he was concerned these were just two confrere knights, serving a three-year duty. The term "prince" was a backhanded insult. The fact that the Emperor had requested that they should be seconded here was barely acknowledged. So, it would appear, were specific instructions from the Abbot-General that Manfred's words should carry the bishop's authority. Manfred had been told that the Order, here in southern Sweden, behaved as if it was a law unto itself. He was seeing the proof of it.

The proctor-general obviously didn't realize that he'd come to change that.

Manfred did nothing to clarify this either. He said nothing, just docilely walked out into the courtyard. Erik, who knew his charge well, braced himself for trouble.

Von Tiblaut hadn't yet got the measure of the prince of Brittany. Perhaps, as others had in the past, he mistook Manfred's stolidity for oxlike stupidity. "Don't keep us waiting in future," he said irritably. "You, too, Hakkonsen. And I don't want to see that pagan weapon again. Is that clear, Knight? Put it in a saddlebag or dispose of it."

"I have no pagan weapons," said Erik, his voice icy. "All my arms are wielded in the service of Christ, and the Godar Hohenstauffen." He turned to his mount, pointedly ignoring the order. No wonder there was trouble here between the Danes and the Order, with this stiff-necked, petty, self-important ass in charge.

Von Tiblaut goggled at him. Obviously no one had disobeyed him for many years. But perhaps something about the way the Icelander had spoken made him keep his peace, for now. However, his eyes were narrowed, thoughtful.

He might have been even more thoughtful if he had realized that Mecklen, one of the quiet knights sent to accompany the prince, ranked as an Archimandrite proctor, and that three of the other ten were senior proctors, from Bohemia. They were traveling as mere ordinary knights, and to all appearances were a bodyguard for the nephew of the Holy Roman Emperor. On the ship from Copenhagen, Mecklen had explained matters to the prince. "While they concentrate on you, Ritter, they won't watch me. And the bishops of the order are also concerned about what happened in Venice and what appears to be happening in Sweden. They'd like matters seen to, firstly, because this threatens the order, and secondly, because the current situation seems to have aroused the wrath of the Emperor. We don't need any more of that sort of trouble."

"I am authorized to act with both the Abbot-General's and the Emperor's authority," Manfred had said, in a deceptively mild tone.

Mecklen had not been deceived. Nor had he been angered. "Indeed, and I am here to lend force to your actions within the Order, and if need be in the service of the Emperor. Unless we are needed, we shall simply be your personal guard, assigned by the Abbot-General. But we are here to report back to him."

They rode onward into the hinterland, toward the rising forested hills of the Småland borderlands. In the distance you could see that the dryer ridgelines were spiky with pine, with the wetter valley land covered, by the color of it, with spruce. Looking around, Erik could see that the country here had once been thickly forested, too. Some of the fields were returning to scrubby birch and aspen patches. Still, the potential for an ambush of a heavily armored mounted column was limited here, on the largely open flatlands. True danger would start along with real afforestation. Without allowing his vigilance to drop, Erik gave more attention to the fields. He looked at the straggly remnants of a strip of pease. Compared to the stark, steep, unfertile beauty of his native Bokkefloi in Iceland, this land was a farmer's dream. But there was no mistaking that there was poverty in the wooden peasant huts. Something was wrong here. The farms closer to the coast had been far richer.

Manfred had plainly noticed, too. "Are these Danish lands?" he asked.

One of the knights shook his head. "No. These are the lands of Ritter Von Stelheim. He was a confrere knight in the chapter house at Lödöse. He bought the lands from the Order when he had finished his time."

Manfred's heavy eyebrows lifted fractionally. "They're in poor heart for a place that is potentially so rich."

"These Götar make useless serfs," said the knight, scathingly. "You have to beat one to death for every one you can get to work. And half of them run off over the border."

Erik made no comment to this sally, except to raise his eyebrows slightly.

The Breton prince shrugged as if it meant nothing to him. Indeed, it was only because Erik knew Manfred well that he could spot the tightening around his mouth. Erik kept his own tongue between his teeth . . . with difficulty. Things were very different in Celtic Brittany or in his own Iceland. Even in Swabia, the heart of the Holy Roman Empire, beating a serf to death would have had consequences. But the Knights drew the bulk of their numbers from the eastern frontier. Such conduct was not uncommon there, but there the differences east or west of the border were slight. If anything, you were worse off as a peasant in King Emeric's Hungary, than in either the Empire or the Grand Duchy of Lithuania.

A little later Manfred asked casually, "And the lands nearer the coast. Don't they have the same problem with their peasants?"

"They did. But mostly it is Danish settlers there now."

"Ah," said Manfred and they rode on in silence.

Erik knew the explosion was merely being delayed. That night they were once again ensconced in a wooden fortress chapter house, on the edge of the Småland hills. As soon as they were in the privacy of their assigned chamber, Manfred allowed himself to erupt. "Stupid goddamned Prussians! They're running a private little land grab here, and turning this frontier into a war zone. No wonder the Danes are furious with them."

Erik shook his head. "It's not just a problem of the Prussians. After all, we served with a couple of good ones in Italy. Men like Falkenberg. It's a rot in the Knights of the Holy Trinity. The Knights are supposed to be an arm of the church. To help the spread of the word of Christ. To defend the people of the Holy Roman Empire against the pagans. Here they have become oppressors. They have become a force which drives people away from the church. If the rumor is true—a force motivated by monies paid to the order for seized lands."

"And Charles Fredrik has given me this mess to sort out," said Manfred sourly. "Maybe staying in Mainz would not have been so bad after all."

Erik stood up. "Come. Bring your quilted jacket and the rapier. Let's go and put in some practice in the lower hall."

"I've spent the whole day in the saddle and the mad Icelander wants to go and fence . . ." said Manfred grumbling on principle, digging in his saddlebag.

Erik shook his head. "I don't. Or at least that is not my first purpose. You're going to need to sort the wheat from the chaff here. Let's see whose minds are not too set in stone to try a bout or two with a rapier instead of a broadsword."

"Ah." Manfred nodded, taking the round-edged and buttoned blade from his gear. "Well. Get your winnow then. Let's go and bruise some wheat."

Within the bounds of the Holy Roman Empire, in the Italian states, Aquitaine and the Celtic League of Armagh, gunpowder weapons were becoming increasingly commonplace, and the heavy plate-armor was far less used. The rapier had largely superceded the broadsword, and the style of warfare, too, was changing. But in the pagan northlands, and on the eastern frontier, times had not yet moved onward. Steel plate, spiky and angular to deflect pagan magics, the broadsword and the lance, the mounted knight and the massed charge were still effective against the undisciplined waves of largely unarmored and unmounted barbarians with throwing axes and greatswords. At least . . . on the flatlands.

In the lower hall a number of knights were working at pells and a knight-proctor was drilling an unfortunate group of squires. There was a sudden drop in the clangor when two unarmored knights entered the hall. Then, with ostentatious effort, the drill noises resumed as Manfred and Erik went through a series of stretches and then lunges.

"Why do you bring these little willow wands here? Have you not the thews to wield a true knight's weapon?" sneered one of the knights at last, taking a break from hewing a defenseless hardwood pell into kindling.

Manfred looked at Erik and raised an eyebrow. Erik nodded almost imperceptibly. This one would do. He was older than most of those here, and obviously a pack leader. Erik had noticed him conferring with Von Tiblaut earlier. "I don't suppose," asked Manfred in a diffident tone, "that the good Ritter would care to try a bout?"

The heavy-browed knight snorted. "Me? Von Mell prance around like some ponce of a southern dancing master? No, thank you. Why don't you try a man's weapon instead?" He held up his broadsword.

"Why," said Manfred easily. "I believe I would like to." He stepped over to the Ritter and examined the sword with all the appearance of interest. "Which is supposed to be the sharp end, Ritter?" Smothered snorts and chuckles competed with the all but stilled noises of training.

The heavy brows lowered further. "You are trying to mock me."

Manfred clapped an arm across the man's shoulder. The fact that his hand happened to rest on the knight's neck was purely incidental. "Not I," he said sanctimoniously. "Did I say anything about dancing masters? Come. Let me try this weapon." And he took it from fingers rendered suddenly nerveless, because of the extreme pressure on a point in the Ritter's neck.

Manfred felt the sword's balance, weighing it in his hamlike hands. Erik watched with some amusement. Manfred and the broadsword were a natural pairing. He had the build and the wrists for it. And he'd been training with one for longer, and with better masters, than any border Ritter would have. Manfred turned on the pell.

"Dia Coir!" he thundered. It was a textbook stroke, on the turn with a full bodyweight follow-through, perfect to the detail of exhalation and the war cry's force coinciding with the strike. The top of the pell leaped and bounced across the floor. Manfred stood calmly inspecting the blade. He handed it back to the open-mouthed knight. "See that you get a proper edge onto this thing. It'd do as a butter knife right now."

Embarrassment had turned the heavy-browed knight's face to a shade of beetroot. Now the blood drained away. He was white with fury. Erik tapped him on the shoulder with the rapier. "Let us see how your butter knife can do against my willow wand."

"Are you mad?" demanded the knight, thrusting his blue jaw at the lean-limbed Icelander. Manfred's display of might had made him wary about that newcomer, but this foreigner looked easier meat. He was less bulky, if a little taller.

"I promise I won't hurt you," said Erik reassuringly.

"I meant that my sword is neither rounded nor buttoned," said the Ritter through clenched teeth. "And unlike you, I am armored."

"Ah. Well, I shall just have to keep out of the way of it then," said Erik, stepping back and assuming guard.

Ritter Von Mell took a deep breath. "Let me show you what a true weapon can do. Once I've disarmed you I will give you a long overdue hiding with the flat." He stalked toward Erik.

Erik moved aside easily from the blow intended to knock the relatively frail rapier spinning. The next blow was, if anything, harder, delivered with real anger. Twisting his blade from sixte into a croisé on the furious swing, Erik used Von Mell's momentum to angle the broadsword downward to nick the floorboards. As it did this, the rapier flicked upward to touch the Ritter's throat.

"You are dead once. Do you wish to continue?" asked Erik, dispassionately.

For an answer Von Mell wrenched his blade out of the floor-boards and swung it at Erik's head. Erik sidestepped. For the next ten minutes he continued to dodge, using Von Mell's rage and strength against him, while the entire lower hall watched. Occasionally Erik proved that he could have killed Von Mell. Then, as the Ritter began to seriously tire—he was, except for his helmet and boots, in full armor—Erik began to apply a dreadful lesson, both in swordsmanship and respect. The armor might have saved Von Mell some bruises. It did nothing for his dignity, especially as he received swats across buttocks with the flat every hundred heartbeats or so. Erik Hakkonsen took training to the far edge of fanaticism and a little beyond. He was scarcely even breathing hard. His opponent was staggering, barely able to raise his sword tip. Von Mell was, of course, carrying many extra pounds of steel plate, and a heavier weapon. But he was also not in particularly good shape. Erik did not give him a second opportunity to call a halt.

Eventually Manfred did. He did so by the simple method of taking Von Mell by the neck-piece and sitting him down, hard, in a clatter of steel. Then he twitched the Ritter's broadsword away from him. "Hasn't he sweated enough, Erik?"

"There is still tallow to melt away from his ribs," said the Icelander critically, looking at the knight—who had made no effort to get to his feet again. "However, I hope I have stripped some from between his ears. In future, Ritter, try thinking before you speak."

"He taught me that lesson the hard way, too," said Manfred with a guffaw. "Now," he said to the crowd as he handed the sitting knight his sword again. "Are you all going to watch us or do any of you care to try one of these . . ." he held up a rapier, " . . . willow wands."

There was a long silence. Then one of the knights—the one who had been drilling the squires earlier, stepped forward. "I believe I would."

He was a broad-faced fellow with a square chin and a somewhat crooked nose. Unlike most of the blond Ritters, his hair was an indeterminate brown. There was something about the set of his chin that said that this one was no loudmouth pushover. Von Mell had accompanied them from Lödöse. This was a knight of the local chapter house. Here was someone posted to a border chapter house—and he had been drilling squires—never a popular task. Von Mell had stood close to the proctor-general's confidence. This knight was from the opposite extreme. Erik regarded him carefully. He had potential.

"Certainly, Ritter," Manfred said easily. "I'll give you a hand getting out of that breastplate, if you like. The quilted jacket will save you from getting more than a bruising."

The knight shook his head. "Perhaps tomorrow I will try that. What I would like to see is more of that work with the point. I noted that you, Ritter, used the point a great deal. Is it really effective against armored men?"

Erik nodded. "When used with precision, yes. But you must remember that by and large it is not our foes who are heavily armored, and that firearms—aye, and even crossbow quarrels— render armor an expensive, heavy ornament."

There were faint gasps at what amounted to near sacrilege to the knights. But the broad-faced one acknowledged this with a serious nod. "But in mass combat there is little time or place for precision. And our foes here mostly use throwing axes, spears, and greatswords." He felt the balance of the rapier Manfred had handed him.

Erik liked the lad more and more by the minute. He'd often wondered whether the physical effort of carrying all that steel robbed the brain of needed nourishment. The knights were long on honor, generally long on piety, and a little short on mental flexibility. "True. Although there is always a place for precision, even with a battle-axe. But the foes of the Church we are sworn to defend . . . will not always be the foes you stand against now. This new weapon hones and broadens the skills of a knight. Hold it thus. Posture is somewhat different, too. See."

They worked at it until the vespers bell. And this knight showed no sign of exhaustion. He handed back the rapier. "Perhaps again tomorrow, Ritters," he said, hopefully. "Do you make a long stay here? Have you been stationed here?"

So the run-of-the-mill knights of the local chapter house knew nothing of who they were—or why they had come. Well, even the proctor-general of Skåne didn't know all of it, although he might well guess, as he had chosen to accompany them. "We're on a sort of tour," said Manfred easily. The locals would suspect that they were no ordinary knights anyway, by the very fact that the proctor-general had ventured out into the cold.

CHAPTER 4

Kingshall, Telemark

air was sweeping. Yard sweeping was normally a thrall's way of passing time "constructively" engaged so that he would not be sent to do something that required more energy. Cair regarded it as a necessary evil to be completed as quickly as possible. He'd found that, in his case, few people would come looking for him in his makeshift 'workshop' in the smelly shed behind the hide store. He had several other matters he wished to attend to, today. He had been gathering some old hooves and broken horn pieces, and he wanted to make some spirits of hartshorn. Hartshorn was known and used to revive ladies who felt faint. Cair also knew that there were other, less savory possibilities for the substance. Apparently a similar substance had once been distilled from camel dung in the temple of Jupiter Ammon, in Libya.

Queen Albruna came walking across the yard area, with Signy a few steps behind her. As usual, when in the presence of her stepmother, the princess's shoulders were hunched, and her eyes were downcast. As usual, too, although there were several ladies and serving women accompanying the queen, it was Signy who was carrying the fine porcelain bowl full of rose hips. The bowl was none of the coarse local work or even stoneware from the Empire. By the looks of it, it came from far further east. The queen was apparently on her way to make rose-hip cordial.

Working with food would have been considered beneath most noblewomen, but medicines were different. Albruna was talking loudly and cheerfully. Cair stepped respectfully aside. The queen was not someone that anyone would dare to annoy.

Signy stumbled. She caught her toe on a cobble, and merely spilled two or three of the rose hips. The queen rounded on her. "You clumsy girl! Can't you do anything right? You nearly dropped my bowl! I told you how precious it was."

Cair saw how Signy cringed. And the queen turned on him "You. Thrall. Take the bowl from her. Even a dirty stable-thrall can do the job better than you, Signy."

So Cair dropped his birch-twig broom and ran to take the bowl. Carefully.

It was blue and white, patterned with dragons, but not in the usual serpentlike Norse tradition. He carried it as if it were made of thinnest Venetian blown glass—and indeed that would have been cheaper. Something this fragile, that had traveled this far was rare indeed. He carried it across to the stillroom—where such medicines as the Norse had, were made. Bundles of herbs hung from the roof, drying. The shelves had various bottles on them. Cair peered curiously—he'd never been allowed in here. Unfortunately, all the labeling was in Futhark. He set the bowl down with care, his eyes taking in details. Cair had become an adept thief since he found himself here. Most of the things he stole, true, were ill guarded. They were not things that any thrall might want. This place—other than some of the glassware, and that was poor stuff, too—had little to tempt him.

The women had all crowded into the small room. The queen was famed for her simples, and they'd come to watch. Cair found that his way out was blocked by several Norse matrons who would have made fine pier bollards or bulwarks against any Atlantic storm. Short of pushing through them, he was trapped in this corner. The only clear space was around Signy and, of course, the queen.

The queen handed her stepdaughter a glass beaker with finely chopped herbs in it. "Signy, pour the walnut oil in there—up to the first mark on the glass. Now, obviously the magical healing essence . . ."

Cair watched the princess hold the beaker out at full arm-stretch and squint at it, and then pour carefully. Still peering intently.

The queen exhaled angrily, breath hissing between her square teeth. "You foolish girl! That's far too much oil! And now both the oil and the herbs are spoiled! You infuriate me! Can't you do anything right? I do my duty by you, trying to teach you what a princess of the blood should know. And do you even try?" She tore into Signy, who just stood there, biting her lower lip, her face white, bowed beneath the onslaught. Was this the same young woman who fearlessly mounted warhorses in the stable, and who would kill an old dog, herself, to give it the best surcease from pain that she could?

Cair decided that it was time to intervene. Quietly—and the women were all watching Signy being shredded, so none would notice—he pulled the adder from his ragged pouch and dropped it to the floor, just to the Signy-side of the plump apple-cheeked matrons. It lay there, the malevolent-looking black zig-zags patterning down the dorsal side making even the dead thing look dangerous. One of the other thralls had killed it this morning out in the fields, where they'd been set to moving stones to ready the land for the plow. One of the others had brought it to him. They all brought him the oddest "gifts"—from misshapen roots to odd mushrooms. Sometimes even he was at a loss as to what to do with them. The snake hide he'd thought he would make into a bracelet. Perhaps he might milk out the venom—that might prove useful, too, he'd thought. Well, this was a better use—there was venom enough here. He pushed forward and groveled at the queen's feet, contriving to stand on the snake's head in the process. "Please, Mistress Queen," he quavered in his very worst Norse. "Is snake. Not princess. I kill. Crush head." He pointed—creating shrieks and retreat. "I bump Princess Signy. My wrong, Queen. Not she."

The queen stared at the snake. Then at Signy, and then at Cair. Then at the snake again. Cair had a sinking feeling that she at least wasn't fooled about how alive it had been a few moments back. But she was the only one in the room who hadn't been taken in, judging by the sounds of alarm.

"What a brave thrall," said one of the women, looking in horror at the snake.

The queen schooled her face into the semblance of a smile. "Get up and take it away, thrall. What are you doing in here, anyway?"

"I carry bowl," said Cair, humbly.

Signy spoke up for him. "He doesn't speak very good Norse, Queen Mama. And I don't think he did bump me. He's a good hard worker. He just doesn't understand well."

Cair created a distraction by picking the snake up, and flicking it with his thumb so that the tail waggled about. Rigor had set in but he doubted that many of his audience would notice. The women shrieked obligingly. "I take and throw. Sorry I bump she," he said, making his way through a miraculously clear space to the door.

He escaped with the adder, and went off to throw it away, much amused. The queen might be suspicious, but what could she do?

He found out later. One of the burly guards came down to the stable with a whip. And grabbed Cair by the arm. He pointed with the whip at four of the other thralls. "You. Take his other arm. And, you two, his legs. If I get kicked, you'll get beaten, too. Pull that tunic up."

The guard laid into him with the whip. A slave can be punished at whim. Cair should have remembered that.

"Stop. Why are you beating my thrall?" Signy demanded.

"Queen Albruna told me to, Signy," he didn't even address her as "princess"—rank disrespect. And he laid on another stroke.

"He's my thrall. I'll say if he must be beaten."

He swung the whip down. "I take my orders from Vortenbras or the queen. Not you. He's to get twenty strokes. Go to the queen if you like." The guard seemed to find that very funny.

Signy stared at him in helpless fury. And he raised the whip again. She grabbed a bucket yoke from against the wall, and swung it at him.

He attempted to dodge, but that had two unexpected consequences. The first was that he pulled in against Cair—who bit, hard, into the flesh just above his knee. And thus the return swing of the yoke caught him on the side of the head, instead of his whip arm.

It was a good solid oak yoke, intended to allow a man to carry two buckets of water. It hit the man with an audible crack, too. Signy was small, but not weak. The guard let go of Cair. The thralls already had.

Cair pulled down his tunic, and weighed the options. If this Norse bear of a man attacked Signy . . . well . . . he needed some weapon. But his tongue was always his best form of sword. "It would be hard for the king not to have the head of any man who put a hand on his sister—even in front of thralls," he said, clearly.

The man growled, feeling the side of his head. And Cair realized that he was not quite alone in his fight. The dogs that had inevitably followed Signy around growled straight back at the guard.

"Any minute now and they'll start barking," said Cair calmly. "Then the whole pack of them will be here. They'll tear you apart."

The hulking guard looked at Cair, obviously not knowing quite how to deal with Signy. "Thrall. I've been sent to beat you. I'll go and fetch some of the others and finish the job properly."

Cair shrugged. It hurt like hell. "Enjoy explaining to them that a woman bested you. I'm sure that will make them all respect you."

"You've beaten him," Signy's voice shook slightly. But she stood her ground and held on to the yoke. "Your mistress is not going to count the strokes. Now, go before I whistle. That will indeed bring half the dogs in the hall here."

The guard straightened up. "Just you wait, thrall."

"Oh, I will," said Cair, with a confidence he was far from feeling. "But I won't have long to wait. Ill fortune is right behind you. You are a doomed man. I read it in your future."

The guard snorted. "Insolent thrall. How dare—"

"I mean no disrespect. I do but see what I see," said Cair, loftily.

The guard snorted again, and stalked out.

Cair smiled. It cost him no small effort to do so.

"Back to your work," said Signy to the open-mouthed thralls standing staring.

The others hastened away. "It might have been better just to let him finish beating me, Princess," said Cair, quietly.

"Probably," said Signy with a grimace. "He will come back, thrall, with his companions. And Vortenbras won't listen to me."

Cair bowed. It hurt. "I will deal with it, Princess. He just caught me by surprise."

She looked more worried rather than eased. "You shouldn't have done that trick with the snake, thrall."

Cair attempted not to smile. "But it was a very good one, Princess. The ladies screamed so well."

For the first time ever, Cair saw Signy smile back at him. He decided that a beating had been a small price. She shook her head, almost unbelievingly. "You are very impudent, thrall. But you will get badly hurt."

"I'll do my best not to, Princess. Could you tell the stable master to tell all of us to move the dung heap to the far paddocks tomorrow? Later? Please, my lady?"

She bit her lip. Looked suspiciously at him. Then nodded. "Later."

It was an unpleasant extra job that would take many hours. Cair winced at the thought. And he'd have a sore back for it, too. In the meanwhile he had a lot of preparation to do. If he knew human nature at all, either the guard would be back just as soon as he was sure that the coast was clear, or he would come in the morning after he'd done some brooding. Cair thought it would be wise to disappear for now. Signy's ceiling hideout would do nicely. He took someone's saddle along for company and began to quietly cut stitches with a sharp little fragment of iron he'd made with patient rubbing on some stone. The other part of what he did, he knew that the princess would disapprove of. But the horse would recover.

When evening drew on he slipped out of his sleeping area. Nobody—by now—would dream of mentioning the fact to anyone in authority. He left his carefully caraway-scented bedding and took a long, cold, obstacle-filled walk—dragging a small sack of caraway behind him. He then walked back to the stables. Cair dared not sleep, but instead sat, thinking. Before cock-crow he made himself busy with mucking out. The horses did not approve of the change in pattern, but by the time the thralls were straggling across the garth to the kitchen for their morning rations he'd moved himself off to the dung heap, and had begun loading up the cart.

Presently, the yelling told him that the hue and cry had started. He smiled and went on loading dung. If anyone had actually looked around the back of the stables they'd have seen him there. Soon he heard the dogs, baying, giving out that they had the scent. Cair went on loading. He had the better part of a cartload of dung done before the other thralls, still talking in excited little knots, came around the corner.

They stood there gawping. "But . . . you've run away," said Thjalfi.

Cair shook his head at them. "Run away? I have not. Who would have mucked out for me if I was not here? I couldn't sleep for the pain from lashes. So I came to work early. I've done a great amount of work while you've all lain on your pallets." He pointed at the manure. "See."

The thralls did. He got the feeling that a good few of them wanted to come and touch the manure in the cart just to make sure that it, and he, were real. "But . . . they're out there hunting you," protested one of the thralls who worked in Vortenbras's section.

Cair shrugged. "I can't help that." He noticed that one of the hindmost thralls had sneaked off, doubtless to tell someone. "Come on. Let's get the job done, before it gets too warm and flies drive us all mad."

Thus it was that when the stable master came running around the corner, Cair was once again just a thrall, loading muck. "You," the stable master called him out. "What are you doing here?"

Cair looked puzzled. "Shoveling horse manure, master," he said humbly. His clothes and hands bore ample testimony to this. He was willing to bet his bouquet did, too. Most unlike caraway, it would be. "Ask the others. I had done nearly a cartload by myself. It's what I was told to do. Do you want me to do something else?"

The steward plainly found this a bit too much for his small mind. "But you were missing. You've run away."

Cair contrived to look shocked. "Oh no, master. I'm a good slave. I just started work early. My back was sore and I could not sleep, master."

"He does things like that, Svein," said Signy, who had come on the scene, quietly. "I think he's mad. But he's done his horses, and by the looks of it done a lot of the work I told you to get them to do."

The stable master swallowed as if his mouth was suddenly too dry. "But the dogs followed him. He has run away."

"He didn't run very far, by the looks of it," said Signy, coolly. "I wish the rest of them would run to the dung heap as eagerly."

"But . . . but . . . I set the king's men to hunt him . . ."

Signy raised her eyebrows, tilted her head. "Well, whatever they're hunting, it's not him. You'd better saddle up, so that you can go after them and tell them they've been sent on a fool's errand. If you wait until they've wasted half a day on it they'll be furious."

"They're going to be furious anyway," muttered the man. But he left in haste.

Cair settled into the work. Never had shifting horse dung—even with a sore back, seemed so sweet. And he collected quite a bit of saltpeter in the process. It quite made up for being underslept and very hungry.

Later, the news trickled down. One of Vortenbras's guards had had an unfortunate accident that morning. His cinch had broken midjump, and he had tumbled headfirst into the broken logs and briars. The man had been brought back to the hall on a hurdle, with a cracked head and a broken arm. And his horse had kicked one of the others. That rider had also taken a bad fall.

Cair looked sorrowful. "I did warn him," he said. He'd take things very carefully for a while. But the seeds of rumor were planted. And well watered.

CHAPTER 5

Kingshall, Telemark

Jarl Svein, Hjorda's emissary, was back from Stavanger. Rumor had it that Hjorda's coffers were very full right now. A fleet from Vinland to Flanders had been intercepted, apparently. Doubtless reprisals would follow—but for now Hjorda had gold to burn. Or at least to spend on a bride-price. And, if they'd paid it over to Telemark, the vengeful fleet wouldn't recover it.

Signy made her small, stiff bow to the sleek-looking man. He bowed extravagantly. And well he might. If King Hjorda had his way, she'd be his queen.

For a day, at most—but then he wouldn't know that. If she managed to do it right, that was. There were times when she doubted she'd even get that right.

Signy drew some cold comfort from the knife in her sleeve. It was dedicated to Thor, not Odin. Most of the aristocracy gave some worship there, although Odin was their lord, and the warriors and even the thralls gave more deference to Thor or Frey. The hammer thrower was something of a direct god—but he was an honorable one. Odin's repute was less savory in these matters. Her oath was sworn on Thor's ring, and the hammer inscriptions on the knife.

"Princess," said the jarl reverently. "I am delighted to make your acquaintance. You are everything I was led to believe."

As I have heard you and my stepmother talking about me, that is not a compliment, thought Signy. But she did not allow her face to betray her. "Indeed," she said, frostily.

"Signy," said Queen Albruna, with a honey-dripping smile. "I have wonderful news for you. Your betrothal! Of course the formal announcement and the presentation of the bride-gifts will take place at the banquet tonight. Such joy for you, my dear! Although I will be sad to lose such a dutiful daughter . . ."

"Think of it as gaining a son," said the jarl, somehow managing to keep a straight face. Hjorda was older than the queen.

"Say how happy you are, Princess," said the queen.

"It is my duty to say so," said Signy, even though she knew that this would bring down Albruna's wrath, later, in private.

The jarl chose to ignore this snub, and to continue with more platitudes. He probably had practice. King Hjorda had sent three wives to the burial mound already. "It will be a joyous occasion, joining two ancient great houses."

Hjorda's line was oh . . . maybe a generation old. His father had been a forsworn murderer, too. An ancient great house, indeed. Signy found herself unable to dig up a reply. Besides the lump in her throat was getting in the way of talking. How could Vortenbras agree to this? Queen Albruna wanted her out—so long as she got as great an advantage as possible from her stepdaughter. But Vortenbras! He knew how much their father had hated Hjorda. How could he? But she was a princess of the house royal. She knew where her duty lay. And she knew the sure course to honor, too. She retreated to the corner of the room. Typically, her step-mother's chambers were cold. She pulled her shawl tighter around her thin shoulders and waited for the next horror. It wasn't long in coming. One of the ladies-in-waiting drew attention to the tambour frame the queen had set down. The queen's embroidery was always exquisite. This piece, executed in gold and silk thread, particularly so. It was an as yet uncompleted needle-picture of the death of Brynhild. The admiration in Jarl Svein's voice was genuine. "It's a work of art, Queen Albruna. What they call nué, or 'shaded gold' work in the Empire. The princess is a notable needlewoman. She's been well taught."

Albruna laughed musically. "I'm afraid not, Svein. That's my current piece. Poor Signy shows no talent for this sort of womanly art." Looking across the room Signy could see her own poor effort on a stool by the fireside, where she was sure that she'd not left it. From here she could see every crooked stitch. It was in coarse flax thread, but that was all she found she could work with.

"Signy, do show us your piece. Or perhaps you could sing for us?"

Signy wished desperately to be elsewhere.

The knife came down in a vicious arc. Thrust deep into the softness.

Signy lay there, sobbing, with the knife clutched so hard in her hand that the haft's wire-binding cut into her hands.

She could kill a bolster. But could she kill a man? Even one as vile as her bridegroom?

CHAPTER 6

A chapter house on the Svear borderland

After the rapier winnowing, Erik and Manfred walked across to the main dining hall, to take the evening meal together. The monastic knights lived simply. In theory, anyway. Erik had found it true enough in the chapter houses he and Manfred had served in on the eastern frontier. But here, as at Lödöse, the food and drink were more what one expected in a minor nobleman's manor.

Their fencing companion chose to come and sit across from them. "So," he said, "I gather I have been fencing with people of high degree—who expect special treatment, although this is contrary to our oath."

His voice was guardedly neutral, but he had chosen to sit with them although there were other vacant places.

Erik pushed at the platter of highly spiced pork in front of him. "Is this food specially prepared for our benefit, then?"

"I'm enjoying it, if it is," said Manfred cheerfully. "It's a sight better than the food at Norburg in Prussia was. Not a patch on Venetian cuisine though."

The broad-faced knight looked a little taken aback. "No. This is about the usual standard. I was surprised when I joined, too."

"You should try the houses in eastern Prussia," said Manfred with a grimace. "We were there for our novitiate. They

45

eat nothing but boiled cabbage, turnips, and gruel half the winter, I swear."

The local knight looked distinctly surprised. "I did not know that you had served a novitiate just like the rest of us, Prince Manfred."

Erik's shoulders shook slightly. "He did his best not to, believe me. He certainly did his best not to."

"Yes," said Manfred, ignoring him loftily. "I ate boiled cabbage, turnips, and gruel . . . In between praying and drilling. Or drilling and praying. Your abbot here must be an easy-going one."

"He probably doesn't have reprobates like you to plague him," Erik said, dryly.

The Ritter looked somewhat taken aback. "They made a prince drill and eat cabbage?" he said bemusedly. The idea of the cabbage especially seemed beyond him.

Erik could support that, anyway. Cabbage was something that should forever be removed from the diet of anyone who was going to be confined to armor. "As you said earlier, the order sets aside worldly rank, Ritter. The archbishop himself decreed that Manfred should be just another knight, anonymously enrolled." Erik smiled wryly. "Unfortunately, the prince just hasn't stayed anonymous enough. Word leaked out. People have a problem with leaving off the title, as the Emperor doesn't look kindly on *lèse-majesté*, and we're just serving our time as confreres. They think that next year they might have to please explain why they treated the prince like a lummox who eats too much," he said, pushing the pork platter away.

Manfred reached across him and helped himself to some more of the meat, anyway. "I have a big body to keep up. And I've a lot of cabbage and gruel to get over. To say nothing of the drilling."

"Oh. That was not the impression that the proctor-general gave me a little while back." The Ritter gave them a brief embarrassed smile. "I've been hauled into our abbot's office and told to watch over you and stop you infecting our squires with silly newfangled and undisciplined ideas. I am the proctor of instruction."

"Usually a penance position," said Manfred. "Erik here was given the same task—until they realized that he liked it."

The broad-faced man acknowledged the hit with another smile. "Fortunately, the abbot hasn't caught on to that yet. I was worried that that was why he'd called me in. I was told instead to come and converse with you, and to report back. It is not something that I am accustomed to being asked to do."

So, thought Erik. This was a "fishing" mission. The knight proctor was not too sure which side of the conflict he stood on. So, instead of being a good spy he was letting them know what he was doing here.

"Well, Ritter, let us introduce ourselves formally, seeing as you have orders to converse with us," said Manfred, letting his amusement show now. "I am Manfred of Brittany. The morose one complaining about good food is Erik Hakkonsen."

The knight nodded. "My name is Juzef Szpak." There was something very . . . odd about the way he said it. As if expecting trouble, and ready to meet it halfway if need be.

Only the very observant would have noticed any change in Manfred's manner. But then, Erik was very observant. It had kept him alive, and, because of this, he'd tried to train his charge to be observant too. Sometimes he even thought he'd succeeded. "Well, I am pleased to make your formal acquaintance, Ritter," said Manfred easily, giving him a friendly buffet and a grin. Manfred was plainly going out of his way to be engaging, and to treat Szpak as an equal. "You've the makings of a fine rapier artist."

There was a slight lessening in the tension in Szpak's shoulders. No answering smile, yet. "It is good training. But I think I am too big, Prince Manfred. This Ritter here," he gestured at Erik, "makes me look like an ox."

"Well, he tells me I look like a cross between a donkey and a fat slug," said Manfred. "Szpak. It sounds like a Polish name. Is it?"

"I am Polish, yes. My father was a merchant from Danzig," said the Ritter. His voice was even. His eyes said, "make something of it, even if you are a prince."

No wonder he was in the abbot's black books, thought Erik. The Pomeranians and Prussians from whom the knights now drew most of their membership were the most feudal and downright medieval in the Empire. The Junkers would just *love* a Pole, and a self-confessed son of a merchant, to boot. It was different in Venice, Iceland, or Vinland, where "nobleman" and "trader" were often synonymous. Here a true noble took at sword's point and would cheerfully kill for implying he might sully his hands with vulgar chaffering. This Juzef must be a tough lad to have even made it to being a knight-proctor.

"You've fallen in bad company associating with all these Prussians," said Manfred, plainly also understanding this. "Speaking as a Breton who has fallen in with an Icelander, I am an expert on bad company."

"You *are* bad company," said Erik, pushing his trencher aside and standing up. "Come and talk to us in our quarters, Ritter Szpak. Seeing as you have orders to do so."

"Satisfy my curiosity," said Manfred, once they'd reached the privacy of the chamber that he and Erik had been assigned to. "Just what is a Pole doing here in among the Knights of the Holy Trinity."

Juzef Szpak looked at Manfred thoughtfully. "You do not wish to know what a merchant's son is doing polluting the ranks of the noble order?"

"I'm a Breton," said Manfred digging in his saddlebag. "Things are not quite the same as in the Empire among the Celts, for all that I've spent a lot of my life in the court at Mainz. After all, Erik's father sells ponies and goats. And I put up with him," he said with a good-natured grin. Manfred pulled the metal flask that he'd been looking for out the saddlebag, unstoppered it with his big square teeth, and offered it to the startled Ritter. "Armor polish flavored with caraway. It's good for you. The caraway is a great antidote to the cabbages you seem so worried about."

The unsuspecting knight took a mouthful. "Whuff . . ."

Erik snagged the flask before Manfred could get to it. "Sheep. My father sells ponies and sheep. We haven't risen to goats yet. And we are here to talk, not drink."

"I can do both, even if you can't," said Manfred. But he made no attempt to take the flask.

Szpak looked at them, his blue-gray eyes round. He shook his head. "The abbot and the proctor-general of Skåne seem to have misled me. I was told you had demanded special deference to your rank, and that you were an idle princeling probably here to cause trouble for the Order."

Manfred snorted. "I'm here to cause trouble, all right. But I've seen more concern for worldly rank among the knights here in Skåne and Småland than in all the chapter houses in the Empire. It's part of the problem here, in my opinion."

The Polish knight-proctor did not disagree with him. "It is not like this in the other chapter houses then? I have only served here and in Lödöse."

"There is always a bit of it," admitted Erik. "It is inevitable, I suppose, as a fair number of the knights are confreres, merely doing three or five years' service. People carry grudges, and a minor landholder has to be wary about, say, offending his overlord's son. But to be fair, the abbots and the senior proctors tend to crush it, hard. They're not confreres merely serving the church for a short time, and the knights have their own lands and charters."

"That doesn't seem to be the case here anyway, Erik," said Manfred. He sat back on the bed. "So, Juzef. Tell me how you came to be here. Tell me about the Knights and their work here in southern Sweden. You were told to nose out what you can. I will tell you directly that we've been sent over here for the same purpose. The Danes have complained to the Emperor Charles Fredrik. There are two sides to every complaint, so I'm here to have a look-see."

"And the Emperor sent someone else to soothe the Danes on her own, which is why Manfred is so irritable," said Erik.

Manfred shook a beefy fist at the Icelander.

Gradually, they got the Polish proctor to talk. Eventually he even told them how he came to be here among the Knights. And they found out why the cabbages elicited such a response.

"Mama came from a good Pomeranian Ritter family. Impoverished, yes. But landholders, who trace their ancestry back sixteen generations. My grandfather had made his fortune dealing in barge loads of cabbages. My great-grandfather was probably a runaway serf. My father still dealt in cabbages, and timber and barley . . . maybe if he'd dealt in fine liquors, or rare perfumes and spices he would have been a little more acceptable. But cabbages!" Juzef waved a languid hand under his nose. "Only the Szpak money did not stink."

Erik snorted. "Isn't it odd how if you pile enough money onto any one spot it loses its taint."

Juzef nodded. "True. Especially when a true nobleman must spend money faster than he can obtain it. My father always said that we never saw them unless they'd come to scrounge. Still, Mama liked to see her kin, and we were happy enough not seeing them that often. But when I was a lad of fifteen, that all

changed. You remember the sacking of Breslau? Jagellion decided
to punch into the Holy Roman Empire, and as misfortune would
have it we were trapped by a party of raiders on the road between
Schweidnitz and Hirchberg. They killed our outriders. My older
brother, Czeslaw, died in the fight. But the rest of us were taken
prisoner. And my father attempted to talk, or, more probably,
buy our way out of it. But he was a devout man, and this lot
were from some of Jagellion's pagan tribes. He must have said
something wrong.

"They sacrificed him. Hung him on a pole with the horse
skulls and hides. Had the knights not come to our rescue then,
my mother, sister, and I would have been next. My mother had
us kneel and pray for his soul." He looked a little ashamed. "I'm
afraid I did not pray for Papa. I prayed for our deliverance instead."
He sighed. "When I saw those three crosses on the banners—the
sun shining on their armor . . . well, I knew then that I owed the
same deliverance from evil to others." There was something very
intense about the way he said that, that said his hero worship of
the order was not quite dead.

He sighed again. "Afterwards . . . my mother went back to her
family: now that she was a very wealthy widow, she was acceptable again," he said dryly. "They were only too glad to use their
influence to get me a novitiate. It got that awkward Polish name
out of the family.

"I wished to be on the Lithuanian front. But . . ." He pulled a
face. "Instead, I was sent here. I thought that I would be defending
the people and the Holy Church against the forces of darkness.
Instead, I seem to be a master of squires."

Erik shrugged. "Without squires, learning to be knights, there'd
be no defense for anyone, Juzef. Someone has to do it."

Szpak nodded. "And the truth be told, I enjoy doing it. But I
don't like training them up . . . so that they can be part of a lot
of minor fights with petty pagan chieftains. So the Order can
acquire more land and some more reluctant thralls to become
serfs on the Order's lands." He paused and looked at them, as if
considering his audience. "If you ask me—and nobody does—all
they're doing is uniting the Götar against us."

"Hmm," said Manfred. "And how goes the pastoral work
among the Götar? We are, after all, supposed to be guards for
the shepherds."

Juzef shrugged unhappily. "The Servants of the Trinity are here, yes. But the monks make poor inroads. There are one or two minor Götar chieftains who have been converted by Danish missionaries with their tribes. They're a thorn in the flesh of the ex-confreres, who claim that their settlements are hideouts for escapees. On the estates the serfs are all herded into the churches every Sunday. But there are still hidden temples to their Wodens found from time to time. There is a Sunday service. The tithes are collected. And that is where it ends."

"And what is the role of the Knights in all this?" asked Erik.

Szpak snorted. "Raids and counter-raids. Petty little skirmishes. We win if they try to fight in the open. So now it's always sneak attacks in heavily forested areas. The Götar jarls and their hearthmen, and a few karls have horses, but mostly they fight on foot. Their horses are smaller and lighter than ours and they're mostly not even shod. When it is a cavalry-to-cavalry encounter we always win. So they choose their ground. Then there are reprisal raids against the nearest settlement." He sighed. "But nothing happens at this time of year, at least. Everyone is concentrating on the big enemy now."

"Winter," said Erik with a wry smile.

"Yes. The weather-wise are saying that as the frosts were late, it'll be a bad one. Last year they said the frosts were early so it'd be a bad one," said Juzef with a shrug. "It's a bad time for the peasants regardless, and a good time for me. I get a lot of skills drilled into their thick heads before the boys go out to fight in the springtime."

"Well," said Manfred, "it'll give me a few more weeks to look around and get a complete picture of everything, before there is too much bad weather to move. The combat side might have told me a bit more, but I think I'm getting the idea. We need a few more weeks to think about what needs to be done here."

"You don't seem to be in any hurry to act, Prince Manfred," said Juzef.

Manfred folded his powerful arms. "My . . . other strategy advisor," he said giving Erik an amused smile, "put it to me like this: When you act on the Emperor's behalf, you'd better be sure, and very sure, that you act according to his wishes. You must act in such a way that any credit reflects on the Empire, and any blame is shouldered by yourself. It's not something you can take lightly."

Erik snorted. "Francesca. I give her credit for managing to get it into your thick skull in a mere couple of years. Anyway, I think we should seek our rest, Ritter Szpak. Tomorrow will be more drill, and we can talk further."

The broad-faced Pole got up. "Yes. Thank you, gentlemen." He bit his lip. "I hope . . . well, I hope you can resurrect my reason for joining the Knights of the Holy Trinity. I was thinking of abandoning my vows. It has been troubling me for some time now. Good night." He walked briskly out, closing the heavy door behind him.

When he was well down the passage, Manfred looked at Erik and said, "We'll need some more like him. But he's a good start, eh, Erik?"

"His being a Pole will not help. The Prussians won't take kindly to him."

"With any luck, come spring, Francesca will have a few hundred Danish second sons ready to join up. We decided that would be the easiest way of soothing the Danes and helping the order. Danes don't have anything against Poles."

"Ah, but your problem may be convincing that Pole that everyone in the world doesn't have anything against him," said Erik, with a yawn.

"True," said Manfred. "But then Francesca said that, in her assessment, our problem here was that the Danes and Knights had nothing to offer the locals. Remember. She was saying how in Catalunia the local barons bought into the Empire, because they kept their lands and it was better than that mad archduke of theirs. Strikes me that we have the same problem with the Poles on the border there. The serfs like the Knights better than Jagellion, once they get used to it. And the Knights are not gentle on them, as you remember. It's the minor gentry we need to look at seducing too. In the longer term this Szpak might be useful there, too."

"She's got you thinking in her terms, anyway," said Erik, sardonically. "Be realistic, Manfred. Jagellion's nobles—even the minor knights—are more hidebound than even the Prussians about their birth. Now, let's get some sleep. We'll winnow some more wheat in the morning, and move on to the next chapter house."

Erik was usually right. But he was wrong this time.

CHAPTER 7

Kingshall, Telemark

The gables of the Odinshof was held up by two massive, ancient, and deeply carved wooden pillars. Outside the grove, the ancient sacred *Vé* circle-grove still stood, the oaks marking the *waerd* of the temple. Every midsummer and again at midwinter the high priest would don *draupnir*, the "dripper"—the heavy, inscribed golden arm ring—and walk the bounds of the *Vé*, walking widdershins around the circle within the circle, chanting the *galdr*, calling the blessing of the one-eyed wanderer down on the kingdom. The sacrifice would be made, and the needfire kindled. Oaths would be sworn and renewed.

It was said that while the circle of wood, stone, and gold remained unbroken, so, too, would the kingdom remain whole.

The screaming carried much farther than the bounds. It carried all the way to the royal hall. Signy bit her lip, knowing that it could not continue much longer. The blood-eagle rite was both terrible and painful. But the victim—with his lungs pulled out of his rib-cage, spread into eagle-wings on his back, and the wounds salted, usually died quickly. The jarl had been both a Vestfolder and an enemy, and, it was reputed, a Christian. He was therefore an appropriate sacrifice. It was a rite that Vortenbras was fond of. He would sever the ribs and pull the lungs out himself. Today three of them would die. One at dawn, one at midday, and one at nightfall.

If possible Signy would ride out. As far out as possible. Hawking, officially, to provide some game for the feasting tonight. Hawking was an activity the dowager queen mother had declared noble and ladylike, so Signy often got away with this. The queen fussed about hats and gloves, declaring nothing so injurious to the feminine complexion as the sun. Albruna avoided it. Signy usually managed to forget either her hat or her gloves, or both.

Today, unfortunately, the queen had been less obliging. When she had come through to Signy's chambers, with three of the coastal jarl's wives in tow, she'd found her stepdaughter already dressed in her riding habit. "No, my dear," the queen had said, with that false sweetness that she sometimes used in front of strangers when addressing her stepdaughter, "Today I need you to join me at the temple."

Signy knew that it was futile to try to resist the honey-sweet pressure that her stepmother could bring to bear. Still, she tried. "It makes me feel sick, Queen Mother." She wrung her hands, and looked pleadingly up at Albruna.

The queen mother always looked like the perfect mother-figure, with her apple-red cheeks, gentle smile, blue-green eyes, thick braided blond hair, and ample bosom to clasp her children to. A part of Signy always hoped that she really would be like that.

"We must show a proper respect, Princess Signy," said Albruna, with just a touch of rigidity in her voice.

Signy had come to dread that rigidity. She bowed her head meekly and said, "Yes, Queen Mama."

The queen mother liked to be thus addressed, at least publicly, and gave her a thin smile. "So, change out of that disreputable garment and come down to my chambers. We ladies will all proceed to the temple together."

Signy noticed that one of the women accompanying Queen Albruna was looking distinctly green herself. Rumor had it that several of the coastal jarls had become Christians in secret. Her father would never have tolerated it, but Vortenbras didn't seem to care. He was keen on the observance of blood rites, which had largely fallen into disuse during her father's rule. But he didn't swear by the Wanderer the way most of the nobility did. It was odd. But then, you didn't question her half-brother Vortenbras. Even as a growing and brutal boy he'd always had the strength of two men. Now that he was full grown, Signy had to admit that he was the image of a true Viking lord. Father had always been proud of his size and strength. Of course, as a girl-child she'd been barely noticed, except when shooting or riding. Then King Olaf had been happy to acknowledge her as his daughter, even if she was a poor scrap of girl. She could ride, really ride, which Vortenbras could not. He always looked like a sack of meal on a horse. And he would turn the most placid mare into a restive thing. Signy had always desperately wished that she could change herself into a boy, and one with Vortenbras's thews. If the queen mother had had her way, the princess would only have ridden when strictly supervised, on the kind of horses Albruna preferred: one step above a fat donkey. But King Olaf had given in to the queen on everything but this. "She's my daughter, dear. She has the right to ride anything that she can, in my stables." If he'd said it once, he'd said it a hundred times. And she could still remember how he'd always gone on, with his characteristic baying laugh. "And that means every horse I have. They follow the little thing around like dogs." So she still got to ride, to hawk, and to shoot. It had become taken for granted that she would, and although Albruna had done her best to restrict it since the king's death, Signy still did. On horseback she did not feel useless.

But today, in an ill-fitting green dress of heavy brocade that she needed a thrall to get herself laced and buttoned into, she would sit through the chanting and drinking of blood oaths, and desperately wish herself elsewhere.

There was a polite knock on the door. Only the thrall Cair ever knocked like that. The other servants tended to be through the door by the time they'd finished knocking. Mind you, he was making headway there, too. At least they knocked now. She had decided it was probably best not to ask too closely about what her newest slave was doing to the lackwits, slackers, and her stepmother's spies who had been given to her as servitors. He was something of an enigma, this thrall.

Cair bowed, polite as always. "I have brought something for you, Princess." He took a neat cloth package out of his ragged pouch.

That pouch amused Signy. He was her thrall, and she'd given him permission to carry it. It was as grubby and ragged as any item a thrall might own. Yet she'd caught a glimpse of gold in it. And that certainly wasn't all it held. Signy had decided that the man was a magpie. He had anything from birds' eggs to bundles of old cloth containing gods alone knew what. He didn't need the pretense of a ragged pouch to keep the thralls' fingers from exploring it while he slept. They were all terrified of him, and especially that pouch. The house-thralls avoided him, pulling their skirts aside when he walked past, but he'd made her part of the stables shine. If he was a *seid*-witch, the more power to him. Cair was possibly the only person that Signy felt she didn't have to watch her tongue with. Since the snake incident, he'd had a few more whippings at Albruna's order. The queen always found some pretext, but basically it was because the queen did not approve of even a mere thrall treating Signy with deference. It hadn't appeared to worry him. Or change the way that he behaved.

Signy knew that the raid which had brought him here had been an utter failure, bringing back a bare handful of slaves. It had been in breach of the truce oath too: a shameful thing, even if Vortenbras claimed otherwise. So what if the Emperor was a Christian? An oath sworn on Odin's ring might not bind the Christian, but it ought to bind both Vortenbras and Telemark. But then Vortenbras had territorial ambitions and wasn't about to let an oath stop him. Some successful viking was needed to get a following. A great raid would have drawn every second son, every malcontent and troublemaker from across the thirteen kingdoms, and Sweden and Denmark, too, to Vortenbras's standard.

It had failed.

So, now the king was displaying piety instead.

Signy took the parcel from the thrall Vortenbras had rejected as too old, too sick, and unable to speak a civilized language. The more fool her half-brother. The man had learned Norse with the speed and eagerness of a salmon that wanted to spawn. His accent was a little odd, but he was fluent. And, she had to admit, he was as clever as a fox to boot.

She looked at the little bundle with a raised eyebrow. This new thrall was one of the few (if not the only) person, besides the dogs and horses to whom she could cheerfully say what she liked. "What's this, Cair? A potion to make me vomit on the queen? She'll have me whipped again."

Cair smiled crookedly. "But wouldn't it be worth the whipping, Princess? No. It is just some clean beeswax."

She looked quizzically at him. "To chew. Or to make candles from during the rites?"

He shook his head. "There is a story of a Greek hero who saved his ship from sirens—beautiful singers that lure sailors to their doom, Princess—by getting his crew to plug their ears with beeswax. The sounds distress you. With your hair braided as it is over your ears, no one will ever know. Even the queen will not notice."

"If she talks to me she will."

The slave-thrall shrugged. "She doesn't talk to you, Princess. She talks at you. Just nod and say yes. She'll never know the difference."

Signy had to smile. This thrall did that to her. He was nearly as good as a dog at it. He didn't seem to know his place, or care that he was of a lower order—but he treated her as if she deserved great respect. She'd have thought that as an outlander he was confused about her status, except—well, he certainly wasn't stupid. "The queen would have you whipped for that, Cair."

He tapped his forehead. "A good thing that I made sure that she wasn't listening, Princess. She is down in main hall. She's got long ears." He waggled his hands beside his head of odd, curly black hair. "But not that long," he said, stretching his arms up and waggling his hands at full stretch.

Signy found her smile had grown to a laugh. "Yes, but she has her spies. You'd better get away from here before Borgny comes to help me with my dress."

Cair assumed a look of deep sadness. "Borgny is very unwell. Little Gudrun is on her way up to assist you."

Borgny was one of the queen's pets, and one of Signy's worst tormentors. Little Gudrun was too timid to torment anyone. She was nearly as small as Signy. The princess looked suspiciously at the thrall. He smiled enigmatically.

Signy shook her head. "The queen will surely get rid of you," she said, quietly. "She always does. But if, as I have been led to expect, my marriage to that pig Hjorda of Rogaland is to come in the spring, I'm determined to take you along. You're too good a thrall to deserve less. I'll need at least one thrall for my pyre." She smiled at him. "And that would give you entry to Odin's halls, which no thrall can expect, otherwise."

He seemed a bit taken aback. But that was not really surprising.

It was quite a privilege, normally only accorded to the servant of a lifetime.

Later, she sat with the royal household as the priest walked around Odinshof, flicking blood from the altar bowl with his *hlauttein* twig of mistletoe. The broad gold arm ring seemed almost too heavy for the old man. Well, it was said to be a harsh duty to have to wear the *draupnir*. It rested normally on the huge altar block, and was only taken up for the swearing of oaths and other stern duties like this.

And the beeswax seemed to have worked. This time it was her stepmother who looked a little sick, and pale. Signy hoped desperately that her stepmother would go off to her estates near the border to recover. Kingshall was always easier to survive when she was away.

CHAPTER 8

air found what the little princess had just said one of the most puzzling things he'd yet encountered among these uncivilized primitives. If he'd understood it right she'd just, with the air of someone conveying a huge privilege, decided to have him on her pyre when she got married.

Weddings around these parts plainly involved more than just a little bed warming! So he took himself back to the stables and to Thjalfi. The thrall might be a few pieces short of a full set of chessmen in his head, but he was an invaluable source of information. And because he was more than a little slow, he was easy enough to pump unobtrusively.

"Brides get burned?" The thrall shook his head. "No, not unless the groom works too hard on his wedding night and dies. Then she may climb onto his pyre with him. Much honor to the wife. Very romantic," he said, dreamily. "Ancient heroines like Signy—she who was married against her will to King Siggeir, the King of Gautland, and then had her vengeance, and was burned beside him."

Cair swallowed, beginning to understand the context of this Signy's statements. "And who else? I mean . . . tell me about the way you would burn a great jarl or his lady."

Eagerly, the thrall began a lengthy description of the burial of King Olaf. Painstakingly he listed the grave goods and the food that even thralls had got to taste. Eventually he came to: "And,

59

with the king we put six serving girls and six thralls. It is a great honor," he said, hopelessly wishful. "Thralls go to Odin's hall to serve there!"

It sounded like the sort of privilege that Cair felt he could go without. But he'd better learn to understand their religion and society. He'd been avoiding doing so previously. Looking back, he could see that he'd been stupid. Disdain was all very well, but you had to know your enemy.

Over the next week Cair tried to absorb the religion and culture of his captors. The more he learned the more he decided that these Norsemen were crazy. They believed everything had either a spirit, or a little gnome, or a troll occupying it. Giants made natural phenomena like storms or earthquakes happen. Ha. Stupidity. To someone like himself, a firm believer in real cause and effect, doubly so.

He'd even sneaked into the pagan's temple for a look around. Well, he'd bribed one of the door wardens. Even in a slave society there is some money floating around. Some of it inevitably found its way to a worker of charms. "We thralls don't go there! But Vilmut will let you sneak in in the early morning when he is on duty. Albrecht is always asleep then," one of the girls had told him. "He will let you in for a copper penny. Two if you want some of the holy ash."

"The holy ash?"

She giggled. "It's no use to you, outlander. You're a man. Or at least, we think so. It is powerful fertility magic. Especially from the Yule log. That is what the priests scatter on the fields at the Beltane feasts."

So, in the pale dawnlight he had gone and parted with a solitary copper penny. The ash from the kitchen hearths would do just as well for the things he needed ash for. He suspected the ash from there would do just as well for the foolish women, too. The crude soap he'd made with it might even help fertility. At least they might smell less and thus attract someone to assist with conception. Soap was still an imported luxury here.

This particular temple was dedicated to Odin. There were others around, but it appeared that the one-eyed god was the darling of the Norse ruling nobility. Thor held sway among the warriors, and was even venerated by the thralls. But Odinshof here was strictly for the nobility.

It was a pretty poor place for all that. Cair had looted far better. The only piece of gold in the place was a solitary, chunky, crudely engraved bracelet, rather like the ones that a fair number of the warriors wore just above the elbow. It lay, quite unguarded, on the middle of a huge slab of stone in the middle of the floor. An earth floor, yet! The rest of the place was wooden, and every surface was carved. The only exception was the back wall, where the fire burned—which was just the rock of the place. The image of their god was old and wooden, too. He might be the Lord of the Nobles, but Cair thought that he could use a dose of gold leaf. He looked more like a sneak thief than a god. Still, the monastic orders would pay for these idols. The monks believed them imbued with magical power. Cair treated that assertion with the scepticism it deserved, but, well, if they wanted to part with good money . . . He studied the carvings. The stains on the huge rock—it must weigh three hundredweight at least—suggested that blood sacrifice was practiced here. In the grove, on angled poles, he'd seen evidence of horse sacrifices, anyway. Skulls and hides. It seemed a waste of good animals, as he doubted that they'd have the common sense to give this Odin the unsound beasts.

They were remarkably gullible, he decided.

The other thing he decided was that Princess Signy needed his help. Badly.

He started working on a few suitable "miracles." And doing a little unobtrusive dyeing work on Signy's wedding robe, secretly looted from the kist in chambers. It would now change color with body heat . . . a simple trick that should convince both her and any others. As for the rest: he had been collecting sulphur from the dried-out ponds next to the mine up on the hill, and saltpeter was something that the horse-dung heaps had provided. And charcoal was easy enough. Making vitriol had been tricky— glassware or even glazed pottery was hard for a thrall to come by, even one such as himself. But the shed behind the tannery was now transformed into quite a laboratory. The thralls were all in terror of what he did there, and the smell of the tanning kept others away.

The only question was just how much time he actually had. He was an astute observer of people. He'd managed to keep the peace in a fleet of corsairs, to direct their internal pressures at an external foe. There were storm signals building up here.

Vortenbras had added to his pack of hearthmen from across the petty Norse kingdoms—and beyond. He had a fair number of disaffected Danes and Svear, too. A bad lot, in Cair's judgment. At the moment Telemark appeared to have weaker enemies all around her. The small kingdom had a peace treaty with the Empire and the Danes, but was more or less at war with its neighbors. Only the fact that they all hated and distrusted each other stopped them from allying and destroying Telemark.

CHAPTER 9

Telemark and Trollheim

In the mountains of Norway, some trails lead where they appear to. Others lead nowhere. A few lead . . . elsewhere. Don't follow those if you wish to return. Miners digging copper and fine silver in the mountains of Telemark know that this also applies to unknown galleries that they break into from time to time. No miner would go wandering down those galleries. Instead, wisely, they block the holes with heavy stones, and look to follow the ore-body in another direction.

Sometimes something will shift the stones.

Then it's a good time to go delving elsewhere entirely.

Only a trail of mine-tailings in among the stunted trees, and on the rock slope above an old, lichen-encrusted bautarstein mark this spot. The driven stone is not a large one. But it is very, very old. And it is coarse-grained gabbro, while the rock around is a pale and fine-grained granite. It is well off the trail that leads through to the next valley. There is no trail to the hole in the rock wall, and its old spill of mine-tailings. But if you look carefully you will see the mark of bears. It is a dangerous place to wander.

In the misting rain the file of *björnhednar* had carried their mistress in through the mine and downward. Ever downward. Across the bridge that is called *Gjallarbru*, and out into her country. Bakrauf breathed the air of the place, drawing strength into herself from it. Much of her magic was derived from here and she needed to return from time to time. They marched across the river—a mere braiding on the sandbanks now, and onward to her castle. The pillars raised it and she was borne inward.

Soon the troll-wife was on her throne, its posts carved with dreadful bears and the runes of binding. She sat and waited, preparing herself, repairing herself. Sometimes sunlight was inevitable. Troll-folk of lesser magical skill could not have protected themselves against it. Normally she'd have drawn on the strength of the half-aflar in the Odin rites, but somehow this had been denied to her this time, despite her charms and the thrall bracelets. That was worrying. So was the situation. So she waited. Her son would come when he had killed and eaten. Together they would have to try a working. She'd considered raising the draug from the peat again, but had decided to go deeper. Further.

At length her son shambled in. There was still blood on his muzzle.

Bakrauf could see through the mask of humanity that Chernobog had assumed. Grand Duke Jagellion had been overmastered by the Black Brain long since. For a human to attempt to control such a one was rank folly. In the longer term, she and the other creatures of the wider dimensions played for greater stakes than mere geographical control over pieces of the human world. But there were resources and power to seize. And there were the supernatural forces that opposed them both to be dealt with. One day they would struggle for supremacy. Here in her own place, the troll-wife feared not even Chernobog. In the wider world it might be different, and in his realm he could destroy her instantly. But for now they would cooperate. She and her son had designs on the north parts. It suited Jagellion to have a threat to the north of the Holy Roman Empire. The Svear were ripe for amalgamation. The Danes and the Imperial Knights in Skåne could never hold them, if they and the Norse unified. Besides, the Danes and the Empire were at each other's throats at the moment. The Norse and Svear could exploit that. Denmark, too, had people who yearned for the old ways and the old days. They could harry the Baltic, and the Empire's west coast was virtually naked. A new Viking age could be born.

Jagellion would not oppose this—although his own territories would abut theirs, if they succeeded. And his magician and aide-de-camp, Count Mindaug, was almost too expert in western and northern magics for his master's good . . . if his master had merely been Grand Duke Jagellion of Lithuania.

Mindaug might . . . or might not be aware that his master had been absorbed by the demon. But when Bakrauf explained her problem to him, he did understand that at least, no matter what he knew about his master. He explained: "The constrained dead cannot lie, lady. But they do not always speak the whole truth. The 'draupnir' you speak of is more than just an arm-ring. Such items become the repository of generations of sympathetic magic. In a way it is the embodiment of the place itself. Forget trying to break the oath. You would have to shatter the very rock apart before that could work."

"And if I destroyed it?" she asked venomously.

"That would work, of course," said Mindaug. "But it would probably be easier to destroy the land itself. On the other hand, such symbols are usually protected, but they have geographical limitations. Remove them from their places of power and you may as well have destroyed them."

She shook her head. "The arm-ring cannot be removed from the temple *waerds*. There is a curse on it, powerful enough to affect even nonhumans such as my son and I. We tried. We used our tool-creatures, and they, too, failed. I thought that if I could bring it here, I could deal with it."

Mindaug bared his sharpened teeth. Looked thoughtful. "If you could desecrate it in some way . . ."

"How? My son and I are not able to tolerate something that could hurt such a thing . . ." Bakrauf paused. "I suppose we could get others to do it. Powerful Christian mages. And of course the oath must be renewed with the winter solstice."

Jagellion, who had sat silent through the consultation, rubbed a hand across the place where his eyes would have been, spoke now for the first time. "The simplest would be to avoid the oath renewal—if you can. The arm-ring may compel such a thing, just as it placed under ill fortune your earlier plans."

Bakrauf's son growled. It was a terrible sound.

CHAPTER 10

The morning brought a rider from Lödöse to the dining hall. One who had come in the night, now, when nights were an ill time to be riding. Erik noted the new arrival in the dining hall when they had stopped to break their fast—after a good two hours' weapons drill.

"Who's he?" asked Erik, as the Polish Ritter came to join them.

Szpak looked. He raised his solid bar of eyebrow. "Nothing passes you by, Ritter. He came from Lödöse late last night, and sat closeted with the abbot and the proctor-general. He was once a knight with the order. He has family interests in Copenhagen, I believe."

Erik smiled wryly. "Noticing things is a bodyguard's job. My father started training me up for that when I was about five, Juzef. And I might say that nothing seems to pass you by, either."

The Polish proctor shrugged. "Secrets in a monastic order are few and far between, Erik."

"He's got all the hallmarks of a bearer of news," said Erik, suspiciously. "There is something afoot, Manfred. Word out of Denmark about what you're actually here to do, at a guess. I think we need to gather your escort. Now. They're not locals."

Manfred looked at his half-finished platter. "You're getting worse than Sachs at seeing evil under every cobble." He was never at his best before breakfast, and Erik had been using him as a training model since before dawn.

The call to arms came just after breakfast.

"At least they had the decency to let us fill our bellies first," said Manfred quietly to Erik as they stood in the courtyard, listening to the abbot, along with all the other men under arms in the chapter house.

"Very considerate. Such reports of raiders always come in at times designed to fit in with normal routine," said Erik sardonically.

"Hmm. I suppose we'd better offer to ride along," said Manfred, thoughtfully.

"Breakfast improved your temper, anyway," said Erik. "Volunteering to ride out, yet."

"Well, it isn't actually raining, at the moment," said Manfred, looking at the sky. "And it is easier than being used as a demonstration dummy by you."

But there was absolutely no need for them to volunteer. The proctor-general of Skåne was generous enough to volunteer them for the mission. "I have requested that the abbot make a space for you in the troop that rides out," he said. "You will be in no danger, but I wish you to see firsthand what sort of atrocities these pagans practice."

"They have committed some atrocity?" asked Erik. There had been, well, a note of surprise in the hushed comments among the knights in the courtyard. It was late for such raids—mostly these were aimed at reprovisioning at the enemy's expense. Once the grain had been gathered in, but while cattle were still on the hoof, was the preferred time. It was a lot easier to drive off beef on the hoof than in a salt cask. Martinmas slaughterings were well behind them now. Things normally settled down for winter.

"Atrocities are always committed," said the proctor-general.

From what Erik knew of raiders anywhere that was probably true enough.

Erik and Manfred mounted up and rode out with the column, with Mecklen and three of his companions unobtrusively behind. Erik noted, to his surprise, that the Polish proctor of instruction, Juzef Szpak, had also ridden along. He found a reason, a little later, to ask him why.

Szpak looked faintly embarrassed. "I . . . told the abbot that

I wanted to go on watching you. He told me it was no longer necessary. So I leaned on one of the young fellows who was among my better—if more troublesome—squires last year to feel sick and give up his place to me."

Erik looked at him with narrowed eyes. "So, your abbot told you it was no longer necessary—but you decided to go on a long ride in the cold anyway. Why?"

Szpak looked awkward, and mumbled "Because I don't trust him. The Svear don't raid at this time of year. He handpicked the knights himself. He doesn't usually do that—one of the proctors does. They're a mixture of a few of the worst Prussians and a lot of green youngsters. I owe it to my boys to watch over this lot. There is something going on."

"I had decided that, too," said Erik, grimly.

But for the rest of that day nothing happened. They spent the night in a heavily fortified border manor and were in the saddle at first light heading toward a smoke plume. A smoke plume to the northwest in—according to their worried host—a stable area. One where there had not been trouble for over a year. Szpak confirmed this. It was not an area where he'd even been.

A man on a hard-ridden horse met them en route. It was Ritter Von Naid—once a confrere with the order himself.

Raiders had struck one of his estates the previous night.

"I had a lucky escape," explained Von Naid. "It's a small estate, near the border. I was there yesterday. I had a problem with the accounts and I took my steward and my strongbox back to Narnholm—my main estate—with several of my servitors from the border estate to help me guard it. This morning a servant came with the news that the place had been sacked. Several of my people are dead, and goods and livestock have been looted. My men have gone to see if they can find the culprits' trail."

CHAPTER 11

Telemark: a dale near Kingshall

Fifteen sheep slaughtered!" Vortenbras seemed to take it as a personal affront. The fact that the terrified karl had also reported the death of his shepherd seemed irrelevant. The royal party had been on a hunt close enough for the man to accost them. Only naked fear could have made him interrupt royal personages in the pursuit of pleasure. But from what he described to his overlord, he had reason for that fear. "Yes. Their throats torn out. The monster drained the blood out of them for his ale!"

"Sounds like a rabid wolf to me," said one of the nobles, dismissively.

"Lord. No wolf can break down a good oak door. No wolf tears just the liver out of a man," said the karl obstinately, fear lending him the courage to gainsay his betters.

"We'll ride up and have a look," said Vortenbras. "We can hunt wolf as easily as deer."

Signy, well back in the mass of riders, said nothing. She'd heard stories like this before—horror stories. But the other incidents had always happened in far corners of the kingdom. This little valley was virtually on their doorstep.

It was a beautiful little spot. Sheltered and quiet. The last autumn leaves still clung to the apple trees beside the stone hut.

The door was made of coarsely rived oak, probably made right here on the holding. Each of the planks were at least one hand thick. Something had smashed it in as if it were no more than parchment.

One of the huntsmen examined the dead sheep. "Its throat has been slashed, Your Highness, not bitten out."

"A man did this?" asked Signy, looking at it. "A man with a knife, perhaps?"

The huntsman looked doubtful. "Maybe. But why at least four times?"

Vortenbras and two of his personal guard and several noblemen had by now dismounted and gone into the hut to look. They found something that both the killer and the karl had missed: a child fearfully peering up from the root cellar. The little boy was not six years old and plainly far gone into terror. But he was able to tell Signy in a low, sobbing whisper about the thing. The monster. "It was big. So big it nearly didn't fit in the house. And white, with claws and teeth ..." He started sobbing uncontrollably. Signy wished desperately that someone who had some experience of children was there to help her. Then the karl who had brought them word picked the little urchin up. Hugged him. "I've a son of my own, lady," he said, gruffly. "He needs to be held right now. This boy lost his mother a few years back. His father was all he had. I'll see to him."

They found the claw-footed tracks—each print at least two hands wide, with the claws cutting like spikes into the turf. That was easy enough. They set the dogs to it. But the dogs kept flying from the scent and coming back to seek the company of the horses and hunters. "Dogs don't like it," commented one of the huntsmen, nervously rubbing a hammer amulet at his throat.

They weren't the only ones.

The trail ended at a sheer rock wall. They rode around it to try and find where the creature had gone, but failed.

It was a subdued and frightened group of hunters that returned to the stable that evening. But other than to offer a sacrifice, there was nothing further that could be done. Vortenbras and his men scoured the countryside for several more days, and Signy had her solitary rides constrained.

It also brought her, finally, to the private conversation she'd been seeking with her brother. "Why? Father raised us to hate

Hjorda. Rogaland are our enemies. Why must you agree to my marrying the pig? Couldn't you find another midden to give me to? Father would be furious with you."

"Don't meddle in affairs of state, Signy," he growled, looking somewhat discomforted—as he always did, when she mentioned their father.

"This *is* my affair," said Signy, bitterly. "Or do you forget that I am going to be married to that creature?"

Vortenbras growled, "You don't seem to understand what sort of difficulty Telemark is in right now, little sister." He always called her "little sister" when he wanted to emphasize his superiority.

"No, I don't," snapped Signy, anger beginning to override her fear of her brother, "Because you never tell me what is going on. Father always told us about everything. You treat me as if I was some stupid serving wench. Well I'm not..."

"You behave like one. If you would keep out of the stables, and behave like a princess, I might be more inclined to trust you. The truth is Hjorda has us in a very awkward position, Signy. He has sworn pacts with a number of the coastal jarls. For reasons of honor, they will not attack him. Not without some overwhelmingly good reason. Either honor must be satisfied and he must die, as our father desired, or else we need him as our ally."

"I'd sooner die than be wedded to that..." She searched vainly for a better word and had to settle for "pig" again.

"That's your choice, little sister," said Vortenbras turning and getting up. "You've wasted every other opportunity Mother has given you to attract another suitor of high degree. Don't make your undutiful behavior my problem. You've been promised to King Hjorda in the springtime. I gave my word that you'd be there."

"It is your duty, Signy," said Albruna who had come into the room unnoticed. The queen could move silently when she wanted to. "You know what choices the daughter of a royal house has."

Signy felt the weight of her stepmother's presence settling on her. Just being near to her seemed to draw something out of Signy. "Yes," she said dully. At least she was free to kill Hjorda. As soon as possible she found a reason to flee out to the stables. Horses and dogs did not use you. Or lie to you.

CHAPTER 12

Småland

Erik looked at the devastation. Looked down at the ground, and dismounted.

He actually got down on his hands and knees and examined the trodden earth. Then he stood up and stared at their guide. "Ritter Von Naid. Are you sure these raiders were Svear from across the borders?"

"And who else would burn my barns, my hay ricks, and the cottages, not to mention butchering my people?" demanded the Ritter.

Erik stared hard at him. "Who indeed?" he asked sardonically. "All riding heavy, ironshod horses, too. Isn't that odd, as from what I can gather the Götar have smaller horses, which are mostly unshod."

Von Naid blanched, but he obviously thought on his feet. "They steal our horseflesh," he said, hastily. "It is a real problem, here on the frontier. It makes identifying people by their tracks difficult. But my men tracked them to their settlement."

Erik looked down without saying anything. He kicked a piece of horse dung apart. And then used a handy mounting block to get back onto his horse. As the cavalcade rode off toward the Götar settlement, he fell in next to Manfred. "This stinks," he said, quietly.

"Well, you would kick horse dung," said Manfred, with a grin.

"If that was the worst it smelled of, we'd be fine," said Eric, grimly.

"So what do you think is going on?"

"I'm not sure yet."

Half a mile on they met with four men—Von Naid's.

"We followed them, milord. They thought they'd hidden their trail. The cattle tracks were easy enough. They're in a settlement over that hill there—about two miles from this place. Captives, horses, and cattle."

Manfred sidled his horse over to Erik. "Three miles. But we heard about this bunch of raiders from nearly thirty miles away. Mighty good information system they have."

They rode on through forested country, and at length stood looking down at a rather scruffy little hamlet next to a ford and a small dam and mill. It had a palisade, but the gate was open.

"Well," said the hard-bitten proctor who led the group, drawing his sword. "Let's ride down and ask some questions." By the way he said it, it was going to be questions reenforced with—if someone was lucky—the flat of that broadsword.

"Do you think that's altogether wise?" said Erik. "They've seen us. They're not closing that gate. This is either an ambush or they're innocent. Either way there are better ways of approaching this."

"I am in command here, Ritter," said the proctor. "I'm used to handling these Götar. Leave it to those of us who know. Out swords, Ritters." And there was a steely rasp of his orders being obeyed.

He began to lead off down the hill at a brisk trot. And an arrow arced out of the thicket below them to their left.

It hit a horse. The animal screamed and the rider went down with a clatter.

The proctor half turned, saw, and yelled, "Charge!"

The knights put spurs to their horses.

And Manfred bellowed, "HOLD!"

Manfred had the kind of voice that would even penetrate a charging knight's helmet. Erik joined him in a second bellow.

It was chaos. Of the thirty knights, several were still careering down the hill. Some were wavering, half turned in the saddle—and a fair number had turned back.

Then, at a full gallop, Szpak caught up with the leading proctor.

And knocked him out of the saddle with a mailed fist.

"Hold," he yelled, too, turning his horse. Facing the oncoming knights with his sword in hand.

Mecklen had produced a small horn. "I think I will sound the retreat, Prince Manfred?"

Manfred nodded, and the horn call sounded. That brought all the knights back.

Erik was busy studying the scene. Things were happening down at the village. Hastily someone was closing the gate. Below them, the proctor who had led the charge was staggering to his feet.

"What cowardice is this?" roared one of the older Ritters. "Now we'll have to ram that gate."

Szpak, riding up behind him, knocked him off his horse too. He pointed down at the hamlet. "There's a cross on that building down there, fools. It's a Christian settlement."

"They're pretending," said Von Naid. "They put up a cross and they think they're safe to go out raiding. Burn them, I say. I was a confrere Knight of the Holy Trinity once, and you shame the order. Fritz—you saw them. They've got our captives and kine, they made an unprovoked attack on one of us. Killed one of us." He turned on Szpak. "If you're too cowardly, Pole peasant, I'll lead the attack myself! To me, Ritters!"

"Hold," said Mecklen. It was said with the grim authority of command.

"Who do you think you are to give orders?" said one of the older knights to Mecklen, jerking at his horse's mouth, turning toward the hamlet.

Mecklen leaned over and grabbed the reins. "I am an Archimandrite in the order," he said, "And I am authorized by the Abbot-General himself to give force to the orders of his representative, Prince Manfred of Brittany. You have been ordered to stand. Who are you?"

The older knight gaped. "Ritter Denen."

But Szpak saw more. He saw, as Erik did, that the situation was far from under control. And, as he'd told Erik, most of these young men had seen no action before. "Form up," he yelled. "An orderly formation *now*. You. Denen. Dismount and see what can be done for Ritter Von Aasen. The Knights of the Holy Trinity obey orders from their officers. We do not take them from ex-confreres." Then he turned on Von Naid. "And I'll settle any doubts you have about my courage, on your body, personally."

Most of the knights had been squires under Szpak. Several of them actually laughed, despite the situation. The idea that anyone would doubt the Polish proctor's courage was more than a little ludicrous to them. Almost as ridiculous as picking a fight with their ex-instructor. And they were used to being ordered around by him, so they obeyed, unquestioningly.

Mecklen was plainly used to being in command, too. And he'd had to keep a still tongue between his teeth for some weeks now. He turned on the formed-up troop of knights. "This is one of the most disgustingly sloppy operations I have ever had the misfortune to witness. No scouts. No proper order of march, no forward planning, and no proper military discipline exercised. Now. Someone fired an arrow from that copse over there. You. Proctor Szpak. You seem to be the only man blessed with any brains and military training in all Skåne or Småland. Send out a patrol. Now. See if you can find the bowman. He can't have got far."

"Sir." Szpak saluted and turned back to the knights and began issuing orders.

Mecklen looked at Manfred. "If we could have a private word, Prince."

Erik walked his horse over to Szpak, en route to join Manfred and Mecklen. "Von Naid or his men may try to run, Juzef," he said, quietly.

"I've already spoken to six of my . . . boys," said the Polish knight grimly. "He's not getting away before I've dealt with him."

Erik rode over to the Archimandrite, smiling a little. Their wheat winnowing had brought better rewards than he'd expected.

"Well? Just what is happening here, Your Highness?" Mecklen asked Manfred as Erik rode up.

Manfred scratched his jaw. "I think somehow word came from Denmark about Francesca's activities and what I am supposed to be doing here. A messenger arrived two nights ago, and I think that the local powers-that-be put together a clumsy attempt to get me involved in a really messy butchery of a Christian settlement. Good for blackmail, good for convincing a green and spoiled nobleman that this was a dangerous part of the world and that they were doing the right thing—because to admit otherwise would be to admit to my role in the massacre. I know the Abbot-General has kept very quiet about what we encountered in Venice. The locals might have reached the wrong conclusion about us, and assumed that I'd be shocked by the butchery at Von Naid's estate and take their part in defending the work of the Knots here."

"And?"

"I'm shocked all right," said Manfred. "Shocked no one has got around to hanging this Von Naid. He and his friends plainly considered the murder of a few serfs a minor matter. That 'raid' was conducted by ironshod, wheat-fed horses, from what Erik was looking at. Big ones. That settlement down there has a spire and a crucifix. I'll bet that it is one of the settlements that I was told about—where some minor Götar chieftain has been converted by the Danes."

"And you, Ritter Hakkonsen? What do you think?" said Mecklen. "If the prince is right, and I suspect he is, we've averted a massacre—but we have little or no proof. Prince Manfred did countermand a legitimate order."

Erik shrugged. "If Szpak's boys don't bring back that bowman, I think I may have to track him. The first thing is to send a delegation to that village. See if we can find any cattle or prisoners. And establish whether it is a Christian settlement or not. Otherwise we may have a problem explaining all of this. At best we'll be in trouble with the Abbot-General."

"And Proctor Szpak will be for the high-jump. But I don't think we'll have a problem," said Manfred, gesturing. "Szpak's boys have found the trail of the archer by the looks of it. And I'd say that looks like a priest coming out of the palisade down there."

Mecklen nodded. He called to one his companions. "Proctor Von Stahl. Ride down and see what the man wants."

The proctor did, and returned with a scared-looking priest, complete with a crucifix around his neck—not a local Götar either, by his speech, but a Dane. He was, he explained, a missionary from Copenhagen. And it was a Christian settlement. They were very welcome to search for prisoners or stolen cows, or horses. There were only three in the hamlet, one of which was his.

"They must have hidden them in the woods," protested Von Naid.

"But your men were so sure that they were here in the village," said Erik.

The priest looked at Von Naid. "I know this man. He has attempted to have the people moved. There is the mill and ford he wants. He was here not a week back, making demands."

"Liar," said Von Naid, righteously.

"Go down to the village and ask the Godar," said the priest. "And may God strike me down if I lie."

Twelve of them rode down, weapons sheathed, at Mecklen's order. The village had little place to hide anything, anyway. The women and children were inside the little stave church, praying. The men watched them nervously. And Erik could see that the young knights were cringing.

"I think a little piety is called for," said Manfred to Mecklen.

The Archimandrite smiled and nodded. "Father Björn," he said, "may we enter your church?"

"There is nothing hidden there," said the priest, stiffly.

"We do not wish to search, but to pray, and to thank God for his guidance, and our delivery from evil, Father," said the Archimandrite humbly, dismounting. "People forget that we are but a militant arm of the church. Sometimes we forget that ourselves. Do you think you could ask some of the boys I see to hold our horses?"

The women and girl children shrieked when the knights clanked into the dim-lit church. But the cries stilled when the knights knelt. Erik was aware of people peering in at the doorway.

Proctor Szpak looked at the man that the four knights of the patrol had brought back. "He's been begging us not to kill him," said one of the young knights. "Says his name is Luus. He's a huntsman in Von Naid's service."

"He's a liar," insisted Von Naid. "I dismissed him from my service weeks ago! I see it all now! This is all an attempt to get his revenge. That arrow was intended for me."

Szpak looked coldly at Von Naid. Then at the knights flanking him. "Disarm him, and bind him," he said. "Also those three." He pointed to Von Naid's servitors.

Looking at the old man in his carved chair, Manfred wondered if he'd converted in order to get his soul into heaven before it was too late. He was old and frail, but he still had all his wits about him. He spoke good if precise Frankish. "Von Naid?" He nodded. "He has been here. He has lands just across the river. But the only good mill site is this side. He wants it, but we have the priest here. He dares not just drive us out."

"So he tried to start a little war instead and use us to get rid of you," said Manfred grimly. "People could have been killed. Well, it's not going happen."

The chieftain smiled crookedly. "Yes. Sons, you may come out now. These outlanders mean us no harm."

Manfred should have guessed by Erik's posture that he'd spotted something amiss. But two men with good Swabian-made crossbows were something of a surprise.

The old man smiled. "There will be no killing today. It is good. You will need every man in the spring. There is trouble coming out of the Norseland. Someone has been recruiting young men in the Svearlands." He smiled sourly. "I am an old man now, and an exile with those of my kin that were prepared to follow me. But I, Godar Gustav, still have a few people who bring me word from time to time. One of the Norseland kings has plans." The old man shrugged tiredly. "They will not succeed. But they will kill a lot of people. And me and mine are among those who they wish to kill most."

Manfred nodded. "After this . . . incident, I think you can be sure that the knights will be watching over you. And I think that you will have no further trouble with your neighbor."

There was the sound of cheering outside. One of the old man's sons went to look. He came back, smiling. "They have him. Bound onto a horse like a sack of grain. The people are pelting him with dung."

Manfred smiled, too. "I think we can leave now. May God watch over you."

The old man stood, too, with an ease that betrayed that he was less old than he pretended to be. Well, age lent respect. "I think His hand was over us today," he said quietly. "I was less than sure of Him before this."

CHAPTER 13

Kingshall, Telemark

Signy had got up and dressed herself—as usual, in the dark. Most noblewomen would have failed utterly at this, not being accustomed to dressing themselves, let alone in the dark. At least the years of having the worst, most sluttish serving-thralls had taught her this much. The shabby riding habit, unlike the formal dresses, was something she could get into by herself, with no complicated lacings or hidden buttons. Before she had always laid it ready for herself—another unheard of deed—but lately Gudrun did, such had been the effects of Cair on her staff. The serving women supposed to attend to her were never awake when she got up, but it was not something they would ever admit to Albruna, so it was not a problem. Albruna didn't mind if it looked as if Signy had dressed by guess. Signy didn't mind either, as long as she got out of the hall before anyone was likely to be looking for her. She could ride—and as long as she was back in time to break the fast with the household, no one, or at least no one important, was the wiser.

Today, however, she was greeted by soft rain when she stepped past the sleeping guard on the doorway. It was too gentle to make much sound on the thatch. She would never have time to ride and to get dry and changed before the household was up. She went to the stables anyway. It was—as long as you were prepared to skirt buildings and stick under the eaves—possible to do it and stay nearly dry, anyway. It was early, and only the bake-house thralls were up to see her. Of course she had two dogs at her heel, but she'd long ago taught them to remain quiet. Dogs always seemed to understand what she wanted, even better than the horses did.

As she reached the stable door, someone screamed. And screamed again. And then a third time—a drawn-out shriek of pure terror.

If she'd thought about it, Signy would have run away. But she just reacted, and ran toward the screams. They were coming from the direction of the temple *Vé*. And just short of the grove, the thrall-girl ran headlong into her. They both fell down, the thrall still clinging to her. Panting and gasping "Blood . . . blood . . ."

Three guards came blundering through the rain from the hall.

They checked when they saw Signy trying to sit up in the mud with the thrall-girl clinging to her like a drowning man to a piece of driftwood.

"Princess . . . ?" panted one, still hauling at his leather trousers. "What is it?"

"I don't know. She came out of the *Vé*," said Signy, prying the girl off her. She stood up, brushing ineffectually at the mud. "Stop clinging to my legs, thrall. What's wrong? And stop saying 'blood.'"

But that was all the woman seemed to be capable of saying. She did however point inward, toward the Odinshof.

"We'd better go and look," said the burly guard in leather trousers, tugging his blond moustache.

The woman shook her head and began crawling away. The three men looked doubtful, but leather-pants was made of stern stuff. He began to advance cautiously through the darkness under the dripping trees toward the high gable set against the rock. The others—including Signy—followed.

At the door of the temple they found just what the thrall-girl had been screaming about.

Blood.

There were body parts, too. The two guards had not just been killed, they had been dismembered.

Signy had always wanted to be a battle-maiden. Right now, all she wanted to do was join the thrall-girl.

The great doors to the Odinshof stood half open. And now others from the hall were pressing behind them ... Including King Vortenbras. He thrust his way forward and pushed the doors wide.

Peering around him, Signy saw little in the dimness. On the far side the fire still burned, sullenly. The solid mass of the altar slab was visible, dark and oblong. She could just make out the bowl and the *hlauttein* twig standing on it.

And that was all.

The broad gold arm-ring that always rested in the center of the stone was missing.

The holiest relic, the oath-ring, was gone.

"Bring torches. And call out my hearthmen," commanded Vortenbras. "And keep back, all of you. We'll want no muddling of the trail for the dogs."

Signy found herself excluded, too. She went back to the hall, and made her way back to her rooms to wash off the mud, and to dress in what the queen would declare was a more appropriate style. It might have been more appropriate if she'd had the queen's cleavage and the puffed sleeves had exposed less of her arms. The jonquil shade made her look sallow, she knew. But even here the story followed her, with a terrified-looking Gudrun nervously whispering that the temple had been destroyed and that they would all be consumed by the wrath of the gods.

"The temple is still there," said Signy. "Now help me with this lacing." She heard the sounds of Vortenbras and his men, and the clatter of horses and the baying of the dogs out there. She wished, very much, that she had some reason to go and join them. Vortenbras's crew might fight well with their mouths but they couldn't hunt like she could.

By late afternoon they were back.

But the arm-ring was not. The trail had led up, inland toward the high vidda. And there the dogs had lost it. They'd cast about, hunting hither and thither. But the dogs had been reluctant even to follow the scent in the first place, and had kept returning to the hunters.

By then Signy had pieced together the whole story. The thrall-girl had gone sneaking into the *Vé* to bribe one of the guards to

let her steal a little bit of ash from the holy fire. It was known
to be a powerful fertility charm. She'd found the guard dead and
had fled, shrieking her lungs out.

Even without the evidence of the dismembered guards, it was
plain that what Vortenbras and his men had hunted was not
human. Only a grendel could have done what this beast had done.
Whispered rumor hinted that this was the sheep and shepherd
killer of Rodale, come down to mock its hunters. Or that it was a
creature of the hag of Ironwood, she who was supposed to guard
access to Sverre's northern kingdom of Altmark.

Signy was present when the elderly high priest of Odin came
to confer with Vortenbras. "Whatever took the arm-ring, King,"
the elderly priest declared shakily, "must have no voice, or, with
the curses on the arm-ring, we could have followed it by the
screaming, once the arm-ring left the *waerds* of the *Vé*. And it
must be immortal to carry the weight of years on the *draupnir*.

"I thought the arm-ring gave protection to the wearer," said
the queen mother with the kind of finality that tolerated not
questioning.

The old priest nodded weakly. "It would grant powers to the
wearer, yes, O Queen. You cannot be killed. But the power of
the arm-ring costs the wearer dearly. A year of life for each hour
the power made you whole," He blinked his rheumy eyes. "Any
mortal who stole it would be dead by now. And the arm-ring
must either rest against the altar stone or against flesh. Otherwise
legend says that the *draupnir* will return magically."

That was all very well.

In the meanwhile, the kingdom of Telemark was in ferment.
In less than two months the midwinter solstice would be here.
And amid the feasting and sacrifice, oaths would be sworn and
renewed on the ring.

If there was a ring to swear on.

There was panic among certain houses where old feuds would
be fanned to flames again. There was widespread fear in the
homes of small franklins whose landholdings were attested by
oaths sworn on the *draupnir*.

There was genuine terror in a modest estate a mile from Kingshall, where Count Tirpizr resided. He was a lowly emissary of the
Emperor, in a dead-end job among the Norse in a petty kingdom

in the wilderness. He had one responsibility: to swear the truce oath, on the Emperor's behalf, every Yule. He'd never been much of a success at court, which was why he'd been posted here. And now it appeared that he might just fail here, too. His guards were already inspecting his possessions. Because, if there was no truce between the Empire and Telemark—as of that moment he, personally, was going to be short a head, without ever returning to Mainz to face the Emperor or the states general's fury.

Sheer fright forced him into effective action. He could not just leave—that would never be permitted. But, in case of emergencies, there was a trader in furs and fine liquors who would carry a message. And by nightfall a message was heading south, along with a considerable amount of gold.

Because the Empire would never have entrusted a man as spectacularly inefficient as Count Tirpizr with anything much, his message was only one of five, one of which was only going as far as Copenhagen.

As it happened, any new information that came to the Danish king also arrived with Francesca de Cherveuse, unofficially. Her letter to the Emperor reached Mainz a full day before the next message. Count Tirpizr's message never actually managed to leave Telemark. The fur trader was also in the employ of several others, and he foresaw, quite logically, that Tirpizr was not going to be paying him a retainer for much longer.

CHAPTER 14

Mainz

The Holy Roman Emperor Charles Fredrik was Guardian of the Church, Bulwark of the Faith, absolute lord and defender of millions of souls, from the Spanish marches to the pagan frontier of the Baltic. He was also a man who needed either a far larger desk, or, somehow, less papers, scrolls, books, and letters on this one. He sighed. Tapped the new pile of papers Baron Hans Trolliger had just handed him. "What significance do you attach to these reports, Hans?"

The baron considered his answer carefully. He'd almost had a very short career at the court by assuming, wrongly, that the Emperor would want a yes-man. Only the accident of losing his temper in his first week had revealed the folly of taking this course with the Emperor. It had taught him an invaluable lesson. Once, in a wistful mood some years ago, the Emperor explained: his Icelandic mentor from the Clann Harald, Hakkon, had taught him—with a beating to make sure that the lesson was absorbed—that the truly powerful have no need for flattery. Lesser princes wish to be agreed with and praised to bolster their own fragile position. Real power does not need that.

So Trolliger spoke his mind. As honestly and fairly as possible—because the Emperor would tolerate nothing else. "They worry me, to be honest, Your Highness. We've trouble enough on the eastern flank. The Venetian affair was designed to flank us on the south. This mess with the Danes and the Knights of the Holy Trinity leaves us weak on the whole northern flank. Telemark has become rich with silver mining in the last few years. Strategically it sits in a potentially difficult position, able to raid the west coast of the Empire, and bottle up the Baltic trade. But I don't know how much reliance we can place on the reports. And just how relevant is this item? Surely an oath is an oath?"

"You would swear an oath upon the Bible, would you not, Hans?" asked the Emperor, steepling his fingers.

Trolliger nodded. "Yes, or on the cross, or some sacred relic. But I am not a pagan."

"Indeed?" Charles Fredrik smiled wryly. "That was not the impression Bishop Leofric gave me of you, after your last meeting with him."

Baron Trolliger snorted. "That fool would have burned half of Saxony under us, Your Highness. His theology is weaker than his grasp on reality. And he has no grasp at all of the latter. It's a local custom and it means a great deal to the people there. They believe in it . . . Oh. I see."

"Yes, Hans. The Norse pagans believe that the oath is binding because it is sworn on something *they* believe in. And besides, if Brother Eneko Lopez is to be believed—and the Grand Metropolitan holds him to be one of the greatest students of ecclesiastical magic and the magic of the foes of the church—then venerated pagan items do acquire power. Just as the idols they worship may become more than wood or stone."

"That cannot be true in this case," said Hans Trolliger stubbornly. "If the thing possessed half the powers that this pagan priest claims it does, it could never have been stolen in the first place. I mean, I dare say the locals believe it but . . ."

"But no local would steal it." The emperor sighed. "That leaves a lot of nonlocal enemies, Hans. People who would love to do us ill. I suspect the hand of our old enemy in this. But then I suspect Jagellion of anything that reeks of treachery."

Hans Trolliger nodded, slowly. "But can we rely on these reports? They have not been confirmed yet."

The Emperor picked up a piece of parchment from the chaos of his desk. "I rely on this one, Hans. Not only is it reported to someone else's spies, but this woman has a nose for trouble. This is from Francesca de Cherveuse. The lady whose breasts made you so . . . uneasy." The emperor chucked at Trolliger's discomfort. It set him coughing. When he'd stopped, he continued. "What she's sent me is a confidential report about this incident, as sent to Harald of Jutland. The Danes watch the Norse more closely than we do, for obvious reasons. Harald will be sending us a frantic squall for intervention within the day, I would guess. They'll bear the brunt of this treaty being broken."

"So what do we do, my Emperor?" He knew that the Emperor's health was failing, and that the last thing his master wanted was a war to leave his heir. "We can send troops north to act as a deterrent . . ."

The Emperor shook his head, firmly. "We'll send someone to find the damned thing. Or at the very least find out who stole it. If it is a magical item, we have priests who can track such things. If . . . as I suspect, this is my adversary Jagellion, being revealed may not rebuild this truce, but it should at least improve matters. And I'll send a high-powered and hopefully frightening delegation to Telemark." He rubbed his bony hands. "Manfred should have finished in Skåne by now. I'll send him and a hundred knights. Merely to escort the Servants of the Holy Trinity, of course. Not to let the locals know we can still flatten them with our cavalry," he said, with a laugh that turned into a coughing fit again. He drank some cordial from a flask on the table. That worried Trolliger, too. The Emperor drank too much of that stuff.

Within the hour an Imperial messenger had set out for Copenhagen, with two letters in the Emperor's personal scrawl. One was directed to Milady Francesca de Cherveuse. The other was to be carried with all speed to Manfred, prince of Brittany. Other letters, in Trolliger's neater hand, went to the Abbot-General of the militant order of the Knights of the Holy Trinity, and to the monastic order of the Servants of the Holy Trinity. Requesting—in a fashion that was not quite an order, their assistance on the Empire's business.

It was thus that Brother Uriel, who had served Christ and the Servants of the Holy Trinity with distinction in Venice—when others, such as Abbot Sachs, had fallen into the snares of the evil one—found himself called to the study of the head of his monastery.

He listened in silence while the abbot read out the letter.

"Well, Brother?" asked the abbot, finally, as Uriel offered no comment.

The monk sighed. Shook his head. "You know how I feel, Father Abbot. You sent me to Venice with a pagan relic, nonetheless."

"And you did sterling work there. What little credit returned to the Servants of the Holy Trinity, and those of us of the Pauline persuasion, stem from that."

"We should have destroyed the pagan relic immediately, Father. Then that would not have happened," said Uriel, stiffly. "The same holds for this oath-ring. Such items are not consecrated to the use of the church, and should be destroyed, not retrieved for the pagans."

The abbot rubbed his jaw, thoughtfully. "While I agree with you in principle, Brother Uriel, there are two things to consider here. The first of these is that the Emperor may be right. The evil of the east may have seized this thing. If it is indeed powerful—he likes to gather the tools and symbols of power, Uriel. Chernobog has used the venerated idols and pagan holy places against the Church before. He will again. This may be part of the same thing—in which case it is vital that at least the church should know. The second thing is more secular—we are honor bound to assist the Emperor—especially as we are being entrusted with such a task after having unwittingly colluded with his, and the Church's foes." The abbot sat back in his chair, folded his arms and said, "Finally, Telemark is an area in which we are not permitted to do missionary work. We have, as you know, made some secret converts, but other than that, the kingdom remains committed to heathen gods. This is a Heaven-sent opportunity to display our strength and our faith, if we can do something that they have failed at."

"That is three things, Father," said Uriel.

The abbot raised his eyes to heaven. "I'll tell you a fourth thing, Brother Uriel. *You* are going to Kingshall in Telemark. I have thought, prayed, and even tried scrying about this. My last scrying sent you to Venice. This time I am sending you north. You are a skilled worker of finding magics. I have a letter here from the archbishop. We are sending Brother Ottar—who was a secret convert from Norway before his family were killed and he was forced to flee to Denmark—and also Sister Mary and Sister Mercy.

They are all skilled in the workings of ecclesiastical magic, and at various forms of scrying. Brother Ottar is also a witch-smeller. You have been selected to act as the leader of this group."

Uriel stood up, shook his head, resignedly. "Very well. Will you at least give me your blessing on this, Father?"

"Of course." The abbot smiled. "And, Brother Uriel ... try to open the way for God's missionaries, rather than close it."

So two days of travel later, Brother Uriel found himself in the company of Brother Ottar, a tall, serious-looking man, somewhat elderly and with a little paunch. Together they met up with two birdlike nuns—also of some antiquity. The four embarked on a church-owned river barge, going north. Brother Ottar had more specific details on travel plans. "We are due to meet Prince Manfred in Copenhagen. He is a confrere with the Knights of the Holy Trinity. They are providing an escort for us."

Uriel blinked. "Prince Manfred of Brittany? God moves in mysterious ways!"

Ottar smiled. "Indeed, Brother. I am going back to the lands of the Norse, from whence I was expelled thirty years back. With the blessing of the Empire."

"To find a pagan artifact."

Ottar nodded. "A very old and very powerful talisman, Brother Uriel. I have made a study of them, and of this one in particular. It could be put to use, evil use, in the wrong hands."

"It is an evil thing," said Uriel with finality.

Ottar shook his head. "Possibly not, in this case, anyway. It appears to be a wholly defensive object. It is entirely possible that some powerful neutral is bound to it."

"It does not seem ... from what I have read," said Sister Mary, timidly, "to have been very well guarded."

Brother Uriel shrugged his shoulders. "That implies one of two things, Sister. Either it was assumed that no one would dream of stealing such a thing, or it was believed it had its own defenses."

"It did. Or does," said the other nun, Sister Mercy, grimly. The women were alike in size and shape, but Sister Mercy was as stern looking as the other was gentle. "There are records of an attempt to steal it. According to the chronicles of one Petrus Alberchtus, the thief was found screaming just outside the grove, desperately trying to remove the item and, according to the story, aged and died as they watched. Alberchtus also includes a very precise drawing of the arm-ring."

"Well, perhaps we can use that to authenticate anything we do find."

"A sword thrust will do that," said Sister Mercy. "They tried to kill the thief to get the arm-ring off him—and as fast as they cut he healed. The arm-ring itself was what killed the thief. By then he was in terrible pain. He begged them to kill him. They had to drag him back into their grove, and then help him to pull the ring off. He died before they could kill him. A very old man."

"A strange thing," said Uriel, fascinated despite his disapproval. "It sounds like a charm of healing—yet the pain?"

The timid-sounding little nun thrust her head forward like a curious robin. "Ah. But what if there were two conflicting magics at work?"

"A curse against theft, and a property of healing?" suggested Uriel. "I suppose that could be."

"I think not," said Sister Mercy, shaking her head. "The structure of such pagan charms and their sacred objects is my study. I think the healing is merely an aspect of what the arm-ring is supposed to be: a perfect circle. As such it is a symbol of immortality, and also of completeness. It did not 'heal,' it made whole. And the pain is quite possibly another side effect. It is a key symbol in the pagan community of that land, held in the religious center. It may well be geographically rooted—such things often are. The pain the wearer feels is merely a reflection of the pain the immaterial thing, which is the arm-ring, feels."

"Which makes the thief a very powerful magic worker, at the very least," said Brother Ottar, thoughtfully. "I think we need to ask for guidance, Brother, Sisters."

As the boat moved them downstream, they knelt and prayed. Uriel knew comfort that at least this group of Servants seemed less likely to stray than Sister Ursula and Father Sachs had in Venice.

CHAPTER 15

Småland borderlands

Under Proctor Szpak's orders the column of knights made its way back to the chapter house, only pausing to collect Von Naid's strongbox from his main estate, and to seize certain documents in it. They arrived in the late afternoon. The proctor-general and the abbot both came down to the courtyard. "And now?" asked the abbot, looking at Proctor Szpak.

"We've caught and dealt with the miscreants," said the proctor, pointing to the men tied to their horses—with nooses around their necks, and the noose rope tied to the pommel of the horse next them.

The abbot blinked. "But there is some mistake, surely. That is Ritter Von Naid, who was a confrere here."

Manfred looked at the abbot, and then the proctor-general. "We need to inform you of certain things. It might be wiser if we did this in your office, Abbot Reuno." Mecklen had asked him to keep the matter as low-profile as possible. Personally he thought that it was a mistake. Mind you, it made no difference. There are few secrets in a monastic order. Before dark the story would have spread through this order's ranks. And then, Manfred thought, he could just end up defending these two and Von Naid and his accomplices from summary justice. There were some bad apples here, but the rot had not spread that far . . . yet.

"Later," said the abbot.

"Now," said Erik, who had dismounted.

They stared at him, open-mouthed. "What?" demanded the proctor-general. "Who are you to give orders?"

Szpak and Manfred had also dismounted. "I am the emissary of both the Abbot-General of the Order and also the Holy Roman Empire," said Manfred quietly. "And I am hereby telling Ritter Hakkonsen to take you both to the abbot's office. By force if need be. Dead if he sees fit."

The abbot had half drawn his sword. Erik hit his fingers with the flat of his hatchet. "Do you wish to die now?" he said icily. The abbot opened his mouth to yell—and obviously realized that the troop he'd sent out to take part in a massacre were all looking at him. There was no sympathy in their almost uniform glare.

A wilting abbot, wringing a sore hand, the proctor-general, and Von Naid were escorted to the abbot's office. "I think we will need that messenger who came with the news that sent these two off—if he is still here," said Erik to Szpak. "We will need to speak to him without any possibility of collusion. Hold him out here until we call."

The Pole nodded. "I'll see to it. And see that you are left alone to deal with this." He pursed his lips. "I haven't always seen eye-to-eye with the Order here. But there are some things my brothers will not tolerate." he said firmly, stilling a few of Erik's worries about the knights perhaps trying to "rescue" their abbot.

The door swung shut and the proctor-general blurted into angry speech. "What do you think you're doing? Just because you are the nephew of the Emperor . . ." He let it trail off. "The Order gives no deference to worldly rank."

"These Ritters have excelled in feats of arms in the service of God, the Order, and the Empire," said Mecklen, dryly. "That is why the Abbot-General was prepared to name them as part of his inspectorate here in Skåne and Småland. They act in his name and carry documents with his authority over anyone within the Order. I suggest you hold your tongue until you are told to speak."

It was a long time since anyone had told Proctor-General Von Tiblaut to hold his tongue. He looked ready to explode. But the abbot obviously realized what deep water he was in. He rushed into hasty speech. "But what is this all about? We have done nothing, sirs."

"Von Naid has told us what you conspired to do," said Manfred, gesturing at the gagged prisoner.

"I have never conspired in anything," said the abbot, waving his hands. "Whatever it was was entirely his idea. We knew nothing of it."

Von Tiblaut had still not entirely grasped his situation. "I am the senior officer of the Knights of the Holy Trinity! There are going to be very serious consequences for this."

"There are indeed," said Mecklen. "You have forgotten, Proctor-General Von Tiblaut, that the Order of the Knights of the Holy Trinity owes final deference to God, the Abbot-General of the Order, and to the Holy Roman Emperor, via our charter. You have offended in the eyes of all three of these. You are suspended from all offices of the Order and Church, pending final judgment."

Something about the way in which Mecklen said it dented even the confidence of Von Tiblaut. "Who are you?" he asked.

"Archimandrite Mecklen. I was abbot of Nordwand chapter house, and senior for the Waldenburg chapters, until the Abbot-General made me his Archimandrite-at-large in August." He pointed to the other three older knights. "These are my coassessors and assistants. We are here to lend the force of the Order to correcting what the Emperor has rightly called a mess. Even without this affair, you were due to be recalled and demoted, if not expelled from the Order. Now, I think the Empire and the Order will require more of you. Possibly your head."

Von Tiblaut—ruddy-faced with anger before—was now as white as new snow. "I have done nothing. I don't know what all this is about."

Mecklen looked grimly at him. "A system of payments for lands awarded to ex-confreres—monies the Abbot-General knew nothing about—would be a good starting point. We have spoken to a number of landowners and obtained documentary proof of this, while you watched Prince Manfred. And secondly, an attempt to involve Prince Manfred in a massacre of Christians, including a well-connected Danish missionary. We have a charter to lands—lands awarded to the Christian Götar chieftain Gustav, by the Danish crown—made out to Von Naid. They are signed by you, witnessed by the abbot here, and described as 'lands seized in a violent insurrection.' It is dated a week from now. You tried to get the Empire to take your side against the Danes, by getting us to participate in this act of murder."

The proctor-general shook his head. "I deny it utterly. Oh, the abbot here may have been involved. He gave me various charters to sign when I got here. I didn't check them. Why should I? He is the local authority."

"Liar!" screamed the abbot, seeing himself joining Von Naid as a sacrificial lamb. "I didn't know the money wasn't going to Prussia—"

Someone knocked. It was Szpak with a prisoner. "His name's Meuli. He comes from Copenhagen, or so he tells us. He is an ex-confrere, and has holdings in Skåne. One of the Ritters tells me that he is Von Naid's cousin."

"I had nothing to do with this," said the newly introduced Meuli. "I knew nothing about their plans."

"I think we can ungag Von Naid, and have him tell us what liars his companions are," said Erik.

As the four of them attempted to blame or incriminate each other the story emerged. Francesca's work in Copenhagen had not passed unnoticed, and her conversations with the Danish king's senior courtiers had, in a somewhat garbled fashion, come to Meuli's ears. It had included the information that Manfred was there to decide whether the Empire backed the Order or the Danes in the squabbles in Sweden. The details of the plot had been arranged by Von Naid. That they'd known it would include a massacre of a Christian village, they were all—except for Von Naid—vehemently denying. Then someone knocked on the door, and began to open it.

"We cannot be interrupted right now," said Archimandrite Mecklen firmly, stopping the door with a mailed foot

"I am on the Emperor's business," said the voice outside equally firmly. "You may not hinder those who bear this seal in the completion of their duty." A piece of parchment was pushed through the door crack, and Mecklen hastily stood aside and allowed the man to enter. It was a liberally mud-splattered Imperial messenger. He walked straight to Manfred, bowed, and presented him with a document with the Emperor's own seal on it.

Manfred cracked the Imperial seal. He seemed perfectly calm about it. Only someone who knew him extremely well would have realized he was being deliberately slow and precise. Exercising supreme self-control. Such a message was unlikely to be an order to return for a soirée at the Imperial palace. It was almost certain to be bad news, brought thus by one of Trolliger's special couriers. The mortality of the ruler of the Empire weighed on him. If Charles Fredrik was dying . . . turmoil was inevitable. A bodyguard would rest uneasy until Manfred's cousin Conrad was secure on the throne. Besides, the godar of the Hohenstauffen was important to the Clann Harald. Erik waited, without breathing, watching Manfred read. Why did he read so damn slowly?

Then Manfred exhaled gustily. Erik had obviously not been the only one to be holding his breath. "Well, at least we get to go to Copenhagen on the way. You and I, Erik, are to leave posthaste for Telemark in southern Norway."

"And what are we to do there?" asked Erik, having carefully exhaled so as not to betray his tension.

"Find a thief. And swear an oath," said Manfred, doing his best to smile enigmatically. But the relief turned it into a grin.

Erik noticed the relief also written on the faces of Von Naid, the abbot, and the proctor-general of Skåne. So, plainly, did Manfred. They obviously thought that the matter could now be squirmed out of or covered over. After all, nothing had actually happened . . . bar the death of a few serfs, irrelevant in their minds at least. Manfred shook his head with a kind of stolid finality. "No. The Emperor also said that I must settle matters here before I leave. And I don't believe I need to see or hear any more. Erik?"

Erik drew the sword in one smooth, clean movement. "Their heads, my prince?"

Manfred shook his head again. "No. The Emperor still holds fealty over Von Naid and Meuli, and their men. They must go back to Mainz, I think. It's likely they'll be sent to the Danes for final justice, as I may tell you that my uncle has decided that this territory will officially be ceded to them. I will recommend the settlement of Götar converts in the borderlands. I think that the Danes will agree to that. The Order will remain as guests, retaining a reasonable holding but acquiring no further ones without the approval of the Danish throne. There are, apparently, several hundred new Danish recruits due to join the Order, which will leaven things."

He looked at the proctor-general and the abbot. "Now. As to justice within the Order. The abbot and the former proctor-general—and such Ritters and proctors as are suspected of direct involvement—will be sent to Prussia to the Abbot-General."

He took a deep breath. "Archimandrite Mecklen." He turned to the older knight who had accompanied them from Copenhagen. "You have the authority to act for the Abbot-General. You were sent to lend me authority. I have seen you in the field. Now, I am lending you my authority, here. With the authority vested in me by both the Abbot-General of our Order and of the Holy Roman Emperor, Charles Fredrik, I appoint you as the temporary proctor-general of the Knights of the Holy Trinity for the Pastoral district of Skåne. May you serve God, the Order, and the Empire better than your predecessor. Final appointments here must of course await the Order's decisions, but I will dispatch a letter detailing what I have done, and recommending they consult with you about suitable candidates. I want you to see that Von Naid and his companions in crime are transported, in chains, back to Lödöse. His lands and holdings are confiscated. I shall recommend they be awarded to the Christian Götar chieftain Gustav, as a reward for both piety and to help improve his faith," he said, heading toward the door. "And now, Erik and I must pack. The Emperor does not tolerate delays, and we need to get back to Copenhagen."

Back in their quarters, Manfred sat down on the bed with a thump. "I'm not used to being justice almighty."

"You had backup from Mecklen."

"Yes. I think he'll work out well for the task for now. Better to have an outsider. I'd have preferred to see to the reorganization in person, but Uncle says," Manfred, waved the letter, "we need to be in Copenhagen to await the others. What a hardship that will be." He beamed.

"Give," said Erik, suspiciously.

Manfred held the parchment against his chest. "It's an imperial letter addressed to me," he said, attempting to sound lofty and failing to sound anything but guilty.

Erik shook his head. "Give before I have to make you do so, Manfred. Your wrestling is improving, but not that much." He held out his hand.

Manfred held out the letter. "Look, the escort's not really necessary . . ."

Erik took it and read. And then, with it in hand, walked out to find Mecklen. "The prince omitted to mention that the Emperor has requested that the Order provide 'sufficient escort' for Manfred and various clerics who are being sent to the kingdom of Telemark," he said to the new proctor-general of Skåne.

"I had wondered about that," admitted Mecklen. "Should we say one hundred Ritters, under the command of Szpak? I was impressed by his conduct, for all that he is a Pole."

Erik nodded. "When you hear his reason for joining the order you will be even more impressed, Ritter. He's a good man. The Order needs more like him. United in service and faith, if not in origins—as the Order once was."

Mecklen nodded. "Amen. My father said much the same thing. He was a confrere knight, too. Command experience will be good for Szpak. I have plans for him, here on the border."

"Well, have plans for Manfred, too. He's going to argue about this escort."

Mecklen smiled. "That is to be expected too. I will accompany you two to Lödöse, and we will discuss the matter. I expect the size of the escort will decrease but not disappear."

CHAPTER 16

Copenhagen

Francesca had been busy, busy, busy. Mostly with talking. Or rather, with listening. If you listened politely and occasionally directed the conversation where you wanted it to go . . . Well, she'd found that an amazing number of people were only too happy to give her a great deal of information they'd possibly have been wiser to keep to themselves. Only a fool played at politics and intrigue—dark and dirty games—in ignorance. Francesca never ceased to be amazed at how many fools, even in the highest places, there seemed to be. Vertical diplomacy was possibly even more entertaining than horizontal diplomacy had been. Right now she was practicing her most successful technique: *impress me with how much you know.* "But Count . . . well, I can't mention his name, but a friend, an admirer, shall we say, told me that the Norse were irrelevant, Baron," she said, artlessly. "Of course," she put a hand on the arm of the man responsible for antipiracy measures along the Danish coast, "he's probably not as well informed as you are."

The baron beamed. "That's hardly surprising m'dear. I have more access to privy information than most. And I have a brain to begin with, unlike Count Rothkilde, although I can't fault his taste in conversational companions. But to call the Norse 'irrelevant' is sheer folly. There has been a real problem developing across the

Skagerrak for some time now, and that problem is Telemark. King
Olaf was an honorable man, for all that he was a pagan, but his
son—the man who is on the throne now—has ambitions."

Francesca raised an arch eyebrow. "And no honor? Why should
honor make a difference? I thought the kingdoms over there
were too small and too poor to be a threat to a great state like
Denmark, allied"—she carefully did not say "vassal"—"to the Holy
Roman Empire."

"Ah. Well, you see, Emperor Charles Fredrik forced a treaty
on King Olaf, and it has kept them from warring with the
Empire, or us, or our shipping. But you are right about the
money and the size. Unfortunately, King Olaf turned his military attention elsewhere and before his death had expanded his
little kingdom eastward. Of course, the area is mostly mountains
and forest . . . but one of those mountains happened to be rich
in silver. And the forests make good ship timber. We've got a
problem on our doorstep, all right. But don't bother your pretty
little head about it."

"I won't. Not with someone like you in charge, Baron," she
said admiringly.

He swelled up like a peacock, and told her a great deal
more—not that the treaty was in danger of lapsing—which she
knew already, but of frantic preparations to ready their sea
defenses. Of news from spies among the Svear, where Vortenbras
was recruiting. He almost certainly didn't realize how much he
was revealing, but Francesca was a skilled inquisitor. The Danes
were even ready to call off their feud with the Knights of the
Holy Trinity. For now, anyway.

When she wasn't listening, she was reading—sleeping had to
take second place—but she could not allow this to take away from
her exercise, despite the growing cold. The reading provided her
with precise instructions for a very discreet goldsmith.

Manfred and Erik arrived after some two days of travel, with
an escort of Knights of the Holy Trinity. Francesca arranged that
some seventy minor nobles aand second sons went to watch
them at drill.

The monks and nuns arrived the day after that.

Francesca smiled. "My informant tells me that you would know
Telemark better than most. They say that you passed through

Copenhagen when you fled from there, Brother Ottar. Or should I say Johan?"

Ottar bowed his head. "It was a long time ago, milady. I was a young man. I should perhaps have stayed and died for my belief. But yes. I am from Telemark. My family were killed, burned in our hidden chapel, but I escaped. I sought and found comfort in the arms of the Mother Church. I am not Johan Franklin anymore. I have sworn my vows and found peace. Who told you, milady? Is it wise for the success of our mission that I should go?"

Francesca raised her eyebrows. "I never reveal my sources, Brother. All I will say is that a Danish noble, who had reason to remember you, told me. He is unlikely to tell anyone else. And thirty years, a tonsure, a belly, and a lack of beard will provide a good disguise. No one else will know."

"Except me, Brother," said Manfred. "The Emperor told me in the letter he sent me. And he regards you as our hidden asset, so it is plain that he intended you to go. You'll be safe enough."

Ottar shrugged. "It is not for my own safety I fear, Prince. That is in the hands of God. It is for yours. For all of us who go. But my clan was a minor one, and it is as you say, unlikely that I would be recognized by anyone." He permitted himself a smile. "My abbot granted me permission to lie, should anyone think they recognize me."

"I'd just try and avoid it if I were you, Brother," said Francesca, critically. "You wouldn't be very good at it."

Ottar shook his head ruefully. "True. I can understand why the Emperor himself finds a use for you, milady. You are very astute. I shall, God willing, keep to the truth, by keeping my mouth shut, or at least by speaking only in Frankish."

Francesca smiled and stroked the soft curve of her scented cheek. Manfred had learned to read her subtle signs now. She'd thought of something. Something serious. "It was my understanding that the truce-oath bound Vortenbras from harming emissaries of the Holy Roman Empire. Would they not honor the oath?" She darted a quick glance at Manfred. If she'd got up and said, "Then you are not going," she could hardly have been more clear.

The monk looked utterly shocked. He shook his head, vehemently. "Absolutely, milady! I'm afraid the lack of integrity was the one thing I found difficult to accept here in the Empire. An oath binds. Oath-breakers . . . be they kings or thralls, are outcasts. As much as he might like to, Vortenbras would never openly break that oath. A secret raid, perhaps, that he could blame on rogue elements in his court, on some place that could be argued to be not part of the Empire . . . he might go that far. But the prince could walk unarmored into Vortenbras's court with perfect safety. Until Yuletide, anyway. The worst that Vortenbras could do would be to throw him and the others out of his kingdom. I was born there. That makes me one of his vassals. But that is a chance I would gladly take."

"Well," said Manfred, sitting back on the gilded chair. "You can relax, Francesca. We'll be out of there in a week, if the arm-ring isn't found. So, tell me Brother Ottar. You've been to Kingshall, I presume. What do we expect?"

The elderly, paunchy monk scratched his jaw pensively. "Well, it is not quite like a royal household in the Empire, Prince. The halls are thatched. The place will be full of dogs," said the monk, with a reminiscent smile. "It is much less formal than the courts of the Empire. There are fewer layers of precise hierarchy. It's a bit chaotic from time to time."

"Sounds a bit like Carnac," said Manfred grinning like a shark. "Last time I was home a sow got into the main dining hall. The dogs took after it, so it ran up onto the dais and took shelter under Lady Marchese's skirts. Between her and the pig and the dogs, the table went over. You should have seen the commotion, let alone heard it. I don't know who squealed louder, the pig or Lady Marchese." His shoulders shook slightly. "A very dignified court it was. M'father was the one who caught the pig and hauled it out, too."

"I suppose you were too busy laughing to help," said Erik, with insight based on experience.

Manfred nodded, beaming. "Right you are! So were most of the *duniwasals* there. Marchese is a friend of Mother's from Swabia. She'd been looking down her long nose at the provincials. The men reckoned that it was one fat sow in trouble looking for another."

"Manfred, we're trying to find out about what we can expect in Norway, not about how refined Carnac is," said Francesca. "It sounds as if they might be similar, I admit, from what I've heard."

"Not 'we', Francesca," said Manfred. "My uncle, to my regret, has very firmly said that you are to remain here. He said something about the entire Empire not being able to afford enough furs to send you farther north. If it wasn't for a comment he made later, about me being able to ah . . . catch up with you once the job was done, I'd have said he was trying to separate us, my love."

Francesca looked mulish . . . for a moment. Then she plainly considered just whose orders these were, or perhaps . . . the gray sky outside her salon's mullioned windows. "I suppose I had better obey an Imperial order. However, you'll have to work a little harder at absorbing customs and diplomatic behavior among pagan allies, then. Even if the customs are like those in Brittany."

The monk looked relieved at the news that the prince's leman would not be going to join them. He nodded eagerly. "I have been sent on three missions by our abbot to visit monasteries and sources of pagan literature within the League of Armagh. In some ways the Norse are like the Bretons, yes. The Irish and Scoti have absorbed a fair part of the Scandinavian culture, along with the invaders to their lands. A substantial amount of this has passed on to the other parts of the League of Armagh. To Ritter Hakkonsen here, of course, it would be even more familiar. The nobility and their hearthmen will do things that nobles and knights would consider beneath their dignity in Mainz. On the other hand, they have to. No thrall would be allowed to cut beasts' throats for the midwinter Yule festival."

Erik frowned. "Thralldom is virtually extinct in Iceland. The church frowns on it. The few who consider themselves thralls are more like family retainers these days. But once upon a time a thrall could not even hold sharpened steel."

"It is still like that in Telemark," explained the monk. "As I said, even the slaughter of beasts is not done by the thralls."

"There's a hangover of the same thing in Carnac," admitted Manfred. "My father used to take part in the Martinmas slaughterings, until my mother made him stop."

Erik grunted. "With you out of the place, at least they have one less set of hangovers. But tell us, Brother. It is a pagan kingdom with which the Empire has a treaty. We have orders not to cause offence. What do we avoid? They're idolators—Woden worshipers, aren't they?"

The monk assumed an oratarial stance. "Woden is way the Danes pronounce it. The Knights of the Holy Trinity serving in Skåne took it from them. The word is of the same stem as the old Norse 'Odhinn' or Germanic 'Wouten' or Wotan. It has become 'Odin' among the Norse. Historically the Germanic tribes fractured into isolated shards, each with their own local form of Aesir worship, which vary a great deal. Some, particularly in the territory around our conquests near Uppsala, are truly vile, with a great deal of blood sacrifice. *Oferlundar*, as they are called. Others are less bloody. Odin is but one of their gods—he is, however, the king of the Aesir pantheon. The nobility obviously are very loyal to him. We also believe that they also absorbed several older local pagan religions into the pantheon as they colonized, particularly fertility gods such as Frey. Some of the idols have, we regretfully acknowledge, been imbued with certain magical powers. Some have been possessed by demonic and other spirits. There are scholars who consider each to be an avatar of Woden—"

Manfred held up his hands. "Stop. I see that we have a serious scholar in our midst."

The monk shrugged deprecatingly. "A minor one, Prince. Coming as I did from a pagan land, I knew the old gods had certain powers. I wished to understand how this could possibly be. But both Sister Mercy and Sister Mary are my superiors in scholarship, and Sister Mercy is an expert in the theory of pagan magic."

"And we have Brother Uriel to keep us on the straight and narrow," said Erik, looking pointedly at the goblet of wine in Manfred's hands.

Manfred grinned. "I'd better bone up on my biblical quotations. Saint Paul said, 'Take a little wine for the good of your stomach.' Brother Uriel is a stiff old stick but at least you can trust him not to send you off to brothels, unlike our last guiding abbot." He sighed and patted Francesca with a degree of unmonkish familiarity. "Unfortunately. It did Erik so much good."

Brother Ottar swallowed and looked around for escape.

CHAPTER 17

Kingshall, Telemark

Vortenbras came stalking into the room with a letter in his hand. Signy was glad of any interruption. It might just stem her stepmother's flow. Even her half-brother, looking as if he was about to tear someone's head off, was welcome.

"The Holy Roman Emperor is sending some of his knights and a team of his damned Christian diviners here to 'help' us find the arm-ring, Mother."

Albruna raised her eyebrows. "Tell them no. This is our—your kingdom, Vortenbras."

"I can't," he snarled, his huge hands crumpling the parchment. "Not in terms of the treaty. Not until after Yuletide."

Albruna looked down her nose at him—no mean feat, as he was standing and she was seated at the tambour frame. "Then we must accede with good grace and help them to find out that Sverre's witch has stolen it."

Signy started. Sverre, the grim king of Altmark to the north had been an ally of her father's. To the northwest of him lay Trondheim, captured by the Danes fifty years before. If Sverre had turned against them, then indeed the treaty must be reaffirmed, no matter how much it galled Vortenbras. He was a fool. They'd be in a pincer . . .

"The messenger from Emperor Charles Fredrik is waiting for a reply."

Albruna sighed. "I suppose you want me to help you draft one. Very well. We'll be delighted to have them and their assistants. In fact we'll provide a vessel, safe conduct..." She looked up at Signy. "Signy my dear, you look a little peaked. Why don't you go and take some fresh air. Vortenbras and I will be busy for some time."

It wasn't an opportunity that came often, and Signy seized it with both hands. Still, she would have loved to know more. All she knew was that the priests of Odin were near their wit's end. As she ran up the passage as quickly as she could she heard the queen saying. "Provide a ship to Copenhagen..."

CHAPTER 18

Trollheim

her river was a raging torrent right now. Not even the *björnhednar* could cross it and live. From a quarter of a mile off, the growling roar of tumbling boulders would have made it almost impossible for mere mortals to converse. Bakrauf and the great white monster that was her son had no such problems.

"Call out your hunt to carry us across," he said, staring at the churning water of the Fimbulthul.

Green-eyed and baleful Bakrauf stared at him. "You know the terms of their compact as well as I do. If I use them too often for things like this, then my nine calls will be spent. When I do really need them to bear me away they will come for vengeance, not for orders."

"Call them," he said, his yellow-eyed glare matching hers, unblinkingly. "You won't need them again this year. After *Joulu* they are yours again, for the nine calls of next year."

At length she dropped her gaze. "And how are we to get back? We need to be back by morning," she muttered.

"Fimbulthul is dropping," he said, pointing with a heavy claw. "By morning the *björnhednar* can cross. But we need to consult the easterners. We need to be within our wards before contacting the black brain. Chernobog is not to be trusted."

Bakrauf could not disagree about this. The demon of the East had devoured and enslaved others. It would not let common purpose stop it now. And the auguries she had performed showed hints of dire portent. But the signs were muddled and obscured, as if roiling through a mist of magics. Even she, the mistress of *seid*, could not tell what was coming. All she could see was that it was going to be, in some way, cataclysmic. They had the arm-ring secure and hidden now—and since then the signs had gone awry. The magics involved with that thing were deeper and more powerful than she'd realized. "Very well." She spat. Spittle, earth, and blood were all she needed. That and the words of summoning the bound ones. One of the *björnhednar* could spare some blood.

Soon the enchanted ones came, shrieking and cawing, a black and tumbling mass, appearing first as a squabble of blood-eyed ravens and crows. As they settled around Bakrauf and her retinue, the shriekers resolved themselves from their assumed appearance—into the hunt. Some were things of the nine worlds, others creatures more of spirit than flesh. Blood drinkers, creatures of the night. Crones and pale sylphlike girls with empty eyes. But in exchange for what she had given, they came. Hating her. Fearing worse.

At Bakrauf's command, they snatched her and her escort up. They bore the entire entourage across the seethe and ravel of water, cold hands plucking, not quite daring to tear. They set them down, with spiteful pinches for the bears if not for Bakrauf their mistress, outside the troll castle.

Bakrauf spoke the words of opening, and slowly the hilltop rose on the huge brass pillars. The *björnhednar* bore her within. Trolls, svarts, and human thralls were up and about. The place was full of the smokes and sound of industry, which was as it should be. Her subjects groveled as their mistress passed.

They cowered as her son passed in her wake.

In her throne room the circles were prepared with meticulous care. This was no time or place for haste. Time did not run at the same pace here as elsewhere, anyway. Guardians of flame and ice were positioned.

At last, the blood was spilled and the words spoken. Bakrauf found herself speaking once again to the Grand Duke of Lithuania—or at least to the demon that wore that face.

"My spies have sent me interesting news from the Empire, troll-wife. You've hooked a very big fish with your small machinations."

Bakrauf did not like her works described as small. But she held her tongue. One day there might be reparations. One day. "What big fish?"

"One so big that I will be very generous if he is destroyed," said Jagellion.

Bakrauf smelled trouble. A trap. The Black Brain's "generosity" was infamous. "I say again: what big fish?"

The great scar on Jagellion's forehead pulsed. "The Holy Roman Emperor has dispatched none other than his nephew, Manfred of Brittany, to accompany a group of Christian mages to see the ring found again. This prince has . . . angered me. And his death will weaken the Empire."

Her son growled. It was a horrible sound, deep enough to make braziers vibrate. The guardian flames shivered. "We know that. And his death would bring down the wrath of the Empire on our heads. We are not ready. Not yet. We need to gather the disaffected to us first. Spring is the earliest we can begin the raiding. By next autumn . . ." He growled again.

Jagellion smiled savagely. "What else can you do? Let them find it? That is what my auguries say he will do. Make it appear accidental. Cut off a few heads in ardent apology."

Bakrauf let her breath hiss between her big square teeth. That was what it had all meant! Curses! Black curses! "You hope in vain. Even if we wished to oblige you, we cannot kill him. The magics on the oath-ring will prevent it."

The metal eyes stared out at her. The pulse in the scar on Jagellion's forehead throbbed. Then Jagellion smiled again. "Delay. If you delay enough, until the oath no longer binds you, then you can kill . . ." The grand duke paused, as if something had just occurred to him. "No. Better still. Better by far! Let him disappear. You can be searching desperately for him! His death would be a prize for us, but the Holy Roman Empire could be torn asunder by pretenders and conflicts . . . if he just vanishes." Jagellion's metal eyes gleamed. "Make him disappear, and I will reward you, generously."

"It would have to be generous indeed," said Bakrauf, sourly. "You know what sort of trouble this would bring down on us?

Even here, away from mortal realms, we are not beyond the reach of Christian mages. And it could severely hurt my plans in Telemark."

Jagellion, or the thing behind him, did not seem concerned by her problems. They were, after all, allies of convenience, not choice. "You don't have any other options, troll-wife."

That appeared true enough. She hated being trapped. But there'd be ways to turn this to their advantage. This princeling could be kept as a useful hostage, for starters, once away from human realms where he could be found. And she could engineer things so that their hands were clean. Let some others of the nine worlds carry the blame if finding-magics were invoked. "So what rewards do you offer?" she demanded. Best to bargain hard. She could always renege later. Subtly, of course.

Later, when they had finished speaking, Bakrauf sat back on her throne, pondering. She began to think that there might be quite some possibilities in this situation: if it was played right, both the Empire and the Grand Duchy of Lithuania could be milked. Already Chernobog had given more than she'd expected. And she was the mistress of seemings after all. She began to think in wider terms. She avoided the old gods and their powers. Even dealing with Chernobog was safer, for one such as her. But they, too, might be persuaded to deal for a key to their lost worshipers.

Once all of Germania, Saxony, and Jutland had sacrificed in the groves, too. The smell of those sacrifices must have been sweet. She scowled, sending frightened thralls scurrying. One-eye was not to be trusted.

She sat and considered her options. Seemings and weather magic were her particular strength. Some deep snow might be an advantage. Such things took time, though.

Her son's growl broke her reverie. Well, that would please him, too. He liked deep snow. He liked fresh blood soaking into the whiteness. And if all her illusions and magics failed to lead this prince into entrapment, her son could always take him with brute force. That was his forte.

CHAPTER 19

Copenhagen, Telemark, and elsewhere

It's a historical relic but a fast one," said Erik, looking at the ship provided for them by the King of Telemark.

"It's got no castle worth speaking of," Manfred said, looking at the vessel.

"I've always suspected those of making a ship top-heavy—especially if you're also going to put cannon up there."

Manfred looked thoughtfully at the typical Baltic vessel docked farther down the quayside. "I suppose that's why they make the beam so broad. Like a plump tart."

Erik decided to ignore the last part of that statement. "Well, they can carry a lot more cargo like that."

"Just like a plump tart. And can go down just as easily," said Manfred.

"You're impossible!" said Erik. "Let's go and see if arranging space for the horses will sort your mind out."

Manfred grinned. "Unlikely. I don't feel that way about horses, although I worry about you at times. I've been wondering if a girl with horsey face might appeal . . ." He ducked hastily.

"Being with Francesca again has made you far too light-hearted," grumbled Erik.

"Well, you can be satisfied that I'll be grumpy like you, shortly," said Manfred. "And it is coming on to rain again. Just the thing for a sea trip to Norway. Hello. There is Szpak. He's been drilling those poor bastards day and night since we left Lödöse. I wonder what has caused him to leave off?"

The Polish proctor had indeed come riding down the quay. "Half the town is looking for you, Prince Manfred."

"I deny it utterly," said Manfred cheerfully. "I have an alibi for last night. And for this morning."

The Ritter looked at him with an innocent round face. "Oh. Well, it must have been someone else then. A pity. Those sixteen beautiful young women will be terribly upset, after thinking they'd found their dream man."

Erik shook his head. "You're as bad as he is, Juzef. Next thing you'll be plying him with liquor." The proctor was quick thinking, anyway.

"Well, as it happens I have some schnapps from home," said the proctor.

Manfred beamed. "Lead on! It's just what I need for a nice rainy winter sea voyage with some elderly nuns for female companionship. What's it made of?"

Szpak lifted his chin and said cheerfully, "Cabbages."

"Cabbages?" said Manfred incredulously. "You can't brew anything from cabbages."

Juzef Szpak said in a deadpan voice, "You're not insulting my family brew, are you?" Erik caught the wink as Manfred looked down, slightly abashed. Szpak's sense of humor had been apparent before, but never quite so obviously.

"Uh. no. I have just never had cabbage schnapps before," said Manfred.

Szpak shook his head sympathetically. "The first time is always the best." After a pause he admitted, "Very few people try it a second time. I'll give you some when you get through with meeting the holy monks and nuns. They wish to gather us all to pray."

"I'll probably be grateful even for cabbage liquor after that."

"I'll show you the way. They're at the Chapel of St. Charles." Szpak alighted from his horse and walked with them.

"How goes it with the plans for the horses?" asked Erik.

Szpak grimaced. "Since I managed to get through to that Danish idiot that sending the horses to Danish-held Oslo would be a poor idea, things have gone better. But Francesca promised that it would all be organized in the next hour. She's a remarkable woman, that. She knows everybody."

Erik raised an eyebrow. "You too, eh."

Szpak blushed.

In Telemark, the royal compound at Kingshall was in a ferment. The Court of Telemark pretended, as courts do everywhere, that they were above any comparisons. But it had leaked out that they were expecting an Imperial delegation. Not merely Count Tirpzr but some high Imperial lordling sent directly by Emperor Charles Fredrik. And a group—rumor had it—of Christian clerics! Telemark stood on its dignity. But it also stood on its mettle. Both the royal house and the temples were prickly about this. The halls were scrubbed and dusted from the rooftree to the floor. New rushes for the floors could not be had in winter, of course. But hangings were washed, and house karls and thralls rushed about, scouring and polishing, harried by Queen Albruna herself at times, at her most waspish. Early on, Vortenbras had stamped out in disgust. He'd ridden off with some of his men in search of some sport, rather than deal with the chaos. Signy wished dearly that she could have done the same. Some measure of calm had returned to Kingshall when the queen retired with a headache. But it was near midday by then, and Signy felt as if she—and not just the wall hangings—had been wrung out.

The terrible beast pointed with a razor-sharp talon. He pointed to the crude map he'd scored onto the rock. "Look, Mother. If we take this adit, we can ambush them about dusk. They'll be tired. The bonders' huts will just be in sight below them in the valley—the column will be strung out. I'll cut him loose from the crowd, and between us we can chivvy him down into the kobold lands. Let the little snivelers take the blame."

The plan was typical of him. Direct and without subtlety. But it might just serve. And it would serve her ideas, too. She didn't want the prince dead, for her own reasons and to please Chernobog. She just wanted him "disappeared." She nodded. "He's a big man. The kobolds are always short of labor."

He scratched his coarse white fur. "Kill their slaves quick enough, though. He won't last long."

"Long enough for our purposes," she said with a grim humor.

"If there's trouble, let those maggots take the blame and the pain. When the fuss dies down we can go and fetch him." Troll-wife and troll-son had no doubts of their ability to do this. Conquest of kobold lands would be an easy thing. The only reason that she had not done so before was that the little squits hid in every narrow little crevice and crack when the trolls went rampaging. You could conquer easily enough. But holding the galleries might be another matter entirely. The rat warren was not worth it. "I will send Hati and Járnhauss with you. The snow spells require a great deal of power and even after stealing from the Alfar girl, it tires me. Here. Take this." She handed him a rune-carved bone. The workmanship was stunning, Dwarfish by the looks of it, but neither the troll-wife or her son cared much for the beauty of the thing. "Break it, crush it into pieces, cast the fragments at them and call on my true name. Snow will follow."

He nodded his heavily muscled head. "Good. That will keep his escort there. Heavy snow, Mother. Snow to keep them sitting in a huddle of flea-full bonders' huts until after *Joulu*. Sitting waiting for slaughter, a long way from that accursed arm-ring of Odin. Let them see if they can find it there!"

She swung one of her heavy gray fists at him, catching him on the ear. He was twice her size, but she never let him forget that she was the ruler. "Fool. Never speak the name. Never. He sees far, does One-eye. And mentioning his name draws his attention."

He growled but said nothing. Just looked sullen.

She got to her feet. "Come. Needs must that we go, if we wish to get there before dusk."

CHAPTER 20

Telemark

"I've seen better harbors," said Manfred, surveying the ships pulled up on the shingle. "Actually, I've seen better fishing harbors."

"The rate Telemark is expanding, it'll soon have all of those, too. And other deepwater ports. Stavager and Áslo. Besides, Skien is a good port, apparently. Why they chose to land us here is anyone's guess."

"To make things awkward for us," said Erik. "The Emperor is sending the knights to remind them what heavy cavalry looks like, and they're reminding us how difficult landing them can be. It's a game of sorts." He pointed to the cluster of old men who had come to escort them. "Every one of them is crippled, Manfred. You can bet they're mere lowly franklins, too, by their gear. Vortenbras is toying with you. He's saying that this delegation isn't worth guarding. Learn, Manfred. I wish Francesca was here to teach you all of this. She's much better at these sorts of games than I'll ever be."

"A game that got my gear wet," said Manfred, grumpily. "And now, doubtless, the guides will take us by the most roundabout route, involving half a dozen river crossings, and lots of forest and steep mountainside."

"Doubtless," agreed Erik. "Places where heavy cavalry are going to struggle."

"Humph. Next time my uncle wants a pawn to push around, I'm going to suggest he send you without me, Erik. Well, let's put on a good show for them anyway."

"Szpak is doing that," said Erik, pointing to where the new senior proctor was putting his "boys" through some drill while they waited for the rest of their gear to be unloaded. "That man will go far, I think."

Manfred nodded. "Good instructor. Do they really distill cabbage liquor in Gdansk? Or was he having me on?"

Erik shrugged. "The stuff smelled as if it might be true." He cast a glance at the sky. The heavy cloud looked leaden enough to suggest that only providence could be holding it up in the sky. Snow was coming, or he knew nothing of northern weather. "And I hope they get that kit on the packhorses quickly or we'll need more than even that vile stuff to warm us."

"Why in heaven's name couldn't the Empire's problems take place in sunny Syracuse?" said Manfred. "It's all very well for you. You've got ice in your veins anyway. But there is a lot of me to keep warm, and I've had my skin stick to cold armor before."

"Don't want to be a pawn. Want to be somewhere warm," said Erik, tightening a cinch. "We are full of complaints today. Francesca will still be in Copenhagen when we get back, you know."

Manfred snorted and turned to yell at a couple of porters carrying the canvas-stitched gear bales up the beach. "Move it! We want to be there before this Christmas, not the next one."

Within the hour they were saddled up and riding out. Manfred threatened with snow was a powerful force.

The country they rode through was heavily forested—stands of mixed oak, ash, and elm. Once they left the coast there was little sign of habitation. The trail was rough and underused. Erik was pretty sure that they were indeed being taken by a back route. Brother Ottar quietly confirmed their suspicions. This was the most roundabout way possible, turning a fifteen-league journey into something far longer. The maps he had peered at in Copenhagen had indicated that going by water would be considerably faster. But a few days should still see them at Kingshall—so long as the snow held off that long. Or the wittering old nun-ducks didn't drop dead. Both of the monks could ride—Uriel, like he'd been born in a saddle, and Ottar with grimly determined competence. Perhaps the two nuns were great magic-workers, and scholars.

What neither was, was a rider. Sister Mary could almost stay in the sidesaddle without clinging to the pommel. At a walk. And Sister Mercy was worse. She clung unashamedly. And neither was really of an age to do the journey on foot, either.

They were obliged to proceed at a walk. And to stop to allow the nuns to rest.

And, while their Norse escort had certainly not forced the pace at first, as the afternoon wore on, they began to show signs of impatience and downright worry.

The night was definitely drawing in when they reached a notch leading downward into a valley. "There are houses down there," explained one of the guides—the only one who spoke fluent Frankish. "It is too cold to go farther. Besides, there is a grendel . . . it has killed many beasts and some people," he said looking nervously around at the rocks.

"A grendel . . . ?"

As he said it there was a terrible quavering shriek from up-slope. The elderly Norse escort gave a shriek of his own and shoved his spurs into his horse. Their escort seemed to have one idea only—to see how fast they could get out of there. These Franks could either escort themselves or follow.

"Hold!" bellowed Szpak to several of his knights whose mounts seemed to think that this was a great idea. "Form up. Take station around the prince, the holy nuns, the grooms, and the packhorses. I'll have the hide off any man that panics. Believe me, I am more dangerous than anything you'll find on this hillside."

As if to counter this assertion, a deep, terrible roar came echoing down the valley. It was low pitched enough to spook the horses, and seemingly even to make the rock quiver.

Szpak jigged savagely at his horse's bit. "Prince Manfred. You will remain in the middle of the group," he snapped. "Out lances, Ritters. Except Sonderberg and Von Duren. You draw your swords, gentlemen. Stick with Hakkonsen, the prince and the brothers and sisters. We'll continue at a walk."

Erik could feel the hairs on the nape of his neck rising, as the quavering shriek began again. Something huge and dark was stumping down the slope toward them, wreathed in mist. And Erik knew fear. It was like cold tide surging around them. Horses' eyes rolled. Even with the iron control the knights exercised over their steeds, one of them was going to bolt.

Brother Uriel dropped off his horse. Erik managed to lean forward and snag the bridle as the animal started to run. "Here. Up!" he yelled at the monk.

Instead Uriel was helping Sister Mercy dismount.

"Stay in the saddle!" bellowed Manfred.

Instead Uriel helped the nun down. She fell into his male embrace—probably for the first time ever. But she was already rummaging in a small bag. And singing. It was, unless Erik was mistaken, the twenty-third psalm.

"Damnation." Erik let go of Uriel's horse. A part of his mind said that Uriel was a good horseman. He hadn't fallen off his steed. He'd dismounted deliberately. That didn't stop him trying to reach the frail little old nun—as Uriel was helping the other one down, and Ottar was falling off. Erik decided he'd have her over the crupper. She could haul her skirts up or cling like a sack of meal . . .

The little nun ducked under his hand. It was not so much a case of evading him as scrawling something hastily on the earth. And now Brother Uriel had found her hand. "Sing," he yelled up at the knights. "We are being bespelled."

"Whatever it is, it wants us to run. Hold them, Juzef. Rein in here," yelled Manfred, before joining into the psalm.

Another terrible rumbling bellow came down the valley. But now it sounded less terrible, somehow, above the echoing psalm. The knights stood like a spiky steel wall against the thing that was stumping down the hillside toward them. It was hard to make out what it was, except that it was large and shadowy and surrounded by roiling mist.

"Troll. Or a troll-wife," said Ottar, breaking off his singing in the attempt to light a candle. The wind was no help. Neither was the horse that nearly knocked him over. A squire grabbed that one's bridle. So far someone had taken control of the loose horses, at least.

"You need to set up wards?" asked one of the two Ritters that Szpak had detailed to guard the monks and nuns. "We can use fires." He pointed. There'd been a small landslip here and a snag of dead broken pine was just to the left of them.

"Yes," said Uriel. "Do it." Three squires hastily scrambled off their horses and gathered dry pine, which they put at cardinal points indicated by the monks. "It is a sending of fear."

"And whatever it is wants us scared and running. Or it is herding us down there," said Erik, decisively. "We stand right here. Look. It hasn't actually advanced. It's just trying to frighten us."

The fires were hastily kindled. And the knights stood, the flames reflecting on the bright steel, making a line between the fires they dared the gray menace up the hill slope to attack.

It didn't. The shriek came again. As did a growl. "There are at least two of them—the one we can see up there, and up the right-hand slope the other. It sounds worse. Do we charge it, Ritter?" asked Proctor Szpak.

Uriel answered him. "No. We've raised a ward around us. If they could attack us they would. We will attempt certain spells of banishment now. Even if that fails, the creatures do not like the daylight. We merely need to wait for morning."

"Could be a long, cold wait, especially if the snow comes on."

"It won't. The wind is turning," said Erik, feeling it against his face through the visor. There was a comparative warmth to it. Even a tang of salt.

"Well, we've got lots of firewood," said Manfred.

As he said this an angry flurry of wind and snowflakes ripped at the fires. It sent sparks and twigs flying. It did not damp the fires. Instead they flared brighter. The Servants of the Trinity began chanting in unison. Bell-like voices seemed to be joining them as if from a great distance. The wind died back.

Uriel wiped his forehead. He was sweating despite the chill—it would freeze tonight. "Weather magic. Powerful and treacherous stuff. I hope we have defeated it."

Within the hour it had settled into a siege situation. The grooms and squires had picketed the horses and gathered fuel from the pine snags. The knights had divided up into three patrols, walking their horses along the short perimeter of the fire-warded area.

They prepared themselves for a long, sleepless night.

They were quite correct about that.

Finally, as the sky began to pale, the bellowing and shrieking let up.

They moved out at dawn. There was no sign of the monsters now. Erik and one of the others rode up-slope to have a look. He returned a few minutes later, looking puzzled. "Prints the size of ploughshares. Big bare feet. And a lot of bear-sign. Recent at a guess. Six, seven bears at the least. Odd. I thought bears were solitary creatures?"

Brother Ottar looked wary. "There are tales told of *björnhednar*. Shape shifters, like the *ulfhednar*—the wolf-men."

"Well, perhaps that's what happened to our escort," said Manfred. He yawned. They were all tired. "Erik, I was talking to Brother Ottar here while you went looking at bear prints. He says if we go back a few miles and take that trail off to the west we should come out at one of the lakes. We should be able to hire a couple of boats to carry us. The nuns at least."

Erik nodded. "If we have to ride hard they're going to fall off."

"Sister Mercy doesn't even have to ride hard to do that," observed Brother Uriel, grimly. "The woman hasn't been in a saddle before, Ritter. Sister Mary rode as a child. But Sister Mercy is extremely stiff today. It'll be all she can do to ride at all."

"We've got little choice about it then. Lake Holme it is."

"This king of theirs may not be best pleased about us making our own route."

"Then he should send us an escort that doesn't run away," said Manfred. "I have his safe-conduct here." He tapped his stomach.

"You ate it?" said Szpak with a grin.

"Not yet. It's in an oilskin pouch next to my skin, along with various other documents. But if we don't get some breakfast soon I'll be tempted."

"I was going to ask why you ate alone," said the Pole.

Fortunately, they found a farm shortly after taking the western trail. And once the franklin had been convinced that the outlanders hadn't come to kill him and loot his homestead, he was happy to sell them great rings of flattbrød—round flat biscuits made of pea-flour, barley, and coarse oatmeal—smoked salmon and some weak ale. And with more reluctance, some oats for the horses. There was a lot of winter ahead and he had stock to bring through it.

"It burns us," snarled her son. "It burns worse than that one-eye accursed arm-ring did, Mother. You should have warned me."

She stared at him with cold green eyes. "You'd better get used to it. We'll have to fight more Christian mages and the Knights of the Holy Trinity if we're to have our way. It didn't kill you, did it?" The troll-wife looked exhausted. Having her spells broken had been draining and uncomfortable for her, too. She just hoped that it had hit that cursed elf-get as hard. Hatred as bitter as bile surged in her throat. Well, she'd be rid of the half-breed Alfar soon. It would die. She would no longer be able to draw on it then, but at least it wouldn't be here to gall her.

As usual her son wilted under her gaze. Physically he was even stronger than she was. But he still bowed before her, most of the time. She planned to keep it that way. He dropped his eyes. "So what do we do now, Mother?" he muttered.

"Leave it to me. It will take me a day or two to gather the snow clouds in again. They cannot be at Kingshall in less than three days. I have further spells of hiding and spells of binding to weave."

"Curse their cold iron. I want to kill them. I want to drink their blood."

"And so you shall, son. As soon as I have Chernobog's victim secure. As soon as *Joulu* is over."

CHAPTER 21

Kingshall, Telemark

Cair made sure that he was in a good position to observe the arrival of the delegation from the Holy Roman Empire. Firstly, it was quite amusing. They'd never guess who the ragged thrall watching them was. Secondly, there was a small chance that he could engineer their presence into an opportunity to get away and, indeed, to get Signy away. But he knew her well enough by now to know that she'd never leave willingly. The princess had been brought up in a trap called "duty" and was her own jailer.

He did not have to fake gaping when the knights rode up in neat order, with two monks riding in their midst, and a pair of nuns in a horse-borne litter. The two elderly women looked more than a little sick. Even in the late-afternoon light with the heavy cloud hanging low, the knights' spiky steel armor was almost dazzling. They advanced in neat and disciplined formation—very different from Vortenbras's hearthmen. The Norse were big men, as a rule. These were also big men, on huge horses, in formation. The potential for martial prowess might be what made the rest of the Norse stare. But for Cair it was different. He'd worked out who the bulky, barrel-chested man leading the column was.

Manfred of Brittany. Such a prize! If he had a hostage like that, the Empire would pay Cair Aidin a very high price for his release. Then the humor of it struck him. He was a slave, at least for now. But he still thought like a corsair captain.

Erik looked at the Norse crowd. Typically, he searched for danger, for the unusual. For the threat. It was what a good bodyguard did, and in many ways Erik Hakkonsen had been raised and bred to be the very best. One of the gawping crowd made him pause. He was plainly a thrall—but not like the other open-mouthed slaves staring at them. For starters he was of Mediterranean origin, olive skinned and dark eyed. Most of the ragged thralls were blond or brown haired. Blue eyes were the norm here, too. But slaves could come from anywhere. It was not his appearance that made the man stand out to Erik. It was his posture. That made Erik's reflexes prickle into readiness.

And while the others gazed in awe at the column—this man had been laughing. He'd plainly seen heavy cavalry trooping before. And something about them struck him as funny. That was odd. And, despite the fact that the man was in rags, and not obviously armed, Erik perceived him as dangerous. He mentally marked him down to be watched. The Norse might be scrupulously honorable about the truce oath, but that didn't stop someone else wanting Manfred dead.

It was plain that word had gone ahead—but not far ahead. The Norse kinglet showed signs, to the watchful, of hasty preparation to meet his guests, just as they were escorted into the hall. The Norseman was big. One of the biggest men Erik had ever seen—nearing seven foot tall at a guess, broad chested, with long white-blond braided hair and a beard. He looked as if he could cheerfully have murdered them. Still, he was polite on receiving Manfred's credentials and the letter from the Emperor. Everything was wittered through a translator. Erik decided that it would be unnecessary to point out that his native Iceland had been principally settled by Norsemen, and that Manfred had suffered through some instruction in the language—not so different from the Frankish of the Empire. Manfred had a positive gift for languages. His pursuit of loose women and strong drink had led to his grasping the Italian dialect far more easily than Erik. Doubtless, if there were Norse temptations of the same sort he'd move from rusty to fluent in record time. But for now, they let the interpreter witter. It gave one time to think.

"Vortenbras King he says you are welcome. He apologies for the difficulties."

"Tell the king it was not serious. We are honored to be here, to try and assist you in recovering from your terrible loss," said Manfred, lying with equal facility. Francesca would have been proud of him.

A steward was called and servants led the knights to their quarters.

"Koboldwerk country," said Erik once they were alone. "I'd keep you in full armor if I could. But you will even sleep in a mailshirt."

"They have a treaty with us, don't they?" said Manfred. "Not that I'd trust that big bruiser on the throne too far."

"Exactly," said Erik, grimly. "Even among honorable people it only takes one oath breaker."

"He didn't seem exactly thrilled with the idea that we had come to help him find this arm-ring. What did they call it— *draupnir*?"

"That's it. Dripper." Erik grimaced. "Understandable, them feeling that way, I suppose. Our even trying is something of an affront to the local priests."

"Especially," said Manfred, fishing in a saddlebag and pulling out a heavy golden arm-ring, "as we're going to succeed."

Erik looked at the engraved carved ring, and raised his eyes to heaven. "Francesca, I detect your hand."

Manfred nodded. "She had it made in Copenhagen. It's a good copy of the original—and how many people look that closely at this sort of thing? Now we just have to arrange to find it somewhere. She advised a good layer of mud and a little battering."

Erik shook his head. "My advice, which I doubt you'll listen to, is toss it into a swamp or the gaderobe. As soon as possible. Francesca is a genius at politics—but I wish she'd stay out of physical meddling. She should have talked to the nuns about this scheme."

"Francesca's never been terribly good with nuns, unlike you," said Manfred, grinning. "The old ducks are both all weak-kneed at that manly, clean-cut appearance of yours, and are ready to tell you all sorts of things. We all have our weak points. Francesca's is nuns. The nuns' weak point is you. But this is a good copy, Erik. Good enough to fool an expert goldsmith."

Erik took it and examined it closely. "What it isn't, is a magical object. The real *Draupnir* would be busy killing me right now. I would be unable to let go of it, I would be in mortal agony, and the only way to lessen the pain would be to take it back toward the temple *Vé*. Manfred, everyone knows that. Everyone would know this item was a fake. And then we'd be in real trouble, treaty or no."

"Oh," said Manfred, pulling a face. "Well, I suppose we'd better find the real thing then." He paused. "So how did it get stolen, eh? Some fire tongs? Or a good thick leather glove?"

Erik shook his head again. "You should do your homework, Manfred. It would appear *draupnir* can't be dealt with quite that easily. No, either the thief is dead, which is the theory I favor, because all the guards were killed, or it was magically transported."

"So we're looking for a dead body. And pretty close by if the pain is that intense. You wouldn't think it would be that hard. You'd think the locals could cope."

"Brother Uriel and I were working out how it could have been done. The thief could have been under compulsion of some sort—no one would steal it without that. When they died, the next bearer could have been standing by. It would leave a trail of dead bodies."

Manfred shuddered. "You two are a pair of ghouls. Now we've got to find a trail of weeks-old dead bodies, probably buried, or sunk into one of these lakes, if the thief-master has thought all this out, and planned it that well."

"Possibly," agreed Erik. "And I am sure the locals will have tried every form of augury and magic at their command to find the arm-ring. Obviously someone has hidden it well. So what we thought we'd try is pointing to the thief instead. One of the nuns is good at that."

"Sister Mercy," said Manfred pulling a face.

Erik nodded.

"She looks like she might enjoy thrashing the miscreant."

Someone knocked politely. It was the steward. "My lords, you are summoned to the evening feast. Can I show you where to go?"

They set off up the passage. As they walked, Erik caught sight of the dark-skinned man who had aroused his suspicions earlier. He pointed. "Who is that fellow, friend?"

The steward looked startled. Erik noticed that he made a warding symbol with his hands, obviously without realizing what he was doing. "It's just a thrall, sir. He's the princess Signy's stable-thrall. He's not supposed to be indoors. But he always is," said the steward irritably.

"Odd-looking man," said Erik, fishing.

The steward nodded. "Ugly fellow. He comes from some far-off place, sir. They took him during a raiding voyage. Fished him from the sea, I believe. It's never wise to cheat the sea of its prey."

No more useful information was forthcoming as they were led into the feasting hall of the royal house of Telemark, and to the high table.

The feasting hall might have had all the trappings of a Norse Valhalla, complete with the shield-hung walls, bearskins, rich hangings, and golden—well, thatched—roof, but Da Messibugo's innovations hadn't reached this far into the wilds. The Ferrarese steward's delicate carving was a great success in Mainz, with birds and flesh being neatly cut without the carver even dirtying his fingers. This was more like a scene from an earlier century. Erik realized that if anyone did plan to kill Manfred, dinner would be the ideal time. It was definitely a case of he who stabbed fastest got the best bits. And even the slight girl with the severely braided hair and tight mouth was better at it than Manfred was, and she was clumsy. Erik carefully surveyed the people at the king's feasting hall. Quite a rough crew, by the looks of it. And very free with the ale horns.

Interesting. They were certainly not the courtiers and elder statesmen he'd come to expect in Frankish courts. These were more like a mercenary company, with drinking habits to match. Manfred would look like a man of moderation in this scaff and raff. *Bragar* toasts were drunk, and the evening grew steadily more raucous. Manfred matched the Norse, toast for toast. At least, being foreign, he didn't have to match the boasting. Erik kept himself quiet and watched. There was something about the King of Telemark and his court that made him very, very watchful.

The only person who had been quieter was the slight woman with the braids. Her place at the high-table proclaimed that she must be high-born—most likely the king's half-sister, according to the information Francesca had provided. The woman had answered his questions without looking at him, in as few words

as possible. Words spoken in Frankish, good Frankish. Some outlandish name . . . Princess Signy. Her garb and her manner were
at odds with her position, thought Erik, watching her. Her dress
was citron taffeta, but, in Erik's opinion, badly cobbled. The yellow became her badly, and did not go with the only jewelry she
appeared to be wearing—identical bracelets on each wrist. They
were pretty enough work, little bears holding paws, but hardly the
jewelry of a Norse kinglet's adult sister. A minor merchant's teen-
aged daughter might have worn them with pride. Her stepmother
displayed jewelry enough to prove that the kingdom wasn't poor.
Mind you, bears seemed fashionable here. The queen mother had
little bear earrings.

If the princess dressed as befitted her station, and wore an
expression of less misery, and maybe braided her hair less tightly,
she'd probably be quite pretty. As it was she appeared to be a
spinster in her mid-twenties, at a guess, in a society where marriage by sixteen was the norm. Well, perhaps she was fussy as
well as a bit clumsy. She had a slight squint, he noticed. And
tiny frown-lines on her forehead. She sneaked off early, leaving
the motherly dowager queen to smile blandly at the steadily more
drunken antics of her son's court.

The queen reminded him of his mother—at her worst.

Erik hoped that Manfred would have a suitable headache in
the morning.

And he was not disappointed.

CHAPTER 22

The next day, after breaking their fast, the Knights and the Servants of the Holy Trinity with their divining gear were escorted to the edge of the sacred grove, which, it appeared, was as far as they were going.

Or at least as far as they were going according to the old skinny-shanks pagan priest in his ratty wolf skin, who stood with folded arms, blocking their way. He seemed convinced that his hundred and ten pound bulk was an insurmountable barrier.

Manfred studied the layout of the place carefully. It appeared that a cluster of oaks—the sacred grove, or *Vé*, presumably—grew around a huge tumbled boulder, a rock the size of several cathedrals. Across the fields he could see another such knot of ancient oaks, presumably another temple. The perimeter of the oak grove was marked with driven stones. And, if he understood old spindle-shanks correctly, "No heathen, idol-worshiping unconsecrated priest would come past those stones to profane the holy place."

Manfred had never thought of it that way before, but it was a question of perspective. And old skinny-shanks had the penetrating voice that nature had seen fit to give some older men. Did he have to shout?

Best to do something about it now, before it got any louder. "Brother Uriel." Both the monk and, Manfred noticed, Juzef Szpak, looked in danger of exploding into some very unwise action. "Is it necessary that you actually physically have to go to the place?

Is there no way we can just do it from here? We can try again from each path out of there, or something."

The monk turned to him, shaking his head emphatically. "We need to apply the principles of contagion . . . we need the actual place the accur . . ." Brother Uriel restrained himself with effort, obviously recalling something. "The item. We need something that was touching it. It was lying on an altar stone, apparently. Thus we need the altar stone."

"Does the altar stone need to be in the temple?"

Brother Uriel blinked at the idea, turned to Brother Ottar and Sisters Mary and Mercy. "What do you think, Sisters? Brother Ottar?"

"No reason at all," said Mercy. "Of course the place retains the memories of what happened there—and allowing these memories to be visualized is one of my skills. It will be impossible to perform those magics in some other place, so 'seeing' the deed will be difficult."

"Anyway," said Ottar in a low voice, "I had always cautioned against that. Too much blood has been spilled there. Too much sacrifice and pain. We risk bringing back some *draug* . . . some shades are best left sleeping. Brother, if we can work on the stone in a consecrated space that has never been so defiled . . . it will be safer as well as more likely to succeed."

One of King Vortenbras's hearthmen had translated the idea to Vortenbras.

The king shook his head emphatically. "*Nei!*" He seemed shocked by the very idea.

The old priest, however, found it funny. Something about "it would break the heathen Frank's back and serve him right."

"Excuse me," said the timorous Sister Mary. "It would not have to be the stone itself. We could do a working from dust off the stone. It was done thus with the relics from St. Theophilus's tomb, remember, Sister?"

Sister Mercy nodded. "I had forgotten. Yes. Ask them, Prince Manfred, if we can send one person to gather some dust from the stone."

Manfred turned to Vortenbras, who was looking as if he, too, might just explode any minute. Szpak. Uriel. The priest of Odin—for all that the old geezer looked as if a stiff breeze might knock him over—and this giant of a king. All were braced for a fight. Manfred was used to being the biggest man around. It gave one a new viewpoint to have someone looking down at you. So Manfred spoke calmly, as if he were asking a taverner for another stoup of wine when the fellow already thought he'd had too much. "We will not take our priests inside your holy place, or try to move the stone."

The hearthman translated hastily. The storm clouds over Vortenbras's brow lifted a bit. Old skinny-shanks nodded, and tossed back his ratty wolf-skin cape and lifted his nose, saying something about the true god of noblemen, if Manfred got it right. "We ask though that one of my knights go to see the place where the arm-ring lay. To bring out some dust."

This one gave the translator coughing fits. Vortenbras and the old priest looked thoroughly taken aback and, be it said, amused. However, it seemed that old skinny-shanks was inclined to refuse anything on principle. Vortenbras cut him off mid-tirade, with an imperious wave of the hand. "*Ja,*" he nodded. He looked thoughtful for a moment and then continued. Manfred didn't grasp enough to understand it except for the word "noble."

The hearthman translated. "The prince himself must go. Odin is god for the nobleman."

"Tell them I go with you, or I'm not letting you go," said Erik in the tone that Manfred had learned meant "nonnegotiable."

Manfred turned to the translator again. "I must take my body-guard with me."

Back came the reply. "Only noblemen."

Erik stepped forward. And said something in Norse. The eyes of the translator, the priest and Vortenbras widened. He turned to Manfred. "We will need something to collect the dust on, Prince."

Wordlessly Sister Mary produced a folded piece of fine white linen cloth from the little bag she carried with her.

Manfred took it, and the priest grumpily turned to lead the way into the leafless grove.

Walking quietly behind him between old gnarled trees, some of them with boles the size of cannon trunnions, hung with lichen and mistletoe, Erik said quietly, "So much for the dignity of the Church and the Knights of the Holy Trinity. Do you realize what that translator made of 'dust'?"

"No. What?"

"Dirt," said Erik, sourly.

Manfred's eyes widened. "Oh. No wonder the bastard found it funny."

"Yes," said Erik in a very even voice. "One of the Knights of the Holy Trinity and a prince of the Holy Roman Empire . . . going to clean the dirt off Odin's altar."

"That'll sound good in their next drinking and bragging session," said Manfred wearily. "Oh well, it's done. And what did you do to get them staring at you?"

"They wanted to know if I was noble enough. I told them who my maternal great-grandfather was," said Erik curtly.

Manfred gave a wry half smile. "I didn't know that great-grandparents frightened them like that. I'd have dug out my Great-aunt Olga for the trip. So who was this venerable relation?"

Erik just looked at him coldly.

"Tell."

"Hush." They'd come to the temple. It was cut into the rock of the boulder with a portico-style roof extending out from the stone. The carved wood of the rooftree was black with age and smoke. "Been around for a while," said Manfred, quietly taking in details. Inside, the place was dim, and dominated by the altar stone. It was a back-breaker all right. Set straight onto the earth floor, it must have weighed three or four hundredweight. Manfred wondered if he could have lifted it, let alone have carried it.

"A very very long time," said Erik equally quietly. "Look at the hearthstone." The stone was deeply incised with spiral patterns. The fire burned in what was plainly a natural fissure in the rock, behind it.

The old priest said something, peevishly.

"What does he want?"

"Us to clean the altar stone and get out of his temple," said Erik.

Manfred shook the cloth out. And said: "Keep a straight face, for heaven's sake, Erik," as he hastily bunched it in his big hands.

It was a small, cross-embroidered altar cloth.

"You can actually see where the ring was lying," said Erik looking at the altar carefully. It was indeed dusty. That was inevitable with a floor of tramped earth. "Here, Manfred." He pointed. One could see the faint outline of the arm-ring there in the dust. "Fold the cloth up again. Let's see if we can capture just that."

Manfred held it out to him. "You do it. You've a more delicate touch than I have."

So Erik folded the cloth, and gently placed it on the altar, just over the dust marks. He rubbed just slightly, and picked up the cloth. "Let's get out of here."

The old priest muttered something that was probably "Can't even clean properly." But he was too glad to see them go to make any more fuss.

"What did you mean about those spiral carvings?" asked Manfred as they walked back, Erik carrying the cloth carefully. "You see them in Brittany, too, you know."

"And in Ireland as well. They're no part of Scandinavian Odin worship. That place was a temple long before the Norse brought Odin here."

"Common practice, building your temple or church where another one stood. Establishes that you're the master," said Manfred. "Half the churches in the Empire stand on the sites of old Lundar, apparently."

"Considering that you can't pray without moving your lips, isn't that just what you were doing when I put the altar cloth on top of Odin's altar?" asked Erik, his lips quirking.

Manfred looked a little sheepish. "After Venice and what we ended up fighting there, I take my religion just a little more seriously. Besides, I'd give you long odds that you were doing the same."

Erik acknowledged the hit. "You always were a lucky gambler."

"Well, I hope that this particular gamble pays off," said Manfred with a gesture at the cloth.

They met the others, waiting just outside the ring of stones that marked the *waerd* of the temple *Vé*. "You were successful?" asked Brother Uriel.

"I hope so. There is an imprint of the ring in the dust on the altar stone. I hope we've got that on the . . . cloth," said Erik, handing it over.

By the glint in the monk's eye he knew exactly what sort of cloth Sister Mary had given them. But all he said was, "Excellent! We'll take it back to our chambers and work on it."

King Vortenbras barked out something. Brother Ottar and Erik both visibly paused. "I'm afraid we won't," said Erik. "The king has ordered that you do your ... work in the feasting hall, before all of the company. He's not quite accusing you of chicanery. Yet."

An unfamiliar smile cracked Brother Uriel's stern visage. "The Lord moves in mysterious ways. We were warned against public displays of our faith, but my abbot asked that we should try to open the way for missionary work here. Now, at their insistence, we shall have to show them. Knock and it shall be opened unto you."

Erik fell in quietly behind Manfred and beckoned to the bird-like little nun. "Sister Mary. You're Irish," he said quietly.

She nodded. "In a manner of speaking. My father was a Frankish master miner recruited to oversee lead and silver mines by the Irish. My mother was born in the Bóinne valley. I lived in Dublin until I was a woman grown." She sighed, reminiscently. "Many years ago of course. But the church knows no nationalities."

"Neither do temples, by the looks of it. The hearthstone in there—it was carved with spirals in the Irish manner. You see them in Brittany, too."

The wrinkled face wrinkled into more wrinkles as she smiled. "And farther afield across Europe. Old temples. Some of them rededicated to new gods ... Tell me about the temple. Especially the area where the stone lay."

"It was just across a fissure in the rock. With a big single log smoldering inside it."

To his surprise the old woman ducked her head and hid her face in her hand.

"You do see the symbolism, Ritter Hakkonsen." There was some amusement in her voice. "And some of the other mythos attached to the arm-ring might make more sense now. It was supposed to be born of rock of the temple."

Erik frowned. "But it is gold ... oh, I see."

"Partially, perhaps. You do know that metals are often deposited in fissures, and that gold does occur with silver, sometimes? And Norway produces silver?"

"Er. No. You obviously know more than I do about this, being a master-miner's daughter. But you mean the gold for the arm-ring came from the fissure that's ... well, their hearth."

"Yes. You can see what pagans would make of the symbolism of such an item. I must confer with Sister Mercy about this. The arm-ring, too, may predate the present pagans. It may have a bearing on this."

As far as Erik could see, "bearing" was just a bad choice of words.

CHAPTER 23

Signy had to admit that her curiosity had been stirred by the outlanders. It was not that foreigners were that rare at the court. But, of course, not priests. Or these knights in their spiky armor. She found their strangeness . . . tempting, rather than threatening. They hinted at the existence of a world that was wider than a Norse maid's duty. Most of Vortenbras's hearthmen didn't seem to share her opinion. They plainly found the presence of the knights intimidating. A couple of the more obnoxious Danes had quietly melted away rather than meet them. That was pleasant, too. And the outlanders were well mannered enough. She'd met several of the knights at the stables. They'd been polite—even flattering about her darlings. "It is good to see that the old horses are so cherished, *ja*," said the broad brown-haired proctor, patting a muzzle. He'd instantly moved from "outlander" to "good man" in Signy's estimation.

The only one of them she found alarming was the lean, powerful man who followed the prince everywhere. His eyes were never still. He probably didn't even realize that he walked like a cat. Signy was used to assessing warriors. This one was dangerous. But this morning Vortenbras had escorted them across to the Odinshof. By tomorrow they'd be leaving, successful in finding the arm-ring or no. So Signy was back in the stables. She only had a few more months with the horses, before she was sent to Hjorda to die. She'd make the time as good for her horses as she could.

A thrall came panting in, his eyes bright with excitement. "Princess. The king wants you to come up to the feasting hall. The outlanders are going to try to divine where the arm-ring of Odin is with their Christian magic!"

And here she was in her old riding habit again! And no time to change. She hastened out of the stables. Out of the corner of her eye she noticed that Cair was also walking nonchalantly to the kitchen. She had to smile. The thrall was as curious as she was, no doubt. She had to admit to having wondered how anyone had even dared to try to steal the arm-ring—it was so wreathed in stories of power. It could only be an outlander who would commit such a crime. Maybe one of Vortenbras's foreign hangers-on? Kingshall folk believed that the ring had been here since the beginning of time. It was simply unthinkable for them to dare steal it.

By the time she got into the feasting hall it was crowded, and in the center of the room the foreign priests had already begun their outlandish preparations. She slipped into a corner. But Vortenbras beckoned her across to the royal dais. She'd be able to see better from there. The Christian priests and priestesses had not come to last night's meal. They did look rather like crows in those black and white clothes.

Cair was a worried man. He'd started to smell treachery when he saw King Vortenbras greet Prince Manfred. Cair, of course, shouldn't have been anywhere near the hall when the knights presented their credentials to the king. But servants are so unnoticed.

Cair had captained a ship, and later commanded a fleet of corsairs. Treachery was commonplace among these men. You learned to detect traces of it, in the way men walked and acted. Vortenbras would cheerfully have slipped a knife into Manfred of Brittany, for all that he had been unusually polite. Cair had thought about all this very carefully and reached two decisions. Firstly, the Emperor's reputation was such that if some ill befell his second in line to the throne, someone was going to get badly hurt. Secondly, he'd heard it said that wars were hell on women and horses. He'd bet you could add thralls to that list, too.

Magical rituals were no novelty to Cair. He'd watched his share of fakers in Algiers and Carthage and elsewhere. He'd borrowed freely enough from their patter and occult mysticism to fool these Norsemen, too. This appeared to be more of the same. There was a trick to it. Smoke and mirrors, even if you couldn't see how it was done. Well, perhaps they would succeed. He had always been sure that the piece of chunky gold had been stolen, not by some monster, but by one of the nobles or priests or one of Vortenbras's hangers-on. The whole thing had merely been set up to look like that to fool the superstitious locals. You could rely on them to cloak the whole lot in mumbo jumbo and exaggeration. He was sure that it was an inside job. Maybe the monks and nuns from the Servants of the Holy Trinity could frighten the locals.

Still, watching from a favored place—for a thrall—he had to admit that these Servants of the Holy Trinity were slick. The trick with raising the wards was one worth learning. The chanting had a compulsive, hypnotic effect on the Norse audience—the very air of the place felt prickly with fearful anticipation. With so many people sweating, it was no wonder he was left with a tin taste in his mouth.

Then they were still. And the audience scarcely dared breathe in the sudden silence. The leader of the monks took up a piece of folded white cloth and traced certain symbols on it, first with a few drops of water, and then with a burned splinter from a small chest. He shook the cloth over a large golden chalice of wine. That was a neat bit of loot. Worth more than the stolen arm-ring, in Cair's estimation.

The monks and nuns began chanting anew—with their leader peering into the chalice. Very convenient that. He could claim to see anything. Having steam rise from the chalice was a neat trick, too. Cair could think of at least two ways that that particular "manifestation" could be arranged.

"I see an anvil. A great anvil dripping with blood. The ring is very close to it."

"Tell us more," demanded the queen mother, revealing that she, too, spoke perfect Frankish. "That could be anywhere, priest."

The chalice in his hands began to rock as the queen spoke, and the ward-candles flared. Cair noticed that Princess Signy, standing in front of King Vortenbras, looked ready to faint. She was really being taken in by all of this. Well. Vortenbras was standing right there. He should be able to catch her, that is if the lummox had the intelligence to realize she was fainting.

Wine sloshed, steaming, onto the floor as the priest sought—at least to all appearances—to hold the chalice. "Let that which cannot abide the name of Christ, begone!" He traced a cross in the air, dropping the white cloth in the process, and then seized the chalice with both hands.

It was stilled, but by the look on the monk's face, it was too late.

"There are witches, several workers of magic, in our midst. Doubters and enemies," said one of the little old nuns severely, looking at the Norse crowd from under lowered brows.

How very unusual, thought Cair. *Isn't it odd how the charlatans always claim that it is some unbeliever in the audience who is interfering with their trickery.* He'd thought that the Servants of the Holy Trinity would come up with something more original.

But he had to admit that the little nun's next actions were that. She picked up a short, unornamented wooden staff and pointed it at the cardinal points of the circle. Touched it to the cloth on floor. And then, saying certain words he did not catch, she twirled it between her fingers and threw it upward. It hung in the air and spun lazily. A low moan of terror went up from the crowd.

Cair would have been terrified, too—if he hadn't achieved the same effect with a twig and a strand of horsehair from the tail of the queen mother's fat gray. There were plenty of beams up there, and he was sure that that paunchy monk had the other end of the thread.

"Seraphim and spirits of the air, point us to the thief. Show us the last person to touch the arm-ring," she commanded.

The staff turned. Stopped. Juddered.

Like a lance it flew.

And fell as if it had struck something.

It lay on the dais.

... Pointing at Princess Signy.

There was a collective hiss of horror.

And Signy, her face as white as new snow, fell forward in a dead faint.

Vortenbras stepped hastily away from his half-sister. "Her!" he said pointing at the crumpled figure. "You always said that she was a *seid*-witch, Mother!"

The idiot thrall next to him clung to Cair with terror-born hysterical strength, as Cair tried to struggle forward.

Erik hadn't watched the ritual. Instead he'd watched the crowd. If—and it seemed quiet likely—the thief was here, they might betray themselves.

He scanned the rapt faces, and picked out one in the mob of thralls at the kitchen entrance. That Mediterranean-skinned fellow with the black curly hair . . . and a disdainful half-smile on his face while all around him were in awe. Suspicious. Anyone could pretend to be a thrall, after all. But surely if he were actually guilty he'd be a little more careful about letting his face betray him?

Erik marked him down. Checked the entrances . . . and exits. The guards on the main doors were as absorbed in the ritual as the rest of the audience. Then there was also the arch that led to the kitchens. And a small portal off the dais where the royal family came and went. One guard there. At least he looked alert. Erik prodded Manfred with an elbow. "Exits." Manfred nodded, and Erik felt a small glow of pride. Once upon a time he'd have had to explain. The knights began slowly threading their way to a point between the kitchen and the main doors.

They'd just gotten there, and were behind a solid press of people when Sister Mercy did her divining.

They couldn't have been much farther from the dais.

"Seize her," roared Vortenbras, backing off despite the fact that he was closest to his fallen half-sister.

The slight princess began to sit up . . .

And then chaos broke loose.

It was dim in the hall. It was winter outside, and heavily overcast. Tapers burned in all the sconces. Some light came in from the wide-open double doors and the huge open fireplace.

The tapers flickered in unison. And died.

The double doors swung shut of their own volition.

The fire—several small trees burning—died back to embers.

Several shaggy bear pelts hung around the walls, dropped down. And somehow transformed themselves into huge, real, live, angry bears. Roaring bears, cuffing and flinging anything in their way. They all bore down on the half-crumpled figure on the dais.

In the dim light of the ward-candles—all that still burned in the feasting hall—they seemed gigantic. Monstrous.

As they seized the woman, Manfred bellowed, "Dia Coir!" He held his sword aloft, and it shone like some beacon. "To me, Ritters."

Thrusting their way by sheer weight of steel against the panicking Norse, they pushed forward as the pack of bears squeezed themselves through the small portal that led into the royal quarters.

Erik knew that the light was bad, and the throw was risky, but the press of people all trying to go the other way was slowing them down. The Algonquin war hatchet arced over and over and hit the last of the bears, just as the beast brought both its paws down on the man who had belatedly tried to stop them.

The creature pawed air, and fell.

The knights pressed forward.

Behind them someone had either the intelligence or the desperation to force open the great double doors. Light spilled in. And with this, the fire in the hearth surged into crackling flames.

The knights reached the dais, and Manfred, despite his armor, vaulted up onto it. Erik settled for the stairs—three at a time. The only live people still up there appeared to be King Vortenbras and the dowager queen. The King of Telemark stood defending her, a naked and bloody blade in his hand.

In the doorway lay a bear pelt, and a warrior, who revealed that he wasn't quite dead yet by groaning. The door guard, whom Erik had thought looked alert, was now very plainly dead. Taking a quick glance behind them Erik saw that the monks and nuns were calmly relighting tapers in the wall sconces.

Manfred kicked the bearskin. "There is something in there, Erik."

"Back off, Manfred," ordered Erik, in a tone that even the Prince of Brittany knew better than to argue with. "Brother Uriel!"

The monk came running. Erik snagged a spear from one of the Norse guards who had come trotting up. "There is something inside that pelt. Be ready. It's probably not human."

Uriel took the cross from around his neck, and held it before him.

Erik flipped aside the bearskin with the spear.

It was apparent that the weapons at the ready wouldn't be needed.

The naked man lying there, with Erik's Algonquin war hatchet imbedded in his neck, was no threat to anyone any more.

"*Björnhednar!*" hissed someone.

Manfred stepped over the corpse. "Get your hatchet back and let's get after them," he said grimly.

"Wait," commanded Vortenbras. "My sister is bound to have set traps up there. That is her nature. I will send my men to see if they have fled the royal hall." He pointed with his bloody sword to two of them. "Go. See if they have fled." He looked at his fallen hearthman. Shook his head. "I apologize. It appears that we had the traitoress in our midst all the time." He sighed. "My thankless half-sister. We knew she was a *seid*-witch. We just didn't realize—did not even begin to guess—how far into evil magic she must have gone. She was the first on the scene when the arm-ring was stolen, you know."

"I'm only getting about half of this," said Manfred. "What's he say, Erik?"

Erik translated. And looking across saw that the queen had slumped against the wall. "Is your mother injured? I think you'd better call her women."

Vortenbras nodded. He prodded one of his men. "See to it. The queen is uninjured, thanks be to the gods. I was between her and them all the time. But they only seemed interested in Signy and escape." He rested his sword tip on the ground. "Between the two of us, Ritter, I think it is the shock. She always treated Signy as if she were her real daughter. She had just, finally, organized a suitable marriage for her." He sighed again. "Bad blood. It was always said that Signy's mother was of *Svartalfar* blood. Evil will come out of such mixtures."

The two of Vortenbras's hearthmen who had gone to see if the bear-men had fled came back at a dog trot. "They've gone north, my king," panted one. "Toward the mountains," said the other, gesturing.

Vortenbras took a deep breath. "Get this place in order, Gutheric. You, Hans. Get all my hearthmen together with their war gear. We've a witch to catch and kill." He turned back to the knights. "My thanks. You will excuse me? I must go with my mother. She will need some comfort before I go," he said in broken Frankish to Manfred.

Manfred nodded. "Can we join you? I have thirty good horse-men to place at your disposal."

Vortenbras turned to Erik. "I have not the Frankish to say this. But what if the prince is hurt? The Emperor would be angry, yes? I don't think it wise."

Erik translated. "I'd agree with him, Manfred."

"You would. But Charles Fredrik wouldn't. We'll leave the nuns and a guard of three. The rest of us, including Ottar and Uriel, will ride," said Manfred.

Vortenbras obviously got most of that, bowed and turned to follow the women who were helping the dowager queen.

"Manfred," said Erik, with calmness he didn't feel. "Let them chase their own."

Manfred took a deep breath, and said with the stubbornness Erik had come to know well, and to realize was inflexible, "No. There's more to this than just theft, Erik. This smells as much as that affair in Venice did. You saw those bear tracks when we were attacked on our first night. This is aimed in some way at the Empire."

"I must agree with the prince," said the grim-faced Uriel. "You know that Sister Mary is a witch-smeller."

Erik hadn't. She was far less threatening-looking than Sister Mercy.

Uriel continued. "She says that there were at least three powerful practitioners of the arts here. Three or possibly four. She is sure that some of them at least were women."

"And?"

"Only one left the hall. Unless the bears were practitioners . . . but I think not. They were probably mere tools. Bespelled humans. In other words, Erik, Prince Manfred is probably as safe out of here, as in here."

Erik took a deep breath. "Very well then, Brother." He wished, later, that he'd used the argument of "snow." It might have borne more weight. "But first I want to catch up with one of the thralls. I think he might be able to help us."

"A thrall's not going anywhere, friend Erik. Those bears are," said Juzef Szpak. "We need to get to our horses."

"Well, I'll try in the stables," said Erik. "But I think we'll find that this thrall's run, too. He's neck deep in all this stuff, somehow."

In the sudden darkness Cair had seen the fur-clad monsters seize Signy. Unlike the rest of these superstitious Norse bastards Cair had worked out what they were. By the time the knights got to the dais he was not far behind. He'd got himself close enough to see the one they'd killed. A man in a bear skin—as he'd suspected. And at this point, discretion had kicked in. He was certainly the only thrall still left in the feasting hall. And sooner or later someone was going to notice. Someone might even point out that he was Signy's thrall.

He ducked his head and scurried out, collecting no worse than a casual clout from one of the guards. Once in the kitchen he kept moving. His chess-player's mind had identified several possible moves. At least two of them involved his life becoming rapidly shorter. He was in the stables before anyone else—and up into the princess's hidey-hole before anyone else got there. Even the thralls had sneaked across to the main halls, if not to watch, at least to glean snippets of news from those lucky enough to do so.

He'd organized himself an improvement on the mere ceiling hideout. For years, the stables had just been rethatched on top of the old thatch. The thatch was very thick, and the underlayer was more than a little brittle and rotten. He'd burrowed into the far corner. A dog would have found him rapidly. But getting a dog—except a small, agile terrier—to walk on the poles would be difficult. Besides, he thought it was most likely that they'd go after Signy first. And he wasn't planning to be here if they came back. He'd burrowed in feetfirst, with an old scrap of bark to hide his face if need be, so that he was well able to listen to the stable noises and the excited gossip among the thralls below as they came in. Besides, he could breathe. He'd probably have sneezed himself into betrayal facing the other way. Now he had time to listen, and to think.

The story was already growing like weeds on the dung heap: vigorously, and somewhat misshapenly. Cair was surprised to find that it was growing, at least in the stables, in a somewhat bizarre direction. "It's those black-clad foreigners. Like Odin's ravens." Among the thralls Odin was not popular. Thor and Freya had adoration. Odin—the nobles' god—fear and respect. "Come to stir up trouble among us," the thrall continued to a chorus of assenting grunts.

He was a little more taken aback to discover that it wasn't any deep love for Princess Signy that inspired them to believe it all a foreign plot, but her clumsiness. "She'd spot a hair out of place on a horse halfway across the stable, but she falls over her own feet," said Henri. "What kind of witch is that? Now if they'd told us it was Cair . . ."

"Where is he?" asked someone

"I dunno. He comes and goes about just as he pleases. He was in the stable when they called her."

The sound of boots and loud voices interrupted the thralls. Vortenbras's hearthmen, yelling for horses to be saddled.

And barely minutes later someone looking for him. "I'm trying to find the thrall with black hair." The person spoke Norse, but with an outlander accent.

"We haven't seen him, master," said Thjalfi fearfully. "Not since before . . ."

"I told you he'd run, Juzef," said the outlander, in Frankish.

"Not far, unless he took a horse. Ask them."

"You ask them," the first voice sounded amused. "The language the Götar speak is close enough."

Henri replied without waiting. After all, he was a Frank. "No, master. He didn't steal a horse. He's good slave, master. Very loyal to our mistress."

"Where has he got to, then?" asked the first outlander.

"I think he has gone to try to help the mistress."

"Alone and on foot? He's a crazy fool then," said the second.

"Yes, master. Mad. But he is a magician, too."

There was a snort. "Well, we'll overtake him then, unless he's grown magical wings and flown after them. You can question him then, Erik. Come on. Otherwise Prince Manfred will have left without us, next thing we know."

He listened to the sound of spurred mail-boots walking away. "Better make sure you've got a spare cloak and some boots you can walk in, in your saddlebag, Erik. The prince, too. I think we'll have snow before nightfall, by the looks of that sky."

"I always carry them."

Lying warm in the thatch, Cair wished them all the misery in the world. Outside, horns sounded. Dogs were barking. And Cair at last faced up to thinking about the subject he'd been avoiding.

He was quite sure that she wasn't the thief. He couldn't bring himself to believe that she could have murdered two guards, or even got someone else to do that. Which left him with two questions, the first relatively unimportant: why had the Servants of the Holy Trinity, perhaps working with some of the locals, done this? Politics? Was Signy a pawn in some evil game of the Holy Roman Emperor? But it was the second question that really troubled him: what was he, Cair Aidin, going to do about it?

What troubled him most about this was that he already in his heart of hearts knew the answer. It made no kind of sense. He should take this heaven-sent opportunity to make for the coast. With all the fuss of chasing Signy, they'd never get to pursuing a runaway thrall on a good horse, until he'd got himself onto a boat.

He knew, though, that he'd be behaving like the crazy fool that the outlander Juzef had said he was. But he wouldn't be alone, or on foot. He had every intention of stealing at least a pair of good horses.

CHAPTER 24

Telemark

The trail had been easy enough to follow, but the bears had not made following easy for the riders. They'd crossed the river, forcing the riders to go upstream to where it could be forded and then to ride back until they could pick up the trail again. Then they'd gone into some old woodland, uncut and full of snags and dead briars. A bear could go where a horse would struggle. It was apparent that these bears retained human intellect if not shape.

Vortenbras cursed, "Witch-slut. She always was my father's favorite. She couldn't accept that she wouldn't rule. This kind of thing is typical of her. Typical. Vindictive bitch, she made everybody's lives around her a misery. I should have guessed it was her. And after the way my mother always treated her like a daughter."

Erik made a suitably sympathetic noise. What did you say to a man whose sister had just turned into a witch, a thief, and a murderer?

After nearly an hour's hard ride, the going eased. Erik wondered about that, until he saw that the bears, or shape-changing men, had simply taken the shortest route to somewhere where horses would be nearly as useful as an extra nose—in a room full of skunks. They'd ridden into the end of a dead-end valley. A

144

drystone-walled garth and a hut stood at the head of the valley, and beyond it a steep rocky path headed into a ravine between two granite sheetrock slabs. To add to the cheerfulness of the scene, occasional snowflakes drifted down.

The hearthmen reined in, except for the huntsman, who was busy whipping the dogs in. Men started dismounting with a steady grumble. The huntsman, having completed his circuit of the dogs, came back up to the knights. He pointed at the trail. "Too steep. Much rocks to climb. No take horses," he said in broken Frankish.

"Hell's teeth!" said Manfred looking at the slope. "Not up there in armor."

Erik nodded. That would kill a man, as surely as an arrow through the heart. "Dismount them, Szpak. We'll need to strip to breastplates. I hope they'll wait for us."

The stable thralls left for the midday meal. Cair slipped down from his hidey-hole. Hopefully things would still be in too much flux to have his absence noted. Or, if it was noted, to have anything done about it.

He would have to lead the horses, at least until he was well into the woods. A thrall leading horses would excite no comment. A thrall riding . . . well. A different matter. He had a good hooded cloak and pair of breeches and some boots that might pass for a poor freeman's gear. A knife, too. They'd kill him for that, if they caught him. The biggest problem was that the horses would look like stabled, pampered things, too good for a poor man to own, and his olive skin would betray him, too. So he'd have to try to keep his distance from other people.

He'd decided that a saddle would be worth the attention it might generate while he led the horses and was just busy putting it on when someone cleared their throat behind him. He whirled . . . to face the last person he had expected to see in the stables.

Queen Albruna.

She looked, Cair thought, like a ghost. A shadow of her normal rosy-cheeked blond self. She was alone—also unusual. But she stood between him and his objective. And if he was caught they'd kill him anyway.

Her words robbed him of his resolve. "You will be going to my daughter. I need your help."

Cair stood still. Wary.

She wrung her hands. "Vortenbras and his men will kill her. She makes me very angry sometimes, but she is still my daughter. I cannot let her be killed."

Cair hoped that his suspicion didn't show. Or at least the fact that he was going to brain her with a barrel stave any minute didn't show. "And so?" he asked warily.

"One of my men has just come back. They've cornered them behind Svartdal." Cair knew where that was. He'd been up there with the other thralls to load hay for the stables. It wasn't even a league away. "There is a steep pass up behind it, that leads out onto the vidda. My man saw bear tracks around a cave near a *bautarstein* close to the top. The hunt has gone past the cave but they will find it."

Cair stared at her, wide-eyed. It smelled of a trap. But why him? Was she really just one of those women who hide their feelings behind a mask of bitchiness? "What do you expect me to do, O Queen? I am one thrall. There is an army pursuing your daughter."

"If you tell the outlander knights—tell their leader. I have heard that they do not kill witches who repent," she said wringing her big hands. He'd never noticed how big these were, before.

Sparing witches was at best only occasionally true. But at least she had told him where Signy might be. He shrugged. "I am just a thrall, O Queen. How can I do these things?"

"Don't pretend to be a fool," she snapped. "Take the horse and ride. Just as you were planning to do."

Cair pinched his lips together. "Put your hands behind your back and turn around."

"Why?"

"I cannot leave you free to cry warning. I shall put you in the oat store. They'll find you this evening when they feed the horses."

"Insolent fool. I won't betray you!"

Cair picked up the heavy oak barrel stave. "Turn around, hands behind your back, or I'll knock you senseless and then do it. I don't have time to waste."

Muttering, she did as she was bid.

A very few minutes later Cair was leading two horses down the track that led to Svartdal. Soon a man in a hooded cloak was galloping hell-for-leather up that rutted trail.

Approaching the hay meadows at the top end of Svartdal, Cair tried to formulate his plans, take stock of what he had . . . Which was not much in the way of plans or materiel. Two simple grenades, a worn-out, broken cheap blade he'd bound into a new handle. A small vial of aqua regia . . . a little money. A homemade lucifer. Oh, and the queen's ring. It had seemed too good an opportunity to miss, even if it had started her yelling and he'd had to be hasty about that gag. Plans? None, really. His chess-player's mind found the possibilities either too limited or too wide. And it didn't know why in the name of heaven he was doing this. The cloud was already draped on the mountain like a soggy gray porridge, and was oozing its way down.

The trail of the horses was clear enough even for a seaman to track them. But could he take horses up the pass at the head of the valley? He tried to reconstruct it in his mind's eye. All he could picture was a dark crack, splitting the granite.

Riding around the corner he could see just that. And also a lot of picketed horses.

He rode boldly up to them, picking out from the guards one of the Svear outlanders who'd found shelter with King Vortenbras a few months before. Cair had the impression that the fellow was definitely a bit slow upstairs. Cair swung down from the bay, and produced the queen's ring. He waved it under the fellow's nose. "I have a message for the king," he said, importantly.

The fellow blinked. "The king is up there. They waited for the Franks. They're not far ahead."

Cair nodded. So he'd caught up a little. "Take these horses. I must go up there, too, then. It is an honor for me to be charged with such a mission."

"What mission?" said the slow-wit. One of the other picket guards was walking over. Cair knew it hung in the balance now.

"His medication," said Cair, flourishing the bottle of aqua regia. "And I have no time to waste." He pushed the reins into the man's hand, waved and started jogging up toward the start of the trail.

He didn't look back, or attempt to run any faster.

And somehow, no one followed him.

CHAPTER 25

Svartdal, Telemark

Manfred found that the trail, if you could call it that, would almost immediately have been too steep for the horses. It was more of a scramble than a path. If it went on like this it would be too steep for the dogs. Soon they were climbing up short pieces of snow-capped damp rock—seldom more than the height of a man, but up which the dogs had to be hauled. "Going to be broken legs if not necks at this rate," he grunted, pulling himself up a rock.

"If we're lucky," said Erik, panting. "This looks well planned to me. Roll rocks on us and we're all dead.

"They say it opens up a bit higher up," said Manfred.

"Let's hope so. This is insanity."

They pressed on. The nature of the terrain made it nearly impossible for all to keep together, and it was exhausting going. Manfred knew that nature had made few men as fit, or as powerful, or with as much raw stamina as he had—except possibly the wire-hard Erik. Erik was used to rough-country walking from Iceland and later Vinland, but the other knights were not. They were more used to being in the saddle than in ravines. Erik and Manfred were soon outpacing them, although the dogs and a few of Vortenbras's hunters were still ahead. When they reached the point where the valley flattened out a bit, as predicted, Erik said sternly. "We must let the others catch up."

Manfred nodded. "Let's just move away from this last drop."

So they did just that. Some hundred yards farther on they sat down on a snow-free boulder beside the trail to wait.

It seemed that no sooner had they done so, than the cloud, which had remained reasonably high until then, dropped like a stone.

Worse. As it was closing around them, thick and cold and swirling, Manfred saw that it was spilling into the ravine below. He sighed irritably. "Great. So what do we do now? On or back?"

"Certainly not on. Back . . . well, there are a good few places we could have gone over a cliff instead of down the scramble. So I think we sit tight. Sit tight and be glad that we've got reasonably waterproof cloaks with us. Going anywhere in the mist on a mountain is pure foolishness. We'll go very carefully, sticking together, to see if we can find some fuel and get a fire to burn, if we're going to spend the night up here. But I doubt it. The Norse will come. We'll probably rope the hard sections."

"Meaning those man-bears have got away," said Manfred.

"I suspect so, yes," said Erik. "There are still some hunters and dogs ahead of us, mind you."

"Well, let's get to this fuel gathering."

"Firstly, let's tie ourselves together. You'd be amazed at how easily you can lose someone in this sort of mist. And it swallows sound, too. Here. Tie this thong around your wrist. And we move very, very cautiously."

"We can't exactly fall over any cliffs here, Erik. We saw the place before the mist came down."

"Distances are deceptive in the mist."

Manfred had to admit that Erik was right. Especially in this mist. It was thick enough to be cut with an axe, never mind a knife.

"Hell's teeth. Stop a minute, Erik. My cloak is snagged." It came free with a rip, and curse from Manfred. He liked that cloak.

"See if whatever it was caught on will burn."

"It's got thorns, whatever it is. Part of it seems dead."

The valley was full of snow, away from the narrow central track. It was obviously a fairly barren place, too, but they managed to collect some more dead bushes.

Manfred's foot slipped into a hole and he stumbled and fell, pulling Erik down, too, spilling their precious hoard of sticks. "God's wounds..." Manfred looked at the rock he'd fallen on. Even in this mist it was strange enough to be noticeable. It was plainly worked stone. "This is a bit odd up here, Erik."

The Icelander sat up and dusted himself off. "I suppose it was my idea to tie us together. But I thought I told you to be careful. Hmm." He paused in his reading of the riot act to examine the rock. "It's a *bautarstein*. A driven stone. As you say, odd thing to find here. Usually they're associated with ritual sites. Tombs and the like."

Manfred shivered despite himself. "Great. Stuck up a mountain in Norway in the mist, on top of a tomb. No doubt some Viking ghosts will come and help us keep warm."

"They're doing their best," said Erik mildly. "What you pulled me into appears to be a large gorse bush. Quite a lot of it—the part that isn't imbedded in my face and hands—appears to be dead. So get that knife of yours out and let me have some shavings. We might as well stay right here."

"So long as I can untie this leash."

In the mist nearby, something growled to itself. Something that saw far better than humans in the darkness and the mist. Something that could tell by smell exactly where they were anyway. Something that could move as silently as a ghost if it wanted to. Her weather magic had worked perfectly—this time. The rest of Mother's complicated plots were unnecessary. The *björnhednar* had the *Alfarblot* below ground now. She was still valuable. Even diluted Alfar blood gave certain powers. And Chernobog's prize was within twenty yards of the adit. He'd go and settle for the hunters and their dogs first. He didn't want them coming down here at the wrong moment. It was unlikely anyone would still be coming up, but he'd deal with that, too. He smiled in savage satisfaction. An avalanche of snow and rocks would deal with those foreigners. The Norse casualties were a small price to pay. There were plenty more of those. First he would quickly go and roar at those farther up. And maybe kill a few dogs. He hated dogs.

The mist was a great help, thought Cair, climbing steadily. The Norsemen were stopping the knights from going on. And they were making no effort to be quiet. "Prince Manfred is still up there," said a familiar voice. It was the man who had called him a crazy fool. How right he was.

"So are the huntsmen, my lord," said someone in atrocious Frankish. "They'll bivouac somewhere. There are some caves. This will blow over. I have never seen it come down so fast. Fast come, fast go."

Caves. Cair registered that and moved on up a small rock face. The trail was a bit to his left, but basically it went up. And so did he.

Later he realized that, firstly, he'd been very stupid. And secondly, had he not been so stupid, and had he been in any position to retreat, or even to rest comfortably and safely, he would have stopped. He found himself moving upward simply because staying in any one place was untenable. And sooner or later it must end. Surely it must?

By the time it did, Cair was exhausted. Thrall's food, and a long day, had eaten at his physical resources.

He crawled a bit farther from the steep edge.

And his nose caught the smell of wood smoke in the mist.

As he'd already had a day of avoiding all forms of common sense he headed onward toward it. Most likely it would be some of Signy's pursuit. Right now, as they were set on killing her, murdering them for their fire seemed a fair deal. They wouldn't be expecting him to be creeping around in the mist, and if there were too many of them, well, he'd back off.

Not unexpectedly, the fire had been difficult to get lit. Someone less expert than Erik would have given up. But, now that it was lit, Manfred had to admit that it was very welcome, especially if they were going to spend the damned night on this Godforsaken mountain. And the *bautarstein* made a fair backrest. No Norse ghosts had come to complain, yet. His stomach reminded him that it had been a long time since breakfast, though. "What do you make of this lot, Erik?"

"Deep and murky, whatever it is," said Erik. "Brother Ottar was telling me that that girl is something of a sacrificial lamb. The dowager queen has apparently been offering her to the highest bidder. Apparently, that bid has gone to Telemark's traditional enemy. The girl hates him. Not surprising she turned to the bad."

"Hmm. Sounds like Brother Ottar should be working for Francesca. How did he find all this out so quickly?"

"He stuck his neck out. He recognized one of the nobles at court as a secret Christian who knew him. They've talked. I only found this out on the ride up here, mind you. I didn't suspect her," admitted Erik.

That made Manfred feel a little better about it. "I tell you, you could have knocked me down with a feather when Sister Mercy divined that it was her. She looked like a frightened little mouse of a thing."

"Hush." Erik had the keen ears of a woodsman. By the way he was poised he'd heard something.

Erik got to his feet in one smooth movement and lunged off into the mist.

Manfred followed and was just in time to drop a bear hug around the man Erik was wrestling with.

A bear hug from Manfred tended to stop struggles very fast. But then Erik usually stopped trouble just as fast, if not faster. He hadn't this time.

"Bring him to the fire, Manfred. He nearly stuck me," said Erik.

"If you kick me again, I will squeeze," said Manfred as he carried the prisoner to the fire.

As they got there, Erik gave a low whistle. "It just got deeper and murkier, Manfred."

He stared at their prisoner, intently. "Who in heaven's name are you?"

Cair looked into the steel-gray eyes and knew that he was nearer to death than he'd ever been. He wished desperately that he hadn't reacted to what the man had said. "A thrall, master. My name is C—Karl."

"Who just happens to be creeping around a mountainside in the mist," rumbled Manfred of Brittany.

"Who is good enough with a knife to damn near kill a man with a sword," said the prince's companion, his tone showing that this had surprised him. It was mutual. Cair wasn't used to fighting someone that fast or that proficient.

"I thought thralls didn't get to carry steel?" said Manfred, squeezing slightly. "Eh . . . mister C—Karl? Who also speaks Frankish, in case you hadn't noticed, Erik."

There are times when only the truth will serve well. "I was captured. I was not always a thrall. The knife is a stolen scrap. It was the best I could contrive."

"That's true enough," said Erik, examining the knife. "And he's branded. But I smell assassin, here. Explain what you're doing here. And what is your real name?"

Before Cair could reply something bellowed higher up the valley. The mist stifled some of the sound, but still it was a terrifying noise. "Your friend coming to fetch you, eh?" said Manfred, grimly.

"*No!*" said Cair, anger and fear for someone else overcoming fear for himself. "I haven't got any damned friends. And I wasn't looking for you. At least I thought I was, but then I heard what you said and I wasn't. Maybe Vortenbras is behind all this."

"As a sentence making a lot of no sense, that one is a winner," said Manfred, sounding slightly amused. "I only understood one word of it . . . hola . . . Here it comes." They could hear heavy treads. "What do I do with this one, Erik?"

"Put him to sleep. We can't take a chance."

As he said this, Cair brought both his feet down on Manfred's toes. And head-butted back as he thrust with his elbows with all his strength. Manfred lost his grip as Cair danced free.

"Damn you!" Manfred snatched at him.

Roar! ROAAAAAAAAR!

It was huge. White, except for the terrible redness of its mouth. So close now that you could smell the fresh blood on its breath.

Talons like six-inch knives missed Cair's skin by the thickness of a hair.

They didn't miss his clothing. Had it been anything more substantial than a thrall's ragged tunic, it might not have ripped like paper, and he would have died right there, hauled into a bear hug worse even than Manfred's. As it was he was flung sprawling, to the far side of the fire. He cracked his head against a rock, and the world spun. In the mist, with his head whirling he watched the two knights with their bright swords . . . and the great mass of white fur and terrible claws and teeth. It seemed to be at least one and a half times as tall as the men. It also had a club. Half a tree, by the looks of it. The two knights only had their swords.

And beyond the monster . . . mouth dry, head spinning, Cair

croaked a warning and pointed. In the mist all that you could see was that they were big and misshapen. Like the gnarled trolls of Norse tales. He scrabbled at the fire as Erik ducked under the club and lunged at the white-furred monster.

Erik cut the monster, and it yowled. But it would take more than one blow to stop such a creature. And the others were coming to join their master.

Cair burned his fingers on an ember, and then found a brand. And stared at the *bautarstein* he'd been seeking.

"Back! The cave!" he called, fumbling with his pouch. One of his homemade grenades came to hand. "I'll fix 'em. Back and down," he yelled again. Wishing that his eyes would focus properly, he struggled to light the wick. A powerful arm hauled him back. Which was not at all what he'd meant. "Hell's teeth, fool. Back where?"

"Cave." They staggered back up the slope, and against the odds Cair managed to light the wick of his grenade. He tossed it. But his strength just—wasn't. It fell barely twelve feet away, rolling toward the troll-things instead of their monster master.

"God's blood! It's a grenade. Back!" yelled Erik.

Cair was hauled off with a strength and speed that nearly had his arm out of its socket. They stumbled against a rock face and fell, as it exploded. As grenades went it was not a great one. Still, it did get results.

The earth shook slightly. And it was certainly not from the puny grenade. Soft snow cascaded down on them, and a deep grumbling sound shook the earth in earnest. "Avalanche," said Erik. "Back. Back into the cave."

CHAPTER 26

Erik had heard the growl of avalanches before. But not ones like this one. Erik had been willing to swear that it hadn't been natural. There'd been a dance of odd lights in the mist and a strange sort of music in that grumbling.

Whatever or however the idiot thrall had triggered it, he was really not sure. It must have taken more than that little grenade—there'd been enough noise earlier to start three avalanches. The odd thrall's grenade had made a nice flash and been good for shock value—those trolls had panicked easily enough.

But the avalanche... He was sure that the grenade hadn't caused it.

Running into the cave had left them in an interesting position...

If by "interesting" you meant "stuck." They were going to die of suffocation sooner or later, along with an unconscious man who could possibly have tried to trap them here. "I still can't wake him," he said to Manfred.

"He took a swipe from that thing," said Manfred in the darkness, where he was taking a break from digging.

Erik didn't hold out much hope for the digging. The snow was soft and powdery and simply cascaded back down onto them. And twice now they'd dug... to encounter rock. Perhaps boulders had come down with the snow—or they weren't digging straight. The cave had sloped sharply in and they had rolled and fallen about twenty paces. Erik was also very skeptical about the unconscious man. "That's what it looked like, perhaps, as far as we could see in that murk. But he's alive and not bleeding that I can feel. That seems unlikely, given that I have a gouge in my breastplate and a cut on my shoulder, just from the tail end of one of those blows. I fought with this fellow a few minutes back. He was too good. He had a little homemade knife. I had a sword. He should have died. He should have died, if that thing had really hit him."

"It could happen," said Manfred, doubtfully.

Erik was far less inclined to give the fellow the benefit of that doubt. "You've got to admit his turning up there was more than implausible. He didn't ride with us, so he must have been here before us."

There was a long pause. "I suppose he must have been."

"And he was dead keen for us to get into this cave. Which he knew about!"

"It is pretty damning, I must admit," agreed Manfred. "But I'll swear that thing hit him. And he really seems to be unconscious. I'll get straight answers out of him when he comes around, I think." There was a certain implacability about that tone.

"His being unconscious is mighty convenient for him," said Erik. "But if he isn't, he's the best faker in the world."

"True enough," agree Manfred, who had also tried to wake the thrall. "Well. I can't just sit here and wait for him to come around or for the air in this hole to run out."

"What are you doing?" asked Erik. Manfred's voice had come from farther away.

"Just exploring this hole we're stuck in," came the echoing answer.

Erik's first inclination had been to say, "Well, don't." But he curbed it. He was too inclined to say "no" to Manfred. With some reason, he had to admit. But a novitiate and their experiences in Venice, not to mention Francesca, had made the once-spoiled prince grow up a lot. These days it was far more of a meeting of equals who respected each other, than of instructor and reluctant pupil. Besides, it was nearly impossible not to like Manfred, for all that he was still something of a tearaway. He settled for "Well, let's stick together. It's probably not very big but you never can tell."

"What about the thrall?" asked Manfred.

Erik shrugged, and realized that this was rather a futile gesture down here. So he answered instead, "He's not lying in the snow. He's breathing. I can't get a response from him. I think we can leave him here while we explore around. One of us would be bound to break our necks tripping over something carrying him, for all that I want him to answer some hard questions. If he's a thrall I'm an Ilkhan."

Erik made his way over to where Manfred stood, and they began making their way, cautiously feeling footstep by footstep along the wall.

"It's a lot bigger than I thought," admitted Erik. "We shouldn't run out of air at least."

"Although the stuff stinks a bit, Erik. You know, I don't think this cave is natural."

"Now what leads you to this conclusion?" asked Erik, dryly. "Could it be the relative smoothness of the walls? Or is it some arcane knowledge that is taught to heirs of Carnac?"

"Well, you're feeling better, anyway," said Manfred cheerfully. "I was worried that the slash you took from that thing might have been worse than you were telling me."

Erik smiled to himself. "What the hell was that thing?"

"Hard to tell," said Manfred. "There was fog rolling off its fur. A magical creature of some sort, for sure."

Erik had to agree. The one thing that the Knights of the Holy Trinity had learned—to their cost—was that magical creatures did exist. "It bled, though."

"Yes, I saw that. I think that we might have handled it between us, if those others hadn't been there, too."

"Trolls," said Erik, thinking of the gnarled knobbly things.

"Oh?" said Manfred. "I thought they were stories to frighten children."

"They frightened the hell out of m—"

"Erik?"

Erik would have replied but many small hands held him. Many, many small hands. Several of them were holding his mouth shut. He managed to bite one. It tasted vile. Like swamp mud. But its squeak at least gave Manfred some warning.

Not that that helped him much.

The place was dark. And then there was a hint of light. It grew, but it was no natural light. Instead it was like some eerie marsh light. Cair concluded he was dead. He'd heard of people who had been inside the doors of death describing the tunnel and the clear white light.

Considering the life he'd led he would have thought that it would be warmer. But perhaps that came later. Did the pain stop? His head hurt ferociously. He closed his eyes. Odd that you could still do that when you were dead.

Something touched him. He opened his eyes again. Blinked. The clear white light came from an odd-looking lantern on a pole.

That was not half as odd as the gnomelike thing that held it.

The Norse hell was cold, wasn't it? And what else could this creature be but a devil? A very minor one, by its size. Or maybe he was concussed. He'd hit his head, he remembered. He'd had a seaman on his first vessel who'd lost his wits after a blow on the head from a grappling iron.

The devil spoke. Considering where he was, it was, he supposed, not surprising that it spoke Norse. Well, no more surprising than anything else. "Get up, slave," was something they might say in hell, too.

He tried.

And fell over. It wasn't very far to fall, but it seemed to take a very long time, and consciousness drifted away like smoke.

Later he awoke again, lying on what was, by the smell of it, old straw.

And it was warmer here, but, as his head no longer felt as if it was full of clouds, he was very sure that he wasn't in hell after all. And, he thought wryly, even a mere Norse thrall's heaven would surely have fresh straw?

A little of the cold white light streamed in through a barred grill. He sat up. He felt bruised but otherwise intact. He examined himself. He was still, as far as he could see and feel, intact. His pouch was missing, though. He examined his surroundings as well as he could without getting up. It looked like a cell. Cautiously he stood up. It was as well he did it cautiously, because the ceiling was very low.

Someone had plainly heard him move.

A little ugly goblinlike thing, gray-fleshed and dressed, unless he was much mistaken, in scraps of mole fur, opened the door. Either that knock on the head had permanently affected his brain, or this was some creature he hadn't ever encountered before. The latter was possible. After all, he'd seen for himself apes bigger than a man, that built nests in trees like birds, when they'd gone raiding down south. "Come," it said.

There didn't seem to be a lot of alternatives, especially as mole-fur-clothes was backed up by a lot more of his kind. With, what to them were probably spears. He was led though various hallways, all too low for him to walk erect, until he came to a room where an older, fatter copy of his guide, dressed in ermine, not tatty mole fur, sat on what could only be a throne. Several others sat around the low steps. And in each of the doorways were more. Crowds of them. With more spears that looked sharp enough to make him die the death of a thousand short needles, anyway.

His pouch lay on the stone in front of the throne. Open. The miscellaneous contents were spilled out onto the stone.

The goblin king held Queen Albruna's ring between a gnarled thumb and forefinger. For him it would have made an outsize bracelet.

"Where did you get this?" the king asked, his eyes narrow.

Something about the way it was said made Cair suspicious. And the way it was held. As if it might be contaminated.

"I stole it," he said calmly.

The goblin king began to chortle. So did his courtiers. And the guards in archways.

"That's one in the eye for the old bag," said the goblin with satisfaction, wiping his eyes. "You're a very brave, if very stupid, Midgarder."

"I left her tied up, in an oat store," said Cair.

"Haw, haw, haw! You're a good liar, anyway," said the goblin, sniggering. "What are these other things?" He prodded the aqua-regia bottle with a horny toe.

"The tools of my trade. I'm a . . . sort of magician."

"Haw, haw, haw. And you get caught by the likes of Thallbru?" The goblin king slapped his thighs in delight. The rest of the goblin horde seemed to find it equally funny. "I might just keep you as a joker instead of sending you to the mines."

Cair put the pieces together. Mines. Yet the metalwork he could see was crude. Could he pass himself off as something of an expert on this? He'd never really done much, but it had been an interest. A curiosity. A dilettante's entertainment. Like chemistry, he probably knew more than the locals about it. And he'd found that he could usually wing it on a bit of self-confidence, if they were anything like as gullible as his Norse thrall victims. He was good at this stuff, after all. Some of his tricks would almost have fooled himself, if he hadn't known they were tricks. "My magic is only in the working of metals," Cair said, loftily. "That bottle there is for assaying gold. If it is true gold, the liquid will dissolve it."

The goblin king grinned. "Nothing dissolves gold, Midgarder."

"I will show you if you like. In my pouch you found a coin."

"Not gold," squeaked a small goblin from near the portal. He was a poorly looking creature—head bowed and half groveling already.

The goblin king looked at him sternly. "Give, Thallbru."

The goblin cowered back against the cavern wall. "Not gold. Too light."

"He's quite right," said Cair. "It is electrum, a mixture of gold and silver made up to look like a gold florin. It is a fake."

The goblin king's pale eyes seemed to glow. "Good enough to fool trolls? Bring it here, Thallbru."

Reluctantly, the small goblin produced it from under his skins. Edged forward and gave it to his master, and scurried back. The goblin king looked at it intently and then tossed it from hand to hand. "Too light," he agreed regretfully.

"And a bit harder than real gold."

"Smells wrong, too," said the king, passing the coin in front of his cavernous nostrils. "A pity. You make this?" asked the king, passing the coin to his courtiers. It circulated among them, being carefully examined before being reverently returned to the king.

"No," admitted Cair. "But I could, if I had the tools."

The king smiled gleefully. "Thallbru. A good thrall, this. Too good for the mines. I will pay you for him." He tossed the electrum coin at the little goblin. "Gold!"

"But it's not gold!" protested the little sniveler.

"Haw, haw, haw. Teach you to steal from me, Glibflint."

So Cair found himself spending the next several hours displaying the properties of aqua regia, and talking about wire-drawing and refining. And counterfeiting. He was a thrall, again. But he gathered that being spared the mines was a good thing. He got food, for starters. Gruel, a lump of sour bread, and, as he was already very much in favor, a nice piece of rat.

Juzef Szpak was no quitter. Manfred and Erik, not to mention a dozen Norse huntsmen and hearthmen, their King Vortenbras, and their dogs were up there. The mist hadn't lifted, but with calling and care, and a bunch of picket lines fetched up from the bottom, he had all the knights bar one back together again. Now he was organizing and planning another sortie, despite the Norse warriors telling him that it was foolishness.

He'd got hold of a local shepherd, and discovered that they could go around the narrow pass on horseback. With the well-bribed shepherd as a guide they could even do it in reasonable safety . . . It was just as well he'd got them down, as he had just finished organizing a hunt for the missing knight when snow and a good few rocks came cascading down the gully.

Szpak didn't wait. He and his twenty-five remaining Ritters and Brother Uriel (Brother Ottar being too exhausted in Szpak's opinion) set off with the shepherd to find their way up onto the vidda, and then down into the pass from above. That part of it was rideable, apparently. And as they rode higher, the mist lifted around them and they arrived at the top under the cloud rather than in it.

Near dusk, pushing their horses through hock-deep snow, they found the terrified hunters, hearthmen, and King Vortenbras near the top of the pass, forted up in a cave with what was left of the dog pack. Several of them had been injured, including Vortenbras. In broken Frankish they explained that they'd been set upon by the grendel in the mist.

Now Juzef Szpak knew real fear. He and his men hastened down the gully. He wished that they'd taken the time to redon armor. But he'd judged time to be of the essence. He did not want to lead his men against some monster, just in their mail-shirts. He'd lose some. But he wanted even less to have to explain to the Abbot-General, and possibly to the Emperor himself, that they'd lost Manfred of Brittany and his bodyguard.

Besides, he liked both of them.

Finding a torn body was a shock. But it proved to be a Norse-man. They pressed on, but all they found was a big slide of fresh snow near the top of the steep part of the gully, and Norse warriors and Brother Ottar coming up from below.

"We found Von Strethen," said Ottar, grimly. "He missed the trail."

The Norsemen were examining the new snow slip. One of them called and the knights hurried over. The warrior pointed to huge prints, claw tipped. And from a dead bush nearby, Juzef recovered a torn piece of cloak. The distinctive red cloak Manfred of Brittany had been wearing.

Juzef Szpak sighed. "Back up to that cave. We'll be sleeping there tonight, horses and all. We need to find at least the prince's remains."

It was not a pleasant thought. But that evening, bivouacking in extremely uncomfortable circumstances, the two monks made things worse. "It is possible," said Ottar, "using that scrap of cloth, to divine some clues as to the prince's whereabouts."

"And if he is alive or dead," said Brother Uriel, grimly. "Although we will need Sister Mercy for directional divining.

Juzef took a deep breath. "Brothers. He's dead."

"It's not that easy to kill Manfred of Brittany and Erik Hakkonsen," said Uriel stiffly. "I was with them in Venice. They should have been killed several times there."

Juzef Szpak dug out the fragment of cloth.

He wanted very much for them to be alive.

But a part of his thoughts said, *That means "captive."* Captives of something that had been kept at bay by the name of Christ.

And indeed, that fear was realized.

"Our prayers have been answered," said Brother Ottar. "Thank God."

"Now we can just pray for his safety," said Brother Uriel, whose mind obviously worked in much the same way as Juzef's had.

"Well?" she said. It was snowing, but to a troll-wife that was rather pleasant.

"Well, what?" he growled sulkily. "One of them cut me. Cut me to the bone with iron that burned."

"But are they trapped? I arranged for someone to come and lead them to the cave. I see the avalanche spell has been triggered."

"Oh, so that was your doing, Mother?" His yellow eyes narrowed. "That thrall?"

"It was my doing, yes. Neat, if I say so myself. Even if the queen had to endure the indignity of being locked into the feed store."

He snorted. "That's a joke. And the thrall nearly killed two of the boys. Pieces of them have lignified."

She shrugged. "They'll recover. Or we'll breed more. I've lost a *björnhednar*, and entrapping them is a harder task. I have word from home. The *Alfarblot* is safe in the fortress."

He growled savagely. "One day I will spill the blood from that thing. They should all be killed."

"One day. But for now her blood is worth more in her body than out."

"Soon," he grumbled. "It had better be soon, Mother."

CHAPTER 27

Under Telemark

Erik's biggest single problem in those first hours was not knowing what had been done with Manfred. Their captors had dealt with their struggles by the simple expedient of carrying them and thrusting them into narrow fissures in the rock. It was impossible to fight effectively against the small attackers when you simply couldn't move. He'd been stripped. They'd simply cut off his garments, and then had attached heavy iron manacles to his ankles. Mother-naked, he was dragged out—an abrasive experience. There was light now, dim and white, held in some kind of pole lantern. Erik had had his first good look at his captors as they slapped manacles onto his arms.

They were not a prepossessing sight. They'd been described to him in his childhood. The pointed heads of kobolds were less amusing when you were their prisoner. "To the lead pits with him. There is good work in this one," said a slightly larger kobold—one with a whip thrust into a chain belt. It was a small whip, as he was a small creature. But, as Erik could shortly testify, it stung on bare flesh. He was taken down spiral ramps and cross-tunnels, and then down in a winched wicker cage—into a black hole. They changed winches twice on the way, before he got unloaded at a cross-tunnel.

The work they set him to—in a tunnel too low for him to

walk upright—was backbreaking. He carried lumps of ore, heavy chunks hewed from a vein by small mattock-wielding, glum-looking kobolds. The manacles were a hindrance. He was the only human slave in this section, but by the kobolds' comments, other mines had more. They spoke in an oddly archaic Norse which he'd struggled a bit to follow, but was getting used to. By what they said, the kobolds were resentful about only getting one slave. This they took out on Erik. There was no rest, nor food or drink until the kobolds called it a day. Then Erik was chained to the wall and left there. Alone and in the dark. He was left with a bowl of what could have been soup. Perhaps.

Erik was exhausted enough to sleep. It was warmer down here, but it was still no place to be stark naked. He awoke chilled to the bone, and still in total darkness. One thing was certain. He would die quickly down here. Nothing else—not a way out, or how to start to look for Manfred—was clear at all.

Erik knew that he could ill afford to wait too long before trying to escape. He'd be too weak soon. Mind you, even if he managed somehow to find Manfred and escape to the surface, there was still the matter of clothing. The Norwegian winter would kill them even faster than the kobolds would. He resolved to give it one more day before trying his hand at strangling a kobold with his manacle chains. He spent the time until the kobold mine crew arrived trying to loosen the wall staple he was chained to.

Two weeks of this, thought Cair, and he could take over this place. It had rapidly become clear to him that the kobolds were lousy metallurgists—in fact, lousy metal workers. They bought most of their metal artifacts, despite the fact that they mined most of the ores. Lead appeared to be one of the few things they did smelt. They made no attempt to purify it or to separate out other metals, as Cair knew was possible from visiting the Atlas mines. "The dwarves do that. Clever about that kind of thing," said one of his jailers. "Not good miners like us." As far as Cair had been able to establish that, too, was probably wishful thinking. The kobold workings he'd seen up to now were far from advanced. But he did some fishing around, praising their cleverness and their mines. He trawled for information as to why he should be busy showing them how to make gold-leaf—as a precursor to counterfeit coins—if they normally bought their goods with raw materials. He told them he needed to know so that he could make the right things for them. He struck gold of a different sort.

It was tribute. "For the cursed troll-folk. We wouldn't give the dwarves a fake coin! Daren't! Never! They're too tricky themselves. But, curse her for forever, Bakrauf insists on being paid in Midgarder gold. We find some. Hoards buried. We can smell gold, we can," said the kobold proudly. "We sometimes take some from the Midgarder miners we catch. But they have very little."

"I will need some of the coins to make molds from. The coin will be undamaged and can still be used afterwards. We just need to make dies. You understand dies? You have clay? Beeswax? Let me show you."

"Wax? You will make gold out of wax and clay?" asked the kobold incredulously.

"Not quite. Get me the wax and the clay and I will show you." A kobold was sent scurrying. "Now first we make an impression in this clay of the coin—both faces. The coin comes out. See, there is the inverse of the pattern. Now I will need to stick these together carefully. Melt the beeswax for me."

Cair noted that it was not just humans who did what you told them to, if you told them what to do confidently enough. He also knew that it became a habit. He was determined to establish that pattern. When the first lead coin was cool he took it aside. While muttering and making "magical" passes he took a piece of hammered gold leaf and put a section of it around the rim. Gently, he folded it over the edges and rubbed it until it conformed with the shape. Then he laid a piece of gold leaf over the face and, using a leather mallet and a piece of cloth, gently made it conform to the face of the coin, working it until the join lines disappeared. The coin now appeared gold, except for the lead back-face.

Later the king himself came to inspect and marvel at the lead coin produced by the lost wax method. "Ingenious! We have tried carving the things from gold, but it is very slow."

Even a master of negotiations like Cair had trouble keeping a straight face. He bowed respectfully. "Allow me to show you this, Highness. This is my art. My magic. I make the lead appear to be gold." He produced a lead coin onto which the gold leaf had been affixed.

When he showed it to the kobold royalty, he knew he had them. Had them by the shorthairs.

The kinglet capered in glee. "Hee, hee, hee. Bakrauf. Hee, hee, hee, we will cheat you nicely. Excellent slave! How many of these can you make a day? Ten? Ten or you'll feel the whip. More and you can dine on rat every day!"

Cair bowed again. "I can do many of these at once, Highness. At least twenty! Well, if I can have the tools, certain magical ingredients, and some more space. And some more workmen. One big strong man, at least."

The kobold king nodded imperiously. "See that he gets them. With luck they won't turn the coins over."

"Oh, I will do both sides. I was just showing you how it was done, Highness." Cair did not explain that he was making sure that the king did not think it was real transformation. It wasn't going to last or fool many people for long. Gold leaf was too fragile and too thin.

The king beamed. "Excellent!" He turned to one of his body-guards. "Find me Thallbru. Tell him he has given me a prince among slaves. I will reward him, after all. And see that the slave gets whatever he needs."

Cair had assumed that, if he was still alive, he would get Manfred of Brittany when he asked for a large slave. Other than Vortenbras, there weren't many larger men in Norway. The thought had amused him. Besides, he thought that when they escaped, Manfred of Brittany could be more than a little useful. The knights were still a force to be reckoned with in the world of light and air he longed for.

However, while he was waiting for the arrival of the new slave, conversation with one of his jailers changed his plans.

The guard turned the lead coin over, marveling at it. "Paying tribute is bad enough, but those cursed bear-servants of Bakrauf use our tunnels to go out and into Midgard. Sooner or later trouble will follow. We hate them. We hate them worse than poison."

After a while Cair unearthed the fact that the previous day a bunch of the troll-queen's *björnhednar* had carried a prisoner through the kobolds' halls heading for her place.

Inside Cair's mind a sequence of possible events were worked out. The possibility of mere escape to the upper world receded. He'd never believed in trolls. But strange creatures, like these kobolds, had been discovered by explorers. He'd seen the skin of a giraffe, which was something else he'd never have believed if someone had just told him about it. There was nothing magical about them, any more than anything unknown or not understood was magical.

"Do you ever get flooding problems?" he asked, changing tack, while carefully making yet another wax impression of a coin face.

His kobold assistants nodded gloomily. "All the time. Much heaving of buckets," said one. Cair was a high-status slave. But that still meant that working for him was not something any kobold but the lowest of the low would do. Cair didn't mind. It was easier to extract information from them, and they were far more inclined to do exactly what they were told. They were used to it.

"Ah. Perhaps I can fix this. Send all this water out to the place these *björnhednar* go."

"You can magic water?" The kobold was impressed. "Haw, haw, make it run uphill to troll lands?"

Cair shrugged confidently. "I could send it all the way to Jotunheim if I wanted to."

That was too much. The kobold snorted disdainfully. "You lie too much, slave. Get back to work."

Cair held up the lead coin. "Did I lie about this?"

The idea took a while to penetrate the creature's pointy little skull. "No . . . so you really mean that you can send water to Jotunheim? It is . . ." He looked at his fingers and then at his bare toes, and decided that even with the toes it was too much. He settled for "many many leagues."

"Sure. But big hard magics, that job. Much work," said Cair making a show of wiping his brow. "We can rather send it to the Bakrauf."

"Hur. Good enough." By the looks of it the "much work" had put the guard off. Kobolds and humans felt much the same way about some things.

"But such magic takes much planning," said Cair. "Do you have maps?" he asked calmly.

His answer came with a knotted brow. "What is maps?"

"Drawing of where all the tunnels go. And how deep they are."

The kobold shook his head. "No. What would a kobold do with something like that? We can smell our way!"

"Well," said Cair, keeping his tone bored. "I will have to see the places. The water. The way to Bakrauf's kingdom."

The guard nodded. "If the king says so."

He'd just have to make his own map. He'd already made his own key to the crude locks on his manacles. He'd realized that all of them were identical, fairly rapidly. Simply a bar with a rectangle on the end. He was no expert on locks—the subject had never interested him, but with access to tools he'd modified a piece of thin iron sheet with a bit of patient cutting while his bored guards looked on. He'd hidden it in his hair. That evening, when locked in his cell, Cair had tried it on the manacles. He'd known a moment's real panic when it had stuck. But brute force had triumphed and with a bit of filing he now had "ornamental" bangles that he could lose at will.

Later, the guards brought in another prisoner. He was naked. Cair had glimpsed one other human prisoner in this state in the distance. This man was generously covered in filth. He was big, but he wasn't Manfred of Brittany. His dirty hair had once been Scandinavian blond. Cair recognized the face—the man had once been part of Vortenbras's guard.

He also recognized Cair. "So you were in league with these creatures of the underworld, thrall."

Cair stared at him coolly. "No. I traffic in more powerful sprites. Get him some water to wash in. He smells."

By the time food came, Cair was convinced that Orm, his new assistant, was the stupidest thing on two legs. His reaction to being given a hammer had been to try and attack the kobolds. Cair had been obliged to hit his arm with his manacle chain and knock him down. The hammer went flying and broke several clay molds. Sitting on top of him, Cair hissed, "Idiot. Behave and I'll get you out of here. Do anything more stupid and you can go back to where you came from. Now get up and behave before we get speared." Indeed, dozens of sharp spears surrounded them already. Cair had no delusions. He was being well guarded. A sullen Orm was set to work cleaning up the mess he'd generated. "Thrall's work," he muttered.

"You are a thrall," said Cair crossly. "Now, can you behave with a hammer, or do I send you back to where you were?"

Orm nodded sullenly. Cair set him to hammering gold. Looking at those greedy eyes Cair was glad that the man was still naked, with no place to hide the gold. Here Orm was, half starved and a prisoner—and he saw gold as something to be stolen for sheer greed's sake.

Cair saw a lot more than mere gold that needed to be stolen. But greed didn't even come into the equation.

It was difficult to tell the time down in the kobold warrens. One judged it by meals, which, if one was a slave, came once a day. Orm goggled at their bread and snatched it. Cair let him eat. The kobolds fed him more than he needed anyway.

While Orm was cramming his mouth with bread, guards came to take Cair back to the kobold king. "You claim to do water magic?" the kobold asked.

"I do, yes, Highness," said Cair. "That is what I do. Metals and waters. Mine magic. I was on my way to work on a flooded mine in Germania when I was captured and made a thrall. It is possible to move and part waters. But it is a power-demanding working, requiring some time and a great deal of ritual. The working must be planned and balanced. Protective sigils need to be placed strategically throughout the mine."

The king thought about it. Well, either he thought about it or he just sat there making faces. "And how goes the coin production?" he asked the guard.

"Good, King. He has made over two hundred coins. We'll have the tribute by the end of the week."

The kobold king rubbed his bony hands together. "Then we'll have our hostages back, and Hel take Bakrauf. She fooled us with a seeming in that attack, but never again. We have her smell now. Good, take him to see the flooded shafts."

"I have not named my price," said Cair, calmly.

The king goggled at him. So did the other kobolds. "You thrall. You have no 'price.' We beat you if you don't fix it. Throw you into the pit," threatened the king.

Cair never flinched. "And then I die. Only I can make the gold coins you need. Only I can do the draining spells. If you kill me all my magic is lost to you. But if you pay me I work hard, and well. Because you pay me only when I have done what I promised to do."

The king snorted. But it was a measure of Cair's value that he asked, "What price do you want?"

"My freedom, when I have finished. When the mines are dry."

The kobold king probably thought he was succeeding in looking innocent. "Very well."

Cair bowed low. "Lead me to it. I am eager to begin."

The king did his best not to snigger.

Cair was far better at keeping a straight face.

Manfred was in a hole. Literally. He'd fought the kobolds just a trifle too well. Or maybe they were just furious because his koboldwerk jerkin had wrecked a few knives. So they'd put him to work where his strength would be no danger to them. Where his weight would keep him a prisoner. The rope he had to attach his buckets to—both of water and ore—would not carry his twenty-three stone. And he'd tried climbing the walls to no avail. The blue clayey ore was a broken and shattered mass at the bottom of the volcanic pipe. Water that seeped down and oozed into it also had to be bucketed out. Manfred's current project was to build a tower of the rubbish and climb out . . . before he died like the previous prisoners. He had their skeletal remains for company.

It was extremely odd to look up and see the thrall he'd left unconscious after the avalanche trapped them, staring down at him as he trudged with a bucket of seep water.

The thrall had clothes and seemed to be talking cheerfully to his kobold escort.

It would appear that Erik had been right. Well, he usually was.

Cair found the prince of Brittany's bodyguard-companion shortly after seeing the prince. Erik was fast asleep, and did not appear to wake as they walked past. Cair knew that men like that one were quite capable of feigning sleep. It was something he might have done himself. He did contrive to drop something into the prisoner's empty bowl in passing.

In the long-term aspect of his escape plan, there was a space for Manfred of Brittany. When he got Princess Signy out of this place, Manfred could be either a grateful escort, or a valuable hostage. Cair had plans for either role. If rumor were true, the Hohenstauffens were exceptionally loyal to their bodyguards. Perhaps they understood that loyalty begat loyalty, something that seemed to pass so many people by. Or maybe they just were like that. Cair made a space in his plans for Erik, too. Besides, the man was an exceptional fighter. He could be useful.

So, he noted Erik's position and, besides leaving him some encouragement, simply went on with the map of the passages. It was proving more complex than he'd thought. Still, the kobolds were quite happy to let him measure, pace, and make marks on the parchment in the belief that magical processes always involved a great deal they didn't understand. They sniggered behind their hands at his eager comments about being free when he was done. You don't bother to watch a prisoner who believes that his good behavior will see him free in a few days. Not too closely anyway.

Magic had one other plus: He could demand exotic materials. In fact, to be plausible he had to. Human weapons for instance, to affix to the roof, painted with sigils and surrounded with symbolic items, along with suitable Latin mumbo jumbo. Such a powerful working required a great deal of material and preparation. A great many magical diagrams had to be drawn—in the symbolically varicolored inks that the "water magician" demanded. Cair was finding coming up with difficult and rare items to imperiously demand quite a challenge to his imagination. But, well, that was what magic workers were believed to do, so he did it, and talked inventively about the symbolism and sympathy of each ingredient. At the same time he'd simply had to up Orm's level of knowledge of what he did with the coins. He just didn't have the time to do it all himself, and although the kobolds and Orm could handle the lost wax casting by themselves by now, getting the gold leaf in place had been something Cair had been reluctant to show them how to do. But he could only do so much . . . The idiot was stealing and hiding "gold" coins on his person—in the only orifices available. Did he think that Cair couldn't count? Or cared? At least his looking like a constipated squirrel stopped him talking too much. Cair had promised him escape to get his cooperation.

Cair slept like the dead that night. It wasn't surprising—he felt as if he had walked several hundred miles, most of it stooping. And he couldn't physically fit down a lot of their tunnels. The ones near the surface tended to be narrow, bar a few. Still, he'd been close, close enough to get the scent of pine on the air, and close enough to the place this Bakrauf's bear-people went to, to see gray sky. It played hob with his maps. He'd thought that they were heading deeper underground, and then he saw sky outside. The guards that side of the kobold's warren kingdom had been rare—to the point of being invisible, unlike the area where he'd caught the scent of pine trees. His escort, too close to what they termed "Midgard," had watched him carefully. The ones who had taken him to "Trollheim gate" had been watchful too. But it hadn't been him they'd watched. It had been a lookout for trouble.

"Where are the guards?" he'd asked casually.

One of the escort had pointed. "In the scampers, watching."

"But how do you defend your lands?"

"Fight? Against trolls?" The escort shook his head. "We runs. We hides. Trolls, even when they shrink, are too big for our holes."

Gradually he'd figured it out. The kobolds didn't use the tunnels humans could stand in here, close to Trollheim. They didn't even try and resist, let alone fight back when the trolls came. All the guards did was scamper for safety and give warning. "They sneaked up on us last time," grumbled the escort. "That Bakrauf is a twisty one. She changes. You never know what she'll look like next. We thought they were Midgarders like you."

Cair had said nothing, and just continued mapping. It might take him several more days. There were the deep channels to visit still. Apparently the ore barges sailed down these and out onto the River Gjöll, wherever that was. So far what he'd seen said that the kobolds were not great planners—they'd simply followed ore bodies. The rock was at least in part volcanic, if he was any judge. He'd seen the same structures on Stromboli and Etna when they'd been scouting for raids. The ores tended to accumulate in water fissures. Some of the ones here steamed ominously.

By sheer bloody-minded discipline Erik woke earlier than his captors arrived for work. The staple in the wall was definitely moving a little. It was now a question of whether the soft iron broke, it came out of the wall, or he starved to death first. Or died of thirst. The kobolds seemed convinced that the liquid he got out of that bowl of what was either thin gruel or soup, would do to keep him alive. He felt for the bowl. He determinedly left himself a mouthful each feeding time. He found it. Tipped the bowl into his mouth. There was no liquid forthcoming. He tipped desperately.

Something soggy hit his nose.

He tasted it, cautiously. It was, or had been, a lump of sour rye bread. It was now full of the remains of his soup. And it had a scrap of something thin and hard in it. Flexible but leathery. Erik was already chewing it when it occurred to him that it might just be a scrap of parchment.

That was what it felt like.

Of course he had no light to see.

Bread . . . and a message.

Erik didn't want it lying around, so he tucked it behind his ear. He didn't have many other hiding places. The only thing that this imprisonment and slavery had going for it was that he hadn't—so far—encountered any women while all that he was wearing were a few rusty iron chains. But knowing that somehow someone had sent him a piece of bread and a message, gave him something more precious than food. It gave him hope. He set to work on the staple with a will.

He was able to examine the scrap behind his ear later, while carrying lumps of ore. It was parchment—or had been.

But the soaking and chewing had made the writing illegible.

"There is a human who is interfering with my magical working," said Cair, with irritation, to the guards. "Here, on this node." He pointed at the map.

"We kill him," one of the kobolds said cheerfully. "Show us."

Cair was intensely glad that the kobolds hadn't really got a handle on the maps yet, or he might have been the man responsible for Manfred of Brittany's death. He had nothing against killing him. It just wasn't what he had planned right now. "I don't need him killed," he said hastily. "It's the prisoner in the hole."

"Can't move him," said a senior guard. "Dangerous prisoner. Had koboldwerk vest."

Cair had heard of the fine chain mail that went by that name. It was just a name. These kobolds would have trouble in making a single link, let alone an entire vest. But he'd gathered that there were several tribes and varieties of kobold. These, the mine-kobold, seemed to be at the bottom of the kobold civilization scale. "Oh, I don't want him moved! Just mocked. His spirit is too strong. I need him pelted with these symbolic items." He pointed to several knotted scraps of cloth.

"Won't hurt," said a kobold dismissively.

Cair shook his head. "He must not be hurt, but shamed. Inside each *vestumentum* is a piece of clay." Cair unknotted the bundles, showing them. "It is the symbolism, see. The clothed man of baser clay. And then I put the magic curse words on these little scrolls." Cair couldn't yet read more than the basic futharks—but normal script was something the kobolds didn't use at all.

"So you want us to go and throw these at him?" asked the guard commander.

Cair nodded. "Every day. The shaming takes time. I will prepare more magic missiles."

"Can't we just throw rocks?" asked one of the stupider guards, looking at the missiles. The idea of having to carry the bundles obviously didn't appeal.

Cair shook his head vehemently. "No. That would strengthen his resolve."

The guard commander shrugged. "You're the magician. You, you, and you. Go."

"You've got to insult him, too," said Cair. "At least make rude noises."

"Better wait until the miners go off shift then," said the guard commander. "We don't want to start any fights."

One of the little delights of the wet hole that they'd put Manfred into was the seepage. By the time the kobolds arrived to start work it was usually at least knee deep. The depth varied—his last sleep had been better. But sometime during the "night" Manfred had had a choice of waking up or drowning. Then he had to stand and wait. He'd done his best to make a higher platform, but "no ore, no food" applied, too. So he had not managed that much of a platform—like an idiot he'd given them much of the platform his unfortunate predecessor had managed to build up.

So getting to sleep as soon as possible was an essential. He was tired enough to pass out.

Dreamland was disturbed by something hitting him.

"Yah. Surface crawler!" Whizz. Another missile hit him.

He caught the next one. And just as he was about to fling it back—a good fifty feet straight up—at the jeering kobolds, he realized that it was soft cloth. Cloth? Knotted cloth? A parcel of some sort?

Instead he dodged the next one, and shook his fist at the kobold who had just called him scum. He unknotted the cloth. There was a lump of clay and a piece of parchment in it. On it was written one word in Frankish.

RESCUE, in a neat, precise hand.

Manfred was not stupid. People, he knew, assumed that because he was large, he was dim-witted. He'd cultivated this. It was quite useful at times, and had saved him work at others. Erik had sent the messages and was doing so under cover. He could play along. He collected the parcels, shaking his fist and yelling back at his tormentors.

After a few more missiles they went away.

Manfred realized, as their light receded, that there was one flaw in his cooperation. In the dark he could not read the messages. And he wanted to, very badly. Carefully he untied the knotted cloth. They appeared, by the feel of it, to contain clay. And a slip of parchment. Well, the hole he was in seemed less deep if Erik was at least trying to get him out of it. And these bits of cloth were an unexpected bonus—untied they proved to be enough make a sort of loincloth.

It was only when he lay down to try and sleep again, that he thought of the clay. He felt around for where he'd dropped it. In the dark it was hard to tell one piece of damp clay from another . . . but one of the pieces was only a thin coating of clay covering a wrapping of some sort. Manfred unwrapped it cautiously. By the smell of it, and by the taste, it was—bread! He bit into it ravenously. And nearly broke his teeth. There was something very hard inside it.

By the feel of it . . . a key.

Manfred felt it again, unbelievingly. And then the humor of it struck him. It might undo the manacles, but it couldn't get him out of this hole. Well, it was a start. And he'd bet that it was the first time that any prisoner in this hole had done any laughing.

He finished the piece of bread, eating it slowly, savoring each crumb before he even tried out the key.

It fitted and worked. Liberty was sweet even if you couldn't go anywhere with it.

Eventually he decided that he might as well rest while he could, although his stomach desperately wished that Erik had sent more bread. And a bigger piece of cloth for a blanket. And a bottle of brandy. And a cuddlesome lass. Francesca wouldn't like this spot much, but surely his Icelander could have found a pretty troll or something?

Sleep was a while in coming, but when it did, Manfred slept peacefully and deeply. Water licking at his heels woke him. And a hint of light. The seep had obviously been slower that night. It had only just woken him in time to relock his manacles. As a second thought he pulled off his new loin cloth and stashed that and the key behind a lump of clay against the wall. Somehow he'd find a chance to read the messages on the scraps of parchment and see just what Erik was up to.

But the parchments all said the same thing . . . and advised him to do just what he had done anyway. Play along. The work seemed less hard but more tedious that day.

And this time he wasn't asleep when the taunting and missile-throwing began.

The single light the missile flingers brought with them was pretty dim, but Manfred was encouraged by the words ESCAPE, 2. BEHAVE UNTIL THEN. And this time there were two pieces of bread—even if there was no rope and grapple. Only Erik would tell a man stuck in a pit to behave! Still, he had been considering yanking their bucket ropes down—which he'd been sure would stop the gruel if not bring rocks or arrows down on his head.

It was better than just giving up. But a chance of getting out was better still.

Out on the Telemark mountainside it had been snowing intermittently for the last two days and, looking at the depth of the snow accumulating, Juzef Szpak knew that they simply could not stay here. The knight-proctor had to admit that, as little as he liked Vortenbras, the Norse kinglet had been more than cooperative. Dogs had been brought up, the snow dug over. A cart and then a litter had even brought the nuns up. Sister Mary had tried her wand-divining—with odd results. "It is only effective in a limited range, Ritter," she apologized. "But it does suggest that he isn't in this valley."

The best that the magic workers had been able to establish was that both Manfred and Erik were alive. Alive and chained, somewhere dark.

They could, by moving Sister Mary around, establish where he was. But the locals predicted that days of blizzard conditions were coming.

Szpak knew he had little choice but to retreat back to Kingshall.

CHAPTER 28

Trollheim

$\mathcal{S}$igny had felt her muscles turn to jelly and herself frozen, trapped like a fly in amber, as the Christian witch's divining wand had streaked toward her, and then it suddenly appeared to hit something and fall at her feet. It felt as if the cursed thing was drinking her! She was so exhausted she could barely stand, let alone face this!

The feasting hall blurred as she felt herself swaying. She fell, just as the bear pelts somehow became bears.

When she woke again, she was flying. Or that was what appeared to be happening. Actually she realized that a bear had her by each limb and they were carrying her facedown as they raced through the forest. Tree branches and dead brambles scratched at her. She might as well have struggled to free herself from quicksand—her limbs had no strength.

They raced through forest and meadows, swapping carriers, running on. When they came to the river, Signy thought that they'd have to slow down . . . but instead the bear-creature's leader gestured at the ice-rimmed water and began chanting in a guttural growling voice.

Ice grew as she watched. Splintery spars of it blurred the transparent water, and then hardened and firmed. Soon, amazingly soon, a creaking ice bridge appeared. The bears, claws shrieking on the new ice, scrambled across and ran on. And on.

She recognized Svartdal, and the narrow pass up to the high fells. She'd even been up there, once, with her father. In summer. Her teeth were chattering by the time the bears arrived at a small *bautarstein* in the high valley. They paused there. The lead bear took a pouch that was hung around his neck, sprinkled powder from it onto the stone, and growled some *galdr* words.

Signy watched incredulously as a huge rock slid aside and a cave mouth gaped into visibility above them. They picked her up again and went into the maw.

And down into the dark.

Occasionally she glimpsed light—ghostly marsh light—and heard shrieking and scampering. The bear-men paid it no mind. They just pressed on. Then, at length they emerged, on the side wall of a cliff-hung gorge. They bounded onto the stones of a huge bridge built of perfectly shaped interlocking stone blocks, each block the size of a bonder's cottage. The bridge shimmered as if in the heat, but it was bitterly cold here. In the glimpse she had over the edge the gorge they crossed seemed bottomless. The other side was a bleak place, full of stones and dry grasses. But they rushed on, on and on, eventually carrying her across the braided sandbanks of a river that must be a full quarter of a mile wide in spate. And to a huge bald knob of a hill. There was no sign of habitation, but they were on a definite broad footpath leading somewhere.

From behind a rock rose something that looked like a pile of rocks and scraps of animal fur. Misshapen rocks. With tufts of what could almost be hair ... or coarse grass, growing from the rock top.

It *was* hair. She supposed it was, anyway, because now that it had turned to look at them she could see the misshapen rocks were the features of the troll's face. She screamed weakly. Everyone knew trolls existed. She had just never thought to meet one.

It looked at her. "Mistress says that it must be hooded before you take it into the castle." He held out a leather bag that they pulled over her head. They carried her onward. The smelly leather bag might have hidden the sights from her eyes, but the noises told their own story. There were a lot more people—or perhaps trolls—in this place than the barren landscape had suggested it could carry. A lot of noise, anyway.

Then the bag was plucked from her head, and she was bundled into a cage. It was like a vast birdcage, except for one thing. It was made of wood.

The door slammed shut behind her, and she watched as the bears became men, men in bearskins and not a lot else. One of them locked the cage. The others hauled on the rope attached to a hook on the top. Soon her wooden cage, with a wooden slatted floor, hung thirty feet from the floor.

Lying on the wooden slats, bruised, stretched, wrenched, scratched, and dazed, Signy felt as weak as a half-drowned kitten. The wood she lay on seemed to draw what little life she had out of her, so, somehow, she found the energy to sit up. That was . . . better. But even touching the wood with her hands or her skin made her feel ill. She struggled to her feet. The cage swayed. And she had to clutch the bars to stop herself from falling over. As soon as possible she pulled her hands away from the wood.

Just staying on her feet took every resource she had. But after a little while she felt better. Well enough to take stock of where she was, and to begin trying to work out what had happened to her.

Whatever it was, it wasn't a rescue. The room her captors had hung this cage in was vast and dim. The walls were cut stone. And on a raised dais on the far side, set between carved pillars, was a large throne. The only light in the place came from lamps—stone bowls with wicks set in them—that burned in wall sconces. Still, Signy had never had any trouble seeing fine detail at a distance. It just blurred out when close at hand. The pillars were carved, appropriately enough, with bears. Snarling bears. The faces were not pleasant.

Signy inspected her closer quarters. The wooden slats were wide enough apart to let her put an arm through. She didn't want to touch the bars, though. The only furnishings were a rough wooden pallet. More of this cursed wood? It looked darker. And she was *so* tired. She couldn't stand forever. Perhaps she could curl up like a cat on her boots? Thank goodness she'd been out at the stable and had had no time to change. She stumbled as she stepped across the slats to the pallet, and had to put her hand down on it to save herself. It felt like . . . wood. Harmless. Gratefully she sat down on it, pulling her feet off the slatted cage floor.

It was as if she'd taken a heavy weight off her shoulders. Sighing with relief, she lay down on the narrow pallet and let exhaustion take her into sleep.

Bears and her stepmother chased her through narrow tunnels in her dreams.

She woke up with the cage swaying and being slowly lowered. A team of various-shaped thralls—certainly not all human—controlled the rope. And the throne was now occupied.

The occupant was large, square, and possibly female. The dress would suggest it. The wizened face was curled into a scowl of distaste. Hair, gray and lank, hung down in greasy locks.

"One of the effects of confining you in a rowan cage is that it will affect my magics, too, little half-blood." The last word was clearly an insult. "You see me now without my glamour. Be afraid."

In spite of her circumstances, as she stood on her pallet in the cage, Signy wasn't. It seemed as if she'd spent her life afraid, as if something dark had been stalking her, hanging in the shadows. Now, in a cage, in troll-realms, she was somehow not terrified. It was too late for fear now. "What do you want with me?" There was a haunting familiarity about the troll-wife.

"Your power. Your magic."

"I haven't got any. All I ever do is stop charms working. Every time. Without fail. I don't believe I could make milk go sour if I tried for a week—a week outdoors in summer," said Signy, calmly awaiting her fate.

The troll-wife snorted. "And it never struck you that that was magic, powerful magic? You *Alfarblot* are naturally stupid. Vanir blood mixes badly with human."

But Signy had been proofed against slights and insults by her stepmother. She simply judged distances. She still had her sleeve knife. The bears had not searched her, or robbed her—not that she had much for them to steal. She had her silver bracelets . . . But they'd have had to break those off. She'd been given them when she was a child. She'd grown, but they hadn't. They were charms of protection. If she ever needed them, it was now. "I'm not Alfar. My stepmother used to mock me saying I was *Svartalfar*. It's not true. I am of the house of Telemark. My bloodlines—"

"Your bloodlines are well known to me, Signy. Your ancestors dallied with Alfar not once, but twice. Your mother's mother was *Alfarblot*, and also your father's great-great-grandfather. In you the bloodlines have combined."

The troll-wife knew who she was, at any rate. The throw, aimed as it was through the bars, was not her best. Her best would have put the knife through the evil monster's left eye. The knife hit the troll-wife between the eyes instead.

She might as well have flung a river pebble. She was even more accurate with those, and would have done just as much harm.

The knife clattered to the flagstones.

The troll-wife rubbed the spot between her eyes thoughtfully. "I had forgotten about the knife for Hjorda," she said. "Well, no matter. We'll take care of him in another manner."

The troll-wife stood up. "Leave her without food and water for a day," she said to the troll at the door as she left. "She is too full of herself, yet. And see that she is hauled up again."

The troll bobbed his acknowledgment.

Signy's cage was pulled up again, and her knife remained, a small piece of silver, on the floor of the dim hall.

She was left alone again to ponder how this troll-wife knew so much about her, and about what she'd intended to do to Hjorda. She also wished that she hadn't thrown her knife. It was well known that a troll head was as hard as stone. And besides, she wasn't as good at throwing knives as she should be. It was an unladylike pastime she'd not been able to practice nearly enough. If she'd kept the knife she could have cut through the bars. The only other metal she had were her bracelets.

They hadn't protected her too well yet. But perhaps they had a sharp edge that she could rub away at the wood with. It looked as if she'd have plenty of time to do that.

CHAPTER 29

Under Telemark

Erik had, logically enough, cleared the debris and small rocks from his lying-down spot. When his day's labor was done and he'd been herded along to be chained, he'd gone docilely. They left him with his bowl of gruel. There'd been no more mysterious bits of bread or parchment, but Erik was being docile for good reason. The staple was coming loose. He sat down. Someone had put fragments of rock in his lying place . . .

It was odd rock. Too light. It felt like plaster.

Erik's mystery visitor had been around again. And inside the fake piece of rock was a key and a piece of rolled parchment. After he'd used the key, it occurred to him there might be other "rocks." He felt around, and sure enough there were. But they also contained keys and rolls of parchment, which he could not read in the dark.

Well, at least he knew in which direction to go: away from the pit face. Cautiously, knowing that the mine kobolds could see, hear, and smell better than any human, Erik felt his way along the tunnel until he saw a hint of light. Then he proceeded with even more caution. It was something of a wasted effort. All there was was a solitary glowing globe, set on a rock-shelf. The guard was fast asleep beneath it.

Cair was busy with his last-minute preparations to leave, which was to say he was sitting idle, thinking. He didn't leave things to the last minute.

Then it became obvious that his plans for a quiet departure during that sleep period weren't going to work as well as he'd planned.

He was herded before the kobold king, again. Orm was standing in the background, smirking.

It would have taken a slower man than Cair Aidin not to figure out that his laborer had sold out their escape plan. "This thrall tells me you planned to escape tonight."

Cair managed to look shocked. "Why? I will be free in two days at the most, anyway. Is the water in your mines not drying away?"

The king managed in turn to lie quite well. "Urr. Yes. But this one tells me that you planned to escape with the job unfinished."

Cair drew himself up. "Me? If I was planning to escape, I would have gold coin with me. Search me, and search him." Cair had no coins, gold or otherwise, or anything more incriminating than a key, knotted into his hair. Orm probably had lead coated with gold in his cheeks or in his newly acquired loincloth.

"You are too slick with that tongue, thrall," said the king grimly. "Search him." Cair stood calmly watching as Orm's gloat turned to apprehension. It was his turn next. "They're just with me for safekeeping. To stop him stealing them," groveled the Norseman, when the kobolds produced shiny coin after shiny coin.

"A likely story," said Cair.

The kobold king rubbed his jaw. "Nonetheless, I cannot take a chance. Strip them both. Send this one," he pointed to Orm, "back to the mines. He's a thief, if not a liar." He turned to Cair. "Strip him, and keep him under lock and key."

"Until my work is done," said Cair loftily. "That is our agreement."

"Er. Just so. Until his work is done."

Cair waited until things were settled before pulling out quite a lot of his hair. Every lock that the kobolds owned was the same. In a spirit of neatness, he locked the cell behind him and tied the key into his hair again. Clothing and various other items were stashed in a "magical" display nearby, and he knew where the guards at the various levels were. With regret he had to abandon his old pouch, but he'd extracted most of the valuable bits from it for his new one. He even had his "wand" with its amber eye. With a rope, a bundle of clothes, food, and a good dagger, he set off down. He didn't even have to deal with any kobolds en route.

Erik's victim lay trussed and gagged with his own clothing. And unconscious. Each of the little scrolls of parchment was the same—a map of sorts with the word MANFRED and no clue as to whom his mysterious helper could be. Erik wished he'd been a little more generous with clothing or weapons. He now had a kobold pike, which might do nicely as a misericord, and a kobold light. And a map showing him the way—hopefully—to Manfred. Erik wondered briefly if it was some kind of trap. But why? He could hardly be in worse trouble. And he had an oath to try and honor.

Erik walked on. At length he came to the hole—and Prince Manfred of Brittany.

"What took you so long?" asked Manfred in a harsh whisper, with a crooked grin imperfectly hiding his relief. "And how in hell did you get those kobolds to cooperate?"

Erik felt that his knees had gone weak enough at the sight of the boy, without getting any more sentimentality into the situation. "I've got a key," he whispered back. "I'll need to find a decent rope."

"I've already got the key you sent. Just find something thicker than this string they're using on their windlasses."

That could be a problem. There was an ample supply of ore, a fair number of rocks, a few buckets tied to the cord they used. And no rope. Even all the windlass cords together would not support his weight. Erik knew too well that Manfred had a lot of weight to support.

"I am sorry I was delayed," said a voice from the shadows. Erik whirled, the small sticker at the ready.

The thrall stepped into the light, a coil of rope in his hand. "My former associate betrayed me and it took me some extra time to get here." He tossed a bundle at Erik. "Here. Clothes. Your weapons are hidden farther along our way. I'll set up the rope."

Erik could only gape.

"Get them on," said the bronze-skinned thrall, untying the coil. "We're going to have to move fast."

"We left you for dead," said Erik, fumbling with the bundle. They weren't his clothes, but a miner's leather breeches and a rustic's jerkin. He didn't care.

"It's a mistake others have made," said the thrall, wryly, tossing the rope down as Erik pulled on the clothes. "Boots were something more of a problem. I've got his, but not yours, I'm afraid. They're with the stash."

Erik shook his head. "I'll need some explanations, once we're out of here." The man spoke fluent Frankish, with a hint of an Aquitaine accent.

The thrall shrugged. "Very well. I suggest that you tell your prince to stop trying to climb the rope. He'll get tired and fall, or slip. Rather let him tie himself on. We'll make use of those windlasses."

Erik did.

"Don't whisper. The sound carries farther," said the thrall, rigging the windlass with professionalism.

Erik felt a fresh bubble of unease. Who was this fellow? Erik knew that, too, from Vinland stalking days. He just hadn't thought it through right now. Instinct said to whisper.

They hauled. "Should have left him to get lighter for a few more days," grunted the thrall.

"Be glad he's not in armor," puffed Erik, as Manfred caught the top edge of the hole and, with a scrabble, pulled himself up.

He blinked at the thrall. Tensed. "He's a traitor, Erik. He's with these underground-grub kobolds. Get him."

"I also provided the rope, and the keys," said the thrall calmly. "And I have your clothes. I have been as much of a prisoner as you were."

"I don't trust him much," said Erik, "but someone provided us with keys."

"I assumed it was you," said Manfred, looking uncertain.

Erik shook his head. "I've been chained in a tunnel."

"We can discuss it later," said the thrall. "We need to move now. We have a long way to go."

Manfred nodded. "Let's put it off. For now. Which way do we go to get out of this place?"

The thrall pointed, and they left, the rope slowly falling back down into the dry pit. Some other prisoner might be glad of it.

By the time that they arrived at the swords and the boots, and Manfred's koboldwerk jacket, Erik was sure that they'd never find their way out of this rabbit warren without the fellow, anyway. He seemed to know it well enough. And he was well prepared. He even had water and more of the coarse, sour rye bread stashed.

Cair had to admit that he'd had worse crews. They were tough, and silent, especially the bodyguard. He noted quietly to himself that if the corsairs ever became Manfred of Brittany's personal problem, he might have to cry off raiding the Holy Roman Empire's vessels. He might just be better off killing the man in case he did become Emperor. But first things first. They had to get out of here. "We have something of a problem here." They were at a vertical shaft. "We will need to get up there. And there are guards at the top." Cables hung down to deeper pits. "I had thought we could go up with loads of ore, but the ore baskets aren't moving now. And when they start, the kobolds will be awake and about."

"How far is it to the top?" asked Erik thoughtfully.

Cair checked his map. "About forty cubits. It was the closest I could get us with no guard points."

"A good map, that," said Manfred, looking over his shoulder. "How did you come by it?"

"I made it."

"Where do we get out?" asked Erik, looking at it.

"At the moment it is more a case of 'how do we get out?'" said Cair, unwilling to admit that he didn't know. He hated doing that.

"Erik will sort that out," said Manfred, looking at his bodyguard.

Cair saw that he was busy taking off the boots Cair had stolen for him. "They're a bit loose," Erik said, apologetically.

He took his knife between his teeth and with no further ado tested the cables, selected one, and set off up it like a Barbary ape.

There was a brief shriek from above, and a basket came down. "Noisy," said Manfred. "He's losing his touch. Or missing that hatchet of his." They scrambled into the wicker basket, carrying Erik's boots.

At the top they discovered that Erik had been lucky to get

them that far. He had some seven kobolds prisoner. Several more were never going to cause any more trouble. A glance told Cair just what he did not want to see. They weren't all guards. Some were miners. "They're coming on shift."

"And one got away," said Erik, grimly.

Cair handed him his boots. "Send these prisoners down and then cut the cables. Or kill them. It is time for us to run."

They sent the baskets down and ran. And fought. And ran again. With light on their side, the three of them could hold off the kobolds. But the rock-gnomes poured out of crevices and cracks, pursuing them, trying to block them off.

"How much farther?" panted Manfred, leaning against the wall.

"Close now," said Cair.

Erik peered back down the tunnel. For the moment they'd outpaced the kobolds. He looked ahead. "Got to be blocked, or have a final guard post or something."

"Not here," Cair shook his head. "Not this exit. They're too afraid of trolls."

Manfred laughed. "And that's supposed to be better, is it? Come on. I swear I can feel air movement."

"There's bound to be a last attempt to stop us," said Erik, as they set out again, "even if they are more afraid of trolls."

"Bakrauf is coming to get us," pronounced Cair loudly, reverting to Norse. And then in Frankish, "Walls have ears. Talk about Bakrauf."

To Cair's amusement he'd swear Erik actually blushed under all the dirt. "That's not a polite word, you know."

"I've been told trolls aren't very polite," said Manfred with a grin. "And I'm feeling pretty coarse myself. Bakrauf! Bakrauf!" he yelled, as they raced toward the opening.

The handful of kobolds seemed more inclined to flee than to fight.

They broke out into the light.

And stopped.

They were on a broad ledge, perhaps half an acre wide, on a cliff. Ahead was the ruin of a bridge. Behind them kobolds were coming nervously forward. They might be nervous, but they also outnumbered the three men by fifty to one, and more were coming down the tunnel.

"And now?" asked Manfred.

"I don't know," admitted Cair. "I've never been this far."

"Unless you add flying to your tricks, you're not going a lot farther either," said Manfred. "Even the rope you hauled me out with is far too short. And we left that behind."

The gorge was a good two hundred yards across to the point where the other buttress of the bridge hung. And it was a lot farther down to the ribbon of water.

"There's a trail off to that side," Erik pointed with a bloody sword.

"Let's go."

It wasn't much of a trail, just a narrow ledge sloping downward. But it was better than staying here.

Cair would have liked it better if the kobolds had tried to follow them. Or even if they hadn't laughed and jeered.

Erik led the way down the ledge. It was not wide—sometimes barely a cubit—and without any form of rail, but it was worn, as if others had come this way before. It zigzagged downward, and had been cut where nature did not provide. Looking down Erik could see that there was something of a quay—and a towpath—leading upstream. A couple of laden barges were tied up at the key. And now, kobolds were pouring out of an entry from the cliff onto that quay. No wonder they'd been laughing.

"There is a sequence of hoists inside the mines," said the thrall. "They can move faster than we can, edging along this ledge."

That much was obvious. But at least the rock wall above overhung, so they were safe from rocks or other missiles from above. The water below was dark and wide—and there was no landing on the far side either. Still, in Erik's opinion, that was their best hope.

"Come down," yelled the kobolds.

"Stop here. Boots off, gentlemen," said Erik. "When we get to that far point over there we're going to have to jump. Jump and swim. We'll be upstream of those barges. See if we can get up onto the first barge and cut her loose."

"It looks deep enough," was the thrall's only comment.

"And cold enough," said Manfred.

"You can swim, thrall—I don't know your name?" asked Erik.

The thrall smiled wryly. "You can call me Cair. It is as near as these Norse barbarians get to calling me by name. And I swim well. Better than you, probably. And at least they don't appear to have bows. But they may throw those little spears."

"A chance we'll just have to take," said Manfred. "When we get to the corner, on the count of three, jump together."

The water went beyond just "cold." Cair found that it was almost paralyzingly so. From thirty feet up he went a long way under water. He kicked hard for the surface. The current was frighteningly strong. He was nearly at the bow of the ore-barge before he broke water. He grabbed for it, and missed.

The current was sweeping him on, past it. Distantly he could hear the kobolds yelling, and as he stroked frantically, the cold eating at his strength, he saw the barge swing into the current ponderously, and begin drifting down on him. A rope splashed into the water next to him. He grabbed at it with numb hands and wrapped it around his arms. Suddenly he was hauled toward the barge so fast he actually skimmed out of the water like a dolphin.

Manfred reached down and fished him out. "You might swim better than Erik, but he's more used to Iceland's cold water, by the looks of it," said the big man with a grin. Erik was already at the stern of the laden craft, hauling at a clumsy rudder.

"We want to lighten her a bit," he yelled. "You two had better start off-loading." They got to work throwing heavy chunks of ore overboard into the racing icy water. It was hot work, to counter the bone-numbing cold of the swim they'd had. Erik was plainly feeling the cold, by his color. Cair went aft. "I can steer. See what you can do about drying off your gear."

"Seaman, are you?" said the Icelander, handing him the rudder bar.

Cair nodded. He was a little more wary about what he said, after the swim. For the first time he was able to take a considered look around at their position. The river ran deep and fast, and the gorge was still high and steep walled. The barge had never been intended for this sort of water. He began swinging her away from the main current. Closer to the margins the flow might be slower. Of course there was a better chance of underwater obstructions, too.

Erik wrung the tunic out, and went to help Manfred. "We need some ballast, I reckon," said the prince, working like a stevedore.

"If we hit a waterfall or real rapids in this tub, it won't help," said Erik, tossing mattock-hacked lumps off the boat.

Manfred shrugged. "We didn't have a lot of choices, did we?"

Erik smiled wryly. "My tunnel was warmer and drier."

"Ah, but the fresh air. The views. The company," said Manfred, expansively. "Think how bored we'd be in Mainz. Nothing to do but eat, drink, and seek out brothels. This is so much better for the Icelandic soul than that would be."

"True," said Erik. "At least here I don't know with a sort of horrible inevitability where I will find you. I don't even know where we are right now. Unless you do?" he directed a look at Cair, who was steering, peering ahead.

Cair shrugged. "Norway. Some river called the Gjöll, I think."

Erik paused midthrow. "Gjöll. Who told you that?"

"Those kobold-creatures called it that. With any luck there won't be any rapids or waterfalls before we reach the sea. It is widening ahead. We can't be that far off sea level."

Erik raised his eyes to heaven. "If this really is Gjöll, we're already well below sea level. You don't know much about the Norse, do you, Cair? Where are you from?"

Cair stepped cautiously here. It might be that Manfred or his bodyguard might see their first duty to be to rid the Empire of Cair Aidin, rather than surviving first and taking their mutual chances later. And he no longer underrated these two men. "Lesbos. A Greek island." It was true enough. It wasn't Turkish at the moment. He had been born there. "And other than the fact that the Norse are gullible barbarians, no, not a lot. And I care less."

Erik looked around them and at the water racing under the bow. And laughed. There was not a lot of humor in it. "When you are in their world, Master Cair, the one thing you'd better learn is some respect. Or you're going to die here, in spite of being a good man with a weapon, and as slippery as a stoat. The Gjöll is supposed to be one of the rivers of the underworld."

It was Cair's turn to raise his eyes to heaven. Their view of the sky was at least a bit wider now. "There is usually a real mountain or river at the base of every barbarian myth, Ritter. From far off it is a magical place, an abode of gods. When you get there it is just another river or mountain, lacking in either magic or gods."

Manfred laughed. "We have a hardened sceptic among us, Erik."

"A sceptic that I still want to know more about . . . like what is he doing here?" enquired Erik, going back to off-loading ore.

"Being a fool. I was following Princess Signy." Cair was surprised at the pang that mentioning the little princess brought him.

"A loyal thrall, following his witch-mistress?" There was a hardness in Erik's voice. "Pardon my saying this, Master Cair of Lesbos. I never met anyone less thrall-like in my life. Tell us another one. The truth this time."

Cair bit his lip. "The truth is too ridiculous for even me to accept, Ritter, let alone you. I *am* her thrall. I'll admit I wasn't planning to stay anyone's thrall. But the child is in trouble. I couldn't just leave her to it."

"She's messed with some very black magics, Master Cair," said Manfred, with a gentleness that surprised Cair. "Murders. Politics, schemes, blood sacrifices. Not only men get involved. Ask Eric. Women—even young, pretty, good-seeming women get drawn in. There was a nun, Sister Ursula, back in Venice, who was one of the most evil people in the world."

Cair shook his head. "*No,*" he said firmly, surprising himself with his own vehemence. "I'll believe nearly anyone else could be neck deep in murdering people, or any other kind of scheming in that court. I'm sorry, Prince. You didn't know her at all. But it isn't possible." He grimaced. "I was a stable-thrall. I suppose a murderess might treat old horses like, like their loyalty was worth something, Prince. She was as soft as goose grease with them, and the dogs, too. I suppose a murderess might love her dogs. But it just doesn't fit. She was . . . I don't know how to explain, but I know schemers." He gave a half-smile. "I am one. I could have done it, but not her. It is not possible. All Princess Signy was doing was surviving. They made it hard enough for her to do that much."

"No offence, Master Cair, but according to her brother, she was bitter that she as a woman could not inherit. He said that she was always plotting. That she was rotten to the core," said Erik, in what Cair read as a carefully neutral voice. "The stables did make me wonder. But the Christian mages did pinpoint her, Master Cair. As Manfred said, people are drawn into things that they don't mean to get into."

Cair had made split-second judgments all his life. He'd lived this long by not getting them wrong. He decided that he believed the Icelander—that he, at least, had no part in framing Signy with the theft. "Ritter. I have made myself into something of an expert on 'magic.' It's a lot of trickery. I can do that wand trick myself. Mostly, you play on people's fears. I think you'd all been fed a lot of tales by the princess's stepmother, and the nun decided to see if guilt would spook her into confessing. It wouldn't have worked. Those fellows in bearskins stole her away before there was time to prove her innocence. It was all a fake. A put-up job to allow the real guilty party to get away. With appropriate stories of bear-monsters—that turned out to be men."

Manfred was about to answer when Erik held his hand up for silence.

They could all hear it.

The grumble of rapids.

Big rapids.

Gjöll translated as "scream."

CHAPTER 30

Trollheim, Kingshall, Copenhagen:
various scenes

They did eventually bring her food—dried smoked salmon and water in a small leather bottle, passed up on a long pole. But other than that there was nothing for Signy to do but sit and think. What Signy principally thought about was escape. Eventually, she considered her bracelets. They were very much a part of her. She'd worn them day and night since she was thirteen. The reason was simple enough—they would no longer fit over her hands. The little interlocked bear figurines were indeed sharpish-edged. Would the silver be hard enough to cut the bars of her prison? She doubted it. But . . . she could sit in dimness and brood, or she could try.

She tried to get her hands out of them. And failed.

She tried just snapping them. It hurt her fingers and wrist, and didn't even bend the thin silver. It was a lot stronger and harder than it looked. Perhaps it would cut the wood after all—if she could get it off. She looked around for something she could hook and jerk at it. The edge of her pallet? Or—looking up—one of the bar ends? The woodworking on her cage was rough. Standing on the pallet she could probably reach one of those. But the thought of touching the cage wood made her flesh creep. Eventually, she steeled herself to do it. Gritting her teeth, she pushed her hands through. She hooked the bracelet onto a sharp end, her bare skin burning where it touched the wood. She kicked her feet off the ground, expecting pain. Expecting it to fail.

A moment later she was struggling to grab the bracelet before it fell through the slats. She fumbled it. She was never any good at that sort of catch. But luck was still with her despite her expecting it to fall through the bars, it landed on one, and hung there. Squinting to see it clearly she retrieved it from the wooden slat. The silver proved soft and flexible now. She had no trouble straightening it into a sort of blade.

It was virtually ineffectual as a saw. Eventually she did the same with the second bracelet. This time she had the sense to tie it to her wrist with a thread from her dress.

It didn't cut effectively either. But she felt much better for doing something. Or maybe she just felt much better.

Juzef Szpak was feeling just as much ;a prisoner as Manfred was now supposed to be. Snow was drifting down around Kingshall, thick and soft. It was no longer the near blizzard they'd fought their way back from Svartdal in, but it was still not plausible to go out into the snow again. And, Szpak noted, their quarters were now under guard. Even going to see their horses, they were constantly accompanied.

He'd gathered the monks and nuns in his chamber for a conference.

Szpak found new heart as brother Uriel led them in prayer. The monks placed their candles, invoked the wards of silence and raised a veil of privacy around them, deadening the sounds and muting their voices.

Yes. They were trapped by the weather, and possibly by the heathen horde. But he had been trapped before. And the soldiers of the cross had saved him then. They still had their swords and armor. If it came to a fight, their foes would pay a steep price.

Brother Uriel stood up. "We can speak freely now, Ritter. I warn you, Ritter, that we are being spied on, night and day."

"I had a feeling that was the case," admitted Szpak. "One has to wonder why?"

"All I can tell you," admitted Sister Mercy, "is that there are fewer witches here now than there were when we attempted to divine the thief. But there is still powerful magic being worked, and it has an unwholesome feel to it."

"The weather is not wholly natural, either," admitted Ottar. "Brother, Sisters, something is wrong here. We're definitely not wanted. I overhear things, as the warriors do not think that I can follow their speech. And I have made contact with some of the secret Christians."

"That's risky."

Ottar directed a cool look at him. "So is what they do. And they are not protected, as we are, by a truce oath. At the moment we are in no danger. They are. When that oath is not renewed . . . we may need any friends that we can find. Vortenbras's men are already placing wagers—using your horses as collateral."

Szpak pulled a face. "And I thought that having to explain how we'd lost Prince Manfred was our greatest problem. Well, unless they take us by trickery, or burn us out, we can hold this section of the halls for a while—we can make taking us expensive in the extreme. If the weather lifts we can try to ride for the coast."

"If the weather lifts. The snow is deep out there, and getting deeper, Ritter. We have the sisters to transport, too."

"And meanwhile your scrying has not found either the arm-ring or the prince."

"No. Somehow the arm-ring has disappeared as far as magic is concerned. The spells simply indicate that it is still there, which it plainly isn't. And all we have been able to establish about Manfred and Erik is that they are both alive and very far away."

"The alive part is good news."

Back in Copenhagen Francesca de Cherveuse did not even have that much information. And she was finding it a source of no small irritation. Spies and governments do far more than merely try to listen in on conversations. They also watch things like the lading of ships and the traffic in certain goods. But at the end of the day the best information comes from separate human sources of information, tallying each piece against another, the pieces gradually interlocking to form the entire picture. As a Venetian courtesan, Francesca had been privy to a great many things—including information from disparate sources. Here, in Copenhagen, she had set up her networks, too . . . social networks. The prince's leman was safe to flirt with, politely, although efforts—and they were numerous—to take matters further had to be avoided. Well, men were less guarded with pillow talk, but could still be foolishly informative out of bed.

At the moment it was snowing outside. She grimaced at the view from her window, and turned back to her visitor. She found him a fascinating man even if he could not tell her anything about what was happening in Norway. Most women would not have found Jubal Silvio fascinating—he was elderly, very wrinkled, and not even particularly rich. "Snow. More snow. Snow. Why does it snow so much in the North?"

The wizened man gave a reedy chuckle. "To affront you, mademoiselle." He spoke flawless Aquitaine. He actually spoke some nine languages, and read several more. That was his reason for coming to Copenhagen. In pursuit of rare volumes Jubal had traveled the known world. "Some theorists hold that the North is farther from the sun than the Southlands. A matter of solar angles apparently. An elegant piece of work from a mathematician in Carthage holds them to be correct. But I prefer my theory. And like you, I do not like the stuff. The Venetian spring convoy cannot come soon enough to take me back to Alexandria."

"There are other vessels, Jubal."

"For me, yes. My poor old carcase is not worth much. But for the treasures I have found! A second copying of *Gesta Hammaburgensis Ecclesiae Pontificum*! And in such good condition too. No, I cannot take a chance with that being stolen by Barbary corsairs, for all that they have been less predatory in the last few months. Venetian galleys it must be, regardless of the expense."

Francesca raised an eyebrow. "I can see the corsairs tossing your books overboard, but not stealing them. Pardon my saying so, but they look like poor loot. Not even any gold lettering."

He twinkled. "Ah, but it is the content, not their warped binding and foxed pages, that make them more valued than gold. And there is a ready market on the Barbary coast. Aruj Aidin and his brother may have terrorized the seaways, but they've brought some stability to the Berber. Tunis and Algiers and Carthage are burgeoning places of culture now. As nothing to Alexandria, but still good."

"I suppose piracy pays them well. Perhaps better than librarianship," she said archly.

He chuckled again. "A library's coin is not always gold. She pays in a variety of other bright things. Some I hold as worth more . . . and are harder for the foxes of the pillars of Hercules to steal. Treasures such as your mind, m'dear."

She tapped him with her fan—it was, she thought, a singularly useless fashion accouterment for any other purpose in this climate. "I imagine you say that to all the ladies, who are a lot less flattered than I am. I hear Heinrich with my other guests. Pardon me a moment. I must go and greet them."

Privately, she hoped that it was one of her informants, rather than the head of naval procurement—a noted amateur astronomer—or the bibliophile Count Achen and his vacuous-headed wife. But no word had come from Norway except: snow.

Bakrauf was nearly incandescent with anger. She scratched yet another coin with her nail. A troll-hard nail . . .

Thin gold foil flaked off, revealing the underlying lead. "After them. After the hostages. They've cheated us!"

She knew that it was too late. The little maggots had already crossed the bridge. Its stones had returned to invisibility. Before her people got there the kobolds would be hidden in their narrow twisty little cracks again. She looked angrily and suspiciously at the fake coin again. Where had mine kobolds, not even up to making their own mattocks, got such skilled work from? Her suspicion naturally fell on the dwarves. She got them to make much of her own fine artifice. But, right or wrong, she was in no position to challenge the dwarves. Besides, she'd need their services again herself, sooner or later. They made the *hednar* needles, with which she bound men to the changeling beast-skin, and many other powerful tools. Revenge on the maggot-kobolds would have to suffice, for now.

From her cage Signy watched the furious troll-wife stump out, cursing. She could not help but be glad. They'd been about to lower the cage again. Now all she got was a leather flask of water, pushed up through the bars on a long pole.

CHAPTER 31

Somewhere in the troll realms

Are you going to take over the steering?" Manfred asked. Erik shook his head. "He's a great seaman, whatever else he is. He's even got this bathtub close in to the bank, despite the fact that the current is pulling us toward the middle. The valley has opened up a bit. Rapids might mean that we're coming out of this gorge."

"Or that it gets steeper," said Manfred. Ahead the gorge was misty with spray. Already they had to shout to make themselves heard.

"Contrive oars," yelled Cair. "And get as much weight as you can to the front. We'll see if we can land her."

Erik and Manfred took their swords to levering loose a section of deck plank. This made two rough paddles, but even this and the rudder could not stop the current from wanting to suck their hapless craft toward the strong flowing center. Then they rose up on a huge standing wave, and flumed down it. Cair had the rudder hard over, and that took them skimming past a water-polished tooth of rock. Then into a vast swirl—a sort of maelstrom. At the far edge of this, they struck.

It wasn't a case of thinking about abandoning ship. The impact catapulted them out of the barge wreck and into the water.

They hit the water some yards from the shore—and the flow

was still deep and strong, but nothing like as powerful as in the midstream. Erik found himself washed toward the rocky edge and sucked into a gap between two huge boulders. The gap was fortunately partly choked with driftwood that provided handholds which the slippery, polished rock did not. With a tearing of clothes Erik hauled himself out. His first act was to look for Manfred. The prince was coming downstream fast. Erik ripped a stripped and water-polished spruce from the driftwood and thrust it out to him. Manfred grabbed and hauled. Then, both on the boulder, they looked around for Cair, to see him crawling onto the rocks a little upstream. He was considerably closer to the real shore than they were.

They still had to make their way across several house-to-generous-barn-sized boulders, with water sluicing between them. With some jumping and some driftwood bridges, the three of them finally stood together on the shore, such as it was. It was merely there because several rocky lumps had fallen from the broken cliffs, and were too huge for even this river to wash downstream. They had to shout to hear each other. Ahead, downstream, you could see the huge river seething and fuming across rocky teeth. The kobolds wouldn't come looking for them, or the lost barge.

"We go down, I reckon."

"Ja." Erik agreed. There weren't many other alternatives—up the cliffs would involve a lot of climbing, on what appeared to be rotten rock. The three of them began picking their way down the slimy spray-damp rocks. It wasn't easy going. Several times they had to go back and try another route. But eventually they came to a point where the river reformed into a lake, and the boulders became interlinked with soil.

The valley no longer closed above them. Instead they were under a slate-gray sky. The noise level had dropped off, too. Manfred announced a break by sitting down. "I'm all in." He looked at Cair. "Got any food left?"

Cair shook his head. "I'm afraid not."

Manfred looked at his feet. They were cut and bruised. He grinned. "No food. No boots. Wet gear. I don't suppose you've got any strong drink either? Or perhaps a horse stashed somewhere?"

The man looked as tired as they were. And he was a good few years older than them, too. Nonetheless, he smiled. Erik noted that he was at ease with the prince. He was a very odd thrall—wealthy, powerful men were usually ransomed rather than enslaved. "Patience. We'll get them, but these things take time."

"So. Where do we start looking?"

Cair pointed at the bare feet. "Firstly, let us contrive some sort of footwear. Your feet are too soft for walking barefoot, and more boots are a little beyond me right now."

"Moccasins?" said Erik, reluctantly eyeing his leather trousers.

Cair shook his head. "I think sandals will do. The terrain eases. We should find some planking remains at the waterside. Those will do for soles. I have seen the peasants in Atlas make do with bark, too."

Manfred raised his eyebrows. "You're a widely traveled man, friend."

"Sailors tend to be," said Cair, getting to his feet and heading toward the water.

Erik looked at Manfred and said nothing.

Manfred got to his feet, uneasily. "If he's just a sailor, then I'm an Alexandrine courtesan. Come on, Erik. Let's go and see what fiendish plan our love-struck 'sailor' has for shoes."

"Love-struck?"

Manfred nodded. "In my humble opinion, yes. Be careful around him, Erik. Men tend to be unusually illogical when their balls start thinking; and when their emotions get tied up in it, too, doubly so. Watch what you say about that girl. He's old for it, and if anything that makes a man worse."

Erik nodded. In affairs of the heart—or at least the groin—Manfred was his master. "You be careful around him, Manfred. I know the type. He's a calculator. While he finds us useful—he'll use us. I'd not wager a clipped penny that he rescued us from that kobold mine for any reasons but his own benefit."

"I reckon. Look. He's calling us."

Cair was beckoning. They picked their way across the rocks to him. He had several pieces of pine-planking that he'd hauled out of the water. "You have knives—you need soles. And then we must look to binding. We can cut some thongs off your breeches, Ritter. I have an iron needle. It will serve us in more ways than one."

Cair sat drawing the iron needle patiently in one direction along the knife blade. The other two were still working on their sandals. He had some advantages. For one, as a thrall, he'd walked barefoot for months. For seconds, he had found the planks—and had chosen the best pieces. Now he had time to look around and think. And to avoid thinking about food.

The valley they were in didn't seem to hold much promise of that. There were sparse grasses and dry bracken upslope. Mosses here. It was a bleak place, and what it would be like after dark, temperature-wise, was another matter. Their clothes were wet—to a greater or lesser degree. He'd been lucky—when they'd struck he'd been flung far further than the other two, and had landed in water that was not even three cubits deep. He'd thought he was going to hit the rocks, barely yards from where he had landed. He hadn't even gotten his hair wet, on that second, more involuntary swim. But now he was faced with various questions, the first of which was how, in this apparently deserted land, was he going to find where Signy was being kept? Had that bridge been destroyed after the bearskin-dressed ones had crossed it? Or should his first priority perhaps be staying alive? Perhaps to follow the river—construct a raft? Head for the sea?

He had no easy answers and plenty of doubts so instead he turned to the practical things. He tested the needle. He'd been working on it in the little spare time he'd had before they'd set out. It stuck, weakly, to the iron of the knife. Now . . . a thread from his cotte. The linen was coarse, but it was thinner than the wool of the jerkin. He tied it carefully while Erik watched curiously. The needle had to balance. It worked better if floated on a sliver of cork in water, but hung from something steady, out of the wind, it should give them a bearing. He attached the other end of the thread to a stick and hung it in the lee of the rock.

The needle began to turn slowly . . . as it should. It should steady and point north.

It continued to turn instead. Turn faster.

Cair stared at the spinning needle rather the way a man might stare at a swaying, venomous snake.

They walked downstream. There seemed to be no other logical direction in which to proceed. The gorge had emptied onto a vast rolling plain with hills leading back into the towering, ice-capped mountains across the river. The river, no longer constrained by steep walls, spread out into a broad, meandering flow.

"Some rocks are naturally magnetic, you know," volunteered Erik after they'd been walking for a while. They were all tired and cold. Conversation hadn't exactly blossomed up to now.

Cair shrugged. "Or we have come out at the very place to which lodestones are attracted. Without a sight of the sun or the stars, and no northerly bearing, finding our way around here is going to be difficult."

"True. But we could just head for the smoke," said Manfred, pointing.

Away from the river, across the heath, they could see a thin column of it rising into the cold air.

"Almost certain to be trouble," said Erik, warily.

"Almost certain to have opportunities," said Cair.

"More trouble than being out here when nightfall comes?" asked Manfred, rolling his eyes. "I don't know about you, Erik, but my spine is touching my belly button, we haven't seen any game, I'm cold, my toes are frozen. I'm with our sailor from Lesbos. Even if I suspect he's a Turk."

"Very well," agreed Erik. "Let's walk closer, anyway. But there are only three of us, and I'm not keen on another spell of imprisonment."

"Take it from me, you can't be less keen than I am. That hole made the Empire's dungeons look attractive. And the place flooded the first few days."

"At least you had water."

They set out up the grassy slope and across the heath.

Soon, standing on a low hilltop, they were looking across another wide braided river—not as wide as the one they'd left, but still half a mile of sandbars and channels—at another hill on the far side of the river.

A hill with a difference, though.

Unlike the rounded rolls on the bleak heath that surrounded them and it, this hill had a fair amount of exposed rock. Odd-shaped boulders adorned it.

However, it was the fact that the hilltop was raised on brass pillars that really caught the eye.

The smoke they'd followed wreathed up from inside the hollow hill.

Erik took a long hard look at it, and crossed himself. "Troll hill," he said.

Manfred sat down, taking the weight off his feet. They were looking fairly swollen and ugly. "Do you think they'd give us a bed for the night?"

"More likely to eat us," said Erik grimly. "They're supposed to be able to smell man flesh from half a mile off."

Cair studied the lie of the land instead. "Well, maybe so. But look there. Those look like men to me." A line of ragged figures, carrying buckets, were heading for the water. Something in their posture said "thrall." From here, anyway, they looked human.

"We can cross lower downstream hidden by the bend. It looks as if there would be rocks for cover," said Erik.

Manfred rubbed his feet, wincing. "I thought we were avoiding trolls."

Erik shrugged. "I don't see that we'd smell too different from that lot, even if there *are* trolls in that hill. They've got fire, food, and maybe even horses."

Manfred got up. He was obviously in some pain, putting his weight onto those large feet. Perhaps because he was biggest and heaviest his feet had suffered worst, climbing over the rocks at the rapids. "For horses, I'll even take on a round dozen trolls. Lead on, Erik."

They walked down. It was possible to cross the braided sandbanks without getting wet to more than midthigh. The other side of the river was littered with boulders and flood debris, and in among the flood debris Cair found a broken wooden bucket.

"Ah. My gate pass," he said with a wry smile.

"A bucket?" said Manfred. "It doesn't even have a bottom to it."

Cair assumed a doleful look. "I may be beaten for that."

Erik snorted. "As opposed to just being killed—or made into a thrall anyway?"

"A chance I just have to take," said Cair with a shrug. "I seem to be getting good at changing owners."

"Just how do you intend to get to mingle with the thralls—and how do you intend to get away again?" asked Erik. "I think I had better go. I am a better stalker than most people."

Cair shook his head. "You are a better stalker, yes, Ritter. But you don't walk like a thrall. They would spot you instantly."

"What he says is true, Erik," said Manfred. "You walk like a cat."

Erik acknowledged this, reluctantly. "But you're an unlikely thrall, Cair. You don't fit the part either."

Cair slouched his shoulders and shuffled. "But I can," he said humbly, without, looking up, "master."

"You should have been a court jester or a traveling player, not a sailor," said Manfred, grinning despite his tiredness. "So what are you going to do in there?"

"Check out the lie of the land, find out where we are, steal what I can . . . that'll do for a start," said Cair. "But now I need a bundle of firewood. It'll give me an excuse to get closer. I will get away and bring you news and food as soon as I can. Where will I meet you?"

"Those rocks there," Erik pointed to three large boulders a hundred yards or so upslope. "By the looks of it we should be able to see from the ridge line just beyond that. We'll keep watch."

"Better keep my sword, too," said Cair, unbuckling it. He looked scathingly at it. "Norse rubbish, but better than no blade at all." His stolen knife went into his sleeve, tight-wrapped in a piece of rag. And then, gathering kindling, he set out. He walked along, hidden by an undercut bank until he was nearly at the bucket-filling slaves.

Erik and Manfred watched from the ridge as he meandered to join the tail end of the line of bucket carriers. He calmly set his wood bundle down and, with them, walked off into the hollow hill.

Manfred shook his head. "He's got a lot of gall; I don't know about anything else."

"True," agreed Erik. "I trust him as far as I can throw him, but he's a survivor."

"He's more than just a sailor though," said Manfred, untying the rough sandals and looking ruefully at his feet. "I'd dearly like to know what he was doing in Telemark. Looking at how he organized within the kobold mines, there is no way he couldn't have escaped if he had wanted to."

Erik scratched the bristles on his chin. "I would guess that he is an agent for someone rich and powerful. He's probably an assassin. He might even have been there to kill you."

"He's missed a few good opportunities since then."

"He's a bit confused over this princess," said Erik.

"I must admit I hardly noticed the girl before this lot blew up. I saw her at the feast, of course. A mousy little thing, who looked thoroughly miserable. She didn't look much of anything, let alone a witch."

Erik yawned. "Glamour, or a seeming. It's very much part of the northern magics. Now, you go over to the rocks and stay there. I'm going back down to the river. I saw at least one trout when we were coming across here. Let me see if I can tease one out from under that bank."

"With what? Insults? How do you tease a trout?" Manfred looked content not to move.

"Tickle them. Get a hand under them, flip them out. It takes patience, and tolerance for cold water."

"Even raw trout sounds good," said Manfred. "I'll stay here on the ridge and watch, Erik. I want to rest these feet before we have to run—if we have to run."

Erik looked critically at Manfred's feet. "Tonight, I think we will have to make a fire. We can cook the trout, and contrive some sort of dressing on those cuts."

Manfred nodded. "I'm half frozen now. Tonight will be bleak."

"If this place has a night." Erik slithered back from the skyline and walked off to the water. Manfred remained watching.

Erik found the water bone-numbingly cold but the little red-spotted trout under the bank were overconfident about how it protected them. He had three, and was just getting his hand under a fourth, when a ground-vibrating clang startled him into frightening the fish. He was up and running up the hill before the echo died away.

"They're just shutting up shop," said Manfred.

The boulder-studded hill was . . . just a hill. A little smoke and steam billowed around it, but a cold wind was carrying even that away.

Erik let his breath hiss between his teeth. "Well. I suppose there is nothing to stop us having a fire and some fish now. Cair is stuck in there."

"Did you get some fish?" asked Manfred eagerly, rubbing his stomach.

Erik nodded. "Three—the fourth I lost because I spooked with that racket."

"What are we going to do about the fire? Your tinderbox is somewhere in kobold lands," Manfred pointed out.

"I'll make a fire-drill," said Erik. "There is a lot of dry stuff washed up at the waterline."

The trio of rocks that Cair had pointed out proved as good a camp as they were likely to find. On a dry watercourse, it was hidden in a little fold in the rolling hill, away from prying eyes and sheltered from the icy wind. Water had eaten under the rocks so there was a little overhang. They carted driftwood, and Erik got busy contriving a fire-drill while Manfred cut some dry grass and bracken for their nest.

Erik had been well taught during his sojourn in Vinland. He got first a curl of smoke and then an ember. Shaved dry splinters of resinous pine gave them flame, grilled trout, and some warmth. Nothing could have kept them from the arms of Morpheus. Erik tried to sit guard for a while, but the toll of hard labor, poor food, a hectic escape, and the stress and worry over Manfred over the last few days were just too high. Swords in hand, back to the rock, with a little hidden fire, sleep took them.

If they'd been awake and watching, they would have seen seven huge bears crossing the sandbars. And a huge pile of rocks move to greet the mistress, before opening a narrow portal into the hill.

CHAPTER 32

Trollheim

The thralls were not all human. And neither were the gate guards of the hill fortress. They were at least twice the size of a man, and looked as if they had been crudely carved out of rock. Well, just because there was a thing of substance underneath the rumor didn't make them magical.

The thralls appeared even more cowed and wretched than the thralls at Kingshall. They were certainly not about to ask questions of their troll overlords as to where the extra labor had suddenly come from. Of course they asked him. "I was captured on a raid," he answered as he parked his broken bucket with the others beside the cistern. "I will be ransomed."

"Likely! No one is ever ransomed," said one of the bucket carriers, the biggest by far. He stuck a finger under Cair's nose. "You. I'm Gunnlaug. I am number one here. You will give me one-third of your food. Understand?"

Cair understood perfectly. He kicked Gunnlaug neatly in the belly, and, as he fell, dived on top of him. As they went down, he drew the knife from his sleeve. Closing with the man on the floor, it was invisible to the onlookers. Gunnlaug felt it under his chin, however. "Understand this, Gunnlaug. You *were* number one. Got me?"

The man nodded—very slightly as the knife was pressing into his throat—terror in his eyes. "Good," said Cair. "Now," he slipped the knife back into his sleeve, "you're going to show me how things work. And you're not going to mention that sharp thing or I'll kill you." The man would attempt to betray him, he was sure. But it would take him a little while to pluck up the courage. And Cair didn't plan to be around by then.

The thrall quarters and food confirmed Cair's initial impression: Kingshall's thralls lived in the lap of luxury, comparatively. But, as normal, thralls went everywhere, because they did all the dirty work. An overseer with a whip came hunting for them to do the first bit of that work. Thirty or so of them were marched down stone corridors into the belly of the hill. It was as hot as Hades down here, steamy and sulphurous. The thralls, obviously being familiar with the task, took the sides of a huge pole, which turned the top of a huge brass screw the size of three men. "New men take nearest the screw," Gunnlaug informed him.

Cair punched him in the kidneys. "Don't be stupid enough to lie to me again." He'd observed that smaller thralls were being pushed into place—with the whiplash—close to the screw.

They heaved as troll guards swung their whips. The screw moved, first with difficulty and then with hissing steam and speed, and yelps of fear. Suddenly it spun easily and great gouts of steam shrieked out. Thralls and their troll guards scattered for the relative safety of the walls. The place shook with the deafening noise of impact.

Cair realized that he'd just helped to shut himself into the troll hill. Well, it was an interesting mechanism. Steam pressure. A fascinating idea. He would have been far more inclined to use counterbalancing weights. But it had all sorts of potential.

The thralls trooped out along long corridors and to various places of work. The troll hill was a busy, smelly place of industry. There were forge fires, hammering, the sounds of various forms of manufacture. It looked to him as if the troll hill was gearing up for war. He prodded the now wary Gunnlaug in the ribs. "Where are we going?"

"I clean halls," said the surly ex-number-one thrall. "All new thralls go to the foundries."

Trust this one to have the cushy job. "Things change," he said.

"Today you have me to assist you in cleaning. Tomorrow . . . we will see. I think you might just be going to the foundry—if you give me any trouble."

"Where did they catch you?" demanded Gunnlaug, suspiciously. "You don't behave like a slave. You don't even look like a human. You speak strangely."

"The kobolds caught me in the mines. I was taken from there. Come. Find the cleaning equipment. No more questions, now. I have seen three places I could leave your body already."

Gunnlaug said nothing—wisely. But his eyes widened in shock as he finally got the measure of the man he had tried to bully. "Don't think it is worth it, thrall," said Cair, grimly. "I've friends who would find out, and find you. I've used my magic to tell them already." Cair had been rubbing his amber with the lambswool. He reached out with the makeshift "wand" and was rewarded by a spark, as it touched the thrall.

The man yelped and edged away from Cair. Superstition! He muttered something. It sounded like dokkalfar—"dark elf." And by the looks of it the troll thrall was even more afraid of them than he was of his masters. He plainly thought Cair a spy. Well, he was right, even if he was wrong about whose spy. Cair reached out and pulled out a hair from the thrall's head, as Gunnlaug backed up against the wall. He beckoned. Reluctantly Gunnlaug came forward. Cair licked his finger—and placed it on the man's nose—and stuck the hair there.

Cair muttered a suitable malediction in Latin. "If you betray me . . . that will become a strangling snake and choke the life out of you. If not . . . we'll free you."

The fellow whimpered. But after that he was very, very cooperative, if a little cross-eyed from trying to see his own nose.

Cair was tired. It had been a long, tough day—but he'd had more food and more rest than either Erik or Manfred had had. Having a birch broom to lean on helped. So he was awake when the *björnhednar* carried their mistress down from the small portal in her litter. He kept his head down and swept. It would seem all men looked alike to trolls. But Cair was certain those "bears" were men, too.

His heart raced. He supposed that it wasn't such a remote chance—how many other places were there in this bleak area, after all?

Somewhere in this troll anthill, they had her. And sooner or later, he'd find that place.

The cleaners always do.

Signy watched from her cage high above them as Bakrauf and her assistants marked out the fresh patterns on the floor of the troll queen's throne chamber. Something about the shape that they traced made her feel very ill. She hated watching, but she felt a terrible compulsion to do so. To see what evil was being done. Runes that seemed to crawl with an inner nastiness were painstakingly painted. But she had no idea what they meant. Seven small fires were lit. They burned green and orange, and the smoke rising from them was nauseating.

Small, soft, live things in wicker cages were placed on the flames. They screamed.

Signy had to block her ears and screamed, too. But, horrified, she watched as a dark form coalesced in the midpoint between the flames. It was simply an area of darkness, of shadows where there should be none. Bakrauf was speaking to it. Signy unblocked her ears. She dreaded what she might hear, but not knowing was worse. Besides, putting her fingers in her ears hadn't seemed to help. The shadow's voice was as insidious and unstoppable as poison. It knew that she was there. And, somehow, it was taking pleasure in her discomfort.

"And where is the blood-drinker tonight?"

"My son is keeping control over the other side of the task. The weather magics spells need to be constantly refreshed. You promised to assist, Jagellion. I need more."

"You have power sitting in the cage. Spill its blood and you will have plenty," said the thing of shadow, knowing she was watching. Knowing she could hear. "She has all the properties of a good sacrifice. Give her to that blood-drinker of yours to defile and kill on the stones."

"If I have to I will. But that is valuable coin. I do not spend it easily. You promised me that you would send snow."

"It has a long way to come. But by morning the winds will be over Telemark."

"Good. I fear that stopping the hunt for your prize is entirely dependent on it. The monks and nuns and knights still quest

magically. We've tried to prevent them. You said they were cor-
ruptible. You were wrong."

"Every man or woman has their price, Bakrauf. You just need
to offer the right price."

She snorted angrily. "I'll trade you, Jagellion. Manfred of Brittany for the prices. Or more snow."

"You told me he was in kobold hands."

"I am about to visit a little vengeance on them. They tried to
cheat me. I will fetch him hence."

"Be careful you don't overreach yourself."

By the time the summoning was over, and the shadowy
thing had gone back whence it came, only the emptiness of her
stomach stopped Signy from being sick. She retched dryly. And
sleep was a long time coming, and haunted by nightmares.

Somehow, at the end of the nightmare her stable-thrall was
there, rocking her gently as one might rock a child.

After a while her mind registered that the rocking was real.
As was the voice.

She looked over the edge of her pallet.

Someone was using the long pole to rock the cage.

And was calling her softly.

She shook her head, unbelievingly. It had to still be part of her
dream. She was dreaming she was awake, that was it.

There was no other way that her stable-thrall could be standing beaming up at her.

He grinned, in his usual slightly lopsided fashion. "Strange
birds these trolls keep in their cages, Princess Signy."

"I wish you were real," she said, feeling the tears well up.

"I'm as real as I ever was, Princess," he said, calmly, but
with a rather foolish smile on his face. "We've come to rescue
you."

She gaped at him. Shook her head. "Me?" she said incredulously. "Who sent you?"

Cair smiled. "In a strange way, your stepmother. Before I locked
her in the feed store. I'm afraid I stole two of Vortenbras's horses
for the job. And I have two of the Frankish knights along as well.
An escort for you."

She looked at him, somewhere between hysterical laughter and
tears. "You have to be quite mad."

Cair nodded. "Yes. I think so, too. Here is your knife, by the way." He thrust it into the pole and passed it up. "I found it lying next to the wall there."

She took it eagerly . . . and then paused. "You may need it. I give you permission to carry steel. You are a loyal thrall."

He looked sardonically at her. "Why, thank you, Princess. You keep it for me for now. The locals might not appreciate your authority. I must go—the guard will be back along this passage soon, and the trolls will be up and about, too. I need to organize a few things before we leave. Is there anything I can bring you? Food? Water?"

She smiled tremulously. She had a feeling that he'd been offended by her offering him her knife. Didn't he understand what a privilege it was? What an honor? "You have given me the best thing anyone could. You've given me hope again. Food and water would be wonderful, but be very careful. You are as precious as Korvar."

He waved a casual hand. "I will do my humble best. He's a valuable horse."

That made her laugh. It sounded odd echoing in the huge, gloomy chamber. "I don't think you can be humble, Cair. Go before someone comes."

He winked. "I'll bring food and water. And I'll work on humble."

He slipped away out of the door, leaving her to a solitude that was not quite so lonely. He was the oddest thrall . . . To have persuaded the Frankish knights to let him come along. She wondered if Cair had realized that they wanted her because they believed she was a witch who they would torture and burn. She felt the comforting haft of her knife, clipped back in its sleeve sheath. Well, they'd not take her alive. And if the troll-queen followed the advice of the thing of shadows and darkness, she at least would have a blade to sink into the belly of the blood-drinker.

Actually, she could also use it a lot more effectively than the silver bracelets on the bars. She hugged herself. It was odd to think that someone, not a dog or a horse, valued her enough to come into a troll hill, unarmed, looking for her. He really was as precious as Korvar. She could give a human no greater compliment.

Cair swept aimlessly. His mind was a ferment. First, relief that she was, it appeared, both alive and unhurt. Secondly, at her reaction. Seeing her, smiling down at him, it had been all holiday with his wits. Cair was finally prepared to admit to himself that he—he of all people—was hopelessly in love with the girl-child. And to her he was a loyal thrall, to be trusted enough to carry steel. Not even quite human. To be cherished, yes, as she did her horse. And yet, when he made her laugh in that dark place—it was all right. He would be her thrall, if he could make her happy.

His perambulations had brought him to a familiar scent. Horse dung. He went in. There were eight horses, rough-coated stubby steeds, not the fine Barbary stallions he had in his own stable, but solid creatures, bred to take the abuse of the climate and the locals. There was work to do. So he made himself busy. A little later another thrall came in, looking around guiltily. He nearly dropped the tankard he had with him when he saw Cair. "What are you doing here?" he demanded.

"Brushing this horse," said Cair, in his best imitation of the halfwit Thjalfi.

"I mean here. In the stables."

"I was sent to work here," said Cair. "I know horses. I was a horse-thrall."

"Oh. They never tell me anything. Want some small-beer?"

Cair did indeed. And he also wanted some food and a way of carrying drink. As he took a pull from the tankard, he spared a thought for Prince Manfred and Erik Hakkonsen. They'd be hungry and cold, no doubt. Well, they had water, and some clothes. And he had small-beer, a princess to rescue, and horses to steal. Besides, he had to find a way out and a way to stop pursuit. And while he was about it, he needed to steal some other footware, and some food. He smiled wryly. A thrall's work was never done. He handed the tankard back and went on with his work... just in time. A man came into the stable. A man Cair recognized—one of Vortenbras's crowd of bodyguards. And he wore a bearskin cloak.

The man clouted the other thrall on principle and wandered into the tack room. He emerged with a bridle and tossed it to Cair, who had hastily rubbed dirt onto his face and straw into his hair. Cair cringed and looked down. "The buckle needs fixing. Take it down to the workshops. And you, stop nursing your head and saddle my horse. I'm going to ride out."

Cair scurried out as fast as his legs could carry him. The man had given him an odd look, but said no more. The greatest secret of disguise is to be doing what someone should be doing, but no one wants to.

Erik and Manfred lay on the skyline, watching the troll hill. They spotted the rider, but not where he actually emerged from the hill. "Well, he was right about one thing. Horseflesh," said Erik

"I could eat it, let alone ride it," said Manfred. It had not been the warmest bed for sleeping rough, but compared to the kobold pit, it had been restful. It had never actually gotten dark, and it was still almost half lit. Well, trolls didn't like sunlight so their realm would be like this, according to Erik. But Manfred felt rested enough to face trolls or kobolds or any other Norse creature. Food was another matter. Eric had spotted hare tracks—there was game, albeit sparse, here. But to catch it might be another matter. Eric had been biding his watching time trying to make a snare, when they caught sight of the rider.

"He's coming this way. Do you think it might be the sailor?"

"He rides badly enough to be one."

But as the rider drew closer they could see that he had blond, braided locks, typical of a Norseman.

"Are we going to try and take him?"

"Not unless we have to."

"If he comes too much closer, we'll have to." Manfred paused. "Do you think the sailor might have given us away?"

"And they sent one horseman to capture us? Not likely. Unless the knights' reputation really is slipping."

Manfred grinned. "We're a long way from the chapter houses of Prussia. Maybe he's a messenger from the so-called sailor, coming to invite us to break our fast. A nice sirloin of beef, some kidneys, ham, mushrooms, and fresh bread . . ."

"He must have heard your stomach rumble, because he's sheering off," said Erik. There was some relief in his voice. There was nowhere to easily ambush the man, and a man on a horse had some marked advantages, regardless of who you were.

They watched the rider make his way to the top of the next hill. He began riding back down.

"Exercise," said Erik. "Well, let's see where he goes in." But they were disappointed because the hilltop began to rise on its pillars, slowly and with much rumbling. A great surge of smoke and steam billowed out from under the rim. The rider rode around to what was obviously the front gate of the troll city.

They'd obviously arrived at closing time the day before, because they were able to watch the denizens of the hill come out and go about various tasks, hauling water and driftwood, pulling nets in channels. There was no sign of Cair.

It was a long day, and as Erik pointed out, it revealed the weakness of their position—they couldn't retreat while the troll hill was open, without crossing the river or exposing themselves higher up the hill.

"The question is, Erik, whether we want to get away," said Manfred, seriously.

"You mean in case Cair comes looking for us? I suspect he's been caught, Manfred. And I'm a little wary about relying on the man. He has a habit of coming out of a sewage pit smelling of roses. I don't trust people like that. He looks out for one person. Himself. He'll use us as long as we are convenient."

"That's not what I meant. Our sailor from Lesbos might not be convinced about where we are, but I am certain that we're not anywhere where following the river to the sea and looking for a boat will get us back to the Empire. The only way back might be the way we came. Or where do you think we should go? Which direction? Erik, we can't live forever on a few trout, and maybe, if we're lucky, a hare."

Erik was silent for a while. "I hadn't thought of it like that," he admitted. "If we really are somewhere else . . . and my Icelander kin believe there are definately other places, then we need to look for the known ways back. But this could just be a valley somewhere in Norway. Most of it is still wild in the hinterland."

"Where the sun never shines and a magnetized needle rotates."

"Hmm. Well, maybe we need to move upstream. There is a lot of driftwood in that water. If legend holds true . . . that could be from Myrkwood."

"Myrkwood?"

"A vast forest that is supposed to be the border between the worlds of myth and ours. Or the Bifröst bridge . . . Oh my. I suppose that might have been the Gjallarbrú."

"You're talking Icelandic riddles again," said Manfred.

"You know what Bifröst is—the shimmering path. There for a moment, then gone. It is sometimes called the rainbow bridge, between the world of gods and men."

"No. But I do now. So what was the other unpronounceable?"

"Gjallarbrú. The bridge to the underworld. It is supposed to be huge and guarded by a giantess."

"I guess she must have nipped off for a quick one, and the bridge had fallen down."

"Maybe, like Bifröst, it isn't there unless you walk on it."

Manfred paused. "That would take some faith." He looked around. "The Norse have a pretty cushy underworld then."

"It's a bit more complicated than that. There are parts you don't want to visit."

"Hmm. I'll take your word for it, as long as you work out how we get out of this part." He stared at the line of thralls carrying buckets into the troll hill. "I think you're wrong, you know."

"About Gjallarbrú?"

"No. About our sailor from Lesbos. I think there is one other person he does care about. At least one."

Erik considered this. "You could be right. It would make me take a more kindly view of the fellow."

Manfred shook his head at his companion. "It'd make *me* a damned sight more nervous! A witch with a great hatchet man at her disposal. A hatchet man who is totally ruthless and will always believe she's right and good."

"I suppose so. I still think the better of him for it."

Eventually their long vigil came to an end. The hilltop came down with its resounding crash and wreath of steam. Erik went back to catch some more fish for them to eat. Manfred worked at the fire and their shelter. Erik did well, coming back with five fish, one of which was a reasonable size. Manfred looked at them. Looked at Erik trying to warm up at the hidden fire. Reached a decision. "Let's eat and go scouting."

"What about your feet? They're still in poor shape if we have to run."

"To be honest, they're only getting worse. Some of those cuts are infected. We need to move while I still can. They're not going to heal fast without good food and medication. I'd rather let a horse do my running for me. We need horses at least. And a prisoner to tell us just where we are and how to get out of here."

CHAPTER 33

Trollheim

The thrall quarters were in a ferment. " . . . A great black snake throttled him. Right in front of Eyrgjafa. He was trying to tell her something."

"You were with Gunnlaug, new thrall. Did he tell you anything?" demanded someone.

Cair shook his head mournfully. "He was dabbling in *seid* magic. A man using that! I was afraid of him, when I spotted the charms."

"Charms?"

"I'm a witch seer. If you aren't, then you wouldn't have seen them."

By the time he had embroidered the story, most of the audience were suitably sure that Gunnlaug, the bully of thralls and toady of their troll masters had died a justified death.

The question in his mind, of course, was just what Gunnlaug had said before he died. Superstitious fellow. He'd heard of autosuggestion in witchery of the west-African tribes. They died because they believed that they would, when they had been cursed. This must be more of the same. Still, there was no time to waste. The thrall might have said too much and would certainly have made the trolls a little more wary. The thralls were locked in—naturally. But it would appear that their locks came from the same source

220

as the mine kobolds. He still had his key. As soon as the thralls
were abed, Cair went on a snoop about. He had some things he
needed to gather. If he could get them all together then he'd have
Signy out of here long before the thralls were up and working.

The troll kitchens had stuffs in them that he did not want to
look at too closely. It might not be cannibalism for trolls, but it
would be for humans. However, he removed a stack of flattbrød
from a locked cabinet, and took a bunch of hard-smoked trout and
a small leather flask of beer someone had squeezed out of a cat.
Most of it—barring the flask and three of the flattbrød rings—he
hid in the stable. The flask and flattbrød he took to Signy.

"Cair!" she exclaimed. And hastily put her hand over her
mouth. "I thought you must have been caught," she whispered.
"You must get out of this place. I saw the most horrific piece of
magic earlier. One of the thralls came in here looking for the
queen . . . he spoke to another troll. And as he started to speak,
a black serpent throttled him!"

Cair didn't quite know what to make of this testimony. The light
was bad in here and, well, Signy didn't see close details well, he'd
noticed. Best to deal with the business in hand. "We will be leaving
shortly. I have brought you food and drink. Eat now, while I go and
deal with the hill-raising mechanism. Then I will take you out. I
have found the passage to another small doorway."

And then there was a vast cacophony of noise, and moments
later the passage outside was full of shouting.

"It must be between those two rocks," said Erik quietly. "There
is bound to be a guard. I'll go forward and check it out, Manfred.
You make enough noise for a troop of cavalry."

He slipped his plank sandals off and crept forward into the
dark gap between the rocks. There was a narrow stone arch and
a door.

"ERIK!"

It was only Manfred's yell that saved him. The huge hand
knocked him spinning, instead of flattening him against the
stone.

Erik Hakkonsen was a fine stalker. The Vinlander plains tribe
that had adopted him while he was there were proud of him.

The trouble was, he'd been prepared to stalk men—not stones.
Sometimes when you're on the lookout for mice, you can walk

smack into an elephant. And that was just what he'd done. Those weren't misshapen stone pillars. They were legs.

Manfred, sword in hand, sore feet obviously forgotten, bellowed like a bull, challenging the gigantic stone troll, trying to distract it. Stone trolls—half giant creatures—are not fast, but they are large and nearly invulnerable. As Erik discovered, one could cut the gray silicacious flesh with difficulty—and without much effect. It had taken all his strength, and the blade went in barely a handsbreadth.

It was stuck fast, too. Erik barely had time to dodge back as the troll reached down and plucked it out. It flung the sword away, bellowing loudly enough to temporarily deafen them. Erik ran back, and with the two of them playing tag with it, they retreated toward the river.

And more foes were now coming out of the postern.

Erik and Manfred ran onto the sandbars, and it followed . . . lurching and sinking into the sands.

"This sand is slowing it down, Manfred; let's keep going across."

"We don't have a lot of other choices," panted Manfred.

The stone troll swung a huge fist at Manfred—his feet made him the slower of the two of them—and Erik flung a handful of gravel at the monster's eyes. It stopped with a yowl and pawed at its eyes. Erik snatched up more and threw again.

They'd found its weak spot. It blundered toward them, waving its arms around wildly, obviously not seeing much. "That tree." Erik pointed.

Near the edge of the spit lay an enormous dead pine. Plainly the thralls had been cutting the dead branches away, and now all that remained was the trunk and some whitened branches down the far end. Even half buried in the silt it was still waist high.

Yelling like banshees they leapt over it.

The creature had sound and scent now, even if it could not see. It lumbered forward, unaware that they'd lain down beside the log.

It didn't even see the log until it stumbled over it—and fell headlong into the water beyond.

Water sheeted outward, soaking them. The fallen creature flailed at it, in panic. Erik stood up hastily. The braid of water wasn't that deep . . .

Looking back at the shore Erik realized that maybe the stone troll had been a small problem. The shore was lined with misshapen troll creatures.

In their midst stood what appeared to be a broad, stocky old woman with lank gray hair and a bitter, lined face. She ignored them and instead waved her staff at the river.

Manfred pointed upstream.

A wall of water was coming down at them. They still had at least two hundred and fifty yards of sandbar and channels to cross to the far bank, and perhaps forty back to the troll-crowded one they'd come from. And by the speed of the water that was coming, they didn't have time to get back, let alone sprint to the far side.

Erik saw their only hope. "The tree," he yelled. "To the branches."

They barely made that in time, scrambling up into the skeletal white remains of the branches as the water came surging in a chest-high wave. The water fussed and fretted at the tree, shaking the branches. It shifted slightly, but the flood did not actually succeed in dislodging the great dead tree from the sandbar.

The stone troll had been less lucky, and had gone rolling away with the current. "Well, that's got rid of him," said Manfred. "Now, if we can get out of here before that lot get to us, and if we can mount and ride off, we're away."

"I think we've found Cair's princess," said Erik grimly. "Or some other hag."

"She doesn't look much like that little thing we saw in Kingshall."

"They're supposed to be masters of illusion."

Manfred felt his feet. Looked at the blood on his hands. "I know a few girls who wouldn't mind that ability, without the rouge pot. But I can't see why she'd settle for being a skinny lass, if she can look as she pleased."

"Maybe to avoid being looked at too closely."

"Well," said Manfred, shifting his bulk on the tree branch. He still had his sword, and he obviously wanted to be in a good place to use it. "If this is her actual form, I'm surprised I haven't fallen in love with her myself."

Erik ignored this sally. Instead he inspected the water. "I think

we're going to have to try swimming again, Manfred. It's dropping fast."

"Well, I'm wet already," said Manfred, sheathing his sword. "And
the troll-hag is up to something. Say when. Do we try and stay
together, and do we swim for the far bank?

But before Erik could answer, his muscles froze. He was stuck,
immobile, and unable to say anything, let alone "when."

The trolls that waded across to fetch them simply snapped
the tree branches and carried the paralyzed captives to their
mistress.

Erik and Manfred were dumped at her feet, still clinging to
the branches.

The troll-woman was nearly as tall as she was wide. Her eyes
were very green. "Manfred of Brittany, and his henchman," she
said, shaking her head. "Of all the doors in troll lands to knock
at, you had to choose mine. Others might just have eaten you.
You've saved me a great deal of trouble, you know. Now that I
have seen that the human pursuit of you is not as active as I'd
feared, I was going to go and take you from those little dung-
eater kobolds. And you," she pointed at Erik, "you will make a
good replacement for the *björnhednar* you cost me. I'll have to
find some way of making you pay for my door warden. They are
big and stupid, but they're good watchmen."

Erik and Manfred found themselves being carried in through
the stone door that Erik had nearly been crushed against. The
troll queen spoke a word of command and it swung shut behind
them. The troll hill stank. And the dungeon that they were taken
to stank even worse. They were tossed onto the stone floor, and
troll hands stripped away their weapons. The paralysis remained,
although Erik began to feel a tingling in his fingers.

Cair had moved swiftly when he'd heard the hullabaloo start.
He naturally assumed that he was the cause of it. Being caught in
here would make things worse for Signy. He had located several
hiding spots in his sweeping progress. A man with a broom or
a bucket can go into all sorts of places. Now, only hiding would
serve him. There was no excuse for a thrall to be out and about.
He was into the nearest of his nooks, a store chamber next to
the throne room. This room lacked even one of the smoky lamps
that burned in the passages. He had no knowledge of what was

in there except for what he'd seen in the instant of entering. It was pitch-black. Cair was a self-declared rational man, but this place gave even him the creeps. It smelled of bad taxidermy, and other, less pleasant bouquets. Sulphur was definitely one of the reeks. His brief look had shown him a number of barrels near the entrance that he could duck behind if someone came to unlock the door. In the meantime he peered through the keyhole.

It gave him a view of hurrying trolls. And then nothing more than a crick in his neck. He was about to go out again, when he heard the sound of the return party.

He was able to see Erik and Manfred carried past. He ground his teeth in irritation. More complications! Escape tonight was probably out of the question. He waited. Noise subsided. Curiosity also ate at him. What was this room used for? Eventually he unlocked the door, nipped out, and brought a lamp in. He had to sneer a bit. Magical paraphernalia, by the looks of it. If he'd had this lot back in Telemark he could have convinced them that the sun obeyed him. He noted certain specific items: a stack of bear pelts. And various bottles—sulphur was easy to pick out. Saltpeter he could get from the stables. Charcoal was easy enough. A rack of women's clothes. And here was a lovely supply of bottles . . .

Cair paused. A large jar had a woman's head in it. A blond woman, with a face he knew well. The last time he'd seen her he'd locked her in a feed shed. He shook his head, feeling more than a little queasy. He had disliked Queen Albruna, but this was more unpleasant than he could cope with. He took the sulphur, three jars and, he had to admit to himself, fled from the staring eyes in that dismembered head.

After he'd hidden his loot in the hay at the stables, he stole back to the thrall quarters and slept. Even the fleas couldn't keep him awake. He had a sleep debt of at least a month by now, and it didn't look like he'd be catching up on it anytime soon.

The next day the thralls were abuzz with the story of the night capture. It got somewhat distorted in the process, with the two being anything from warriors from Oslo to Alfar spies. Cair, established as a power in thrall-land by the fact that he'd apparently beaten up Gunnlaug, was treated to a sneak view by one of the thralls whose work took him down to the dungeons. The warder-troll and the head torturer allowed the thralls to look from the stair, through the stone bars, even if they were not allowed into the dungeon. One got quite a good view from the open door. Cair joined in the mocking cheerfully, but kept back. He didn't need to be betrayed by the Franks.

It was another day's work for Cair. Lugging dung, looking for dirty pink saltpeter crystals in it. Cleaning passages. Noting things. Finding the opportunity to grind charcoal and saltpeter. And to curse because his weighting was so imprecise when it came to quantities. Filling bottles. Making fuses was another problem, as lighting them was going to be. The lamps would do while they were in the hill. But outside would be more difficult. He'd yet to find a flint and steel, boots, or weapons. But if he located the bear warriors' chambers, they would give generously, if unwillingly. They owed Signy, and he personally had no objections to collecting from their dead bodies.

Something else happened that day that pleased Cair no end. A column of some fifty trolls, with the troll queen stumping along ahead of them, left in what Cair had decided was midmorning.

"So where are they going, and why are the *björnhednar* not going with them?" He asked Helgi, the stable-thrall, casually. Thralls inevitably knew everything—albeit in a somewhat distorted fashion.

Helgi grinned evilly. "They're off to the kobold mines. I hear that the kobolds pulled a fast one on them. Gave them a lot of fake gold coins in exchange for some hostages. Bakrauf was spitting nails about it."

Cair had to shovel dung hastily to stop himself rolling on the floor laughing. There was a certain justice to it all.

"So why don't the *björnhednar* go, too? Then we could have time off," he said lazily once his shoulders had stopped shaking.

"Huh. Most of the time they leave their horses here anyway. Horses don't like bears much. Now that she's bespelled them, the *björnhednar* smell wrong. They sew that skin onto their living flesh, you know. They scream something horrible," said Helgi, ghoulishly. "The way they treat us you wouldn't think that they were slaves, too. But no rest for us. She only takes them with her and him, to Midgard. And horses aren't much use in the mines—there are too many narrow holes. Anyway, the place is a lot easier without her around. The *björnhednar* drink and dice and leave us alone when she's away."

A little later Cair asked once again with studied casualness, "Does anyone ever escape from this place?"

Helgi snorted, obviously not fooled one bit. "Forget the thought, friend. Where would you go? It's not too bad here in the stables. If you had to work in the foundries, maybe. But everywhere out there is worse. And it'll be winter soon. When the freezing mists come, nothing lives out there."

Bit by bit Cair established that Helgi and most of the thralls were born here, in captivity. Once, long ago, they'd come from a Norway that sounded primitive even compared to the Norway Cair had considered as such. Their seasons appeared a little different, too. Winter had its teeth into Telemark. Well, sheltered valleys existed.

Later he made an excuse to find out where the *björnhednar's* chambers were.

"There are plots against your safety," said Vortenbras. "Rumors that people of your faith were involved in the theft of the armring abound. It is being said that my accursed half-sister was one of your faith."

Szpak stared at the kinglet, "We would of course point her out as the thief if that was the case," he said dryly. The language of the Götar tribes was not so different that the two of them could not converse.

"Logic does not enter into these things," said Vortenbras dismissively.

Szpak continued to stare unblinkingly. He'd noticed that Vortenbras seemed to have trouble looking people in the eye. And right now he felt that the handful of knights trapped here needed every bit of help that they could get. "You have a treaty to abide by and a letter to the Holy Roman Empire guaranteeing us safe conduct."

"Safe conduct to Kingshall," said Vortenbras. "Not liberty to roam my lands. And stop worrying, outlander. If, as you say, your prince lives, then he will be being held for ransom. Doubtless Sverre's men work," he said, angrily. "We could have saved a great deal of effort and time had the Emperor sent me a force to deal with him, instead of an envoy that I must waste my men to protect. You and your men must remain in your quarters."

Juzef Szpak did not offer details of why he was so certain that

Manfred was imprisoned. The fact that the monks had used the shield of privacy to scry for the prince, and had located him, too, finding him in a cell . . . somewhere, was not one he'd gladly share with the gigantic man. Manfred's keepers had moved him, as far as the scryers could tell. But wherever he was being kept was very, very distant, and surrounded by dark magics. Juzef had decided that the greatest danger to his knights, and the holy clerics, was this man. Manfred had trusted him. And Manfred was now a captive.

"On the plus side," said Manfred, looking out through the stone bars at the latest group of thralls that had come to jeer. "At least we're in the same cell, this time. It is warmer and we still have clothes."

"On the negative side that troll-hag knew exactly who we were, and seemed to have a hand in this whole lot," said Erik sitting up slowly. The paralysis had left their arms first and was gradually fading from their legs. It still left them feeling as weak as half-drowned cats.

"True enough," said Manfred easing back to lean against the damp stone wall. "But then it has been obvious that there is more to this than a piece of theft and an accident with an avalanche." He ducked sideways. An apple core narrowly missed. "Why are these thralls taking it out on us? Some of them look as human as you or I."

Erik shrugged. "We're different. We're worse off than they are, and they dare not take out those that really oppress them."

"Uh-huh," said Manfred, "So what do we do now, Erik? Whatever turning you into one of her *björnhednar* means, it doesn't sound too good."

"It means that she will sew me into a bearskin, or rather sew a bearskin onto me."

"Well, it would be warm. I gather it isn't just a fur coat, Erik."

"No, it is actually stitched into the flesh and bound there, from what I recall about the stories of *ulfhednar*. There is more binding to it than mere stitches though. And you're the one she actually wanted, Manfred. You, or rather your role in the Holy Roman Empire, are bait."

"Now I know how the worm on a hook feels," said Manfred. "I'm not bait, Erik. If need be you will kill me."

It was said with perfect seriousness. Erik knew that Manfred had grown, grown a great deal. "*Linn gu Linn*," he said calmly. "And we're not dead yet."

Signy had cut through—but for a sliver—two bars now. It hadn't been easy. She hated to touch the wood, and she didn't dare to leave shavings on the ground. Her dress was now shorter than decency would allow. You could see her calves. She was desperately unsure of what was happening out there. Had her thrall been caught? The idea made her both afraid for herself, and unhappy. She'd never known any human that loyal before. It frightened her a little, too. He had accompanied two knights to find her, all this way and in such danger. How could she explain she wasn't prepared to go with them? Well, he was her thrall. She could just order him to take her away—if he was still free himself. Otherwise, well, loyalty called for loyalty. She would have to see if she could free him. The idea frightened her nearly as much as the idea of jumping down did. It was easily twenty feet to the stone flags.

Just then the door creaked open. Hastily she slipped the knife back into its sheath. She had to put her own hand over her mouth to stifle a glad cry. Cair was still free, and smiling. His teeth were very white in that dark face. He swung the heavy stone door closed behind him. "Good evening, Princess. I'm just stopping by to let you know that I'm getting some labor to let that cage down. I don't think I can lower you safely myself. I need to go and free a couple of prisoners. Then we'll have to break you out of there."

"I've cut through two of the bars."

He beamed. "Better and better. I will just go and fetch your replacement." He stepped out of the door again, but returned barely moments later with something over his arm. "Thrall's gear. I'm afraid we have to disguise you, milady. I've a rope here for you to haul it up on. Where is the hole?"

"I just have to kick them out." She kicked the bars, and he dropped his bundle and caught the falling bar. And dropped it with an air of surprise. "That burned."

"It does." She kicked the second one. He let it fall. "A lot of noise around, still," he said, moving over to the door, steel appearing suddenly in his hand.

No one came, and he came back to under her cage. He kicked the broken bars into a dark corner, and then expertly tossed a rope up through the hole. "There's a plait of straw, a pillow, and more clothes here. If you could . . . um . . . dress it in your clothes and leave it on the pallet. Anyone just looking in will assume you're there. I will . . . just go and organize a last few things."

Signy was grateful that having slatternly servants had meant that she'd learned to dress and undress herself. When Cair returned—cautiously and not looking up—she had to giggle. He was a thrall, of course. But sometimes he treated her as if she was his woman, not his owner. Of course there were scandalous stories of highborn women and elderly husbands . . . but she was a noble. Not like that at all. Was she?

"May I look up?" he asked cautiously

"You can. Can you tell me how I am to get down now?"

"Um. You'll have to jump. I could catch you, Princess."

She had to squeeze through the gap, touching the horrid wood. She had barely the strength to push through and fall.

Shaken and pale, she found herself in his strong arms.

After a while she said: "You can put me down now, Cair."

He did, hastily. And bowed. "Can we proceed, Princess? You are very pale."

He looked rather flushed.

CHAPTER 34

Trollheim

S toop your shoulders a bit more, Princess. Pretend that your stepmother has been sarcastic again." Instantly Cair regretted saying that. Firstly because she looked as if she'd just been whipped, and secondly because somehow her stepmother's head was in a jar next door. Still. They had a lot to do, and little time to do it in. The hilltop had been lowered, and the thralls and trolls were heading for food. Exits would be better guarded later in their rest period—he was not really sure if it was night. He had to press on with speed now, and no one would take her for a princess in that ragged skirt and top and that posture . . . The braided hair would not pass. A piece of folded cloth made a ragged head-kerchief for her.

"Now. At the cells, I will organize the diversion. You will have to go and free the two Franks, while the warder is out of the way. All three of you will have to be out of there, and up the stairwell beyond very quickly. As soon as the warder is in, lock the door. Here is my skeleton key. Most of the trolls and thralls will be at the dining hall. We should have a clear run up the outer passages. The packs are stashed in the stables, hidden in the hay. In case something goes wrong and I cannot join you, here is a diagram showing the way. Head away from the river, as Bakrauf and the kobold raiders will come that way. If something else goes wrong before you can get out—leave the Franks. Let the trolls hunt them, while you mingle with the thralls. You have my key. You can get free."

She looked at him with big eyes. She said nothing, just nodded.

"Let's go."

Head bowed, trying to look even smaller and more unimportant than she felt, Signy walked out of the troll queen's throne chamber and down into the troll hill. Here she was—"Signy you can't do anything right," "Signy you are so clumsy you can't be trusted with anything"—with a skeleton key. His only key. A map which she couldn't read. Instructions she was terrified of having to follow. And it wasn't "Signy you can't succeed at anything." The thrall simply assumed that she would. It was a frightening and somehow uplifting belief. The little hard core of honor that was the essence of Signy Siglunddottir was determined to do it. She kept a wary watch while he set the trap rope. At his gesture she moved past the door toward noisome cells, and waited, willing herself to be invisible.

"The mockers have eased off, and so has that damned paralysis," commented Manfred.

"Which does give us a nice uninterrupted view of the torture chamber," said Erik. "I think, Manfred, that we should take the first opportunity possible to get out of here. You stand in sight at the back. I'll stand here in the shadow next to the door. If someone comes close enough I should be able to pull them close and get at their throats. We'll see if we can get the doors opened."

There was a scream from outside. "Quickly, warder, quick help!"

A moment later someone was at the door. Fumbling with it. Erik snatched and grabbed . . . a thin arm.

He was confronted by a furious face . . . he recognized.

"You idiot Frank! You've made me drop the key into the grating!" hissed Signy in perfect Frankish. "Let go. I've got to try and get it back! Cair is relying on me."

An astonished Erik watched as she ran into the torture chamber, siezed a pair of tongs intended for another, nastier purpose and with a "Thor guide me," knelt out of sight by the door. There was a tearing sound. A few moments later, she was fiddling with the door again. It swung open. "Run. Follow me," she said, dropping the torturer's tongs with a clang. It was a miracle that such a little thing could have lifted them, let alone levered open a grating with them.

Manfred picked them up as he staggered out. Heavy iron things, they must have weighed thirty pounds. They'd been intended for torturing something large. "Close the cell door," she ordered. They followed her to the open stone door. Up the passage was fire and, unless Manfred's eyes deceived him, a troll hanging by one foot, yelling and struggling. "Up the stair. This way." She hauled at them to go the opposite direction, to the stairs where the mockers had stood, just as the troll-warder managed to break free and fall with a crash to the floor of the passage. They hadn't been quick enough. He'd seen them. With a roar he charged after his escaping prisoners.

Manfred hit him with all his strength—which was considerable—with thirty pounds of long-handled iron tongs. He bent the tongs to a forty-five degree angle on the troll's head, and dropped them from his stung hands.

The troll looked puzzled. And then slowly swayed and fell over.

"Cair wants him inside the dungeon, and the door locked," said their rescuer. She was already dragging at five hundred pounds of inert troll—a shrimp hauling a whale. "Come on."

Manfred grinned and grabbed troll feet. "I thought you said she was a mousy little thing, Erik?"

"That was you," said Erik, hauling the other side. "And where is Cair, Princess?"

WOOOMPH!

A huge explosion drowned the end of his last word.

At a brisk trot, out of a fog of steam, came Cair. Steam and pandemonium seemed to be filling the air. He grabbed the troll's arm and helped to haul it the last few yards. Signy locked the door, and Cair reached into a bundle tied behind his back. "You'll run faster with these." He pulled out two pairs of boots. "See if you can get your feet into them. I stole all of them trying to find a pair big enough for you, Prince."

He cocked his head, listening. "And then we must move. We're running behind."

Manfred struggled with the boots and swollen feet. "No good, I'm afraid I won't be running at all."

"Up on my back," said Erik.

Manfred blinked. "Don't be crazy, Erik."

"Do it, Manfred," commanded Erik, "or I'll slug you and have Cair tie you there. I am sworn to defend you."

"I do have horses arranged," said Cair. "We just have to get you there. Up on his back, Prince Manfred. Rather on his back than mine."

Manfred did as he was bid. "Well, I'm lighter than I used to be," he said from his piggyback perch, grinning despite the situation.

"Not enough," panted Erik.

"We can walk once we are in the outer ring," said Cair.

"Hope it's close," grunted Erik.

It was. "I feel sorry for your horse," said Erik, setting Manfred down. "I always have, but now I . . ." Pant. "Understand it at a whole new level."

"Talk later," said Cair, beckoning them onward impatiently. "We have to get to the horses. One is a good eighteen hands at the shoulder."

They made as good a speed as possible with Manfred limping manfully up the passage. Cair led. He carried one of the crude lamps in one hand and a bottle with a wick in the other. Having had one experience with the man's homemade grenades, Manfred didn't feel he needed to meet up with them again.

"What did you do back there?" asked Erik.

"Dropped an explosive down into the water-heating system," said Cair. "They're on a hot spring and they use the steam for raising the hilltop. It won't go up anymore. Not for a long time anyway."

"He's quite mad, you know," said Manfred conversationally, to Signy.

"He's not!" she said defensively. "He's a very, very good thrall. How can you say that when he came all this way with you to get me? I didn't know that it was you in particular that he was going to rescue, or I would have told him to leave you. I'm not a witch!"

"Hush. Patrol coming this way," said Cair. "Use the key to open the door there, Princess."

Signy hastily did, and they ducked inside. It was simply a store-room, and they waited in silence until the trolls had passed.

"With any luck they might still think it was a natural disaster," said Cair. "That's why I wanted it to look as if you might still be in your cells and in your cage, Princess. Come. This way."

He led them on into a stable. And their first encounter with a human. Cair held up a hand, saving the thrall from Erik. "Helgi. You can either come with us or I will tie you up. We're going back to the lands of men."

The thrall looked at them in terror. "Go. Me? No. Hel . . ."

Erik had his hand over the man's mouth. "You have rope?"

Cair produced some thick twine from a pocket, and they bound the wide-eyed thrall, and gagged him. "I would have thought that you'd have killed him," said Erik.

"Likewise," said Cair, digging in the hay. "Saddle up, gentle-men. Halters on the extra steeds. We're taking all of them." He turned to the bound thrall. "Best I do hit you, Helgi. Then you can say that you tried to give the alarm," and he hit him with neatly calculated force.

He handed Erik a roll of material. "Bandage the prince's feet."

Erik shook his head in amazement. "You think of everything, don't you?"

"I try," said Cair. "Life is like a complex game of chess. You can't guess quite all the moves. You will find cloaks and weapons, with the saddlebags. I have a bow for you, Princess."

A few minutes later they were leading the horses down the passage to the small portal.

And at the stone door things finally came adrift.

There was no keyhole for Cair's key-to-all-things.

"She said a word to make it close," offered Manfred, trying to remember. "Ah. *Fjalarr . . .* something."

"*Fjalarr fleggr,*" supplied Erik.

"A password, probably," said Cair looking around, tapping the wall suspiciously.

"*Fjalarr fleggr* just means 'hide trolls,'" said Signy. "Maybe you just have to tell it what to do."

Erik shrugged. Said, "Open door."

Nothing happened.

"Maybe you have to say 'door open,' or some other way," offered Signy. "I wish it would," she said anxiously.

And the stone door creaked open.

They stared at it. Manfred recovered his wits first. "Right. Into the saddle and ride," he said, cheerfully.

Erik held up a hand. "There is bound to be a watchman . . . We got rid of the stone-troll, but there is bound to be something else."

"Right," said Cair. "I will have a look . . ."

"Let me," said Erik. "I, uh, know what to look for this time." He peered out of the doorway. "There is a troll sitting a few yards off," he said, quietly. "I'll distract him, the rest of you ride. At least it is nothing like the stone-troll."

"I'll just block the pursuit for a bit," said Cair. He produced a large clay container, which had a candle attached to the wick. The wick to the clay bomb had been inserted part way down the candle, providing a crude timer. He lit it from the lamp, and placed on the stone door lintel.

Erik looked suspiciously at it. "Let's go, gentlemen, lady. I don't trust that device. I'd rather risk a troll."

They were all mounted, and Cair leaned over so that he could reach the lamp. "I intend to toss this grenade at the troll," he said "Your horses may panic. Hold tight. On the count of three. One and two and three . . ."

And then they were out on the hill slope, urging the horses to run while the watch-troll stirred into bellowing wakefulness. Cair flung his hissing and fizzing grenade.

And then there was no need to urge the horses at all. It was a good thing that all of them were better than average riders.

He rode exceptionally well for a thrall, thought Signy. Not as well as the other two—the tall angular blond Icelandic Ritter rode as if he were an extension of the horse, and the big Frankish one had plainly spent a great deal of time in the saddle. But her thrall had a seat that a fair number of Norse nobility—and most of her half-brother's bodyguard—would have envied. He also, to her shock, had belted on a sword. A trusted thrall might get permitted a belt-knife. Indeed, she'd offered him hers, and there was no question that he'd earned it. But a sword? A fair number of people at the court would have killed him then and there, and Hel take the consequences. But, she had to admit to herself, right now she was glad to have him with her, although the sword was an affront. The Franks she'd freed had been among those who had accused her of stealing the arm-ring of Telemark. True, they were all in the same leaky boat right now.

She pulled her horse in next to Cair. "I have to ask. Who gave you permission to carry steel, Cair?"

For an instant he looked startled. Then he smiled. "It's merely a disguise, Princess. Franks have no respect for someone who doesn't carry one."

"Oh? Their thralls carry edged steel?"

"In war they even allow their serfs to fight," he explained. "A great man needs many people to die with him. Ask the Ritters. Of course I'll throw it away if you wish me to."

She looked at the two knights. Well, it was well known that the Franks were degenerate. "Very well. But you'll have to take it off when we get back among civilized people again."

He smiled. "I look forward to the day when I am among civilized people again."

Somehow she got the feeling he was laughing. He had a bad habit of doing so.

Some hours later they halted at a stream to let the horses drink. "Are they still behind us, Erik?" asked Manfred, tiredly.

Erik peered. He was worried, firstly by the situation and secondly that Manfred should sound tired. The boy had stamina. "I can't see clearly. I think so. This light doesn't make it any easier."

"There are still seventeen of them," said Signy, peering into the murky distance.

Manfred rolled his eyes and grimaced. "Don't they ever give up?"

"Not easily, anyhow," said Erik, grimly.

Cair dismounted. "We have enough of a lead to rest for a few minutes and discuss strategy. To my shame I have planned little but getting us away from that place."

"The frightening thing is I think he really means it," said Manfred. "Help me down here, Erik. I don't want to land on these feet of mine."

Erik helped him down, and Manfred began to unwind his bandages. His feet were indeed a mess. Cut, swollen, purple in places, red and yellow in others. Several of the wounds had begun to go septic and were oozing.

Signy took one look at them, and said, "Cair, do we have time to boil water?"

Cair shook his head. "No, Princess. We need to lose the pursuit first."

"Then have you got any alcohol?" she asked, stepping over to the stream and picking broad leaves, crushing them as she spoke.

Cair dug into a pack. "It was among the things I relieved those fake bears of, Princess." He hauled out a small metal flask. Opened it, and smelled it. Caraway and raw alcohol assaulted everyone's nostrils.

"Good," said Signy. "I will need it for his feet."

"I'd rather put it inside me than outside," said Manfred reaching hopefully. Signy took the flask instead, giving him a dirty look. "You are getting enough poisons in your system," she said sternly. "Look." She pointed to a red line of inflammation creeping up his leg. "You are getting blood poisoning from this. I will need clean cloths, Cair."

Erik noticed that Cair was smiling as he dug in a saddle bag. The edge of the fake thrall's worry had at least been eased. Erik was having to reassess his opinions of the man. He had, after all, rescued them. And he'd treated the thrall in the stable gently—relatively speaking. Still, something about him made Erik's bodyguard instincts prickle. "How did you get all this gear from the *björnhednar*, Cair?" he asked, casually.

Cair grinned evilly, as he handed a piece of fabric to the princess. "They were drunk and I locked them into the sauna. I wedged the inner door and locked the outer one. Good solid doors. When—or if—they get out, they won't be doing anything for a long time."

Saunas were very popular in Iceland. Some even made use of steam from natural vents. "I . . . don't think I want you as an enemy, Cair," said Erik, blanching.

"What are you doing, woman?" asked Manfred warily, and not without reason. She had slipped a very workmanlike dagger from her sleeve, and was wiping it with alcohol.

"I need to open those cuts up, and clean them out. This will hurt," she said with perfect equanimity. "Keep still."

Manfred looked warily at the knife. "Uh. Can't you just use magic?"

Signy pointed the knife at him. "I am *not* a witch. I wish I could do any magic! Do you think that I would need my thrall to come and rescue me if I was a witch? You're a fool. I would have used magic to drive you all away, if I had had any. I would have made *you* into a mouse for insulting me. I wish we'd left you for the troll-queen to give to Jagellion. Now hold still. Try and behave like a man."

"She's the best horse-doctor at Kingshall, Prince Manfred," said Cair, his lips twitching.

She looked up at him. "Maybe you'd better cut, Cair." She frowned fiercely at Manfred. "He may be a thrall, but he has good steady hands. He sees better than I do. And I trust him with my horses." It was apparent from her tone that no higher compliment could be paid.

Erik mulled over this outburst as Cair opened several infected cuts as neatly as any surgeon, or the Emperor's new carving steward, de Massibugo. Signy washed them out with the caraway-scented firewater, and then put the crumpled coltsfoot leaves on Manfred's feet. "We will have to rebandage them with the same bandages, Princess," said Cair. Obviously that would not have been acceptable for one of her horses.

She wrinkled her nose and squinted at them. Shrugged. "It will just have to do, Cair. We'll boil and wash them at the first chance we get. I want to see if I can find some black snakeroot to bathe those feet in, too."

Cair was a proficient bandager, as well as his other accomplishments. Erik noted that the delay had let the pursuing trolls get closer. And she was right. There were seventeen of them.

Manfred stood up gingerly. He bowed to her as she cleaned her knife and slipped it back into her sleeve-sheath with un-princess-like proficiency. "Princess. I owe you my thanks," he said formally, and respectfully. "They feel, well, not too good, but better than they did before. My gratitude to you and your man. I apologize for some of my remarks. You've shamed me. I said things in jest that weren't funny. We thought you were a quiet woman. A mouse. I was wrong." He smiled. "You'll pardon my saying so, but you're more like a lion than a mouse. You might have wanted to leave us behind, but I'd rather have a physician and courageous lady like you with us than half a dozen knights. I was mistaken. I apologize."

She colored. Looked awkward. "It is nothing. You should

mount and get the weight off your feet, until they can be properly treated."

"Let me give you a leg up, Manfred," said Erik.

"He thinks I'm dying," said Manfred, with a grin, accepting. "I can tell. He's babying me instead of bullying me."

Erik climbed into the saddle. "You make pretty speeches to the ladies, but all I get is insults."

They began to ride. Erik had noted that the daughter of the royal house of Telemark rode astride with the ease of an old cavalry trooper, her skirts hitched awkwardly. Erik weighed up Manfred's little speech. The boy was three times the womanizer he'd ever be. And he had an instinct for politics. There had been that mention of Jagellion. These were murky, complex doings, indeed. He could do worse than follow Manfred's lead on this. "My lady. I also spoke a little out of turn. My thanks for what you have done for my Godar's heir."

She bit her lip. And then gestured with her elbow at Cair. "You should thank my thrall. His loyalty in coming with you resulted in you being free instead of in a dungeon. He didn't know that you'd tricked him and come to capture me."

Erik looked back at Cair. And caught a quick shake of the head. Curious indeed. "We . . . have had to reevaluate things, milady," he said disarmingly. "Your man told us you were no witch."

Manfred hadn't seen Cair's head shake. He turned in the saddle. "Master Cair. We owe you our liberty if not our lives. Don't think I am ungrateful, but every time I've sought explanations, we've been plunged into the next crisis. Can I ask now without risking my neck?"

"No, Prince Manfred, not right now," said the man with perfect urbanity. "Because I think we should gallop up this slope while we are out of sight of our pursuit."

And he put his heels into his steed.

Erik had trained with the masters of this kind of skirmish on Vinland's plains. It wasn't a bad point to gallop. The apparently flat, bleak fell had hidden rills and folds, and a canny horseman could keep out of sight, but he was sure that they were being followed by scent. And he was also sure that that little gallop had been because Cair wasn't ready to explain anything.

By default Erik took over leading the party away from the pursuing trolls. Manfred was plainly a little fevered from the sepsis on his feet, and Cair was also obviously no countryman. Thus it fell to Erik or Signy. And Signy, although she had seemed to have fantastic eyesight, did not have any experience of avoiding foes. Erik found the little princess peculiarly naive about some things. One of them was just what sort of man her "thrall" was. She was full enough of her own surprises though. She'd dropped an arctic hare, with a single arrow, at a canter, at two hundred paces. Erik knew that there were very very few huntsmen who could do as well. He knew he couldn't.

Eventually, they just had to stop. They'd gained some time and distance on their foes. Erik judged that spending some of that time on resting the horses and themselves would be time well spent. Besides, he was worried about Manfred. He was not used to the boy being sick.

They stopped in a tiny copse of stunted trees next to a boggy fen patch. Not, except for the possibility of firewood, the sort of place Erik would have chosen, but Signy said that it looked good for the herbs she wanted. The trees, unfortunately, wouldn't provide what they needed for the trolls—good strong lances.

As soon as they dismounted, Signy set off to collect her herbs, coolly giving orders as she did so. "I need a fire. And hot water. We need to draw the poison out of his feet. And those dressings need to be washed and wrung out and dried as well as may be. There's a little forage for the horses . . ."

"I put two bags of oats on the spare horses, Princess. I'll feed them. And see them rubbed down."

She smiled at Cair. "He's a rare thrall."

Erik nodded. "Few knights could organize a campaign as well," he said, trying to keep the irony out of his voice. "I'll give him a hand as soon as I have a fire going. No, Manfred. You will lie down. You can tend the fire once I've organized a firebow."

"There are several tinderboxes with flint and steel. Our bear-men were well equipped," said Cair, unloading horses.

Erik shook his head in amazement. "Never mind knights. There are few quartermasters that organize as well as you do."

"But a number that are even better thieves," said Cair cheerfully.

Erik smiled. The fellow was incorrigible. Even if he felt that he couldn't trust him a finger-width, he had to be amused. "That's hard to believe, too, looking at this lot." He looked across at where

Signy was picking her way along the edge of the fen. "What's your game, Cair? What are you trying to keep quiet about? Why did you want her to believe that you're a good thrall who came along with us . . . instead of the other way around?"

The slight sardonic smile that usually hovered on Cair's lips was absent. "I am content to be her thrall," he said. And it looked as if he meant it.

Erik shook his head, and blew the sparks into a tiny flame. For a while he concentrated on nursing the fire. Then he left it to Manfred and walked over to where Cair was rubbing down the horses with a handful of dry grass. "Give you a hand?" he offered.

"I'd rather you gutted and skinned that hare. I've never done that before."

So, wherever he came from, the man was ignorant of the kind of field craft most ordinary freemen would take for granted. Either he was born a peasant churl—and most of those could gut a poached rabbit before they were breeched—or he'd been born to power and wealth. Or he was an oblate, given to the cloister. But no oblate was that good with a knife. Besides, he spoke Frankish too well. No regional peasant accent—the Frankish of Mainz—with a very slight Aquitaine burr, as taught by a tutor, no doubt. "I'll show you. If you want to pass as a thrall, you need to know things like that."

Cair grinned. "Good idea." He glanced across at Signy, who was still some distance off. "It's to not hurt her, you understand. She has lost everything. I am going to have to take her away from her whole way of life. She was born and bred in this culture, as a princess, bound to her duty. To marry for the royal house, to serve its honor. Now, she has nothing. If she needs a thrall, then I will be it."

"To be honest with you, Cair," Erik said, as he neatly eviscerated the hare. "I'm coming to doubt that 'thief-finding' myself. It is, as you said, out of character. There are more complex magical tests. Things that are beyond fakery."

Cair shrugged. "Believe me, there is no such thing as either magic or being beyond fakery. I'll take her beyond the reach of Telemark or the Empire."

Erik had reason to know that magical powers were real enough. But the reference to "beyond the reach of the Empire" said

Lithuania to him. But no Lithuanian could doubt the existence of magic. Well, a sceptic would find reason to doubt his own senses if need be. There was no point in arguing about it. "Surely her mother would protect her?"

"Stepmother. And she's dead, friend. I haven't told Signy, but I found Queen Albruna's head in a jar in that troll fortress. Anyway, that woman made her life a misery. Honeyed poison in her speech, and constantly belittling the girl. And she'd have seen that Signy's marriage to Hjorda of Rogaland went through, even if I had dealt with this arm-ring fakery. Hush. She's nearly here."

Signy stumbled into view with a handful of herbs. A woman who could drop a hare from a running horse at two hundred paces, who struggled with buckles and tripped over tussocks? An idea came to Erik. He resolved to watch how well she dealt with close objects.

Manfred looked at his feet. To him they looked a fairly unpleasant sight, but perhaps less so than when she'd initially bandaged them. But it hadn't stopped him feeling feverish and shaky. He couldn't afford to sicken on them now. And it wasn't even for something understandable like a sword thrust. There was really no dignity in it. He would be like Lord Arabladan, butt of everyone's jokes because he missed the charge at Salamanca because he had dismounted to ease the pain of his piles.

"What is it?" he asked warily as she handed him a hot and not-pleasant-smelling cup.

"Chamomile and bog-myrtle tea. You have a fever. Drink it."

"Couldn't I rather have some of that armor polish . . . that alcohol?" he asked hopefully.

"No. This is better for you," she said firmly. "Drink it down. All of it."

Cair grinned from where he was chopping a black root into some more boiling water. "She is treating you just like she does the horses. And they recover."

"He's about the same size as one," said Signy. She bit her lip. "It's the only way I can deal with people, Prince Manfred. Drink the rest, now. It is good for you."

He did. It was still vile. They bathed his feet in yet another potion. "Horseweed and black snakeroot," said Signy when he enquired. He wished that he hadn't asked. She poulticed them with more chamomile leaves and boiled his bandages in the horseweed and black snakeroot mixture, before hanging them out to dry on sticks by their fire.

Erik had in the meanwhile been grilling the hare.

"In among your looting you didn't happen to bring any salt did you?" he asked Cair.

"Unfortunately not," said Signy's "thrall." "Please don't beat me, lord."

It was said in jest, but Signy turned on Erik like a vixen to someone threatening her cubs. "He's mine. Nobody beats him."

"I wouldn't dream of it," said Erik respectfully. "Too much salt is bad for you anyway, I'm sure."

They ate. Manfred knew he ought to be ravening, but he ate because Erik looked worried when he didn't. After that Erik took first watch, and they slept wrapped in the cloaks that the mysterious supposed thrall-cum-assassin had allowed their enemy to provide.

When it was time for them to move again Manfred found that the other three had cheerfully conspired to let him sleep through his watch.

"And how are the prince's hooves this morning?" asked Cair. "If it is morning. Funny, I'd read of the land of the midnight sun, but I expected it to be lighter."

"Except that it stays dark in winter," said Erik. "So you aren't there. And how are your feet, Manfred?"

"I'd swear they're better. I'm certainly feeling a bit better. What's for breakfast?"

"*Flattbrød* on the run," said Cair. "The trolls are not more than two miles back. They've not stopped to rest."

"And more chamomile and bog-myrtle tea," said Signy, handing it to him. "Don't pull such a face. Some people like chamomile tea."

"They're welcome to it," said Manfred, drinking it all the same. The look on Erik's face said that resistance would be futile. Besides, it, or something, had made him feel a good deal better. Of course, some protest was obligatory.

They rode out, leaving the hare bones and ashes for the trolls.

It was a long ride across lands that grew increasingly more treacherous and boggy, full of half-frozen hummocks and apparently solid ground where the horses' hooves would burst through into fetlock-deep mud. Black mud, fetid and stinking.

The second time that they'd had to backtrack, Signy sidled her horse up to Erik. "Knight. We need to make for that line over there. The lighter plants. The ground is dryer there." Erik could barely make out the difference in plant color, but Signy obviously could. Erik was no fool, and his brief was to keep Manfred alive. Not to lead the way. So Signy took over. She took them along "trails" marked by plant types that Erik began to recognize after a while as dry-loving. But she could pick them out across a hundred yards of valley. He could only do so from ten or fifteen yards off.

Even Manfred noticed. "You have superb eyesight, Princess," he said.

She shook her head. "Not really. The colors are slightly different. You can only see the plants when you get closer. And I see well enough out here where there is light and air, but put me in front of a loom or a tambour frame and I can hardly see at all."

"I knew a warrior like that in Vinland," said Erik, thoughtfully. "He was long-sighted. Could drop a buck at full range, but half the time he'd miss one under his feet."

Signy colored slightly. "Yes. I do that, too. I'm very clumsy."

"It's not clumsiness," said Erik. "It's long-sight, Princess. I wondered about it when I watched you gathering herbs, to be honest. I imagine that you can see things which are far off clearly, but those that are really close with difficulty and probably not with clear definition. I do believe that you can correct it with eyeglasses."

"Oh no. I tried a pair of those that a visiting Jarl from Vestfold had. They made things even worse."

Riding behind them Cair wanted to kick himself. Hard. He'd had a long-sighted sailor on lookout duty on his flagship. He knew that the condition existed. He also knew just how it could be corrected. Convex and concave lenses. One of them was suited to shortsightedness. The other dealt with the opposite problem. And he'd personally been too blind to see it. Well, Erik Hakkonsen had done the princess no small favor, accidentally. It could be corrected. There were those who made their living by traveling, making eyeglasses. Some of them made things worse rather than better, apparently. But there were those among them who had achieved great reputations from the results they'd achieved.

"I believe there are different types of eyeglasses," said Erik, but Signy wasn't listening anymore. Instead she was staring intently back.

Cair could just make out the dust back across the plain. Two plumes.

"We have more pursuit. Many more trolls are coming," said Signy worriedly.

"Well, I can't say I'm delighted that there are more, but why is that worse than the situation as it is?" asked Manfred. "We couldn't fight off those who're after us now."

Erik shook his head at him, as if disappointed in his charge. "They can divide up and flank us. Drive us like game. They know this countryside. They'll herd us."

"Look for signs of it and break out of the encirclement. That'll be the way they don't want us to go," said Manfred, obviously reciting something he'd been told.

"Well, at least you are thinking. I wondered if you could," said Erik. "Breaking through a flank is always risky, though."

"As I learned off Naples," said Cair, wryly. "Sometimes it is better to come back through the middle."

The next two days on the run proved that the worst fears of the fugitives were correct. There were now some eighty foes harrying them and they were definitely trying to head them off from the forest that was now visible on the horizon. They'd managed to cut some lances for Manfred and Erik, but Cair had contrived himself a troll club—a heavy chunk of basalt bound into a four-foot pole. "If Manfred can club one unconscious, but Erik cannot effectively stab one, I'll leave knocking them over to you knights and settle for hitting them on the head. Preferably from behind."

Manfred had taken a good look at the "club." "Well, I like it—but I think I'll make me something heavier. What I'd like is something more like a miner's mattock."

"That looks like the perfect piece of basalt for the job." Cair had pointed out a long triangular piece, among the fragments they'd stopped next to, It weighed perhaps twelve pounds, three times the size of his own rock. "For someone of your more delicate build, eh?"

Manfred weighed in one hand. Nodded. "Give me a hand with binding it, will you? I tried doing this when I was a gossoon. Thought I'd make me a stone axe. It was a dismal failure."

Cair had cheerfully helped him bind it with neat lashings. Erik was struck by how quick and precise the man was with his hands. If he'd been an assassin, he'd missed a good career as a jeweler, or perhaps a silversmith. But if he was an assassin, he was a well-born one, even if he did not ride like a knight.

By the end of the second day they'd lost one of the led horses in a close encounter, and it looked as if the trolls were going to succeed in encircling them. It seemed that the trolls could go without rest a lot longer than either horses or humans could. Their food for the horses was getting low too. It had grown steadily colder as they'd fled. Little patches of snow lay in the lee edges of rocks, and the larger tussocks here.

"They're going to close on us soon," said Erik, tiredly. "We'll have to try to push out of the gap."

"I suspect that's what they want us to do," said Cair. Erik had found days on the run together had given him more respect for the man. He wasn't nearly as good a rider as Manfred or Signy, who almost seemed to will her horses to obey and adore her. By ordinary standards he was a fair rider, but in this group he was the weakest. However, he made no allowances for this, replacing skill with determination. The only thing in which he exceeded that determination was in straight, pragmatic common sense—and the cunning of . . . well, it was more than a fox. More like a lynx. Erik waited for him to offer his idea. Cair was looking back, plainly thinking.

The land had risen in some low folds with the hills running down toward the forest, with some trees extending from the valleys. They were on a ridge, and could see the files of trolls on either side. "I think we need to go back down there, and then make for the higher hills." The forest lay to their right, and the hills to the left.

"How?" asked Erik, thoughtfully. "Night-proper doesn't seem to fall here. I'd say that what we need is some sort of cover, mist, darkness . . ."

"What about smoke?" suggested Signy.

Erik and Cair found themselves nodding in unison. They'd been cursing the cold wind that took their scent back to the trolls. "It's the best we can achieve, I suppose. It won't be a hot enough fire to kill them. Let's send it back on them and follow behind it. They'll assume we're running on, and will presumably try to get ahead."

Soon the flames were licking at uprooted dead bushes, and Erik was proving what a master horseman he actually was, riding with a burning brand while controlling a restive, rolling-eyed horse well enough to lean down and touch fire to the dry grass. Only Signy felt even vaguely capable of trying it on the other side. Manfred held the horses—to spare his feet—while Cair lit fires on foot. It was not the kind of fire steppe or prairie folk use for herding game; it was far too inclined to go out, and much more smoky. But with brands to relight it and with the wind spurring it into occasional towers of flame in little patches of dry birch, they chased fire before them, back onto the center of the line of troll pursuit, with heavy smoke.

And then it all went wrong.

The first Cair knew of it was a flurry of snowflakes against his bare neck. The sky had been heavy and gray. Now—specifically where they were—it was snowing. Big wet flakes. Blizzardlike. "Hell's teeth. Nothing will burn in this," yelled Manfred.

"It'll just have to do as cover instead," said Erik.

It was doing a better job than the smoke would have. They rode on, keeping together as the stuff drifted down thick and fast. They had barely a mile to cover before they expected to encounter the skirmish line, but Cair thought that they'd be bogged down in the snow before then. He knew little of snow, except that he was sure he didn't like it. Erik and Signy knew snow well, however. "This isn't natural," said the Icelander.

"Bakrauf," said Signy. "She can control weather with her magic."

Cair shivered. "I don't know about magic, but at least it should hide us from the trolls."

"Not likely, friend," said Erik grimly. "They hunt by scent."

"And they love ice and snow," put in Signy.

"They're welcome to it," said Manfred.

As he said this they blundered into a little gully, full of birches, snow, and trolls.

The trolls were just as surprised as they were, but as they'd been riding virtually parallel with the gully, some of the trolls in it were effectively behind them.

"Ride," yelled Erik, spurring his horse, dropping the point of the makeshift lance. There wasn't a lot of time for his horse build momentum, but Erik still hit the troll on the shoulder, and spun and dropped it. The lance shivered and he tossed it aside. Manfred, just behind him, had a clear run.

Signy turned to yell at Cair. Her horse chose that moment to stumble. She was half turned when its right fore struck some snow-hidden obstacle. Off balance, she was catapulted from the saddle.

"Erik!" bellowed Manfred, struggling to turn his horse. He dropped the rein of the led horses and the two of them rode back, to see Cair piling off his horse, running to Signy as she lay on the ground. He had her in his arms.

"She's stunned," he yelled. "Take her." Erik was there moments before Manfred . . . and two trolls. He hauled the landed-fish gasping princess up over the pommel, as Manfred hit one of the trolls with his lance. He didn't have Erik's momentum. The troll staggered but did not go down. Erik reached for his sword . . . and saw Cair slap the rump of his horse. Trolls frightened horses enough. An extra slap they did not need. "Take her away!" As he struggled to control his steed, Erik saw Manfred, his horse rearing, swing his makeshift troll club at the second of the trolls—which was making a grab at Cair.

The horse and the club came down together, as Cair dodged back and fell over a broken birch in the snow.

Manfred's club shattered. So did half the troll's skull.

And it fell like a great tree, onto the man on the ground.

Cair's last yell was, "Ride!"

He disappeared under what must have been at least a ton of troll.

Across the saddle bow, Signy gave a weak gasp and struggled. Erik held her fast and yelled, "Retreat! There are more of them coming."

Signy fought for breath. Fought for freedom. Found herself pinioned by a strong arm. She'd had all the breath knocked out of her by the fall. And hit her head on something too. Even her distant vision was blurred right now.

Cair hadn't so much dismounted after she'd fallen, as thrown himself off his horse and run unheeding past a troll to get to her.

As she tried to draw breath and sit up, her thrall had seemed as tall as Vortenbras. He'd seemed even stronger than her hated half-brother when he had picked her up. She'd felt her fingers close instinctively on his jerkin. And then he thrust her away, upward, letting her be hauled over a pommel.

The horse whinnied and bucked, driving what little air she had in her lungs out again. As the horse turned, she saw Cair, with the sword she'd been shocked to see him carry, lunging at a troll five times his size, yelling at Erik to take her to safety. And Manfred, swinging that huge club, hit the troll. It was bending forward, snatching at Cair. The blow saved Cair . . .

And killed him.

She saw Cair stumble and go down, as the huge mass of troll slowly fell.

Desperately, she willed that he would somehow get free. He must. He must!

With a terrible, unreal seeming slowness, she saw how snow and broken tree fragments sprayed up around the fallen troll, as it landed on top of Cair. Somehow she managed to scream, although it sounded more like a pitiful mew.

She must have fainted, because when she next knew what was happening, she was sitting on a rock, with her head between her knees.

She sat up. Manfred, sword in hand was standing watchfully next to her. "Erik has gone after the rest of the horses. They ran when we did. We're going to have to ride. The trolls are behind us still."

Somehow she couldn't bring herself to care very much. Erik reappeared leading her own horse, Cair's, and one of the spare mounts. "Are you fit to mount up, Princess? They're coming fast."

Manfred tossed her up into the saddle, and, because she did not know what else to do, they rode, switchbacking up the steep hill.

Her mind kept recreating the scene where the troll fell on her loyal man.

Cair had kept a cool head through nearly everything life had ever thrown at him. Now, he panicked.

The broken saplings he'd fallen over had cracked and shattered as the weight of the troll descended onto them and then onto him, pressing him into a snow grave.

He was going to die, drowned, not in the sea, but in frozen water, trapped under the body of his foe.

She looked back at the files of trolls following them. The hills were deceptive, more like steps than hills, leading ever higher. They'd gained enough distance to be able to pause, to take stock.

"He was a good thrall," she said quietly.

Erik felt as if he was a geyser finally blowing. He hadn't realized how much it had been bothering him, and, he had to admit how guilty he felt about misjudging the man. He turned on her, his voice icy. "Princess Signy, you are very astute in some ways. You're good with simples, great with animals. But you don't know people very well, do you? Someone put a thrall-brand on that man. That doesn't make a man a thrall. Not that man, anyway. The only way he would ever have been a thrall was by choice. He chose to serve you. He also chose to die for you."

She was as white as a ghost—but sat stiff in the saddle. Her chin went up as he spoke. "What else could a good thrall do? He was *my* thrall. A thrall must follow."

Manfred turned in the saddle and looked at her. This was not Manfred the spoiled boy-knight, or the Manfred who had emerged from Venice, older and wiser. This was Manfred the prince who one day would give both judgment and justice. "No. That one was no follower, ever, Princess. I misjudged him. Erik misjudged him. And he let you misjudge him, because he believed that it would be easier for you. You were wrong about how he got here. He, on his own, went looking for you. And we followed *him*."

"He came looking for me, alone?" Now Signy looked taken aback. Erik realized that this was alien to her small Norse world. A thrall could not do that. Not without a freeman ordering it.

Erik nodded. "He said to me that you had lost everything, that at least you would have a loyal thrall. He chose that because he wanted you to be happy. Or at least not too unhappy. I think he loved you very much."

Now she had lost her earlier rigidity. Actually, she looked as if she might fall out of the saddle. But Erik was not in any mood to relent. Not when she said, "But I am a princess of the Royal House of Telemark. He was a thrall."

Erik looked at her in silence for a long moment before he spoke. "Princess," he said, "if you were captured on Viking and held for ransom, how many ducats do you think that your captors would ask for your release? What *blot*-price for a royal princess?"

She shrugged. "Perhaps a hundred thousand ducats."

Erik smiled wryly. "An acceptable ransom. Now ask Manfred what his uncle would have paid for the head of Cair Aidin?"

Manfred gaped. "What! Is *that* who he was? A sailor from Lesbos! Huh. Talk about barefaced gall! No wonder he got away with blue murder! When did you figure this out, Erik?"

"At the last. That comment about Naples. That's exactly what he did when the Genovese and the Duke of Naples thought they had him on the run. Remember, the old Fox of Ferrara was lecturing you about it while we waited for Sforza. But I've been suspicious for a while. Can you imagine what a prize you were to him?"

Manfred shook his head incredulously. "Princess. Your *thrall's* head—not attached to his body—would have brought you a cool half a million ducats. And the same again from Venice. Lesser amounts from the Genovese, and I know Aquitaine had a price on his head, too. His brother Aruj might have paid even more for him, alive."

Signy looked puzzled and hurt. And doubtful too. "If he was a noble, then why did he not have his brother ransom him? Who is 'Cair Aidin' anyway?"

"One of the Redbeards," explained Manfred. When that plainly meant absolutely nothing to her he went on. "The brother-captains of the Barbary corsairs. And that is why he could not let himself be ransomed. The Empire and every nation which owns ships on the Mediterranean would pay for the most notorious pirate and raider of the western Mediterranean, dead."

"You mean he was a raider chieftain?" She looked stunned.

Of course such a man would be much respected by the Norse, Erik realized. "I suppose so," he said. "He and his brother also effectively ruled an area the size of about half of all the Norse kingdoms in North Africa."

Signy shook her head again. "But he allowed himself to be branded as a thrall! He worked in my stable."

Manfred pulled a wry face. "He worked in Bakrauf's stable, too. And look what he did to her. She couldn't hold him prisoner. If he worked in your stable—he stayed by choice."

"He was always very good to the horses," she said in a small voice.

Erik suddenly realized that in her odd, terribly limited world, that was as high a praise as she had ever given anyone. Perhaps, as she ever could.

She continued in that odd little wooden voice. "He always said kind things to me. He made me believe that I could do things. My stepmother always made me believe I couldn't." Her chin quivered. "He made me laugh."

This childlike princess had always been emotionally deprived of any real affection, or praise. No wonder she looked so gauche when Manfred had thanked her. "He was a good man," said Manfred awkwardly.

"No, he wasn't," said Erik, regretting his earlier harshness. This child-princess could hardly help her upbringing. At least he understood it. With his own background he had a far better idea of what this Norse ice-maiden would value. "They called him the Lynx of the Sea. I've heard any number of stories. He'd trick his foes, out-think them, arrive when he was not expected. He was the greatest of raiders. The cleverest and best. But the only person he ever was 'good' for, was you, Princess. Remember him with honor."

"You will tell me all the stories," she said turning to Erik, fiercely. "I will find the greatest skalds to have him made immortal. Tell me his whole name again."

"Cair Aidin."

"I had been hoping I could avoid you discovering that, Erik Hakkonsen," said the man himself, hauling his weight up onto the ledge.

"Cair! But we thought you were dead!" exclaimed Manfred, the only one of them not too stunned to speak.

"You were mistaken, but only just." He grinned crookedly. "Just as well, eh? The Emperor will actually want to see my head before he pays for it."

He looked at Signy, who was sitting as if frozen on her horse, looking straight ahead. "What is wrong, Princess?" he asked, gently.

"You're dead. I saw you die. This is just your *fulgyr*. I will not look at it."

"No, I'm alive, truly, Princess." Cair grinned. "You never gave your thrall permission to die."

Her reaction was to bury her head in her hands.

"Hell's teeth," said Manfred, peering over the rock lip. "Look, the trolls are on their way up here. But I still want to know: how did you get away this time, Cair?"

Cair mounted his horse. "I'll tell you as we ride," he said. "I'm very glad to see you have my horse for me. I abandoned one of the spares back down there when I saw that I could save a lot of time by coming straight up the rock band. Besides I'd never have gotten the horse past them. Fortunately for me, you were very visible from below."

Looking back, it was apparent that the entire force that had set off to raid the kobolds was now hot on their heels. This trail had no side branches or possible escapes on it. If it didn't open up—and it showed no sign of doing so—the trolls would capture them soon. The end seemed very near, short of any more miracles. It didn't stop Signy both refusing to look Cair in the eye, and yet constantly checking to see that he was in the saddle, while he explained.

"The troll fell on top of me, all right. Had we been on rock or even sand, I'd have been as flat as a grease spot. But there was a thick snow drift in the gully. The troll pushed me flat into it."

He laughed. "To think I should be grateful for snow. The troll was a lot wider than I was. A lot wider and a lot bigger—and snow must have supported more of its weight than it did of mine. I must admit that I panicked. One lungful of air wasn't going to get me out. I was scrabbling when I hit a tree branch. Skinned my hand—but the branch wiggled. I pulled it. It hit me in the face . . . and there was a hole. I could breathe and I could hear. And what I could hear was enough to make me lie still and breathe. Bakrauf caught up with the ones that had nearly caught us, and she was spitting nails. All I had to do was wait in the snow and dig my way out once they had passed. I found one of the horses and set off after the trolls, and you. And then I saw a way of climbing straight up and avoiding the trolls and getting to you. Very unheroic," he said matter-of-factly.

Erik couldn't believe it. Nothing short of magic and heroism could have got Cair Aidin out of that one. Erik had little doubt both had been called into account.

The trail had become narrower and steeper. They'd ended up dismounting on sections of it which were little more than a scramble up a rock slide. Yet it was obvious, despite this, that the trail was a well-traveled one and that the trolls were pressing hard to catch them. The trail was hemmed with cliffs, and to continue on was the only option.

Eventually the trail did arrive at an end point—a hundred-yard-long valley ending against a sheer rock wall of gray-black basalt. It was several hundred feet high, smooth and sheer, and stretched above the rim of the valley as far as the eye could see in either direction. It didn't look climbable . . . It looked as if even birds might turn around and go the other way.

"And now?" asked Manfred

"The trail leads somewhere."

"I suppose we may as well follow it."

The trail did lead somewhere. It led to the rock wall. It stopped there, as there was nowhere further to go. The trolls were coming on now at a flat run.

"All right. Let's at least go down fighting," said Manfred, drawing his sword.

Erik did likewise.

"I lost mine," said Cair

Signy said nothing. She just held her knife out to him.

"I take it with pride, Princess."

She bit her lip and nodded. Took her bow and set an arrow to the string. Picked a mark.

And the rush halted. And then . . .

"They're backing off," said Signy incredulously. "I don't believe it!"

"I can only think of one possible reason," said Erik, grimly, looking at the basalt cliffs. He'd swear that a part of it had moved . . . it was almost as if an eye had blinked. But if Erik hadn't been looking just there, just then, he would never have seen it. Whatever it was that lay sleeping inside that rock, you surely didn't ever want it to wake up.

Then Erik realized that they were also being watched by a small man, leaning against the cliff. He was swarthy skinned and with a black curly head of hair and a large beard, almost as broad as his wide chest. The look of unholy amusement in his dark eyes was alarming, to put it mildly.

So what had made the trolls back off? The eye in the endless line of serpentine basalt cliff—or this dwarf?

"Three humans and a throwback halfling," drawled the dwarf. "My. What a fascinating gift." He cocked his head inquiringly. "Or are you perhaps not a gift from the troll-people?"

"No," said Cair. "We're just passing through."

The black dwarf seemed to find that very funny. Behind him a black stone doorway swung open.

CHAPTER 35

Trollheim

Bakrauf ground her big square teeth. It was steamy and hot here in her throne chamber. She hated heat. Signy's broken cage lay on the floor. The straw plait and old riding dress had been torn to pieces. "If I get my hands on them they will die by the slowest and most awful means I can devise," she said through gritted teeth.

"Send the wild hunt to fetch them," he said. "We dare not go any farther than we have."

She raised her eyes to the roof. "Fool. You made me use them to cross the river to consult with Jagellion. I have used up all the debts they owe me for this year. If I called them again, before yuletide, they'd come. They'd come for *me*. I need to take Signy and the Frank prince in some other way."

"Well, you can't." Her son almost seemed to enjoy her fury. "The black dwarves will have them now and they're not going to part with them. Not cheaply anyway."

She made throttling movements with her square hands. "Those . . . thieving twisters. The pipes and mechanisms that are wrecked in the geyser . . . The dwarves will make us pay and pay to fix them. And who else could have helped those snot kobolds to cheat us?"

Her monster son paced. "We dare not go against the dwarves. You know what happened last time."

"I know. I know," she said, angrily. "Even those cursed *Ás* make deals with them rather than fight the tricky little rats." She smashed her fist into her palm. It sounded like a gunshot. "What I want to know is, who was the fourth one? Where did he come from? How was he able to get in? How was he able to free her?"

"The thrall who was left bound said that he was a new thrall."

"Those are few enough. A kobold? Or a gnome?"

"A human, Mother. A human from Midgard. Dark of skin and with curly dark hair, like a black dwarf. Does that bring anyone to mind?" he asked, sarcastically.

Her green eyes narrowed. "That's not possible! Simply not possible. He was just a messenger. A thrall. And I used the lightest of enamor entrapment spells on him. Merely a glamour onto his memory of her. Enough to make a thrall do what a thrall would not dream of doing."

He snorted. "Your spell had a far stronger effect on that one than you realized," said the beast. "Sometimes, Mother, you're too devious for your own good. My way—direct and brutal—would not have had these consequences."

"Your way would have had the arm-ring exerting magical forces against us. Just like the raid that the great Vortenbras talked his foolish men into," she said, sarcastically.

"A raid that brought back the slave you foolishly used," he replied. "He must have been besotted with her already, and you had to put an entrapment on top of that."

She was silent for a while. Then she said, "The other slaves taken on that viking . . . they were all men from the League lands. He was the only one even taken in waters to which the Holy Roman Empire lays claim. The truce-oath was broken. He is a curse brought down by that act."

"You attribute the arm-ring far too much power," snorted the beast disdainfully.

She rubbed her heavy jaw pensively. "Maybe not. Maybe I underestimated it. It's a symbol of an old religion, much tied to the land. It was old before Odin worship came to Telemark. I am beginning to think that there is more to it than we realized. I think Chernobog may have misled us deliberately."

"Letting rivals seek their own destruction you mean?" he said, scratching his heavy brow.

"Exactly," she said, her voice grim and cold as ice rime.

"Then I do not think we will tell him of our setbacks. Not until we have recovered the prisoners from the dwarves."

"At least we can be sure that they will not let them go," she said. "They never do."

"But they always offer a way out," he said, meditatively.

She twisted her thick lips into a sneer. "And no one ever succeeds in the dwarf challenges, curse their tricksy little selves. I hate them. I hate them nearly as much as humans."

CHAPTER 36

Copenhagen

Milady de Chevreuse had been forced to change her routines. Francesca did not like doing so. But the winter weather was just too appalling. Furs were all very well, and beautiful and soft, but the wind out of the north cut through or found its way into everything. It was, she gathered, exceptionally cold, even for here. Walking in the snow was ... unpleasant. Walking in sleet was simply out of the question. Her mind turned to Alexandria, where it did neither, where the sharpest minds of the modern world met in a blossoming of culture, art, and knowledge. Where the pleasures of the flesh met the pleasures of the mind on balmy nights ... most unlike this gray sky, gray sea of winter Copenhagen. The food was fattening, one was cold and therefore hungry. And her constitutional brisk walks were curbed by the weather. And now, on this, the first rain- and snow-free day for ages, that oleaginous lardball admiral had to accost her. The man with him looked less obnoxious at least. The furs he was wearing spoke of three things: Vinland, money, and hard wear.

The florid-faced admiral bowed, with a creaking of whalebone corsets inadequate for the job required of them. "The divine Francesca! Your beauty brightens up a dull day! Milady, allow me to introduce my new friend, Fleet Captain Lars McAllin of Vinland."

He bowed, "Honored, milady. What brings a southern flower to these cold northern waters?"

She waved a delicate hand at him. "We go where we must, Fleet Captain. I might ask what brings a Vinlander, and a military man, here to Copenhagen?"

He smiled. "We do what we must too. And what we had to do was deal with a damned pirate. He thought we'd wait 'til spring, but with our Danish friends' help we bearded him in his lair, when he least expected us. We didn't even need the sled teams."

"And which pirate might this be?" inquired Francesca. "One of the infamous Redbeards?

"Nothing on that scale! Besides, although there have been reports that they're starting to harry shipping outside of the Pillars of Hercules, our routes tend to be in northern waters," he said.

"Fascinating! Who then?" she asked.

"A local kinglet. Or should I say, ex-kinglet. We left his ugly head on his gates," answered the Vinlander.

The admiral shuddered. "What a thing to talk about to a lady, Lars!"

Francesca shook her head and smiled warmly on the Vinlander. "It makes an interesting change from on-dits about the affairs of the notables of Copenhagen. It is far too cold to stand around and talk, though. I am making the best of this patch of better weather to take some exercise. Why don't you walk with me and tell me about it?"

"A pleasure, milady. May I offer you my arm?"

Francesca inspected it thoughtfully. "Why, thank you. I have always space for another one in my collection. I do not saunter, Fleet Captain. I walk. I hope that you can keep up."

He allowed himself a look of amusement. "If I fail, you get to keep the arm."

They set off and she said, "I can only assume that you attacked either King Hjorda, Jarl Orm, or King Vortenbras. If it is the latter, I want to know, and the admiral," she gestured at the puffing man, "doesn't want me to."

"The admiral is safe this time. King Hjorda, milady. The ruler of Rogaland. Or should I say the ex-ruler. He won't make the mistake of raiding a Vinlander fleet again," said the man grimly. "He thought he'd be safe until springtime when he and his rats would have gone into hiding and laughed at us from the mountaintops, but we stole a march on him."

"He . . . still . . . got . . . away with . . . the gold," panted the admiral.

Francesca raised an eyebrow at him. "I thought you couldn't take it with you, Admiral?" she said archly . . . to no one. The admiral had sat down, grasping a stone bench like a drowning man clinging to a spar.

"He is a little plump for this sort of exercise, milady," said the Vinlander cheerfully. "And I fear that I may have to learn how to cope with having only one arm."

She laughed. "I'll spare it, provided you don't take too many liberties with it. Manfred of Brittany has a habit of removing undesirable arms," she said. "Now tell me about the gold. A fascinating subject, gold." It was indeed. Gold, not steel, won or lost wars, she'd concluded. Steel decided battles; gold, wars.

"There's not much to tell. Two of the vessels had considerable gold aboard. We recovered—in large part—the rest of our cargoes, freed a goodly number of slaves. The gold, alas, appears to have been spent. Old Hjorda had bought himself yet another bride in the desperate hope of an heir. His third try, poor lasses."

"How odd it is that when noblemen sell their daughters' virtue outright, it is an honorable thing, but should a girl venture on temporary rental, it is prostitution," commented Francesca dryly. "Was the woman relieved to be a widow? I had heard that he was a less than pleasant monarch."

"She hadn't even been delivered . . ." He made a face. "Makes her sound like a bale of fleeces doesn't it? Anyway, several of my fellow captains were all set on taking the raid to Telemark to reclaim the money. But the Danes wouldn't budge."

"Wise of them," said Francesca. "Firstly, the Emperor would not have been pleased. Secondly, where would you raid? Their king's seat is far inland, for just that reason."

He looked startled. Plainly he hadn't expected a pragmatic and well-informed reply. But he took it in his stride. "And Vortenbras is a tougher nut to crack, milady."

She nodded. "So tell me, has the map been rearranged? Are the Vinlanders and Danes attempting to hold Stavanger at least?"

"They'd have liked to. But it appears that they're wary about it. The enclaves at Oslofiord and Trondheim appear to have provided a few bloody lessons."

"So Rogaland is now a kingless state? A place without a ruler?"

He shrugged. "It could be described like that."

"And that," she said, detaching her arm from his, "could be even worse for shipping and the region. Now, if you will excuse me," she twinkled at him, "a little more really brisk exercise is called for."

Later she took up the issue of Rogaland with the earl of Fyn, a far more intelligent and able man than the admiral.

"My dear Francesca," he said consideringly, "I must tell you that military adventurism is seldom as well-paying as it might appear. The Norse do have queens ruling, from time to time, but you'd find it even colder and less cultured than Copenhagen."

She rapped him over the knuckles with her fan. "Silly man. I have no intention of being queen—at least, not of some howling wilderness. As for military adventurism: *I* know that, and *you* know that. But do others who might blunder in know it? A power vacuum is a dangerous place."

"Relax, m'dear," he said, cheerfully. "The jarls are still there, even if Hjorda has gone. His own claim to the throne was tenuous, which was another reason he wanted to marry this girl. Her maternal line are among the strongest claimants. And, on the basis of precedent, his betrothed wife-to-be could be enthroned anyway. It won't be the first time a woman has been widowed before she's been wedded."

"I have gathered corpses make for quite complaisant husbands," she said, removing his hand. He was a great source of information, but a terrible old lecher. Fortunately, he could take no for an answer, at least temporarily.

That evening she composed a letter to the Emperor that contained several nuggets of valuable and potentially dangerous knowledge. She'd tried to gather information about the late Hjorda's betrothed. But information on Princess Signy of Telemark was scant. Apparently she was a slight girl, quiet, reserved, and very much under the spell of her powerful step-mother. Old to marry among the Norse. At twenty-four she was nearly on the shelf.

CHAPTER 37

Aurvangar

ere, on this side of the black stone doorway and down the long passage they weren't—strictly speaking—prisoners, or slaves. The captivity in Aurvagar was a little more subtle, if far more effective. They were free to leave at any time. The black dwarf had cheerfully showed them the open doorway to the cave chamber he'd escorted them to. "Feel free to pass through," he'd said with a giggle, pointing at the landscape outside that doorway.

And then he'd left them. By the time they looked around he was gone.

Somewhere of course must be the entryway that the sniggering black dwarf had showed them through, but none of them had been able to find it. You could hear the sounds of industry: hammering and clanking. But the labyrinthine passages never led to it, just back to this solitary cave room. Company—like food and drink—was remarkably scarce. The volcanic landscape outside the door showed no sign that anything had—or ever could have—lived out there.

Perhaps the dwarves liked an endless aspect of ash and glassy black rock. Erik was sure that he didn't. "We shouldn't have let them take the horses," he said.

"How could we have stopped them? And what would we have fed the horses on?" asked Manfred. "They seemed friendly enough."

He was not referring to horses.

"As friendly as someone who is in total control can afford to be," said Cair, sitting cross-legged against the wall. "I suppose they're waiting for us to ask for help. There will be a price, of course."

Erik was sure that the corsair admiral was right. And if childhood stories were to be believed, the price would be high . . . and tricky. "They have a reputation," he said in Frankish, "of playing games. Of deceptions."

"What else can we do but to play along?" said Cair.

"Force," said Manfred, looking around in a fashion which indicated that he thought they were being spied on.

Signy snorted and looked at him scornfully. But she said nothing. Just looked down at her feet again.

"Um. I gather that's really not a good idea," said Manfred, looking chastened. Or, thought Erik, doing his best to.

"I don't think it would be wise," said Erik, carefully reverting to Norse. "We really wouldn't want to fight with them. We'd do better to bargain for our freedom."

"Very much wiser," said the black dwarf, grinning and leaning against the wall—where he definitely hadn't been a moment ago. "Come and talk to the others." He led them out along the same passage that they'd tried at least five times before and through into a smithy. There were two other dwarves at work there. One, thought Erik, looked like the dwarf who had led them into this trap in the first place.

"Still here?" he asked, looking up from his engraving. "I thought you were just passing through. Seems like they've got a bit delayed eh, Sjárr?"

The other dwarf slipped a shimmering sword into an annealing bath with a hiss that almost, but not quite, hid his guffaw.

"We seem to have got a little lost. We could use some assistance," said Manfred evenly.

The dwarves looked at each other and chortled. Erik might have been tempted into something premature and foolish if it hadn't been for the way the dwarf still held that hammer. You do not pick fights with a blacksmith, not even a small one, if he uses a hammer that size, one-handed. "Really? And how would you pay for such assistance? We do not provide anything for nothing. And we do not accept payment in promises," said one of the three.

This, thought Erik, *is where things get difficult*. He and Manfred had not a brass farthing between them. He doubted that the others did either. Mind you, you never could tell with Cair Aidin. "You seem to have already relieved us of our horses," he said mildly.

"Your horses?" The dwarf grinned. "You can have them back—if you pay for their feed. Food is pricy around here."

"And horses eat such a lot," said one of the others with mock sympathy. "Now, what skills do you have to offer us? Or money or rare gems or precious metals will do."

"All I have are these," said Signy, holding something out. "I offer them for free passage to safety for my man here."

Cair saw how Signy held out the narrow bands of silver. So: he was still "her man," and she was offering her only jewelry to free him. He recognized them as the bracelets she'd always worn. "They are supposed to be protective and magical."

One of the dwarves took the broken silver bracelets into a calloused hand. "Our work," he said professionally. "But it has been broken." He sounded surprised by that. He handed it on to the one who had been engraving. "Here, Fjalarr. What do you think?"

That dwarf held it up to the light. And then placed it into a solution in a glass beaker. Cair noticed the glassware. His eyes had already roamed across most of the equipment in this room. They were master metalworkers; that he could tell. But the glasswork looked of poor quality—greenish and barely translucent. A fine tracery of bubbles formed about the silver. The two dwarves shook their heads in unison. "Not worth much anymore, halfling," said the one called Fjalarr. "The runes are rubbed out, most of the enslavement and the leeching spells are gone. It would cost more to fix again than they're worth."

He hauled it out of the liquid with a pair of forceps, shook it off, dipped it in what Cair decided was probably water, and tossed it back to her. She fumbled the catch. The dwarves laughed, setting Cair's teeth on edge. Now that he understood the problem of her long-sightedness . . .

"We'll give you their value in silver," said Sjárr. "The work is worthless now. We'll pay to know how you got free of them, though. They were supposed to never come off."

"And what did you do to the runes?" said the third dwarf, the one with the long nose.

Signy had the honor of a long line of Norse jarls and kings, and, regrettably, the business sense of a rabbit, decided Cair, as she answered: "I broke them on the rowan-wood cage. And I tried to cut through the wood with them."

The dwarves nodded. "Ah. That stuff is poison to your kind. We never thought that you'd go near it."

It might be superstition, thought Cair, but at least she could have sold it! What else was superstition for?

"And you?" said the dwarves to Manfred. "Going to offer us an ox, are you? Like yourself, hee, hee, hee."

Cair could not help but appreciate the irony of it. Manfred of Brittany was trapped in the same way that he had been. If he were to give them any indication of his true worth, they'd keep him very securely indeed. Or . . . sell him to a worse enemy. "I have my sword. I'm a good armsman," said Manfred. "So is Erik."

"We've no use for those. Who would fight with us?" said the fourth dwarf, dismissing this out of hand.

"I am a maker of glassware," said Cair. He had blown glass before out of curiosity, when visiting a glassworks. It hadn't been that successful, but he could do at least as well as whoever made that lopsided bowl. It also had their interest.

"A valuable trade," said the engraver, Fjalarr, approvingly. That was good. "We'll have to make your challenge harder." That sounded bad.

"Challenge?" asked Cair cautiously.

"It's tradition," explained Fjalarr. "We agree to cancel your debts and let you go, if you succeed at a task we appoint you to. An interesting task. Draining a lake or something."

"Perhaps with a thimble?" enquired Cair, who felt he was getting to understand the dwarves. He'd also picked up on the fact that they were prisoners.

"Yes," said Sjárr "That's one we've had before."

"I'll take it," said Cair eagerly.

"Ah. No, we'll think of something else this time," said the engraver, thoughtfully. "We'll show you to your jobs in the meanwhile. And you, halfling, what can you do for us? You Alfar do fine work, if you can be brought to it, although we don't like to admit that anyone does anything as good as us. Weaving perhaps? You like living materials, usually. Not good with metals."

She stamped her foot. "No. I am tired of being called 'Alfar' and I don't weave, spin, embroider, or anything like that."

This amused the dwarves even more. "But you are Alfar, or at least a half-blood," said Fjalarr. "Now, come with us." It was distinctly an order.

Cair was led to a small cave that had a furnace and various tools. "The last glassworker we had was a kobold. He wasn't very good. He was also too ambitious in his challenge. Out-eating Eldr . . . He burst." The two dwarves who had accompanied him roared with laughter.

Cair looked at the tools, the furnace, the materials. He was hard-pressed not to giggle himself. The one thing he wasn't see-ing was a blowpipe.

"To make good glassware I will need certain other things," he said calmly. "A short iron pipe for starters."

"Make yourself one. The ironworks are through there." Vitr, the long-nosed dwarf, pointed.

Cair looked shocked. "I'm a glassworker. I can't work with iron." He'd probably be more comfortable with the stuff than glass, the truth be told. But he had a feeling that the truth might just serve him badly.

"We have something suited to your talents, half-blood." The shortest, and plainly oldest of the dwarves was mocking, but there was just a trace of wariness in his voice, in the way he looked at her, as he led her down the passages. He'd said least in their foundry room, but þekkr was plainly the senior dwarf, along with Fjalarr—the dwarf who had brought them through the serpent wall. (She recognized it. Perhaps the Icelander also had. To her thrall and Manfred it had just been rock, not a monster.)

Signy wondered why they should treat her any differently. There had been no sign of respect in the way they treated anyone else. Perhaps this was something she could make work for her, and the others. She was still terribly confused about Cair. He was a thrall . . . branded and clearing dung. He was also a captain of raiders, a jarl, by the least comparative reckoning. Yet he'd been content to be her thrall. It was easier to think about this "Alfar" that they flung at her head. Her stepmother had called her that, too. So had the troll-wife. "Why do you call me 'Alfar' all the time?" she said, stopping.

The dwarf shrugged. "You use glamour. We can see through it, of course. But we can see you as you really are, lady. You cannot hide from us."

Glamour. A magical ability to appear as something you were not. But she remained inherently truthful. "I don't, as far as I know, use any such thing. I am myself. I have no skills at any form of magic, although you all seem to think I have. Everything anyone ever tried to teach me went wrong."

"Midgarders' teaching?" said the dwarf with a curious lift to his shaggy eyebrows. "Humans?"

"Who else?"

"And you say that they kept telling you that you were Alfar and could do magic? And you didn't want to?" asked the dwarf, grinning evilly. "You do realize that you were bespelling yourself, don't you? You willed it thus. Alfar magic doesn't work quite like Midgarder spells. Clumsy things. Full of words to focus their puny powers, which mostly come from interbreeding with nonhumans anyway. But few Midgarders have as much Alfar blood as you, lady. Alfar need only the will, not the words and symbols. Those can help of course . . . but not if you do not want them to work. Besides, those thrall bracelets would have channeled most of your power straight to your owner."

"Thrall bracelets?" she asked, fearing that she knew the answer.

"The silver bracelets you tried to sell us. Those who wish to keep Alfar as slaves use them."

The idea shocked her. A slave? She was of the royal house! "You say that you made them. Why do you not put more on me?" she demanded imperiously, holding out her wrists.

The dwarf shrugged. "It is not necessary. You're not a slave here. You can leave if you fulfil your challenge, lady. To the *Alfarblot* that should be simple. We'd have to let you go home. We want no quarrel with your kin. But we have to honor our traditions."

"Let me and my companions go home to Telemark," she said uncompromisingly. The dishonor of having been tricked into a 'thrall bracelet' still rankled.

"Telemark?" said Þekkr, curiously. "Not Alfheim? We have little to do with Telemark. The arm-ring protects it." The dwarf tugged his beard. "Very well. If your Midgarder companions win their challenges they may accompany you over the bridge. Otherwise, we'll just let them go." He seemed to find that funny.

With sudden insight she understood. "You enslave them with hope."

"Of course," admitted Þekkr. "The strongest chains are the intangible ones."

"The sound of a cat's footfall, a woman's beard, a mountain's roots, a bear's sinews, a fish's breath, and a bird's spit," she quoted, remembering the ingredients that had gone into the chain that bound Fenrir, which Odin had sent his servant to fetch from the dwarves.

The dwarf nodded. "*Gleipnir.* The open one, because belief is a strong chain. That was one of ours."

They'd resumed walking and had come to a place where, suddenly, the torch-lit passages opened into a hall with sunlight streaming in through the crystal roof. A stream kept the air moist.

At one time the raised beds in here must have been verdant. Now, straggly and sickly plants sparsely populated them. Þekkr gestured at the beds. "Our skills lie with metals and rare gems. We do not make things grow."

That, thought Signy, was obvious. Someone, once, had set this up as a herbiary. Someone who knew and loved plants. The biggest problem that she could see was straight neglect. "I see," she said neutrally.

It obviously didn't fool the dwarf. He grimaced, which did nothing to improve his ugly countenance. "Yes, *Alfarblot.* We know. But you are good with live things. We are not. Plants should stay dealt with, not need constant fussing. Sjárr and Vitr were all for making them out of bronze and emeralds instead. But they do not cure as well."

"This is my challenge? To make this grow?" She could perhaps do that. The idea made her feel strangely eager, actually.

She plucked a weed and absently shredded it between her fingers, reducing it into three stems and plaiting them. The dwarf looked at her. And at the plait. "No," he said, "That is just a little repayment our guests could do for us." He pointed to an archway. "Come, I will show you your challenge."

He led her down the passage to a small cavern opening out onto the bleak landscape.

What Signy saw there made her blood run cold. She could face axe-wielding trolls or a view of Hel and its freezing mists, but this frightened her.

It was a tambour frame, with a half-finished piece of Nué gold-thread embroidery on it. From here, halfway across the chamber, she could see that it was set with perfect, neat little stitches.

She knew that from close up, it would be a blur.

"Our last guest left with her work unfinished," said the dwarf. "Considering that Alfar lasses are so good with their fingers, and that you want to return to Telemark of all places—I thought it would be appropriate."

Signy looked at the untidy plait in her fingers and realized that she'd entrapped herself. And then she looked at the tambour frame, seeing the stitching and the cartoon, really seeing them properly and not just as a terrifying task, and absorbing what the picture being stitched was of.

It was a grove of young oaks. In front of them sat various magical creatures of the woods, all staring intently at a slab of stone ... and at a fissure in the great rock beyond it, which had smoke issuing from it.

She was horrified to realize that she recognized the fissure.

The temple, so ancient, blackened and smoke-impregnated and filled with carvings that looked as if they'd been old when Odin was a boy, was not there.

However, on the altar stone, the great arm-ring was in its correct place. That part of the embroidery had been finished. The arm-ring shone with the finest of gold thread. The embroidery was masterful, and that part was perfection itself, down to the shadows.

She'd seen it lying on the stone, just like that, gleaming as if from some inner light.

In this embroidery it was, however, aggressively unadorned. Simply a plain band of heavy hammered and polished gold without the runes.

She looked at the cartooned outline of the rest. And blushed, despite the situation.

The scene was bluntly erotic. The cartoon had not minimized the huge phallus. The male did not look human ... in other details as well.

"A family portrait, perhaps," said the dwarf, sardonically.

"It's been stolen," she said, slowly.

"What? Your ancestor's picture?" said the dwarf. "I promise you it's ours. The artist got that far with our gold."

"I mean the arm-ring. It is the arm-ring of Telemark, isn't it?"

"What else could it be?" said Þekkr. "And it can't be stolen any more than you could pick up a country and slip it in your pocket. It has too much magic hammered into the metal."

"The altar stone is empty. I saw that myself," insisted Signy.

"Ho! It's a neat trick, if you can do it," said the dwarf, and vanished himself. She heard him snigger, but could not see him.

That evening Cair found his way back to the chamber—somehow the passages had led back there. There were a fair number of other "guest workers" in the labyrinthine workshops of the dwarves, but once they'd been called to the kitchens to get their food, the others had all gone their way, walking as if they were going somewhere—and then they had just not been in the passage when he turned a corner. Cair was tired of the tricks. Tired of his attempts at making glass, too. He'd had some success once he remembered that glassmakers added potash to lower their melting temperatures. He'd been quick enough to remember that they'd used arsenic to clarify their glass. He recalled finding it amusing at the glassworks in Oran, that a poison should lurk—apparently harmlessly—in fine, transparent drinking glasses.

He'd burned himself several times today, but not quite as badly as his clever mouth had. Why had he picked on glasswork? He was a dabbler. A man of wealth and power who had found science more amusing than philosophy or religion, the other fields open to a man who wanted slightly more intellectual pastimes than drinking and fornication. Too late he'd established that there was a big difference between watching and doing it yourself, under pressure.

He saw that Erik and Manfred were back already, organizing bedding for themselves.

"I got our saddlebags back," said Erik. "Yours and the princess's too. Trust you to organize a cushy job, Cair." He didn't sound angry or suspicious about it, anyway. "I'm working furnace bellows."

"And I am carrying ore to the smelters," said Manfred. "So what sort of 'challenge' have they given you, sailor from Lesbos?" He seemed to find that title funny.

"An impossible one, naturally," said Cair, sitting down, and stretching out his tired limbs. "I have to make a bird out of cold iron."

"Doesn't sound impossible," said Manfred with some interest. "I know more about blacksmith work than a prince should." He grinned. "I ran tame in the smithy in the castle at Carnac. Smithing is still reckoned near-noble work among the Celts, no matter what they think among the Franks. We're primitive and proud of it."

"The catch is that it has to fly and sing," said Cair, sourly.

"Hmm. Tricky little devils, aren't they," said Manfred. "I'm supposed to get into a cave . . . The entry is a hole the size of my fist. The rock around the hole is slightly chipped and pitted. They said that the last challengee was a troll who hit it with a mattock for forty years. They said I'd have to do a powerful lot of ore carrying to sweat down enough. They seem to find it very funny," he said with a dead straight face that Cair had learned meant he didn't find it in the least amusing.

"Mine is a rock that even Manfred could not lift, if I told him that there was strong drink underneath it," said Erik. Cair read something in that tone, too. Erik very carefully wasn't saying something. The tall Icelander came and sat next to him. And wrote on the cave floor with a piece of charcoal, PULLEY.

Cair nodded. And rubbed it out. "They're fine artisans, but their equipment is a little primitive," he said, reaching for the charcoal.

"Magic," said Manfred stretching his limbs. "Which I know you don't believe in, my skeptical friend. But it makes them lazy."

Cair nodded. "It certainly makes people's wits weak, my trusting friend from Brittany," he said. He wrote EXPLOSIVE FOR MAN-FRED on the cave floor. Even if they were watched—as seemed likely, considering, the Frankish words and alphabet should disguise things well. Also, perhaps as a measure of their power, the dwarves seemed to care little if their "guests" did try to escape or explore. That was a lot more frightening to Cair than physical chains had been.

CHAPTER 38

Kingshall and Copenhagen

"Weapons drill again?" Brother Uriel seemed surprised.

Juzef shrugged. "What else can we do, Brother? Like praying, extra drills do no harm. Besides, unless I'm mistaken we're doing two things with them. The first is to frighten a bit of respect into Vortenbras's hangers on. And the other is, I suspect, to inspire several of your 'secret Christians' with a strong desire to join the order. Just making a judgment on the number of young men who have found an excuse to speak to me, the interest in being a knight in the service of Christ may be bigger than their interest in being a monk in the service of Christ. I've told them about having to eat cabbage and live in chapter houses in Prussia, and fight howling demons from outer darkness, but not even the cabbage could put them off."

"You make a jest of God's work, Ritter. You are also part of a monastic order."

Juzef Szpak was feeling in a poor mood for being lectured. "Many a good thing has been done with a light heart, Brother. And I think it's up to God to judge whether my jests serve him better than your moralities. They see that our swords and our faith are not jests, for all that they outnumber us twenty to one. They intend to murder all of us, if we do not manage to leave before Yuletide. Yet my men drill calmly. It frightens them and impresses them. And maybe I will be able to get you and the clerics away if the weather lifts. If not, we'll go down fighting. I'd hoped the secret Christians among the locals would have been prepared to help us get away. Instead they seem prepared to fight next to us, but they think that our getting away is hopeless."

"What of the prince and Hakkonsen? We know that they still live."

Juzef shrugged. "At the moment I can't get my own contingent of men out of Kingshall, let alone go looking for them. I am not looking forward to telling my superiors that we lost them, but my duty to you and the Empire is still to be done."

Francesca frowned at the letter from the Emperor. She usually avoided frowning—there was nothing worse for leaving lines on your face. But this handwriting . . . Why, oh why, did the Emperor insist on doing any correspondence he considered vital himself?

She knew why of course. She had employed enough spies herself to know the answer to that. But it would make it easier to read if he did have someone he really could trust and who could write properly! Well. The content and orders were explicit enough. She sat and penned the letters to the necessary people. It was probably going to be expensive. Looking out of her windows she was sure that it was going to be cold. But she'd better go herself. She pinched her chin thoughtfully, and sat and wrote one more letter to a Fleet Captain Lars McAllin of Vinland. He could be useful. Probably also expensive, but if the Emperor wanted his nephew in one piece . . .

She tinkled a delicate glass-and-silver bell.

Poor little Heinrich could go out in the cold and deliver the letters.

CHAPTER 39

Aurvangar

"I have found out where the arm-ring of Odin has gone," said Signy, on her return. She brought with her a strong smell of the stables.

"Where?" asked Manfred.

"Nowhere," she said. "It has just been made invisible. It is still there, touching the rock."

Erik shook his head. "It would have to have been made intangible, too, Princess. We put a cloth onto the altar to collect dust. We'd have seen the bump, surely?"

She rubbed her forehead tiredly. Erik noticed that it had a dirty streak on it. "Oh. Well, that's what the dwarf thought."

"And what challenge have they given you, Princess?" asked Cair, handing her a cloth and a clay dipper of water. You had to admire the man's thoughtfulness, admitted Erik. He'd managed to get their saddlebags. But Cair had brought water, and given the small woman exactly what she wanted most. Erik had decided, back when they'd been eluding trolls, that he'd rather have the Barbary corsair on his side than against him. Looking at him now, he decided the best way to be sure of that was to befriend this odd little princess. Besides, he was getting used to her. She had her blind spots, but she was as true as sword steel. Courageous in danger . . . a very different person to the one he'd met at Kingshall.

Her problems seemed to lie more in a lack of experience with life rather than in anything else. And her "thrall" had enough of that for both of them. He watched as she washed her hands, and then face, delicately as any cat, not answering him.

Finally she said quietly. "I can't do it. And it makes no difference if you do yours either. They will let you go. But there is nowhere to go. It's just to keep you docile. To keep you hoping. But even if you all succeed, you will just have to come back. There is no food out there and there is no way out of here, unless you cross their bridge. And they will only let us cross that if I succeed. And I can't."

"I believe that you can do anything, Princess," said Cair, firmly, taking the soiled cloth from her hands as if he'd been a body servant all his life.

"Not embroidery," she said, forlornly, looking like the dejected girl-child Erik had first seen back at Kingshall.

Cair stood like a statue, looking at her fixedly. And then a savage grin spread across his face, the grin of a fox looking at an unguarded henhouse. "A shame that," he said, hastily hiding the smile. He gestured at the open cave-mouth "Let us take a little walk in this pleasant hell hole. Take the air."

They walked out, and Erik located the perfect spot for conspiracy. It was a narrow ledge—a splinter of the black, glassy rock that hung some twenty feet above the valley. The ledge ended just beyond Erik, and by dint of Manfred scattering glassy gravel back along the ledge they had a spot which not even invisible listeners could approach silently. They sat kicking their legs in space, with Manfred tossing rocks at the valley, as they talked idly about their day. "The plant beds require water and fertility. The soil is spent. So I have been bringing horse dung to it," explained Signy.

"You, Princess?" Cair nearly fell off the ledge in apparent shock.

"Who else?" she asked.

"I will try to arrange something . . ."

He looked ready to leap up and do it. She put a restraining had on his shoulder. "Cair. You showed me that you could shovel horse dung and remain a man. I remain a princess of Telemark, whatever I do."

"But . . ."

She shook her head firmly. "We do what we must. Is that not

what you said to me? Besides . . . in a way I have always been a thrall."

Manfred cleared his throat. "There are no invisible folk below us. I've been tossing rocks in a pattern that would have laid them out if they were. What did you want to talk to us about? You two can argue horse dung later. Personally, I don't think carrying ore makes me less of the heir to Brittany, although it does smell better than horse dung, Princess."

"You are right," she nodded. "It is in the blood. But there is honor."

"There's ends and means to achieving those ends," said Erik. He'd shoveled horse dung himself, after all. There was little enough labor at Bokkefloi. "There's nothing dishonorable about horse dung. But can we get back to your next fiendish plan, Cair, so we all know what we're in for this time."

Cair nodded. "I think we will speak Frankish," he said quietly.

"I'm still not betting that this is safe, either," said Manfred equally quietly, still throwing more rocks at the valley below them. "The dwarves have certain skills we can't match, Cair."

"Well, then we must just go around them," said Cair. "The princess made me see that."

"How?" she asked, shyly. "I don't think they will let us cheat . . . Besides, that would be dishonorable." Something about the way she said it told Erik that an oath sworn by this Norsewoman would be utterly binding.

Cair nodded. "Not cheat, or not in any way that the dwarves do not accept. Each of the challenges has a loophole. They are possible—somehow. Manfred simply has to get into the next cave. There is a tiny hole, in adamantine-hard rock. He could never fit. But there is no exclusion that says he has to do it that way. Someone tried to cut their way through with a mattock. We'll try a more direct method. The rock Erik has to lift—a lever will do that."

"I have to hoist it higher than my head," said Erik.

"A lever, and then a pulley system. Something you have already thought of."

"Could work," admitted Erik.

"And, Princess, the problem is that you cannot see close-work?" asked Cair.

She nodded. "If you can make me a device so that I can work at a distance, say seven feet, it would be easy."

"It would be pretty difficult to control a needle seven feet long," said Erik, managing to keep a straight face. "I have a feeling that you want to make some kind of eyeglasses, Cair."

Cair nodded. "Yes. And I think I have an answer to my challenge, too. But it is all contingent on one thing." He turned to Manfred. "I will contrive that you and your man return to your own people, but I need your oath, before I will."

Manfred looked faintly amused. "Oath?"

"Yes," said Cair. "I am increasingly of the opinion that it would bind you. Princess Signy is here because of a false accusation. She may have to flee her home. I want you to swear to me that you will grant her sanctuary in the Empire, and escort her there, protecting her with your arms, if need be."

Manfred chuckled. "You don't want a pardon yourself? A truce between Cair Aidin and the Empire? I'm just as well placed to offer and to honor that."

Cair raised an eyebrow. "And deprive my fleet of its legitimate prey? No, Manfred of Brittany, forget the play-acting of ordinary negotiation. I read horse tracks well enough to know that you and Erik came back for me when I was lying under a troll. I'll give you a truce until we're free of this place, or rather, until the princess is safe. And don't pretend that it isn't within your power, or that you still doubt her innocence."

"I am not a cow that you two can chaffer over," said Signy, crossly. "My stepmother treated me like that. I see now that it was a mistake." She pointed at Manfred. "Cair is my thrall. You are bound by treaty to stay your hand from me and my property. Attempt to capture or injure him and I will hold you forsworn. I am not leaving Telemark. I shall live and die in it."

Manfred nodded to Cair, his shoulders shaking slightly. "I'll swear your oath. I think you've got enough problems of your own. I might even see if I can persuade Uncle to pardon you for what you've done. He puts a high value on Erik. I'm not so sure about me."

Cair smiled sardonically. "But then I would have to forgo my ransom for the two of you. And I don't catch prizes like this every day."

Signy looked sternly at him. "You're to leave them alone. They're also protected by the treaty."

"Very well, Princess," said Cair, meekly. But no one was fooled by his meekness.

"And what do you say, Erik?" asked Manfred, looking at his mentor-bodyguard's frown.

Erik shook his head. "I say we should get out of here first, and then back to Empire lands, before we worry about it. And the Godar Hohenstauffen wants your thick head attached to your shoulders. The oath that Cair asks will probably mean he has reason to keep it there. I think the Emperor would consider it a small price to pay."

"The sage has spoken," said Manfred, grinning. "Very well. Now can we get back to those beds? Mine is calling me. And I have a feeling that Cair will leave us with no sleep in the near future. He seems to like doing that."

They walked back to the small rock chamber that served as their quarters. They'd eaten, courtesy of the dwarves, and sleep, too, came swiftly. At least there was no apparent danger of being killed in their sleep here. The dwarves would far rather they worked themselves to death.

The next day Erik managed to find time to walk beside Manfred as they set off to their various labors. "What do you make of this situation, Manfred. This oath? And our 'witch'?"

Manfred grinned. "He's more of a witch than she is, if you ask me. Wand-pointing thief or not."

They walked in silence. "I've thought of something, Manfred. That wand—who did it point at?"

"Her."

"Did it?"

Manfred pursed his lips. "It did stop abruptly, but there was no one else, really."

"There was someone behind her. Directly behind her."

"Vortenbras?" exclaimed Manfred. "He stole his own oath-ring?"

Erik nodded slowly. "It came to me when Cair said that he would not swear a truce-oath with the Empire, and deprive his fleet of its prey."

Manfred bit his lip. "Son of a . . . Vortenbras is big enough to kill a few guards. What about his mother?"

"She's dead. Cair saw her head in a jar, and he's not the kind of man who makes mistakes, Manfred. I imagine Vortenbras sold her to this troll-wife, Bakrauf."

"A nice man, Vortenbras," said Manfred, wide-eyed.

"Indeed. I'm sure he planned to kill Signy, too."

Manfred rubbed his big hands. "Well! I think the Empire might want a rival claimant to the throne of Telemark, badly. Uncle will be very pleased with that oath, even if we have to see that Cair succeeds in getting her out of Telemark. I don't think that the Redbeard is accustomed to failure. But we'll still have to give him what help we can."

Erik blinked at him. "She is a woman, Manfred."

"So was Queen Ethelbertha, despite the way she looks in the woodcuts! I knew that all the history my tutors droned at me had to be good for something, one day," said Manfred, with immense satisfaction.

"Ethelbertha didn't have a brother."

Manfred stopped walking. "If I tell our sailor friend from Lesbos about what Signy's brother tried to do, I don't think she'll have one for long. I wouldn't mind giving him a hand, actually."

"We've a treaty to abide by," said Erik, dryly. "Otherwise you might just have to beat me to it."

That evening Cair arrived again before Signy. He looked tired but triumphant. He held out a small piece of glasswork. "It's far from perfect Venetian glassware. But it is transparent—thanks to a little arsenic provided by our hosts. They were very concerned I might season their pottage with it. But Sjárr and Vitr are most impressed with my skills." He chuckled. "I gather they're going to give someone else the poisoned glass to drink from though. They're going to be as disappointed as Bakrauf in her coins."

"Her coins?" asked Erik curiously, examining the little beaker that Cair had made. It was, as Cair said, far from perfect. But the glass was thin and clear, barring a few imperfections and bubbles.

"I made fake coins—lead with a gold foil covering for the kobolds," he explained.

Manfred shook his head. "Why did you even bother with piracy? Now look, Erik has a theory he wants to discuss with you. We think that the diviner might have pointed to Vortenbras as the thief, not your princess. He was standing right behind her."

Cair raised his eyebrows. "I almost wish I believed in divining."

"Magic's real enough, Cair," said Erik.

He shook his head. "Magic is just something that people don't understand and are too lazy to think about."

He was also openly doubtful about Vortenbras sacrificing Queen Albruna to Bakrauf. "He's very dependent on her, Manfred. She's the planner. He's the Viking ideal—but she does the thinking. If you told me that she'd organized it I might be more inclined to believe you. She probably did and then fell foul of the troll-wife."

"Vortenbras told us that his sister was a schemer who had been embittered by losing the throne, remember," said Manfred. "Now that's pretty patently false, and those *björnhednar* bear-men worked for Bakrauf. So they must have been in league with each other."

Cair nodded. "She—Queen Albruna—had Bakrauf's ring. I took it off her."

Erik blinked. "He's a man of many parts, Manfred."

Manfred yawned. Grinned tiredly. "And I'm still inclined to think that maybe he's a magic worker, by the tricks he pulls. How would you have stolen that arm-ring from the temple, Cair?"

The swarthy man grinned. "I'd have hidden it in the thatch of the temple until the hue and cry was over."

"I told you he'd make a better witch," said Manfred to Erik. "I had a look at my challenge today. It appears that we have two hours a day to work on it. Digging a tunnel around should work. It'll take about twenty years at two hours a day."

Cair shook his head. "It is a bit more complex than 'two hours.' The dwarves will allow you to stay on," said Cair, "after they've fed the 'guests.' I asked today." He pulled a face. "I talked at length to Sjárr and Vitr. I'll admit that they're a lot sharper than the trolls or the kobolds. I could almost like them."

Erik was sure that he heard a small chuckle from the far side of the room.

Cair continued smoothly. "Fjalarr is another matter. He thinks he's clever sneaking about, but he should bathe more often."

Cair stared pointedly at the floor next to the far wall. And then nodded... "That's got rid of him, for now."

Eric followed the man's pointing finger and noticed a layer

of chalky dust. And also saw the small footprints in the dust. "Powdered limestone. I claimed I needed it for the glass."

"You can hardly deny that's magic," said Manfred. "Invisibility, I mean."

"Watch me," said Cair, tapping the wall carefully, where the dwarf's footprints neatly appeared to walk through it. He looked a little startled. Tapped further across. It sounded identical. Coming in from the other side of the cave, Signy stared at him in puzzlement.

"His brain has finally overheated, Princess," explained Manfred, cheerfully. "He's hoping someone is going to say 'come in,' and show us the way out."

"Oh, I know where that is. I saw it today," said Signy. "The Bifröst bridge. It's beautiful. And I have something for you, Cair." She held out a handful of dirty pink crystals. "This is what you collect is it not? I've watched you."

"Walls have ears, my princess," he said, looking startled.

"Not now," she smiled. "I've found that I can see them if I want to. Fjalarr was the hardest, but they're visible now that I know how to look."

Erik looked at Manfred, and said nothing. But that look conveyed a fair amount of alarm. Maybe, just maybe, she was a witch after all. Or at least, as the dwarves said, not entirely human.

Signy had had the strangest day. The first strange thing had been coming through to the herb conservatory and finding green shoots peeping through the soil that only yesterday she had been determinedly but inexpertly forking dung into. She'd seen thralls doing that, and never realized just what hard work it could be. But she had such a lot to think about, that the hard physical labor had been a release of sorts. An exhausting release, as she found. Thralls did this every day? No wonder they got beaten so often to make them work. But she'd worked and thought, and wheeled more barrows of dung to the garden, and petted the horses a bit. It came to her that there were worse things to do—like embroidery. A large part of her mind had been taken up with thinking over both what the dwarves and Cair had said. It had been much easier to think about what the dwarves had said, and even what the cartooned outlines of the picture on the tambour frame had shown. Virgin princesses weren't supposed to think about that sort of thing, but she'd seen dogs and horses, and been curious.

He was a thrall. Not a man. Yet, here she was, working like a thrall. If a princess could work like a thrall, forking dung, then could a raider captain not do the same? Honor could be regained. And when his eyes rested on her she felt like a woman, not a thrall or a princess. Did a brand destroy a man forever? Thralls were freed. It was rare, but not unheard of.

Maybe such a person could become a franklin. Or a trader.

But they did not associate with the royal house.

A part of her said that she did not care.

She turned her thoughts elsewhere, hastily, when this happened. This morning she was turning them to the real possibility that she could indeed do magic. She was well enough versed in the patterns of planting and harvesting that happened around Kingshall to realize that plants do not appear overnight, not even with the most liberal application of water and all of the horse manure in Norway. She found herself singing in sheer delight when she saw the first shoots, not the formal ballads that her stepmother had insisted on, and that she'd hated, but a strange, wild tune that seemed to come from somewhere deep inside her. The words were in a language she'd always known, never used. The conservatory was a wonderful echo-chamber and there was no one to hear her ... and to her amazement the green shoots were actually growing as she watched. Leaves opened.

She stopped, staring.

"Powerful *galdr*!" said the dwarf from the corner. "You are worth far more than Bakrauf has offered. She'll have to increase her price."

"You would sell us all to Bakrauf?"

"No, she just offered for you and the big one. We'll consider her offer for him, for all that he's a strong worker. But she undervalued you. She said she'd buy the glassworker, too, if the price was right. But he's not for sale. Too useful."

"None of us are for sale," she said firmly.

He laughed. "That is not really for you to decide, half-blood. I doubt if my brothers would sell you for less than the *brisingha-men* itself. But Midgarders ..."

"Are mine," she interrupted sternly. "Oath-bound. And I will sing such a *galdr* over your halls that everything here will wither and die, if you try."

He snorted and laughed. But she got the feeling it was more for show than in disdain. "We'll decide."

He vanished. She found herself wishing that she knew where he'd got to, and then to her further surprise she saw him as a wavy outline, near the stable passage, scowling at her. He looked far from laughter now.

And Signy, with not the vaguest idea of how to sing to anything but the herbs, and not at all sure of how she knew how to do that, felt good about herself. It was a feeling that continued throughout her day. Not even moving loads of dung could take it away. It was only when she looked at the tambour frame with the half-finished embroidery that it faded a little. But it still felt as if she had discovered a small spring somewhere in the desert inside her. She'd found loyalty—she would venture no further than that, yet, and she'd found that she could do things. She found that she was not useless, and that she could make things live and grow. The spring had been forcing a trickle upward in her ever since Cair had handed her the key to free the others. It was moistening ground, and shoots were beginning to grow in her, too. There were seeds that had been waiting, dormant but alive, all her life.

Signy wanted to help her companions. Loyalty was as much part of her as breathing. She would not let them go back to the troll-wife. Not if she could prevent it. But in her heart of hearts, she didn't really want to go back to Telemark either. Not to the half-dead existence she'd tolerated, not knowing anything better.

In his glass foundry Cair had not been feeling very good about himself. Blowing glass was a lot less simple than watching others blowing and trying it out under expert supervision had been. Even faking coins had been an easier task. And he had to make clear glass somehow. Clear, clean, bubble- and flaw-free glass. And then somehow he had to make an iron bird that could fool these dwarves that it both flew and sang. He had an idea about the singing. Well, whistling anyway. But flying had him flummoxed for the moment.

He'd realized that he was being watched, and somehow knowing that had made him work better. He patted and shaped the gather of glass on the end of the pipe against the piece of polished stone he'd found to make do instead of flat metal for marvering. He began to blow. And turn it slowly . . . It expanded without bursting or unevenness. He put it back into the furnace, hoping that the watcher would go away. But he felt they hadn't, so he pulled it out of the furnace. It had sagged slightly, so he shaped it against the stone and then blew it some more. He'd learned by now that the glass retained heat and must cool slowly. The glass bubble was carefully heated again and flattened on the base. And then he used tongs from the furnace to shape a rim into it, before taking it off the blowpipe.

A Venetian apprentice glassblower would have laughed at it. The watching dwarves had cheered instead. "Elgerr used to make models out of clay and dung, put them on a metal rod, and then dip them in the molten glass," said Sjárr.

"Or he made some small clay molds he pressed the glass into," said Vitr. "But the blowing produces finer and thinner glass items than he did. And it is much quicker, too. He used to take forever picking out the model, too. Do it again, we want to watch."

"It doesn't always work," admitted Cair. "Sometimes they break."

The dwarves grinned and nodded in unison. "It happens to all of us. Try."

So Cair tried. And this one was even better. The third one broke, but by then he'd delighted the dwarves enough to get them to agree to provide arsenic. They found the idea very funny. "You can make one for Bakrauf as a gift," chuckled Sjárr.

So he'd got his arsenic. And discovered that it did clarify the brown tint in the glass and make it more transparent. Getting from there to a polished convex lens was still a large step.

"We don't really have much use for beads," said Vitr looking rather scornfully at the clay concavities Cair was pressing molten clear glass into. "We want containers that can hold acids, particularly."

"These are not beads, Your Wisdom. They're tools for my fine-work. Maybe they'll be useful to you, too."

The dwarves were, true enough, holding them as prisoners, but Cair found that, compared to the other denizens of what he was convinced was a gray-skied Norse hinterland, he could get on with them. Artifice was a compelling fascination for the dwarves. Well, he found it that way, too. The three of them argued about acids, and how they worked, as he polished the best concave glass pieces. Of course their ideas were rotten with magic, but they were ingenious thinkers all the same.

When he put two of the concave lenses together and produced a bubbly and uneven magnifying glass—the two dwarves were excited enough to go and fetch a third one. Þekkr was quick enough to grasp the principle immediately and also to work out the need for a uniform curvature on the lens. He promised a metal die for this and agreed that Cair's work deserved a bellows man and an assistant to keep the furnace temperatures even. The dwarves were happy with the magnifying glass—But Cair was not. He knew that they were a long, long way from an adequate lens.

"It's not easy. I'll want a man who understands my language and needs. Erik would do fine. Some moron like the kobold people gave me is worse than no one at all."

The dwarves sniggered. "That's typical kobold, isn't it?" said Þekkr. "Pointy-headed idiots. You can have him."

By the knowing look the dwarves gave him, they knew he was up to something but obviously weren't worried enough to care. It was all part of the game to them.

Either he'd prove them wrong, or he was the one who should be very, very worried.

He settled for being uncomfortable about it.

Manfred didn't really mind carrying ore sacks. He wasn't about to tell anyone this fact, but it was not overwhelmingly hard work. Tedious and moderately strenuous, yes, but not too much so. And it left his mind free to work. Many people made the mistake of assuming that because he was big, he couldn't think, or at least not about anything above his belt. That suited him fine.

Having people underestimate you is always useful.

He occupied himself during his last trip in working out just how long they'd been captives—or rather how long it had been since they'd blundered into that kobold hole. It was a difficult exercise. For part of it there'd been no decent measure of night and day at all. But, unless he had it wrong, they had six to eight days before the truce sworn on the arm-ring was null and void. And assuming they'd moved in a straightish line, they had to be a good many days' travel from Kingshall. Probably at least as much as the eight days.

That led him on to pondering just how to deal with the situation between Cair Aidin and Princess Signy. Signy, yes, could make a good foil for her half-brother if the treaty was annulled and Telemark was free to pursue its expansionary policy. The Danes and the Empire could stop it. Probably. Provided the little Norse kingdoms stayed divided, and provided that the Svear stayed out of the mixture. Even then there were just too few people to seriously challenge the might of the Empire. But they could bleed the Empire white, while others attacked. Conquest of Norse lands would be easy enough, but occupation in these mountains and forests would be near impossible. So it would be containment: expensive, difficult, and sapping of resources that were needed elsewhere. Signy had overheard Bakrauf in communication with Jagellion. It was undoubtedly all part of a far bigger geopolitical game that the Grand Duke of Lithuania played against the Holy Roman Empire. Manfred wished that Francesca were here, and not just for the obvious, physical reasons. Not that that would not be, well, more than pleasant, but also because these sort of political machinations were meat and drink to her, just as combat was to Erik.

He wondered how Erik was getting on with the corsair. That was an even bigger problem than the Norse, really. Cair Aidin was the enemy of the Empire. Both from religious convictions and also as a raider that had cost the Empire and all the Mediterranean states dearly. It would in some ways have solved a lot of Manfred's own moral dilemmas if the man had indeed been squashed flat under the troll.

Manfred wondered if Cair's presence was yet another one of Jagellion's machinations. He also wondered, with wry amusement, how Signy was going to get around her noble scruples to bed Cair. He knew that look of old. And most women—hell, make that most people—could persuade their minds to do what their hearts and bodies wanted to. Manfred had often thought that if he could have harnessed all the mental energy he'd put into the subject himself, he'd have been able to out-think Francesca.

Erik watched Cair—he had a delicacy of touch, did the corsair, that was totally out of keeping with his bloodthirsty reputation. But then, there were many things about him that didn't actually add up to the image that the Empire had of the raider. Erik began to suspect that it was not beyond Cair to cultivate the rumors. "Now, if you can press down gently and evenly on that, Erik," said Cair.

"I'll do my best, but you'd have done better with Manfred for these technical tasks. He likes fiddling with metalwork and I've seen him pull apart the trigger mechanisms on guns for fun. I tend to regard artifice as something to use, not to play with."

"I'll probably get him in here as well, as soon as I find some work for him. The only thing I'll fail with is the princess in here. The dwarves are very pleased with the way she's making their garden grow. They'd like to keep her."

"From what I can gather, they usually do end up keeping people," said Erik. He paused and then decided to speak his mind anyway. "Look, Cair, at the moment we are together in this mess. We owe you our lives—I've not forgotten that. But if there is a threat to Manfred I'll have to kill you. I also think that your mind and clever fingers are our best chance at getting out of here. So why don't the two of us cry a truce? You've decided that you can trust Manfred with the one you hold most dear, and you're right about that. I've decided I can trust you. I can trust you that far anyway," he modified.

Cair nodded. He couldn't speak as he was busy blowing glass. But when he put it back into the furnace before marvering it a second time, he said: "A fair deal. I was going to propose it myself. And Erik. You understand far more about the culture Princess Signy is trapped in. If I am killed will you do your solemn best to see that she escapes from Telemark?"

It was Erik's turn to nod.

They worked on, Cair with visibly growing skill. It would take months before he was half as good as a Venetian apprentice, but his work had far eclipsed the efforts of the kobold who had been his predecessor. The dwarves looked in from time to time, and seemed well pleased. Cair and Erik got through a lot, and even found time for work on Cair's bird. Well, actually on a glass dropper that Cair made, that he insisted would work for part of the "song." And they made a selection of lenses, which Erik found himself set to polishing. It was like polishing armor, but even more tedious. Still, Erik heard more about just how Cair had ended up as a thrall, and of how he had ended up in the kobolds' hands.

"I think you were a pawn in Queen Albruna's hand," said Erik thoughtfully.

"I suspect the same. But she's dead now."

"You're certain that was her head you saw?"

Cair nodded. "Absolutely. I haven't yet found a way to tell Signy. The woman made her life a misery, and probably betrayed her to Bakrauf, but she was still the only mother Signy has ever had. Or ever knew, at least."

CHAPTER 40

Trollheim

Bakrauf snarled and crumpled the message.

"They have discovered something of the value of their prisoners." She ground together her huge teeth, teeth which had crushed human bones before. "I told you we should not be so hasty in offering to buy them back."

"What else could we do?" asked the monster she called her son. "Anyway they never do let anyone go. Not really."

"Except for Alfar," said Bakrauf. "They don't try too many of their tricks on the denizens of Gimlé's Halls. And she's got a lot of that blood, curse her."

"You mean they might let her go?"

"Might," admitted Bakrauf. "They keep on the good side of the Alfar, curse both of them. Of course gold talks loudly to the black dwarves. They will risk a lot for more gold. But they might just let her go. With the dwarves you never can tell."

"So what do we do?"

Bakrauf shrugged. "There are few places where they can be returned by the dwarves to Midgard. Only three in Telemark. We must have those places watched. In the meanwhile our plans proceed. Trolls must be bred, our allies here and in Midgard marshaled. Weapons must be made."

"And the hill-raising mechanism must be fixed."

Bakrauf ground her square teeth in rage again.

CHAPTER 41

Aurvangar

Signy moved the little piece of glass that Cair had handed her away from her eye ... and nearly dropped it. "Everything got closer! It's magic!"

"There is no such thing, Princess," said Cair. "Just science. Understanding how things work."

"But with this I can do close fine-work," she said, her eyes luminous with excitement.

And so it was. Experimenting with a number of the lenses they found one that allowed Signy to see, clearly, what her fingers were doing. They had made a little wire holder for it. Signy marveled at her own fingers' deftness, now. The picture that was taking shape under her needle seemed almost alive. Now that she could see what she was doing, needlework was no longer a horrible chore. She could enjoy it, too, and finally see what other women had enjoyed about it. The gardens were flourishing—other than trips to pet the horses, she could work nearly without interruption on the embroidery.

In fact she had to slow it all down so that they could finish together. The dwarves, particularly Þekkr, came in to look and often to talk. They seemed fascinated by her, and she used this fascination to get a great deal of information from them, particularly about things magical. She was rather proud of herself. The deft fingerwork left her mind free to ponder many things. She reached certain conclusions over time, and, eventually decided to act on them.

That evening while they were sitting on what Erik had named "the council ledge" she explained. "I have learned a great deal from Þekkr about the arm-ring. I will not call it the arm-ring of Odin, but by its old name, Gullveig the Dripper. She was bound to the altar stone and within the *weard* stones of the Vé. She is powerful for both good and ill. The *weard* stones restrain her. Only at the time of the ancient sacrifice can the ring leave the stone, and then only to greet the *weards* so that she may know them. They are smaller, symbolic versions of old *bautarstein* that encircle the ancient kingdom. She guards them and they guard her. Taking the arm-ring from the stone magically is almost impossible . . ." Signy paused. "So there is only one place it could be," she said, calmly.

"Where?" asked Manfred.

"Touching the altar stone."

"It's not invisible," said Erik firmly.

Signy shook her head. "No. It is not. But it is there. Touching the stone."

Cair was quickest, beating Erik by seconds. "Under the stone?"

Signy nodded. "It is the only place where it could be, as I said. It must remain in the center of Telemark. At the spiritual and symbolic center."

Manfred looked at Erik, tilting his head on one side. "I reckon that answers the 'who did it?' question, too."

"My half-brother," said Signy in a matter-of-fact tone. "No other man could have lifted that stone." She paused for a moment. "Without those pulleys you're working on, that is."

There was a silence. Signy realized that they were all waiting for Cair to speak. After some time he did. "You know I don't believe the superstitions," he said. "Yes, I know it fits your theory, Erik, of whom your Christian mage was really pointing to with her wand trick. I know, too, that Vortenbras was itching to get out of the treaty he had with the Empire. But superstition is a question of belief. So even if the superstition is just that, Vortenbras may have known it and believed it. So he could have done the deed. And, true enough, only he could have done it. Unless Manfred of Brittany had sneaked in to do it?" enquired Cair with a lift to his eyebrow.

"Er. No."

"Good. I would have hated to have broken my oath and killed you. I'm getting quite fond of the way you grind charcoal," Cair said cheerfully.

"Well," admitted Fjalarr, glumly looking at the magnificent piece of artwork, "you've fulfilled the challenge, fair enough. I must be honest, this piece, superb though it is, is poor exchange for our gardens."

"I've done my best to see that they endure," said Signy.

Þekkr cleared his throat. "You wouldn't like to consider staying on? You and the glassmaker. He's clever for a Midgarder." The dwarf looked as if he was having his teeth drawn, but he had made the offer. "We could even consider better terms . . ."

Three months ago she could have asked for no more. To be needed . . . No, to be wanted, for her skills and for herself. "You're better without me here. I see too much," she said with a mischievous smile.

They looked at each other. "We wondered why you stayed," admitted Vitr. "You could have walked out so easily."

"As you said, intangible chains are the strongest. And loyalty binds me."

"Oh? We thought it was something else," said Sjárr, his spark-eyes dancing. "Well, let us go and see if that can hold you here, if he fails."

"He doesn't fail," she said with a calm certainty.

She was surprised that she had admitted that she knew who they were referring to, and even more surprised that they knew. She'd even toyed with the idea of calling him to her sleeping mat . . . That would have been an almost unthinkable concept, three weeks back. It was perhaps a good thing that the Franks were here.

In two sections, the steel disk went in through the hole. Manfred had fun attaching the two pieces together in a space where two hands did not fit, but at length the plate blocked the hole completely.

Vitr clicked his tongue. "Big and dim," he said, laughing. "The idea is to get through, not to block it up." He came up and, standing on tiptoes felt the welded bars that now protruded through the hole. "Or are you planning to hold on to these and pull it out?

Manfred shook his head. "Just wait and see how dim I am, Vitr."

The dwarf laughed again. "I can already see how big you are."

The second, outer, heavier plate and the black powder had Vitr rolling on the floor with laughter. "Oh my, Midgarder. This is priceless. Magic, no doubt." His expression said exactly what he though of Midgard magic, or at least of Manfred as a practitioner of it.

Manfred looked tolerantly at him. "I'd stay down there. Or come a lot farther back around the corner preferably. The sort of charm I'm going to work here will very possibly twist that beard of yours into knots popping out of your tail end."

Vitr sat up. "Wait. I must fetch the others. This is too good to miss."

"Sure. Can I fetch my friends, too?"

Vitr gave him a stern look. "Don't be silly, now. They're busy. And so should you be. We've got another load of locks for the kobolds to finish. I talked with Fjalarr about that piece of Midgard 'magic.'" He pointed at the metalwork. "You're wasted carrying ore. It's into the foundry with you, lad."

Manfred knew he ought to treat the "promotion" with disdain. But it was flattering, coming from the black dwarf. He had time to carefully lay a trail of the black powder that Cair had mixed so precisely. It took them nicely back around the corner. Manfred knew little of explosives—he was a Ritter, not a bombardier. All he knew was that this was dangerous stuff. It was mildly funny, though, that the corsair was distinctly envious that Manfred got to play with his toy. Manfred grinned to himself, thinking of Cair behaving like a mother hen last night. "It is that the powder is tightly enclosed, you understand. That is why it must be rammed in a cannon. Otherwise it just burns. And for heaven's sake, Manfred, be careful with the stuff."

"You aren't."

"That's because I have some idea of what I am doing," Cair had said loftily, and in Manfred's opinion, untruthfully. There was a certain amount of devil-may-care luck involved in Cair. One day it would run out on the man—or that was Erik's theory. Manfred reckoned that Cair would simply produce the next plan, and if that failed, go on to the next . . . as long as his explosives didn't blow him up to an accounting with his maker.

Manfred knelt, and hauled out his tinderbox. "Here," said Sjárr, "you want a spark?"

"Yes," said Manfred and then looked up just in time. "Hey. Come away from there." Vitr and Þekkr were heading around the corner, toward the explosive. And the trail of powder was fizzing and burning along behind them. "This way! NOW!" He yelled in a voice that brooked no argument, that could have brought walls down by itself, without gunpowder.

The two dwarves turned. Vitr jumped, seeing the fizzing trail burning behind him. Manfred had lumbered up to the two, grabbed one startled dwarf in each hand and flung them as far as he could up the passage. They were remarkably heavy for small men. He dived after them himself, nearly impaling himself on the very affronted Vitr's dagger.

Then . . . the charge exploded. Vitr dropped his dagger. A piece of the roof dropped, too. None of them heard it. Belatedly it occurred to Manfred that a cave was also a good enclosed space.

As if by magic—and it was entirely possible that it was—Fjalarr appeared. He was saying something. Manfred couldn't hear anything right now. But he seemed reassured by the intactness of his brothers. Then others appeared—humans and other workers, with Erik and Cair in the forefront, and Signy a little farther back, all looking worried and then relieved. Saying something because their lips were moving. Manfred allowed himself some of the choicest expletives of Venice in describing Cair. Manfred couldn't hear them, but by Cair's grin, he could.

Manfred couldn't lip-read too well, but he was willing to bet the fellow said, "I told you so."

Hearing was beginning to return now and they all walked cautiously around the corner to where the dust was settling slowly. Someone had the intelligence to bring along a lamp from the wall sconce.

And to his horror, Manfred saw that the wall of adamantine still stood. The metal plate was somewhat buckled. He touched it gingerly, and it fell with a clang to the floor.

It still stood! After all that! He kicked it in disgust. And had to leap for safety as the admantine wall fell down in a shower of cracked crystal. Well, a large part of it fell down, along with another piece of roof that came with it, in sympathy.

"I hope," said Þekkr, "that your attempt at the fulfilment of your challenge is less exciting than your companion's efforts." He seemed to find it funny.

Erik looked darkly at Cair. "It'd better be."

"Good," said Sjárr, his grin like a half-moon in his black beard. "I'm not standing too close anyway. Not after last time."

"I still think we should give them back to Bakrauf," said Vitr with an evil chuckle. "The old troll-wife will be paying us through the nose for repairs from their last efforts. I shouldn't have thought she'd want them back. I mean, they've cost us a priceless wall of adamantine so far. Now we'll have to get someone to put it back together again."

"She must be crazier than we thought to be prepared to buy them," agreed Sjárr. "Well, Midgarder. Go to it. Tell us if we have to duck."

Erik dusted his hands. If something did go wrong he'd be flattened. "This is just simple mechanics," he said with a confidence that he wished was real.

The biggest problem had been to find something to attach the pulleys to on the roof. Erik had noticed that the passage was wider at the top than the bottom. The three iron-hard poles could not—without being lifted and turned—come down.

"The lever is good," said Sjárr. "We understand those. But the rest is . . . interesting."

"Watch."

Using the enormous pole as a lever, Erik rolled the rock onto the net bag. If that broke he'd eat it—if he wasn't squashed flat. He'd tied those knots himself, and every good Icelander boy had done his time fixing and making nets. A net spread the load.

Now it was attached to the pulley. They'd tested these as exhaustively as possible. But there was no real way to test them on that rock—or with the rock's weight. And the rope was locally braided stuff. Who knew how strong it was?

Still. The pulleys were threaded. He hauled. The rope cracked alarmingly. Erik could feel veins standing out on his forehead.

"You don't have to haul it right through the ceiling, you know," said Vitr. "We like it. Can we have these devices? You've no further use for them now?"

Erik was so startled to discover he'd done his task, that he nearly dropped the boulder on himself. Lowering it gave him time to think.

"I'll bargain for horses. And to save us time arguing I'll settle for four of ours."

Vitr chuckled. "It'll save us feeding them anyway. Interesting principle, that double pulley."

The air was full of colored smoke. Cair brushed his bird with feathers and muttered in what, unless Erik was much mistaken, was Latin.

All four of the dwarves watched curiously as Cair readied the metal construction for flight. It looked, Erik thought, like a vicious kingfisher. Cair had carved the body out of soft wood and then cut it in half. Each half had been pressed into the molding material and the impression filled with wax. Then Cair had patiently hollowed the wax and used gypsum to fill in the hollow. Then he used his "lost wax" casting skills to cast the two halves. Careful soldering had joined it all together, with the glass paraphernalia inside. The only opening now was the throat. It was a work of art, Erik had to admit. The wings were separate and solid pieces of thin artistry. Only the join—a thin leaf spring of the finest and most flexible sword steel that Cair had been able to scavenge, was rather unlifelike. Still, it meant that when you tapped the wings they "flapped." The eyes, made from a broken amber bead Cair had produced from his pouch, seemed to glow with life. Cair had put his heart and soul into this piece of work, and he was a craftsman and an artist born, by the looks of it.

It might be very impressive, but Erik still didn't see how in the Hades it could fly or that Cair could even pretend it that did. He also knew Cair had very little time to do whatever he was planning to do. The bird had a bellyful of hot coals that should very soon melt the solder or start it whistling—he was not sure which would come first.

Cair chanted in Latin as he attached the horsehair cord to the bird's legs. He appeared as calm as any man could ever be. Only the professional bodyguard could pick up the small signs of tension, the slight nervous mannerisms.

"It has to fly properly, not be whirled around your head," said Sjárr, looking suspiciously at the horsehair cord.

Cair nodded. "If I was going to do that I would have attached the cord to its wings. This is just to restrain it from flying away before it sings. Now. You interrupt my preparations."

Erik could hear the faint hiss of steam. So could the dwarves. "What's that?" asked Fjalarr, eyes narrowed.

"Merely the magics beginning to work," said Cair. "Now. *Aves per aspera.*" Holding it by the legs he raised the bird above his head.

The hair on the back of Erik's neck prickled as he saw the wings lift and snap straight again. They were vibrating slightly.

And then Cair flicked it up. Well, that was how Erik saw it. It might have looked like someone releasing it, too.

The bird hung, flapping its wings, just under the cave roof. Then began to whistle as water from Cair's dropper dribbled onto the plate of now very hot iron within and turned to steam, with nowhere to escape but through the whistle just inside its throat.

Cair turned to his hosts. "My challenge is done. Now take us to the princess, and let us go."

The dwarves stared in incredulous delight at the iron bird. Erik had to prod them to get their attention. Cair had warned him that the whole thing just might explode.

He'd had enough of Cair's experiments with explosives for a lifetime. Anyone who didn't want that to be a very short lifetime should have that attitude.

Manfred and Signy were waiting with the horses. The dwarves had refused to let them in "because she might assist" and poor maligned Manfred "because he might make something explode." Huh. Did they ever have the wrong sow by the ear.

Bifröst bridge shimmered. It certainly didn't look in the least like a bridge. It looked like a rainbow. If he hadn't been quite so expectant of explosions behind him, Cair would have never ever ventured onto such a thing. Well—except that Signy had already stepped onto it, and her horse was prepared to follow. Horses would follow her anywhere. The rest of them were not so privileged. They had to blindfold their horses before walking out onto a bridge that felt solid enough beneath your feet but looked to be made of light and air.

"I do not believe in magic," said Cair, firmly not looking down. Those were clouds down there.

Erik was plainly suffering from similar problems. Or at least one problem, perhaps with being above the birds on a shimmering transparent bridge of many colors. "How does a man who doesn't believe in magic make a metal bird fly? What's that except magic?"

Cair snorted. "Magnetism. I had put a lot of magnetic ore on that rock shelf in the roof. That's what the leashes were for. Had I not anchored the iron bird down, it would have stuck to the roof."

CHAPTER 42

Telemark

Praise the day at evening;
a wife, when she's been burned;
a sword, when it's been tested.

—Hávamál

They stood on the mountaintop in the weak sunlight of a crisp winter morning.

"If I ever have to do that again," said Manfred, solemnly, "I need to be so drunk that I can't recall the first time. Remember that, Erik. I'm relying on you." He turned to Signy. "I don't suppose you know where we are?"

She nodded and pointed. "Yes, of course! This is my own country. I have ridden over most all of it. Kingshall is down there. You can see the smoke." Indeed it was clear against the pale sky, speaking of warm hearths and the places of men—far from trolls, kobolds, and black dwarves.

"So what do we do now?" said Manfred. "We've no idea of the date, and it seems very likely that if we take you down there, Signy, they'll kill you first and ask questions later."

"I am not afraid to die," said Signy proudly.

"Then either you need your brains taken out and mended, or you need to grow up and stop talking such nonsense," growled

301

Erik, who had not entirely recovered from crossing a bridge of rainbows, light, and air yet. "Death is an uncertain country, and we've got a fair amount to achieve before things are set to rights. We've got to get the arm-ring out from under the stone, and get the culprit dealt with."

"In the meanwhile, I think the need to survive is the immediate problem," Cair pointed downslope. "We're not unlooked for, it would seem."

Looking down the hill, they could see a party of warriors who were pointing back up at them, and grabbing for weapons and rushing for horses.

"Either we're after Yule, or they're not planning to pay much attention to the truce," said Erik, wishing for armor, a good lance, and his Algonquin war-hatchet instead of a stolen sword that he didn't like the balance of. There were at least twenty warriors down there—and one was already on a horse, heading away, obviously a messenger going to bear news to someone, probably Vortenbras.

Manfred grunted sourly. "So much for a quiet arrival."

"Well," said Cair. "I doubt if we could have sneaked in. It would seem the dwarves tipped someone off about our coming."

Erik shook his head. "Not likely. Think about it, Cair. They'd have been up here, instead of camped down there if they'd known for sure. Most probable thing is that these were sentries. Bifröst joins to this world at certain known places. Mostly mountains."

Cair nodded. "So. I think we run?"

"Not very fast in this snow," said Erik. "The only clear trail is where they're coming up—and look at how they're sliding."

Signy snorted. "They're Vortenbras's foreigners. No local would try coming up an ice flume. Look." She pointed at the cut logs stacked off to their left. "The loggers come up here in winter and send the logs down the gully to the lake. In summer the logs would have to be dragged out—a long way around. So the loggers come up with barrels of water when it starts to freeze at night, and pour the water down the gully. It freezes and the logs slide all the way down."

Cair had already dismounted. Erik held his hand over his eyes. "Oh no!"

Manfred jumped down grinning. "Hell, why not? Even if it isn't after Yule if someone is stupid enough to get in the way of a log, that's their problem. That should even the odds a bit. And there doesn't seem to be anywhere to run to, except the bare patch on the top of the mountain. There simply isn't enough forest here to hide in. Let them get in the way at their peril."

"Ah," said Cair. "But what if we simply got out of their way, instead of them getting out of ours, in the same way? Lift that one so that we can lash it onto this one."

"I said 'Oh no!' because I recognize that evil look in his eyes," said Erik. "Can't you see what he's planning?"

Manfred paused in what he was doing. "Are you proposing to sled down on them, Cair?"

Cair nodded. "Down and past. There seem to be some horses in their encampment."

"Do you have any idea," asked Erik, "just how fast and how dangerous a sled like that could be? Sliding down an ice chute?"

"More dangerous than staying here?" said Cair, sardonically. "My head and the princess's are already forfeit. You two they might spare. Stay if you choose."

"He's got us out so far, Erik," said Manfred, hefting the logs with Cair. "Give us a hand."

"It's how close-run his crazy ideas have been that is worrying me. There are absolutely no explosives involved here, are there, Cair?"

"I have a few glass grenades saved for emergencies," admitted Cair. "This could become one if we don't get away."

Erik dismounted. "Given that sort of choice, an ice log flume is the safer option," he said wryly.

The warriors had about three hundred and fifty yards of snow to struggle through, and the leaders were down to the last fifty when Cair's latest mad invention was ready. Three logs were lashed together, the lead edge coarsely chopped into an upward-facing point. There were several leashes or reins to cling to.

They hauled it to the lip, just a few cubits away from the stack. And heaved it over. It didn't instantly begin sliding, but bogged down in the fresh snow. "We'll have to run with it. Get it moving," yelled Manfred, grabbing a leash and hauling, while below them the warriors attempted to urge their horses forward.

Cair's contraption began to slide. Reluctantly at first, and then with increasing pace.

"On, everybody!" Manfred shouted.

They dived for the logs, clinging, as the makeshift sled bucked and bounced over small obstacles, gathering speed, building momentum.

Fortunately—for them—the warriors had moved out of the gully a long time back and had been making their way up the sides of it.

The log sled passed them traveling faster than a crossbow bolt, in a shower of fresh snow and screaming. Erik knew he was but one of the screamers. The sled leapt like a salmon and did not quite flip over. And hurtled onward. Surely no mortal was intended to go this fast—blinded by snow—and live!

Yet they did . . .

The sled slowed. And, wiping the snow from his eyes, Erik realized that Cair's crazy idea had had several unexpected consequences. The first one was that they had absolutely no chance of taking horses from their enemy's camp without a long trip back. The second was that if one unladen log was intended to reach the lake, three logs, plus the weight of four humans would go farther. A lot farther. The sled was still slithering along and the far side of the frozen lake was now looming, coming up relatively fast. The occupants of the small manor on the far side of the lake were disappearing into the trees as fast as their legs could carry them.

As a getaway device, the only two faults Erik could see were that it had carried them far from horses—and affected Manfred and Cair's brains.

"That has to be the greatest experience of a lifetime! A sport of kings!" said Manfred cheerfully. "I wonder if they'd mind if we went up and did it again?"

Cair patted the sled proudly. "And imagine if we could harness that speed. A ship moving that fast to Vinland! Why, we were moving faster than a gazelle . . . faster than a leopard, even."

"Why don't you just get them to fire you out of a cannon?" asked Erik, unclenching his hands from the makeshift leash. And then, seeing the look in Cair's eyes, he hastily said: "*No*. Forget I even mentioned the idea. Not that I'd mind firing you out of a forty-eight-pound bombard, but you would probably find some perfectly good reason for us all to join you. Now come on. Let's see if we can find some horses before we get joined by that bunch of warriors."

They didn't find enough horses. But they did at least find two sturdy horses and a sleigh. "If we live through this lot, we'll pay them for it," said Manfred. "Now let's get out of here before the owners get back, or those warriors get here."

"I wonder how something like this would do going down the ice flume?" said Cair speculatively.

Erik closed his eyes in horror.

"They'll be able to track us easy enough," said Cair, looking back.

"Not for long," said Signy, smiling. Being back in Telemark made her feel . . . complete. As if she'd been missing something and had not known it was gone all these years, but now it was back. Perhaps it had been the thrall bracelets. Perhaps it was knowing that she was able, and valued. Perhaps it was both. But the crisp cold air was as heady as wine. She felt ready, right now, to challenge the entire world, let alone her half-brother. They swung onto a sled trail cut with the runners of many other travelers. "It's the main road to Kingshall," she said cheerfully.

"Uh. We might want to go a little cautiously," said Erik.

"We are still before *Joulu*—yule as you say it," said Signy. "The decorations are still up on that manor door. No good housewife would leave them there after the holy night."

"There are occasional bad housewives," said Manfred. "And a bit of caution costs nothing. I wouldn't be in the least surprised, Princess, if there were orders to kill you on sight. I'd like to avoid that. Erik will doubtless insist on returning this equipage, and cleaning blood off them is such a job."

Signy hadn't come to terms with anyone wanting to kill her. It just seemed impossible to accept that her old life hadn't belonged to someone else. "I suppose you're right, " she admitted. "Well, what do we do now?"

"Find a spot to lie low and send a scout out," said Erik. "Me, I think. I could pass for a local." He looked sardonically at Cair. "So long as I wasn't pretending to be a thrall, that is."

Cair chuckled. "A local franklin. Long on pride, even if short a few pence in the pouch."

"Describes the Clann Hakkonsen perfectly," admitted Erik. "Now, all we need is a place to lie low."

"I know just the place. It was where the man and his sheep were murdered by the monster in the fall," said Signy.

"Just our sort of place!" said Manfred. "Maybe it has a few trolls, too. Or kobolds... Lovely, peaceful part of the world, this!"

"It'll mean that no one goes near it now," Signy said, as sternly as possible. "I wouldn't like to spend a night there myself. And Erik has put me in mind of something, Cair. You'd better give me that sword and my knife again. It is bad enough that I am in trouble, without someone hanging my thrall for carrying edged steel."

Cair couldn't say that it felt good to unbuckle the sword. It made him feel naked. But in an odd way she was quite right. His thrall brand was quite visible. A thrall might easily be punished for no good reason. But killing one was wasteful. And, while he might be a better swordsman than most, he knew that his deadliest weapon was his mind. With that and his hands free he might just achieve a lot more than he could have by relying on the sword as his first option. The sword was the choice of those who could not think.

He handed back her knife with a little more reluctance. "Be careful with the blade, Princess. Whatever you do, don't touch it or eat with it."

"Why?" she asked, looking at it.

"There is crushed arsenic stuck to it with a mixture of flour and water," admitted Cair.

Erik turned to Manfred. "I said he looked like an assassin!"

Cair acknowledged the hit. "I am an exemplary one, giving away the tricks of the trade. I used arsenic to clarify the glass, and I thought that having a few extra surprises in store never hurt," said Cair with a laugh, as they took the sled off the main trail into new snow and off toward the abandoned bonder's hut.

Now they had shelter—and two horses, and a sled, but they had no other tack. Erik tied off the traces, making himself reins, but he would have to ride bareback. That in itself was no problem to Erik, but it would make him stand out.

The other problem was food. But after Erik had ridden out, Cair found the dead bonder's apple barrel. Manfred munched as they sat and watched for trouble. "You couldn't find his ale barrel, too, could you?" asked Manfred cheerfully. "Not that these aren't good apples. Just that they'd be better as cider."

Cair had to sympathize a little with Erik, trying to mentor Manfred.

Erik was a long time in returning. But eventually he came. "Our timing is good and bad—it's *Joulu*—Yule tomorrow. It's bad, because if we'd been faster we might even have got into Kingshall. But it looks like Vortenbras has every warrior he can find guarding Kingshall and the Odinshof. Rumor is flying. I even had a chat with another franklin. Signy, you are the Hag of Jarnvid, by the way. You descended from the mountain on a snow snake that killed a hundred warriors this morning. You are coming to disrupt the Yule celebrations and thus destroy Telemark forever. You and I, Manfred, are evil *fylgjur*, not truce-protected men." He pointed at Cair. "He is a *Svartalfar* and evil to the core. The warriors have orders to kill us all first and ask questions later."

"But . . . we never killed anyone!" protested Signy.

"When did the truth ever get allowed to spoil a good story?" asked Erik with a shrug. "Kingshall is shut siege-tight, and the rest of the knights are trapped inside it."

Signy bit her lip. "At a guess," she said, "after the ceremonies in the Odinshof, Vortenbras will kill your men. If there is no arm-ring, the oath will not be renewed."

"Then we'll just have to get there before these ceremonies are over, won't we?" said Manfred.

Cair realized that they were all staring at him.

"Me?"

"You. Even if it means putting up with your explosives," said Erik.

"I don't have much left. But why me?" Cair found this amusing. They were all capable people in their own right, after all. And up until very recently they'd regarded him with some suspicion. He had to admit they had justification for that.

Erik found it smile worthy, too. "Because doing the impossible, or at least improbable, is your sort of trick."

Cair shrugged. "I just look at things slightly differently."

"Well, look at this one differently then," Manfred said firmly. "I'm open to suggestions, Cair—even including explosions, as Erik said. I've men I owe loyalty to, as well as my duty to my uncle and the people of the Empire."

Erik, after working with Cair, had found he could read when the corsair was dreaming up something particularly fiendish. Cair's eyes took on a lazy half-lidded look. And when he started to smile it was a good time for wise men to go elsewhere.

He was smiling now. "Tell me about this ceremony, Princess. It involves a new fire being lit in the temple, doesn't it?"

CHAPTER 43

A snowy vidda, Telemark

Conditions were not ideal for raising a *draug*. Moonless nights and thunderstorms were the best. And the time—so close to *Joulu* when ghosts, *disir*, and *draugar* walked anyway—gave them far too much liberty. But Bakrauf did not have the latitude to choose her times. She needed to find Signy and her companions, and find them now. So she had raised him up, hoping that the cold had kept good people indoors.

The troll-wife looked at the *draug* with vast distaste. It was not only that burial in the bog had not been kind to King Olaf. She could endure the sight of his peat-stained visage with equanimity, if not pleasure. He'd held out against her spells far longer than any mortal ought to. It was what he had said that had angered her. The constrained dead do not lie. Some may take a positive pleasure in telling the truth. They could, she knew, be selective about which truths they told.

"She can hold *draupnir* without pain. It is her birthright. She can set its bounds."

"You didn't tell me that," said Bakrauf, accusingly.

King Olaf's chest gurgled swamp water. "You didn't ask. She is of my blood. He," the *draug* gestured at the hulking monster that was her son, "is not. I know that now. You could fool me when I was alive. Not anymore. She will avenge me, Bakrauf. She will

309

cleanse your filth off our clan's land. She will undo the shame I have brought on my house with that." He pointed to her son.

Too late she raised a hand to try to stop her son hitting the *draug*. His claws tore into its face and throat.

That was what it had wanted. That would give the dead king a way to deny her the information she needed. Curse it. And curse his stupidity! It was a corpse, and could feel no pain. But now he had seen to it that it could not speak either. It would take much tedious sewing to have it fit to use again. And she did not have the time.

Instead, she must muster her forces around the arm-ring. They only needed a little more time and the oaths sworn on it would be gone like last night's dinner.

She got to her feet. As for its prophecies: *draugar* could only know what the earth they lay in knew, and what the dead knew. They did not know the future. At *Joulu* the truce-oath would be gone. Each of the surviving Christian knights could be sacrificed. The blood-eagles would be pleasing to Odin.

"Come," she said. "We still hold the key. They must come to us, and then we can deal with her."

"And the thrall," said her son grimly.

She ground her big square teeth. "Definitely. Especially the thrall that did so much damage to my castle. I want him maimed, like the smith Völund. His dying must be a long, slow, and shameful thing."

"If I catch him it will be so, indeed," said the great white monster.

CHAPTER 44

Telemark

Deep inside Telemark, Fleet Captain Lars McAllin of Vinland's dogsled teams surged ahead, scouting. The horse-drawn sleds were slower. McAllin swore by those dogsleds and those small bombards of his, but Francesca liked having the solid Danish soldiery in their sleds along as well. Several of them had volunteered—with remarkably little persuasion—to serve as confreres with the Knights of the Holy Trinity. It appeared that the Ritters had impressed while in Copenhagen. And the fact that they were under the command of a young Pole, not a Prussian, had helped still more. As long as the vile weather held off, the expeditionary force would be a surprise visitor to Kingshall. Foolish penmanship in that invitation from King Vortenbras gave them at least a semilegitimate reason to be there. If it proved less than acceptable, then Francesca knew that they had enough force to race through anything but serious opposition.

One of the Danes came back to her sleigh—the tip of her nose protruded from a fur mountain.

"Bad news, I'm afraid, milady," he said apologetically. "The lake hasn't frozen hard enough to cross it, as we expected. It'll mean going back a bit to where we can definitely cross."

"And that means a further delay. You do know that we're racing against time here," said Francesca worriedly.

"Yes, milady. You've said." The Dane smiled ruefully. "We should never have taken directions from that one-eyed man, but he seemed trustworthy. He said that this would be shorter."

Francesca sighed. "Well, we just have to do what must be done then. I hope we're not going to be too late."

"We'll do our best, milady," said the Dane.

CHAPTER 45

Kingshall

Kingshall and the Odinshof were surrounded by a triple ring of warriors. Nothing was going in and nothing coming out. But this was *Joulu*. One thing had to pass through. The *Joulu* log must be kindled with needfire and fragments of the old log. The priests carried the huge oak log, garlanded with green swags, in through the barrier. And the warriors stood respectfully aside, allowing the priests clad in their wolf skins passage toward the Odinshof. Without the kindling of the fire on the *Joulu* log there would be no fertility for the fields, no protections against harm.

All across Europe variations of the same ancient pagan Yule ritual, sometimes with a little Christian top-dressing, were taking place.

Nobody would have dreamed of stopping it. Not for anything.

"It's sacrilege!" Signy had protested, when Cair had pointed this out.

"Why?" asked Manfred, grinning. "As far as I can work out, your corsair doesn't plan to blow up the log, or stop it getting to the temple. All he wants to do is to join in the hard labor of carrying the thing. You'd think they'd be grateful. And to be honest, Princess, none of us are of your faith, and so it is not sacrilege to us. And I need to get into that temple. Erik and I are going whether you do or not. I've helped to carry Yule logs in Carnac. No gods flung lightning bolts at me."

She looked at him, amazed. "You have? But you're Christians!"

"It's part of a pre-Christian tradition that has endured," explained Erik. "It still happens all over the place."

"But then you must know that no woman could do that!" She colored. "It's . . . it's men's work to carry Odin's holy log."

Manfred, of course, caught on quickest. He gave a shout of laughter. Patted Signy, with a great deal too much familiarity, thought Cair. "Don't worry, my dear. I'm sure if I were Odin I'd *insist* on female log-carriers."

Erik joined Signy in blushing. "I hadn't realized the symbolism. They scatter the ashes over the fields, don't they? You can just pretend to be carrying. We'll put you opposite Manfred. Let him do all the work."

Cair was the only one who had kept a straight face. "Princess, what would be better? To wait here, and be hunted at their leisure, or to go and beard them in their lair?"

Signy lifted her chin. "The latter of course, but can't we do it in a more . . . some other way? It . . . it doesn't seem honorable."

"And to allow Vortenbras to succeed is honorable?" asked Cair. "We can try an open charge, but that would just end up with us all dead. Or we can join the priests at dusk. Who counts priests? They're like flies on a corpse."

"But surely they'll notice us joining them?" said Erik, ever pragmatic.

"There are wolf skins here," said Cair. "Not very well tanned by the smell of them, but then that's just too bad. We can disguise ourselves—there is not much more to Odin's priests' garb that we can't deal with in the twilight. I will arrange a little distraction and then we can join the procession."

"Explosives?" said Manfred suspiciously.

"Well, gunpowder anyway," admitted Cair. "No big explosions. I have some interesting new experiments I haven't tried out yet with additives to the powder. Finely ground iron. It has interesting effects."

Erik and Manfred looked very distrustful.

Tch. He hadn't killed them yet, had he?

"As the senior representative of the Emperor's delegation you must lead your men to the temple," said Vortenbras smoothly.

Juzef Szpak could cheerfully have pushed his sword through the big self-satisfied bastard's spine. They'd planned to hold a section of Kingshall against all comers—and short of the Norse setting fire to their own halls, they'd have been the very devil to dislodge.

Now, by following the pretenses of the truce, they would be forced into leaving their security. Well, the Norse would still pay a very steep price for their treachery. If he had a hundred knights on horseback they'd have had a real fighting chance. "We will be there. Dressed as befits the occasion."

"Good. I will be going to the temple now to spend some time in solitary vigil for my sister. She may have been evil and a witch, but she was still my sister. Or that's what my mother says. I will have a thrall sent to fetch you at the appropriate time. Your heathen priests must of course remain here. We cannot have Christian priests defiling Odin's temple."

Juzef drew himself up and touched the cross on his surcoat. "We knights are part of an order militant. We are as much priests as they are."

"Oh." That gave Vortenbras pause, but not for long. "Well, I dare say it will not matter in an hour or two. Let them see a real god's temple then."

"We've seen the true God's temples," said Szpak, stiffly. What was the point of this pretense? "Let them go, King Vortenbras. What are they to you?"

The Norseman snorted. "You will learn," he said, as he turned and left.

Juzef Szpak looked at the departing man, eyes narrow, thoughtful. There was no point in assuming a defensive stance in the temple. So he, personally, was going to see if he could save his brothers back in Småland and Skåne and Prussia a lot of dying later, by killing this man. When trouble broke, they would not form a defensive circle, but a wedge, and they would try to reach the Norse kinglet. He went to inform his brothers-in-arms.

He was not surprised to find the knights in agreement with him. He was considerably more surprised to find that the Servants of the Holy Trinity were pleased to go to the temple. Uriel looked down his long nose at him when he suggested otherwise.

"God's service asks not how little we can do, Ritter. It asks for our all. We are secure in his arms," said the monk dryly.

Szpak wouldn't have minded being secure in twice the number of Ritters, too. On horseback.

The mist swirled thickly through the bare oak branches of the *Vé* when they marched in perfect formation to the temple. The temple was full of warriors—Vortenbras's personal guard, and the nobles of Telemark.

As the knights took up their positions inside the temple, a party of Odin's priests and their acolytes in their wolf-skin cloaks came in carrying the huge log between them, on short strops of grass-woven rope. Behind him Szpak heard one of the nuns draw breath sharply. "Witchcraft!"

Coming, as it did, from a witch-smeller, that was no typical priestly accusation to be taken with a pinch of salt. Especially when Juzef recognized the scruffy large man on the far side of the log . . .

Erik thought Cair's fountains of smoky yellow sparks would probably have been an adequate distraction, even without the mist and the fast-descending winter night. When the mist lit up with sparks and hissing fountains of fire, several of the acolytes who had been rounded up for the heavy lifting had run, shrieking. In the pandemonium, joining the procession in their places had been almost ludicrously easy.

Disguises had been harder. Men here wore beards and long hair. Signy had had to undo her tight braids—that was easy. The glorious cascade of white-gold hair that this released was not masculine, however. Beards had to be contrived with a little help from the horse manes. Breeches had to be found for Signy: The bonder's scanty wardrobe had not been removed, and his spare breeches were available. But they were barely a disguise. They accentuated her narrow waist and broad hips, as the dowdy riding habit had not. And with her hair loose and framing her face, she looked far more feminine. It accentuated the high cheekbones, the fine structure of her face, and those deep blue eyes, which Erik thought were looking more Alfar by the moment. He wondered why he'd never noticed it before.

All that her horse-hair moustache and beard did was to make them all laugh.

"You'll have to put on a glamour to fool them," said Erik, regretting the words as soon as they were out of his mouth.

Strangely enough, that just made her smile. It was the kind of smile that made men do really stupid things, like walk into walls. By the look on Cair's face, he was ready to walk right through them for her, right then. "I'll have to do that," she said calmly.

"I might suggest a hat as well," said Cair, regaining his composure. "Or a hooded garment such as the late owner of this place has left."

Maybe it had been the hood Signy wore. Or maybe she'd cast such a glamour over all of them that even Cair's display of sparks was unnecessary. But no one even questioned her right to be there. None of them got a second glance.

The party of priests—real and false—walked in through the dripping trees of the *Vé* grove. They stepped in through the carved doorway of the Odinshof to face the waiting crowd.

"Looks like they've had nothing to do but polish armor since we left," muttered Manfred to Erik. But that was real relief in his voice, at seeing Szpak and the rest of the escort grimly arrayed for war—here, where he had least expected their support.

The log was set down, and the old high priest of Odin had doddered forward with a *hlauttein* twig in his hand, when Manfred stepped forward. "Greetings. King Vortenbras. We have found where the arm-ring has been hidden."

Vortenbras's jaw dropped as he stared at Manfred and plainly recognized him. "Wha . . . seize him."

Manfred held up his hand. "Hold. We still have a truce. You, Vortenbras, are still bound by it," he said, grimly. "Bound by an oath sworn on the holiest symbol of all Telemark. Break it if you dare."

The Norse stood frozen. Only a few of Vortenbras's malcontent ragtag foreign camp followers stepped forward . . . and realized that no one else had. They stood, too, uncertain.

"We need witnesses." Manfred turned to the elderly priest. "The arm-ring of Telemark cannot be taken outside the temple *waerds*, without extreme pain. It will return magically to the altar stone if removed from contact with it. It is never worn except on Midsummer Day and Midwinter Night."

"Yes, outlander," quavered the old priest. "That is correct."

Manfred pointed to the altar. "Yet it isn't lying on top of the stone, which means there is only one place it could be, if this is all true."

Erik and Manfred seized the altar stone and heaved together. Slowly it came up from the earthen floor.

There was a hiss of indrawn breath.

Pressed into the hard earth was the image of an arm-ring-shaped object.

It had been there, all right.

But it wasn't there anymore.

Cair had taken the opportunity presented by Manfred's show-manship to melt back into the shadows. He wasn't watching Erik or Manfred. Instead he was watching Vortenbras . . . and somebody else.

Queen Albruna.

Her head looked just like it had in the jar in Bakrauf's castle.

He was less surprised than Manfred or Erik when the arm-ring turned out to have been removed. Vortenbras's face betrayed him. Cair could predict the next moves—and none of them were good for Signy or for him.

Signy looked at her stepmother in the same way that she'd looked at the dwarves when they tried to disappear. The image of the apple-cheeked, comfortably plump blond woman blurred and shivered as if viewed through a heat haze. But Signy was horrified to see that it was still someone she recognized.

Erik spoke. "This is plainly where the thief hid it. Has this place been unguarded since then?"

The old priest shook his head. Peered rheumily at the hole under the stone. "No. A priest and four guards have been here every hour of the night or day since the holy object disappeared." His voice quavered slightly. "We tried scrying . . . augury. All the signs *did* say that it was in the temple. We've searched. But no mortal could lift the stone."

"Can we put it down now?" asked Erik, making something of a mockery of that statement.

Manfred nodded. "On the count of three, mind toes."

They dropped it.

And the leader of the Frankish knights spoke. "King Vortenbras said that he came here to meditate in solitary this afternoon."

The old priest blinked. "But he is the king. It is his right."

"He is also the only man I've seen who could possibly have lifted that stone alone," said the man, Szpak, she thought he was called.

The deathly silence that followed was broken by Queen Albruna. "The witch must be here, too, Vortenbras. The one in the hooded cotte."

Signy felt all eyes turn to her. She pulled the hood off, shook her hair free, and for the first time in her life feeling every inch a royal princess. Now that she knew and understood that she'd been a prisoner, and magically oppressed, it was easy. Now she understood why her stepmother had abused her, too. Albruna—as she'd called herself—had been afraid. Signy lifted her chin and stepped forward, speaking loudly and clearly. "Yes. I am here. I am free of those who captured me, who would have seen me killed for *their* theft and *their* murders. Who have falsely accused me. Who have also sought to dishonor and break the truce my father swore to."

She pointed. "I name you, Vortenbras, as the murderer of the guards of Odin's temple. They would have known and trusted you. You were their king. You gained access and killed them, unsuspecting. The arm-ring was not stolen. It was hidden under the altar stone by the only man who could lift the stone. The outlander Christian magicians pointed to the thief—not to me, but to the person who stood behind me. You. Vortenbras, I accuse you. You are a murderer and a thief. You came here alone this afternoon. You insisted on being alone. Show us your upper arms, if you dare."

Vortenbras laughed. "Make me. I am still the king. I rule here. I give the orders here."

But Signy could feel the crowd in the temple draw toward her. She could hear the fear behind her supposed half-brother's bravado.

But she'd not accounted for her stepmother. "A woman? Even in men's clothing? Touching the holy log of Odin? That is sacrilege."

Manfred and Erik were back among the knights now, but Manfred of Brittany spoke up for her. He was an honorable man. "Strictly speaking she was not touching the log," he said loudly.

He might as well have tried to stem the tide. The *Joulu*-log ceremony was an older and far more powerful part of the life and belief of the people than any mere royal machinations or murder could be. On this rite the fertility of the whole land depended. There was a murmur of fear and horror. And with her new-awaked sensing of magic, Signy knew that these were being manipulated. But she did not know how to counter it. She saw that the Christian mages were trying something. But it would be too late for her.

"Take her to the tree," said the high priest, his old voice cracking with rage. And she found herself swept along in a tide of priests and warriors. Carried outside the temple.

The tree was ready for the sacrifice. It was a strong young tree, just outside the temple doors, its bare branches stark in the light of the torches they carried out with them. A stout rope was attached to it, and it was bent.

It was something of a signal honor they were paying her. Kings died thus. King Vikar had, to appease Odin for his people. She held her head up high as they put the rope around her neck. She would show them how she could die, even if she'd never had a chance to show them how she could live.

"Tell them to let go of me, damn you, Szpak," said Manfred, furiously. "We've got to save that woman!"

The four knights that Juzef had detailed to the task did nothing of the kind.

"Prince Manfred, we cannot intervene," said Szpak, sternly. "We cannot take up arms against the Norse without breaking our oath."

"The devil take that oath, man." The struggling Manfred had dragged all four knights to the door of the temple. "They're going to kill her. And I persuaded her to do what they plan to kill her for. Erik!"

But Erik wasn't there.

When Erik Hakkonsen had heard the queen mother speak, he'd looked at her in some surprise. He did not, by this stage, expect Cair to be wrong. She was dead and her head was in a jar in Bakrauf's Trollheim castle. But she appeared alive enough, and spreading her poison. It certainly looked like her, down to the detail of the silver bear earrings.

It was that final detail that overcame what he was later convinced was a magical compulsion. With a snarl he'd leaped away from the other knights. Albruna was still standing up, regally, smiling as if she had not just sent her stepdaughter to her death. She had seven bulky Norse guards with her, but they were in front of her. "I need your cross," Erik said to Brother Uriel, in a voice that brooked no argument.

Uriel did not hesitate to give it to him.

Taking it, Erik ran up the shallow stair between the banks of seats, and grabbed her, pushing the cross against her as he did so.

"Got you, Bakrauf!" he yelled, grabbing her from behind.

The cross did have an effect on her glamour.

It might have affected her magic and her strength too, but these were vast, anyway. She writhed and swung a blow at Erik that very nearly leveled him. The second fist hit his other cheekbone. Erik saw stars, but still held on tight, managing to pinion her. He was dimly aware that the seven guards had turned to bears, and that Manfred was calling him. The bears weren't his problem. The knights and several of the Norse nobility were dealing with them.

Then Brother Uriel was there, also sprinkling holy water on her. She hissed and spat like a fire in a rainstorm. And subsided like one, too. Glowering and furious.

Cair had been swept along with the press of men heading out of the temple with Signy.

He had no plans for this. Only determination . . . and a last fire and smoke bomb he hadn't used when they joined in the Yule log procession.

All this had been his idea in the first place. And now, she was going to die for it. He lit the fuse from someone's torch. And tossed it into the crowd. The bomb was designed for show, not harm, but right now it was all he had.

He hit the warrior nearest to him in the pit of the stomach and wrenched his poleaxe away from him.

"A rescue!" he yelled. "Signy!"

With the rope around her neck Signy saw Cair, like some Viking berserk out of legend, fighting his way toward her. Men scattered, or fell. This was good and fitting. Cair would surely go to Valhalla, to be part of Odin's host, thrall brand or no, fighting like that. It would seem that no one could stand against him and his companion.

Her heart sang with pride and joy.

Cair realized as he fought his way forward that two things had happened—the first: his bomb had plainly not gone off, and the second was that he had at least one comrade to help him. The whistling iron bird dove at his foes, slashing at them with its long, sharp beak, or with the talons he'd cast for it. He had no time right now to question the logic or the possibility of it: it was here, and Signy needed their help. The fact that it was indeed a magical creature, or else it could not possibly fly and attack his foes, was irrelevant.

All that stood between him and Signy now were Vortenbras's hearthmen. The Norse locals were too superstitious to attack. There were of course still a lot of hearthmen.

"I want him alive," bellowed Vortenbras, holding a spear to Signy's side.

That suited Cair down to the ground. People who had to try and keep you alive were a lot easier to kill.

"You can maim him. I don't mind if he loses limbs. But keep him alive."

Manfred let his arms go slack as if he was going to stop strug- gling. Then he wrenched them free, just as Vortenbras yelled, "I want him alive." Damn. If they only sought to capture the gallant idiot, Manfred had no excuse to break his oath.

Then when Vortenbras said the second part he knew that he was right.

"Prince Manfred! Our oath!"

"The hell with it. My honor!" roared Manfred.

And then . . . there was the sound of sharp trumpets shatter- ing the air.

It was Signy. Who would have thought that a human throat could have produced such a sound?

Signy screamed. It was a sound of pure fury and anguish. How could Vortenbras? Hel take her half-brother. If Cair died in this battle, fighting for her, then they could die together as was right and fitting. Odin would never deny a fighter like that a place in Valhalla.

Instead, Vortenbras had decided that her man—and there was no denying it now: he was her man—must be maimed, so they could not even be together in Valhalla.

She shouted into the sudden silence as the crowd turned to stare at her, using the words that King Vikar had used, centuries back. "If I am guilty of anything, let Odin's will fall as it may. Otherwise, I will exercise my will."

And abruptly the air was full of birdsong and warmth . . .

And the strong tree that was bent to hang her as an offering, shrank and became a sapling. The stout rope became frail calf-gut, and the spear Vortenbras thrust furiously at her turned into a weak reed and snapped.

Signy stepped free. Weapons fell from several hands.

And then Erik struggled out of the temple, his arms still tight around the troll-wife. Bakrauf had half burst out of Queen Albruna's gown, exposing a row of white, sowlike teats to the crowd.

A collective hiss of horror went up from the warriors.

"The troll-wife," said Erik in the silence. "Bakrauf. The source of all these troubles."

"Sorcerer! What have you done to my mother?" bellowed Vortenbras.

Erik looked him straight in the eye. "Queen Albruna is dead. Her head lies pickled in a jar in the troll-wife's castle," he said. "This one has taken on a seeming of her." He grunted as Bakrauf struggled in his arms. "She is a mistress of glamour. We need chains to hold her. Cold iron. Fetch them."

"Let me help," said Szpak calmly. "The arms of armored men will do. Von Gersinger, Alendorff. Take her. One in front and one behind. Hold her tight."

"Better put your visors down, Ritters. She bites," said Erik. Both of his eyes had already begun to swell.

Signy walked forward and took Cair by the arm and led him forward, a broken poleaxe in his hand and a strange metal bird on his shoulder.

"It's that thrall!" exclaimed Vortenbras. "A thrall that has taken edged steel! Attacked his betters! He'll do for the blood-eagle."

Signy looked coolly at her half-brother. "He has every right to take up steel, Vortenbras. He was *my* thrall. *My* property, and I have freed him, as is my right. You will have to look elsewhere for victims."

Cair's showy firework chose this moment to go off and shower them in sparkling yellow stars.

Signy held tightly to Cair. But she did not choose to run or even retreat.

The metal bird on Cair's shoulder whistled, took off, and flew above them.

No one else stood their ground—except for Vortenbras. "Get up," he snarled at his men. And such was the sheer force of his personality, or his hold on them, that they listened. Warriors got to their feet, looking sheepish, looking scared, but still looking to Vortenbras.

"I still rule," Vortenbras said coolly. "Understand and remember this. The kings of Telemark cannot be removed except by death. I have decided. Hjorda is dead and you, Signy, are an impediment. You will be sacrificed to Odin. A fitting royal sacrifice to cleanse this temple of the heathen Christian filth trespassing in it. I will kill you with my own hands if need be. And this time your witchcraft will not stop me." He looked at the knights. "The arm-ring of Odin is missing. The truce-oath will not be renewed." He looked hard at them, daring any accusation, any back-answer.

Cair had an answer. He threw the broken poleaxe like a javelin. It hit Vortenbras on his unprotected throat.

And Vortenbras did not die. He pulled the blade out and snapped the remnant of the shaft off, dropping it at his feet.

The blood stopped flowing and the cut healed as they watched.

Vortenbras spat blood . . . and laughed. "You cannot kill me. But I can and will kill you, thrall."

Cair's reply was to pick up a piece of the axe shaft.

Manfred found his arm being tugged furiously by the two nuns. "We need you," said Sister Mary.

"Now," said Sister Mary, tugging harder.

He shook his head. "Not now. I need to kill Vortenbras."

Sister Mercy snorted. "You can kill him fifty times over. He has the arm-ring. The magic of the thing will simply mend him."

Sister Mary explained. "We need to get him to take the arm-ring off. The only way to do that is to use your strength on one of the *bautarstein* which mark the *weard* of the arm-ring." The birdlike little nun looked at her companion. "We cannot do it."

Manfred drew a deep breath. *Think. Do not react without thinking.* Erik had said it a thousand times. "I'm sorry. Show me what you need done."

The mossy rock had been imbedded in the soil a long time, but it was no match for Manfred in this mood. Clutching it like some stone baby, Manfred ran back through the crowd, thrusting them aside.

"Place it so that he is outside the *weards*," clucked a panting sister from his wake.

Manfred didn't run into the hearthmen and drop it. He simply threw it from there. Fortunately for them nobody was hit by it.

As it touched the ground, Vortenbras, the Viking ideal . . . screamed like a woman in labor. He dropped his sword and clawed at his arm, tearing the rich cloth, yanking at the thick golden arm-ring that was revealed. The Norse kinglet pulled it off, shrieking.

It lay there, gleaming in the torchlight.

"Now we know, indeed, who stole the arm-ring," said Brother Ottar, speaking Norse, his voice strong in the silence.

Vortenbras shrugged. Standing back from it, he retrieved his sword. "I cannot avoid the treaty between Telemark and the Holy Roman Empire," he said. He turned on Signy—and the crowd. "But nothing else changes. The kings of Telemark are kings by blood, and cannot be removed except by death."

"Yet they must face challenge by the jarls. Trial by battle," said Signy. She turned to the nobles of Telemark. "Who will remove this king for us?"

Vortenbras laughed. "Who here will dare to meet me?" He held up his sword. "I am the foremost warrior in all Norseland. Face me, if you dare."

Not one of the Norse uttered a word. "I will," said Manfred.

"Or I will," said Erik. "I am a better swordsman."

"But your eyes are half-swollen shut," said Manfred cheerfully.

"Comes of kissing troll-wives." He'd pay for that later, but it was worth it.

"I'll do it," said Szpak.

The old priest had come forward, nervously. He reached for the arm-ring, but it burned him. Still, it rolled against the *waerd* stone. Manfred wondered if this was the thing heading itself back to the altar stone. Wringing his burned hand, the priest said feebly. "You can't, outlanders. You are truce-sworn."

"I'll do it," said Cair cheerfully as the metal bird landed gently on his shoulder. "I'm not sworn to any truce. And I owe you for this brand, Vortenbras, and for the mistreatment you have given the princess."

Vortenbras looked down at the corsair. "You may not be a thrall but you are not noble. Not a landholder," sneered Vortenbras. "I almost wish you were. I would enjoy killing you, for all that you are undersized."

"Before these witnesses, I gift you my mother's holdings, Cair Aidin," said Signy loudly.

Manfred saw how Vortenbras's eyes widened. "Cair Aidin?" he said, staring. "You? The corsair? The Lynx of the Pillars of Hercules? You? Here? Do you know my agents have tried to contact you, or your brother Aruj, to suggest an alliance? North and south we could harry the seaways."

Cair laughed, calm and seemingly amused. "I'd sooner bed a viper," he said, dismissively.

"And I would ally with no man who would let himself be made into a thrall," sneered Vortenbras.

Cair grinned, white teeth bright in his dark face. "Ah, but I am a freeman now, Vortenbras. A landed freeman of your own country. I have the right to my sword. But it was lost at sea. I'll need another blade to fight you with."

Vortenbras snorted. "You can have any blade in the kingdom. It will do you no good. I'm going to hamstring you and make you into a thrall again. Your death will be slow and obscene."

"Very well." Cair turned to Erik. "Do you have a rapier? Not a broadsword. A proper rapier."

Erik nodded. "Yes. A Ferranese blade from the hands of one of De Viacastan's journeymen. You can have the use of it with my blessing. In fact, you can have it. Fair payment for services rendered."

Cair nodded. "Fair payment indeed, Erik. I thank you. Have someone fetch it for me, please."

He turned to Signy.

"I ask one boon, Princess. Can I borrow the knife you gave to me as my main gauche?"

She nodded. Drew the blade very carefully from her sleeve sheath. "Here. You are a free man, Cair. A nobleman of Telemark. Use it well." Only Manfred was standing close enough to hear her say, "I will join you cleanly my beloved. I will be beside you in Valhalla." She plainly did not believe anyone could defeat Vortenbras. It was also clear that none of the Norse did, either.

He bowed. "Thank you, Princess. I am honored." He took the metal bird from his shoulder. "I gift you my bird in return. I suppose the dwarves said that I must make it, not that they could have it."

Cair turned to Manfred. "I understand the honor the princess does to me . . . now. Nonetheless . . . you have an oath."

Manfred grinned. He had had enough lessons from Erik—and the two of them from the Venetian armsmaster, Giuliano Dell'Arta—to know that size wasn't everything. Speed and skill were. "I'm not going to need to honor it, Cair. But I would."

Cair smiled, and felt the balance and weight of the knife, holding it up.

Vortenbras snorted his disdain at the knife. He drew his huge two-handed sword. Well, it would have been a two-handed sword for any other man. He looked at his half-sister "I'm not an old dotard like Hjorda, Signy. Maybe that would have killed him. Not me."

Signy smiled at him, showing her teeth like a vixen defending her cubs. "You hoped for that end for me, Vortenbras. You and that thing I called mother. You called me *Svartalfarblod* and called me a *seid*-witch. Why are you not afraid that I will bring my magic down on you now?"

Vortenbras snorted. "You're too soft. Besides, I have my own powers."

A panting man arrived with the rapier, and a commander of the guard from the perimeter.

"We hear a large number of dogs out in the mist, King Vortenbras," said the commander.

"Deal with it," snarled Vortenbras. "The problem you were

supposed to avert is here already." He pointed at Signy. "And find the men who let the *Joulu* log through and kill them."

"You'd better wait until the issue of kingship is decided before you do anything rash," said Manfred to the commander, whose eyes opened wide, plainly recognizing the speaker. "But you can pass the word on to your men that the arm-ring has been found."

"Who asked you to speak?" snapped Vortenbras, looking furiously at Manfred. The veneer of polite court manners was peeled away.

"I don't need your permission, kinglet," said Manfred, trying to make Vortenbras angry. In a fight, an angry man was less cautious. It might offset the advantages of reach and weight that Vortenbras had. He had not forgotten that the corsair had almost bested Erik with a homemade knife. But Vortenbras was presumably skilled, too. "We found it on the thief and murderer's arm." He pointed at the culprit as the commander gaped.

"Are you ready?" said Cair calmly, inspecting the rapier, trying its balance.

"You might as well wait for the death," said Vortenbras to the guard commander, but the man had already scurried away.

As Cair raised his blade in salute, the cloud tore open and the light of a full moon spilled down on them. Vortenbras wasted no time in such niceties as a salute. He simply swung. It was the kind of blow that could have severed a spine—if it had hit. It did not.

Cair had moved. And lunged and slashed in.

"First blood to the outlander!" exclaimed a coastal landholder.

"He is not an outlander," said Signy. "He is Jarl Cair of Telemark. He is now of our land. He is mine," she said fiercely, as the two circled. "I will bury him with honor. I will climb onto his pyre with him."

"I hope that's planned for the far future, Princess Signy," said Erik comfortingly, as the fighters whirled and sought advantage. "He's got the edge on Vortenbras, you know, Princess. See, Manfred. That's the Lozza double riposte."

Looking at Signy, Manfred realized that she'd expected Cair to die, and die quickly. He saw how the blood was draining from her cheeks, and she bit her knuckles as she realized that, as much of a legend as Vortenbras might be, there was always someone as deadly. Before, she'd had a grim certainty. Now she knew the terror of hope. Cair's metal bird moved on her shoulder, half-opening its iron wings. She petted it instinctively.

Fear.

Cair realized that something was very wrong. He felt fear. Bowel-melting terror, in fact. His mouth was dry. He prickled with cold sweat.

This was . . . wrong. He'd never been afraid in a fight before. Before it started, yes. That was perfectly normal. But once combat was joined it melted away from him. Now . . . he was terrified, terrified enough to make his sword tip waver.

As he circled, looking for an opening—and wishing he could turn and run—a part of his mind said, *If you can make metal birds fly, if Signy can make gardens blossom and trees shrink, this bastard can also use magic against you. He can make you afraid.* And with that, he began chanting to himself in Latin. He used the only words that would come to him. And in the background he heard the monks and knights singing, echoing somehow the silent words his lips were forming " . . . I shall fear no evil, thou art with me . . ."

Like the ebbing tide, the fear receded. Vortenbras swung wildly at him again. There was no skill in the big Norseman's stroke. Just brute force. Now, facing him coolly, Cair sidestepped it with ease. A few moments back it might have killed him. But without the fear to aid him, Vortenbras was no swordsman. Now Cair knew with a clear certainty: fear was the key. If Vortenbras was able to turn his foes' bowels to water then he didn't need skill. No wonder the Norse were terrified of him. He made them scared, magically. Somehow he created fear until rationality drained away from his foes and panic set in. And panicked men were easy to kill.

Well, now that Cair had worked it out, it was Vortenbras's turn to feel terror. Cair knew that there was no point in prolonging the agony. Lunging and twisting, he slashed the Norse king across the wrist, severing tendons. Vortenbras dropped the sword.

As Cair came in for the coup de grâce, Vortenbras threw himself sideways and, with a squeal, grabbed the arm-ring. Vortenbras was now back inside the *waerd* line with it, and began to heal.

With a desperate lunge, Cair knocked the arm-ring out of

Vortenbras's hand again. It rolled back next to the *waerd* stone again.

"Pick it up, Cair," screamed Signy. "Don't let him take it again . . ." and her voice trailed off.

Cair did so, snatching it up and pushing it onto his arm. Inexorably, he advanced on Vortenbras. "It ends here," he said grimly. "I am not afraid, Vortenbras. You've failed. You are going to die."

But what had shocked Signy into silence was that her half-brother's image had gone hazy, and was shifting, changing. Clothing split and tore and icy mist hissed off the white-furred beast that now stood before Cair. It stood at least fifteen foot high. One paw hung limp, but something this size did not need both. It also had a mouth full of long white teeth—a mouth now open in a roar.

"Grendel!" said a shocked voice in the sudden silence after that roar.

Mouth open, the grendel charged down on Cair.

Cair used to entertain himself on shipboard by throwing knives at a target. He seldom missed.

He put Signy's arsenic-laden dagger right into the back of the Vortenbras-grendel's throat. And, as the grendel caught him, he rammed Erik's sword home into its belly, up into its heart. Hard.

The last thing he heard was Signy screaming.

CHAPTER 46

In search of warmth. Kingshall, Telemark

The Norse captain looked at the dogsleds, and the bombards ... and the woman who was beckoning to him. He decided that reason might be the better part of valor—his troops had largely deserted him, running to watch the fight at the temple.

"Good evening." She smiled dazzlingly at him from her nest of furs. "We've come about this missing arm-ring ..." she said in passable Norse.

"Oh. It's been found, milady," said the Norseman, relieved.

"Excellent!" Francesca buried her second spare copy deeper into the furs. She gave the Norseman the benefit of her best smile. "Then, if you could be so kind as to direct us to some place where we can get warm, and inform Prince Manfred of Brittany that Francesca is here. Emperor Charles Fredrik has been worried about him."

The smile nearly robbed the warrior of speech, which, in Francesca's opinion, was as it should be. "Uh. Certainly, milady. He's ... he's at the temple right now. I'll go directly ..."

She put a gloved hand on his arm. "No. It will wait ... at least until I am somewhere warmer."

If the thing had been found and Manfred was—apparently—intact, there seemed little point in further intervention. Certainly not tonight, in the cold.

"What's that noise?" she asked, as the air was suddenly filled with a sort of clashing drumming.

"It's a celebration, milady."

CHAPTER 47

On the stairway to Valhalla.
Kingshall, Telemark

When Erik saw Cair go into that death clinch, his heart had fallen to his boots. In Vinland he'd seen a dying grizzly take a man into its embrace once. And this was much bigger than a grizzly bear.

He and several others—Manfred, Szpak, and Signy—and a metal bird rushed forward as the grendel fell, claws still tearing into Cair, who was underneath.

With a wail of despair, Signy flung herself onto her grendel half-brother and hauled. Manfred added his considerable strength, pulling it over. And Erik and Szpak pulled the arms apart.

Cair had made sure and doubly sure that it was dead. It was probably dead before he'd lunged up through the belly and into its heart, and had been trapped in that death hug for his pains. That didn't stop the metal bird from pecking the grendel's eyes out. Cair's ragged cotte was shredded—Erik saw the white of splintered bone in among the blood-streaming rags.

Weeping, Signy pulled her man free. "You can't die! You can't!" she gasped, holding on to him.

She pressed her head to his breast and clung, her golden hair spread across his bloody cotte.

All was still, but for her sobbing. The Norsemen stood respectful, silent.

The silence endured.

And then Cair's arm came up and around her.

And Erik saw that a golden circle surrounded his upper arm, and that the terrible gashes on it were already healing.

The arm-ring made all things whole . . .

The rheumy-eyed priest of Odin muttered, "Sacrilege." But he said it very very quietly.

Signy lifted Cair. You wouldn't have thought such a slight thing would have had the strength, but perhaps she drew it from her will. That was large enough.

She got him to his feet.

And as he stood, swaying, still held upright by her, the watching Norsemen began hammering the pommels of their swords on their shields, cheering wildly.

Cair raised his free arm. It was healed, and the arm-ring gleamed against the dark flesh. The Norsemen stilled.

He cleared his throat. "Do you not kneel before your new queen?" he asked loudly.

There was a stunned silence from the huge crowd. "I will challenge to single combat any man who doesn't," he said coolly.

And throughout the *Vé*, and into the field beyond, warriors knelt.

Fight someone who just killed a grendel, single-handed . . . and lived?

I don't think so, even if he is an outlander with a thrall brand.

"Long live the queen," said Manfred, with a grin to Erik and Szpak. "You wouldn't have a drink about you, Juzef? Even that cabbage liquor would do."

The two knights manhandled Bakrauf toward Kingshall. Behind her she heard the cheering.

He was dead, then. Grendel would not free his mother.

Spittle and blood were all she needed to call her hunt. She would extract such revenge on the stinking little *Alfarblot* . . . She bit her cheek and spat, calling.

The hunt came. From a tumble of ravens and crows the children of darkness took form. Tonight of all nights they were easy to summon. This was the longest night. The night when even the dead walk.

As the two knights yelled and dropped her, Bakrauf realized that the hags and sylphs and creatures of darkness had come for her.

Not to carry her away to safety, to her own place, but to extract their awful revenge for her entrapment.

It was not quite *Joulu* midnight yet.

Her own shrieks were lost in the roar of adulation for the new queen.

And the knights' attempt to come to her rescue was thwarted by a *draug*, blundering toward them out of the darkness. They turned to defend themselves as the thing that had been King Olaf lurched toward them, dripping. It was somehow managing to laugh with that ruined face.

On this the longest night, when *draugar* and *disir* walk . . . He was only dripping his way to his ship mound, where he wished to rest, when her spells were broken. He felt them fall and tear from the very fabric of the earth that he was part of. When the hunt came . . . he was ready.

As he retreated from bright swords and cold iron—that could not hurt him anymore—he knew what passes for satisfaction among the dead. His daughter would rule now, which was as it should be. Frightening a couple of heathen knights from rescuing the troll-wife who had murdered him and usurped his throne for her monster son was a pleasant way to ensure his little Signy's rule. And Odin himself would have appreciated the irony of it all.

He could rest now, with honor, in his ship mound. The hunt would shred her into gobbets and scatter them across the nine worlds.

The golden circle lay on the altar stone as if it had never been removed. The old high priest picked it up, muttering. But oaths must be sworn. And *Joulu* waited for no man or new queen. He slipped the arm-ring over his bony elbow. "Let Odin bear witness," he said, solemnly. "To oaths sworn on this, his symbol, the oath-ring of Odin and Telemark." He scowled. She'd insisted that he put that last word in. She claimed the ring *was* Telemark. "The oaths will absolutely bind you and yours. Step forward those of you would swear on the holy symbol."

The new queen did. She still wore ragged and blood-stained clothes. Men's breeches! But neither the priest nor the Norse nobility would have dreamed of letting any sign of disapproval show. That new jarl—best never to think of him as a thrall again—had already made it painfully clear that he would personally deal with even the faintest sign of disrespect.

But the oddest thing was that, despite her clothes and having her hair wild and undressed, like some great golden-blond halo from one of these heathen Christian ikons, she looked like a queen. She did not need that watchful-eyed grendel killer of hers standing watchfully behind her to get respect. Already some of the Norse ladies were surreptitiously unpinning their hair. Imitation is the sincerest form of flattery. And suddenly a lot of women who had followed the false Queen Albruna's lead in their comments and manner to her stepdaughter wanted to do a bit of flattery really, really badly.

It didn't seem that she'd even noticed. But then, the true ruler need not. Toad-eaters are what those of lesser legitimacy need.

Her imperial counterpart's gear was equally shabby. But he walked like a prince, too, even if he was not wearing the armor of his fellows. He wore honor instead, and it shone brighter.

The oath was sworn.

And at the end of it, the queen turned to her outlander ex-thrall jarl . . . and laughed.

He looked as if he'd bitten one of those foreign spices. A peppercorn.

Many other oaths were sworn.

But there was no blood-eagle sacrifice at the end of it.

The old priest thought rulers should stay out of religion.

The crowds were dissipating, heading toward the warmth of the feasting hall. Groups of Norsemen, still stunned with the knowledge that they had been there, walked, talking in low voices. They had actually seen what the skalds would sing of across the Norse kingdoms. And they had really been there to see it . . . Already the stories were beginning to grow, by the snatches that Erik overheard.

Manfred took a deep pull of the flask Szpak had sent someone to procure, as they joined the drift back to Kingshall. "That's vile," he said cheerfully to the Polish Ritter. "Well, we're done. Sweden sorted out. Arm-ring found, treaty ratified. Now I can get back to Francesca in Copenhagen. I know she'll have a good hundred young Danish second sons ready to become confrere knights. You can trust Francesca to have it all wrapped up."

"She's here," said Juzef. "She arrived while all the excitement was going on, along with a load of Danes and Vinlanders. I heard about it from one of my men who got the news from one of the Norsemen."

Manfred grinned even more broadly and quickened his stride. "Well, what are you waiting for? Let's get across there. This is even better than that sailor from Lesbos's magic tricks."

As he said that, Erik paused, midstride. Then the Icelander started to laugh. And then laughed some more. And sat down on the snow to laugh, clutching his aching sides.

"What's wrong with him? He's had hardly any of that schnapps," said Szpak, looking puzzled.

"Cair's magic tricks," spluttered Erik. "Weren't tricks."

"What?" asked Manfred, frowning.

"I just figured it out," said Erik, clutching his knees, beaming like an idiot. "Cair, the sceptic who didn't believe in magic, went through huge performances to fake magic—which always appeared to work . . . Which, considering that he was an amateur, is surprising. Impossible, really."

Szpak looked curiously at him. "You mean you thought he was a fake?"

"Yes, *he* thought he was a fake!" said Erik, struggling with his gravity. "And he believed it so hard he convinced the rest of us. But he'd fooled himself. He was going through the rituals of magic, without believing they'd work. He thought it was his tricks working. But it wasn't. It was the real thing. Oh, priceless!"

Manfred's eyes narrowed. "That bird. Signy is a witch all right, and not quite human. But she wasn't even there when he did that bird—and you two hurried out before it exploded and the dwarves found out that it was a fraud! And then it came flying to his rescue. Oh, priceless indeed!"

Erik nodded. "No wonder he always appeared able to do the magical! No wonder he always managed the improbable! He must be kicking himself. Our too clever, chess-playing, think-every-possible-move-ahead corsair missed something basic in his calculations. He got it all wrong ... And now he's a Telemark landholder, obliged to let the richest prizes he ever saw go."

"What are you two talking about?" demanded Szpak.

Manfred hauled Erik to his feet, helped him dust snow off himself. "About, among other things, me having to explain to my uncle that the corsair captain Cair Aidin is now subject to a treaty with the Empire and that a price on his head would be diplomatically awkward."

"And that price is not about to be collected by any Norseman," said Erik, shaking his head, ruefully.

Then it was Manfred's turn to start laughing. "But I think Charles Fredrik is going to be pleased with me after all. No wonder that smart Turk was looking so sour at the oath. As one of Signy's citizens and landholders, he's just forsworn attacking not just us, but the Empire's shipping, too. Priceless! No wonder Signy was laughing. She's a smart woman, that. She's kept him home."

Erik grinned. "All right. So it *is* all done then. I agree. Now all we have to do is get out of Norway."

"As fast as possible!" agreed Manfred. "Away from trolls, kobolds, real fake magicians, and too-clever women. To somewhere warm."

Juzef Szpak grinned. "That's a nice thing to say when I have to go back to Småland!"

"Ah. But you will have your cabbage liquor," said Manfred comfortingly.

EPILOGUE

In the last few days, Cair—or Jarl Cair, the Grendelslayer, Lord of Numedal and Amdal, as he was now respectfully known—had come to realize that his princess, free of her past and confirmed in her power, was able and clever as well as beautiful and kindly. He loved her more than ever. And now he had this message . . .

"She wishes for you to come, alone, to the stables, Jarl," said the respectful warrior. "She said to tell you it was to discuss her impending marriage."

Well. She was a queen. Not free to marry or even love of her own choosing.

It was a long walk to the stables.

She was, naturally, waiting with the old horses.

There were, as usual, four or five dogs at her heels. Well. He had a bird that ate live coals on his shoulder. She'd returned it to him, and bade him keep the dagger. Her steel, given to him as her champion. By now, she didn't need him as that. She was the darling of the nation, both adored and respected.

Instead of the fine dresses that she wore nowadays, she'd dug out an old riding habit from somewhere.

It tore at him. In his heart he knew that he was still her thrall, and would always be that.

"My princess," he said, and knelt.

"Cair," she said tenderly, raising him up. "I wanted to talk to you. To talk to you away from the court and the people. To go back to the time and place when you were my only friend. When you, I realize now, planned to run away with me. To kidnap me, if need be, to save me. If I'd known then what I know now, I would have gone with you, corsair."

"I only wanted you to be happy, my princess," he said humbly. He would always be humble with her. A thrall was.

Her eyes were luminous as she looked at him. "But I am not a princess anymore, Cair. I am the queen of Telemark. And I am known as an *Alfarblot* witch. Queens must marry for power." She took a deep breath. "Witches . . . witches are different. We do not fear them here in the north. But people believe the only fit husband for a witch is another witch. I know, now, that I can work magics on things that grow and live. You weave magics into whatever you do with inanimate things. Yet you claim to not believe in magic. I could not marry a man who claims not to believe in what I do, or in what he does."

Cair took the bird from his shoulder. It looked at him with glowing amber eyes that had once been a broken bead. He'd come to terms with the fact that he'd made some misjudgments about both the Norse and about magical matters. "A good scientist is always prepared to reevaluate matters on the basis of new evidence . . . If you rub his nose in it," he said with a wry smile. He flicked the bird up to fly, and folded her into his arms. Flying in a circle above them, the bird began to sing.

"For you, my Alfar queen, I will be all of mankind's witches," said Jarl Cair quietly, to his beloved.

GLOSSARY

Archimandrite: A senior rank in the Knights of the Holy Trinity, just below that of a bishop. Derived from the person who is in charge of a number of monasteries.

Arm-ring: also temple-ring. Well-attested pagan religious item. A heavy ring worn above the elbow. Some of these were "consecrated" and worn by the priest-chieftains, and solemn oaths were sworn upon them.

Aesir: The principal ruling pantheon of Norse gods. Some sources divide these into Aesir and Vanir.

Alfar: Elvish.

Altmark: Kingdom to the north of Telemark.

Aqua fortis: Nitric acid.

Aqua regia: Nitrohydrochloric acid. Very corrosive, will dissolve metals including gold.

Aurvangar: (wet-gravel plains) Place where dwarves live.

Bakrauf: Troll-wife name.

Balefire: (evil fire) Ritual fire kindled with certain hard fungus.

Bautarstein: (driven stone) Upright stone monument.

Bifröst: (the shimmering path) Bridge between the lands of gods and men. Sometimes interpreted as a rainbow.

Björnhednar: (bearskins) Shape changers into bears.

Brisingamen: (the flaming necklace) Freya's most precious possession.

Brynhild: The Valkyrie whose mistaken marriage to Gunnar gave rise to the tragic events in the Völsung saga. She casts herself onto the pyre of the man she wished to marry. One of the "examples" held up to Signy.

Disir: Goddesses associated with the dead.

Dokkalfar: Dark elves.

Draupnir: (dripper) Arm-ring. A legendary one from which other rings (or wealth) were supposed to fall.

Draug: Ghosts or walking dead. Literally corpses that walk. The only way to "kill" a draug is to cut its head right off, place the severed head between its buttocks, and cremate it.

Draugar: Plural of draug.

Eldr: (fire) Giant name. The Scandinavian skaldic culture had a wonderful tradition of "kennings," plays on words, with multiple layers of meaning. Anthropomorphism of natural forces and objects was the norm. So it is possible that eldr was both a giant and the personification of fire. Eddic poems were expected to be multilayered and were appreciated for that.

Fimbulthul: River, "terrible/mighty Thul."

Fjells: Sharp or rounded peaks.

Franklin: A freeman who is not a noble (archaic term, 14–15th century).

Frey: Chief fertility god. One of the Vanir. Usually portrayed with an enormous erection.

Freya: The sister of Frey, her province is love and sex. Her most infamous exploit was sleeping with four dwarves in order to obtain the Brisingamen.

Fylgjur: (fetch) Protective spirit.

Futhark: Runic script.

Galdr: Chants—spells.

Garth: Enclosed courtyard.

Gjallarbru: Bridge between Midgard and the underworld.

Godar: Both chieftains and priests.

Gimlé's halls: The halls of alfar.

Götar: Occupants of Southern Sweden before the Danish invasions.

Gjöll: lit. "Scream"—a mighty river dividing the Midgard from the underworld.

Hag of Járnvid: Hag of Ironwood, a giantess who fosters the wolf who will one day devour the sun.

Hati: Troll-name, meaning "hateful."

Hjorda: The king of Rogaland to the west of Telemark.

Hlauttein: Aspergillum.

Iron vitriol: Hydrated ferrous sulphate, which was then distilled to produce sulphuric acid.

Jarl: Earl.

Járnhauss: Troll-name (lit., iron-skull).

Joulu: Yule, an ancient pagan festival, long predating Christmas, which Christmas has usurped, taking many of the customs. The date is taken as the point at which the sun begins to win against winter (the winter solstice). Customs relating to the kindling of fires, often wheel-shaped ones to symbolize the sun, or phallic ones, occur across the length and breadth of Europe.

Jötunheim: The realm of Giants, bordered by Járnvid.

Kobold: An underground-dwelling Germanic/Nordic gnome, known to give miners a hard time.

Lesbos: An island in the Aegean, near to the coast of Turkey. Its claims to fame are that the term Lesbian originated from there, via the poet Sappho, and that it was the original home of the Barbary corsair Brother-Captains Aruj and Khayr (Cair).

Martinmas: The 11th of November—Saint Martin's Mass, by which time the winter slaughterings were to be done and salted away.

Midgard: The one of the nine worlds that Norse myth believed men lived in. All of the worlds are interlinked "places" and not "worlds" in the way we think of them as globes hanging in space. The Norse world was a multidimensional place.

Moonling: One who has been moonstruck. The moon was believed to cause lunacy. Often applied to those whose wits were a little lacking.

Needfire: Fire kindled by friction, without the use of any metal, believed to be necessary for certain magics.

Oferlundar: Sacrificial glade.

Pease: A generic middle ages term for any form of bean or pea.

Seid: Black magic only practiced by Odin and women.

Signy: Another tragic heroine, who eventually burns willingly with her husband King Siggeir, although she was unwillingly wed to him.

Sjár: (sparky) Dwarf name.

Skald: Bard or court poet. A revered person in Norse society.

Svear: Generic term for the Swedish pagans.

Troll: (giant or monster) Not the sort that lived under bridges and ate billy-goats. Huge, powerful, and capable of assuming "seemings."

Thrall: Slave.

þekkr: Spelled with its proper *thorn*, which isn't "just an English *th*" and never should be substituted with such. Editors who want to change it shouldn't blame the copy editor or typesetter—they know better and cringe when they see a *thorn* substituted with "th" by mistake or misunderstanding. *Thorns* are pronounced as a "hard" *th*, as in *that*.

Ulfhednar: (wolf-skins) Shape changers to wolves.

Vanir: Fertility gods who fought a war with the Aesir, exchanging hostages, and becoming part of the Norse pantheon. It seems that the Germanic tribes spreading across Europe and Scandinavia absorbed and incorporated older and different religions into their own. This myth possibly has its origins in an actual war between two tribes of believers in different gods.

Vé: Sacred grove.

Vidd: High plateau.

Vitr: (smart) Dwarf name.

Völund: Legendary smith who was captured and hamstrung and imprisoned on an island from whence he escaped by constructing a pair of wings.

Wanderjahre: Journeyman years.

Woden: also Odhinn, Woutan, Wotan. Woden was the Danish way of naming the king of the Aesir; known as Odin among the Norse.